Chimera

A PSYCHOLOGICAL THRILLER

BY

CHUCK MORGAN

Chapter One

2002…Calvin Walker

The woods behind the high school are alive with movement, but only if you know where to look. From the outside, it's all shadow and undulation, soft shapes where trunks and branches shiver together, dense enough to swallow you whole if you step just five yards from the path. They call this the "greenbelt," like it's a nature preserve or something, but nobody in their right mind comes out here after dark unless they're looking to score, smoke, or get laid. Or, in my case, to practice.

Up at the stadium, the metal bleachers thrum with post-game chaos, band geeks packing up sousaphones, moms gossiping about next week's bake sale, and the quarterback's dad screaming at the coach for benching his golden boy in the fourth quarter. All that is nothing more than a distant pulse now, reverberating through the trees in slow waves. I keep to the periphery, walking heel-to-toe on the deer trail I mapped out two weeks ago. Every time my boots land, the crunch of leaves vibrates through the bones of my shins.

There are two girls tonight, one blonde and one a dark silhouette at the lot line. They peel away from the others like stray lambs from the herd, giggling about something nobody else heard. I'd like to believe they're completely oblivious, but you can never assume total stupidity. Even prey animals develop a sense for things that stalk. I keep my breathing steady, thumb pressed against the notch of my windpipe, counting each inhale and exhale like I'm timing a shot. My right hand slips inside the pocket of my cargo jacket, fingers wrapping the textured handle of my hunting knife. I don't take it out, not yet, but I trace the outline of the blade with the tip of my index finger, learning it all over again. The edge is so sharp it wants to open me, but I don't let it. Self-control is the only thing that separates the hunter from the idiot with a weapon.

The girls are halfway down the embankment now, laughing louder. The blonde lights a cigarette and passes it to the other. The smell of dope wafted through the air. I watch the flicker of the lighter, the way it makes her face flare up for an instant, all bones, and acne and black eyes. She's the one who said she'd bring tequila to the after-party, but I know she never did. She's been dry all night. That's why they're here instead of a hundred yards over, where the party is already dying. They're looking for privacy and something to make them feel alive.

They're talking about a teacher, I think. I catch phrases: "fucking psycho," "wouldn't even let me go pee," "did you see her shoes?" It's the same old complaint parade, but I listen anyway. Details matter. I note the timbre of their voices, the way the blonde's tone spikes at the end of sentences. She's the dominant one or wants to be. The other is quieter, always a split second behind on the laugh, always needing to catch up. That's why she lingers at the tree line, looking back over her shoulder every few steps.

I keep to the shadows, counting their paces and matching mine to theirs. The trick is to lag two steps behind, always in the angle of their blind spot, never directly opposite or parallel. That way, if they turn, I freeze to merge with the scenery. In my peripheral vision, the stadium lights flicker and die, leaving only the sodium-orange haloes of the parking lot lamps. The game's over, and now it's the empty echo of what happened. The woods belong to me.

The wind picks up, and with it comes the scent of marijuana and cheap perfume. I time my breathing to the gusts, inhale on the wind, exhale on the quiet, letting their odor blend with the loam and wet rot of fallen leaves. I count heartbeats. I imagine mine as a red line running side-by-side with theirs, waiting for the perfect convergence.

They stop near the creek, the place where the old fence collapsed and kids go to make out or piss in the dark. There's a patch of bare dirt there, littered with bottle caps and half buried condoms, evidence of all the other animals that passed this way. The blonde flicks her cigarette and looks up at the sky, breath frosting in the cold. The other girl, the quieter one, pulls her jacket tight and looks at her phone, and back toward the stadium.

I know what comes next because I've rehearsed it a hundred times in my head. The blonde sits on the log, cocks her head, and tells a story, something about her stepfather, or maybe a rumor about a freshman who OD'd last year. The quiet girl listens, nods, pretends to care. She glances at her phone again. I glide in closer, cutting through the underbrush with the softest possible steps, body low, eyes level. The knife is out now, blade pressed flat against my thigh, not gleaming, but hungry.

I wait until the blonde stands to pee. That's the break. She hands her purse to her friend, mutters something sarcastic, and steps behind a thicket. The other girl stands awkwardly, scanning the woods for movement, not expecting to find any. I hold my breath until the blonde's footsteps fade behind the brambles. Now.

I lunge. The first ten feet are a blur, a rush of wind, a slick pulse of adrenaline, boots barely touching ground. The quiet girl doesn't even see me until I'm behind her, my left arm snaking around her neck, elbow clamping down against her larynx. She's lighter than I thought, or maybe it's the surge of energy in my limbs, but she lifts clean off the ground as I squeeze. Her phone clatters to the dirt. She makes a sound, like a startled rabbit, not a scream but a short, panicked gasp.

My hand is so tight on the knife that the hilt creaks. She flails backward, stomps on my foot, and my toenail cracks, but the pain is distant, secondary. I focus on the way her windpipe collapses under my elbow, the fluttering panic of her heartbeat against my chest. Her head thrashes left and right, and she tries to bite me, turns her mouth and snaps at my forearm. Her teeth scrape denim, and I let her. Every detail is information. I slide the knife across her throat, and blood sprays out, covering the leaves. I set her gently on the ground and tuck her head forward.

Chapter Two

Her friend, the blonde, hears the commotion and calls out, "What the fuck, Casey? You, okay?" There's laughter in her voice, but it dies quickly when she rounds the thicket and sees her friend sitting on the ground, her head resting against her chin, blood pooling on her lap. She doesn't see me standing to the side, next to the tree.

For a second, time expands. I see everything, the way the blonde's face freezes, her mouth open, and half a scream jammed in her throat. The way her right foot slides backward, looking for balance or maybe a way to run.

I move towards the blonde, who sees me out of the corner of her eye. She tries to run, but I'm faster. She swings the purse at me, a desperate haymaker, but I raise my arm and block it. There's something solid in there, a bottle of nail polish, maybe, or a heavy keyring, but it doesn't stop me. I grab her wrist, twist it until she drops the purse, and shove her face-first into the gravel. She sprawls, knees scraping open, but tries to crawl away. I kneel on her back, pinning her down. She screams even louder now, begging. "Please, please, please." The words come out in a torrent.

I let the blade dangle inches from her ear, letting her see it. Her whole body seizes, breath coming in short, wet bursts. She smells like dope and fruity lip balm and something else, a high sharpness that's all terror.

I glance back at the woods. The quiet girl is still on the ground, hands pressed to her throat, but she's watching, eyes wide and round and shining in the dark. I wonder if she can see my face. I hope she does.

The blonde tries to buck me off, but I'm heavier, stronger, and more practiced. I lean down, mouth close to her ear, and whisper, "It's almost over." Not because I mean it, but because I want to know what she'll do. She sobs, trembles, goes limp. That's the signal. She's ready.

I press the blade against the nape of her neck. She flinches but doesn't scream this time. I raise the knife, pause, and draw a quick, precise line across her throat. Blood spurts onto the ground. She shudders, and her heart hammers through her ribcage as her heart tries to compensate for the loss of blood.

The creek isn't much, two feet deep, a foot across, lazy as a drunk. The moon shatters on its surface, scattering silver splinters through the reeds. I kneel, washing blood from my fingers, and the water turns pink, then pale again, like nothing ever happened. The cold numbs my hands but not the raw nerves running up my arms. My heartbeat is wild, a jackhammer in my ears, but my hands are steady, fingers moving with the careful patience of someone tying a fly or setting a bone.

Behind me, the woods have gone silent. Not empty but waiting. I listen for movement, but there's nothing but the tick and shift of the creek, the way it tongues the rocks and carries away the evidence. My jacket is sticky with blood and mucus. It clings to my forearms in black patches, already going tacky, but I resist the urge to scrub it all away. The sensation is part of the process. The residue means I did it right.

I run my thumb over the edge of the blade, testing for nicks. There are none; the knife is still perfect. The handle, though, is smeared and slick, and I make a mental note to clean it with bleach as soon as I get home. I flick water onto my face, rinsing off any streaks of blood that might have sprayed onto my face.

I moved back to the girls. The silence in the woods is disturbed by the distant hoot of an owl and the buzzing of mosquitoes. I pause for a minute to savor what I've done. What I've just done hits me like an air pocket, one moment turbulence, the next calm so absolute I don't recognize it. I expect an aftershock: panic, disgust, at least a tremor of second thoughts. Instead, an eerie, total vacancy settles over me. I stand there, one hand still sticky, the other holding the knife loose, and it's like I'm a mannequin in a window display, posed to look like myself. I look at the bodies, at the red pooling under their chins and the way the leaves soak it up, and there's nothing. No gloating, no triumph, not even the animal thrill that was supposed to be the whole point. I'm not afraid, not sorry, not even especially proud. I just am.

The dumb part is, I always imagined the first kill would be a kind of awakening, a key turning in a secret lock, gears whirring into alignment, the old wall between me and everything else finally crumbling. But there's no transformation. No spirit leaving the body, no demon taking my place. Only a slow, weightless clarity, like waiting for your reflection to blink and realizing it never will.

I study the scene. There's blood everywhere, but not as much as you'd think. The quiet girl's hands are still clamped to her throat, even though she's already gone, and her nails have gouged deep purple crescents into her own skin. The blonde is face down in the gravel, but her legs are twitching, some stubborn fragment of refusing to believe it's over. There's a smudge on the back of her jacket, mud, or maybe the print of my knee where it pinned her down. I crouch beside her and flip the body over; the head lolling at a wrong angle. Her eyes are open and so blue they almost look fake, like a doll's.

I check my pulse out of curiosity. It's normal. No racing, no explosions in my chest. The thing that registers as real is the cold, the way it chews at my knuckles and makes the blood on my hands go stiff and black. I wipe them on the inside of my jacket, on the moss, and in the creek, but the color stays under my nails. I'm not sure I want it gone.

I glance back up the slope. The woods are quieter than before, not even a breeze to rattle the branches. I listen for sirens, for footsteps, for the angry mob that always chases you in the movies, but there's nothing. I could stand here all night, and no one would ever know.

I kneeled over her and pinned her arms with my knees. Her chest heaves, and I watch the frantic rise and fall, the way the fabric of her shirt stretches and sags with every breath. I pull the blade from my belt and hold it up, letting the moon catch on the steel. She whimpers, kicks, and falls silent. It's over.

I cut the T-shirt away first, a slow draw from neck to navel. The blade parts the cotton like it's nothing. I slice the bra next, right between the cups, the elastic snapping open, exposing perfect breasts.

I make the first cut fast, a horizontal slash across her chest, right below the clavicle. Blood beads instantly, bright red against the white of her skin. I watch the blood run, pooling in the hollow at the base of her throat. It's mesmerizing, the way it flows slowly, now that there's no heartbeat to move it along, obeying only gravity.

The second cut is vertical, intersecting the first to form a cross. Not a Christian cross, more like the old ones you find in Viking books, a crossroads, an intersection of fates. I pressed the blade deeper this time.

But I'm not done. I carve a spiral into the intersection, starting at the center and working outwards, letting the blade do the work. The skin parts in delicate, even arcs, and there is a strange satisfaction at the precision.

I finish the spiral and sit back, admiring my work. The symbol looks clean, almost deliberate, a message only I understand. I have no idea why I chose the cross and the spiral. I might have seen something similar in a movie, or it might be something I saw in a dream. All I know is it feels good to carve it. I wipe the blade on her shredded shirt. The blood is still flowing, slower now, congealing at the edges. I watch her eyes, looking at how they've clouded over, and a weird peace settles over me. Like everything is in its right place.

Chapter Three

Arranging the bodies is not about hiding them. That would be cowardice, a retreat from what I've accomplished. It's about presentation, about making a statement. I start with the blonde. I straighten her arms, place them flat at her sides, palms up. I cross her ankles, aligning them with the torn hem of her skirt. I tilt her face to the sky, closing her mouth with gentle pressure on the chin. She looks peaceful now, like she's fallen asleep in a field.

For the quiet girl, I folded her arms over her chest, her hands meeting at the base of her throat. The blood no longer flows but is pooled in the hollow between her breasts. I tug her shirt open to expose the crosshatch of bruises at her neck, the imprint of my forearm. It's important that people see how she died, what it took to end her. I brush a strand of hair from her eyes and wipe my fingers on the damp grass.

The last step is the ritual. I pull a black marker from my pocket. A Sharpie with a chisel tip, bold as a tattoo gun, and kneel beside the blonde. I draw the spiral cross again, this time on her wrist, making the lines thick and unbroken. I feel compelled to add the hand-drawn cross. Not sure why, but I see both crosses clearly in my mind. Something is telling me they both need to be there. The skin is cold and resists the ink, but I press harder, leaving a mark that will outlast the blood. With the quiet girl, I do the same, careful to center it on her wrist like the stamp from a club or concert. When I'm done, I step back and admire the symmetry.

My breathing slows. The adrenaline fades, replaced by a dull, humming satisfaction. The work is done. I scan the clearing one last time, checking for anything out of place. The cigarette lighter, the phone, the purse, all accounted for. I leave them near the bodies, trophies for whoever finds the scene.

The symbols are my way of assuring them safe passage to the afterlife. I retreat into the trees, moving quickly but without panic, following the creek until I reach the bridge near the highway. I stop under the overpass, heart finally slowing, and check myself for evidence, blood, hair and fabric. There is nothing evident in the dark, but I'll look closer once I get home.

***

I slept a dreamless sleep and woke up refreshed. I replayed the night in my head, frame by frame, analyzing what went right and what didn't. There's room for improvement. I should have secured the first girl better. Next time I'll take one victim instead of two. Two was too many, and things got sloppy. I won't let that happen again. Next time, I'll bring zip ties or tape. Something to keep the victim still. The knife worked perfectly, but I need to practice the spiral more, make it cleaner. It's important to get the details right. Otherwise, what's the point?

Sometime this morning, they'll find the bodies, and the world will be a slightly different place. The first cut is always the hardest. After that, it gets easier.

When I was finished with breakfast, I pulled the hunting knife from my belt and wiped it clean in bleach water. The blood came off in thick clots, dark as motor oil. When the blade shines again, I hold it to the light and check for flaws. There are none. I slide it back into its sheath and exhale. I grab my backpack and a different jacket and head for school. The sound of the washing machine wiping away my adventure.

I head to where the bodies were found. The cold is absolute now, crisp enough to sharpen every smell and sound. The woods are hollowed out, silent, like the whole world is holding its breath. I follow the crowd as they move through the woods. It looks like everyone from the school is here, as well as all the neighbors. Someone should have brought coffee. The parking lot is full of police cars with flashing red, white and blue lights, and an ambulance sits idling at the path. Its doors open, waiting.

Distant voices float through the trees, faint but growing. Someone is calling their names, students are crying and parents are yelling at the police, wondering if the community is in danger. The panic, the confusion, the way their voices shatter the silence. It's like the conclusion to a story that's been writing itself for years.

The blonde is where I left her: arms splayed, knees crooked, shirt peeled away to bare the cuts across her chest. The cross and spiral are already scabbing at the edges, blood sticky and black in the early morning sun. Her eyes are closed, lashes tangled in tears. She looks surprised, even now. That's what I wanted.

The other girl, the quiet one, lies on the ground where I left her. Her eyes are still open in fear, and the spiral cross on her chest is a thing of beauty, if I must say so myself. I wonder if she realized she was dying, or if her body simply gave up and left her behind.

I stop next to a group of my friends and stare at the police activity. No one is talking. We all stare. The air is fresher here, untouched by smoke and noise and human sweat. I breathe it in, letting it fill me. There is no fear, no guilt, not even relief. It's a kind of curiosity, an eagerness to see what happens next.

The police push us back as they surround the scene with yellow tape. We linger a while longer and head towards the school. The principal will tell us all later at the assembly that returning to normalcy is the best thing we can do right now. I completely agree. Behind me, the woods keeps its secrets, at least for a little while longer.

Chapter Four

I never trust the digital clock in my car. It runs three minutes fast in the cold and two minutes slow once the engine warms. Every morning before I park, I recalibrate against my watch, a dull, heavy Omega I stole from my father's dresser the day after he died, when nobody in the house could muster outrage. The timepieces match: 07:16, which means I have exactly nine minutes before the target leaves her house.

I jot the change in my field notebook, a calfskin Leuchtturm1917, black, gridded, German, and mark the date, time and atmospheric conditions: overcast, 48°, wind out of the west, 7mph. I draw a new isometric sketch of the house across the street. It's the same as every other morning, a suburban ranch, mid-century, painted an optimistic turquoise, but I note the Halloween decorations taped to the storm door, the growing mildew patch on the gutter, and the cluster of pink bicycles abandoned by the mailbox. Her dad's SUV is gone, which means she'll take the shortcut through the Dwyer's yard, emerging on Greely at 07:28.

I check my mirrors. The engine idles smoothly, and my reflection in the driver's window is exactly as I left it, hair cropped to regulation length, shirt pressed, and jeans clean. My eyes are bloodless. I look like every other high-achieving parasite in the senior class, which is the entire point.

I set the pencil, a Uni Kuru Toga, 0.3mm, gunmetal gray, back in its dock and review the night's log entries. The handwriting is immaculate: tall, straight letters, no embellishments. The target stayed up past 01:00, the phone-glow visible from the south window. At 01:22, she flicked on the kitchen light and opened the fridge, extracting a Yoplait and some kind of bottle, probably water. At 02:08, the master bedroom light came on, illuminating her mother's outline at the window. I add a note about the dog, nine minutes in the backyard, barking at nothing, returned inside without incident.

Every observation and every deviation from routine go into the notebook. By page 43, the system is so granular it predicts her movements to within ninety seconds. I diagram the route she'll take to the bus stop, highlighting points of cover and potential witnesses. When she emerges, right on schedule, she's wearing a blue windbreaker, her hair is in a tight braid, and her backpack is on both shoulders. I note her posture, her pace and the eye contact she makes with passing cars. No eye contact today. She's thinking about something else. The notebook absorbs it all.

She walks with purpose, head tilted low, as if the sidewalk is a chessboard and she can see ten moves ahead. I watched her for twenty-four seconds. I move my gaze to the second-floor window, where a curtain stirs and a woman's silhouette surveys the street. I mark the time, 07:30:14, and cross-reference it with Tuesday's entry: MOTHER AT WINDOW, DURATION 18 seconds, PHONE TO LEFT EAR.

There is no phone today. I file this under ANOMALY, underline it twice, and scan the house for changes.

A UPS van stutters up the block, the driver already scanning porches for Amazon packages. I photograph the license plate with my phone, just in case, and upload it to a hidden folder. No detail is too small, and I do not believe in coincidence.

When the target is safely out of sight, I start the engine and pull away, blending into the carpool swarm like an afterthought. I don't follow her. I never do. The point is not to be seen, but to see. I take the long way around the block, roll past the target's house again, and note the empty driveway, the unmoving mailbox, the dog's nose pressed to the bay window. I log the time: 07:38. There is no movement inside. Her mother's SUV is no longer parked in the driveway. The morning is still.

After school, I return to my observation post. It's a different car, this one a battered gray Civic with a dead air freshener and the seats forever dusted in dog hair. I park two blocks away, in the alley behind the Kroger, and walk the rest of the route, blending into the herd of teenagers slouching home with energy drinks and vape cartridges. I duck behind the same hydrangea bush as yesterday and watch the house with field glasses, careful to time my glances so they look accidental.

The target's room is on the east side. From here, I have an unobstructed view of her desk, her bed, her bookcase. At 16:04, she drops her backpack on the floor and changes shirts, moving with a brisk, awkward economy that is both efficient and adolescent. I record the make and color of the bra, the motion with which she closes the curtains, and the way her fingers linger on the string for half a second before letting go. I wonder if she knows she's being watched. I suspect not, but it's an open question.

From a leather case, I remove a collapsible mechanical pencil and a fresh notebook page, and I sketch the floor plan of her room, labeling points of ingress and egress, measuring distances by thumb-width and triangulation. Her windows are double-hung, with latches on the lower sash. The screen is bent on the left side, a possible weak point. I estimate the interior door is hollow-core, easy to force, but the carpet would muffle the sound.

She reappeared at 16:21, hair now down and her phone pressed to her face. She spends twelve minutes on the bed, scrolling before she throws the phone at the pillow and kicks off her shoes. I capture the moment in the notebook, DEEP SIGH, HEAD IN HANDS, 16:33, and draw a box around it. This is the window of opportunity. Most girls her age would kill for privacy; this one barricades herself in her room, leaving the house empty.

I cross-reference the family's weekly routine. Her mother's shift runs until 18:00, and her father is on a business trip to Dallas until Sunday. The little sister is at cheer practice until 19:00. I confirm these times against previous logs, check the school calendar, and highlight the gaps in yellow. The next forty-eight hours are the best chance I will get.

Back in my car, I examine the preparation list I taped to the glove box:

— gloves, nitrile, medium, powderless

— disposable shoe covers (2 pairs)

— entry kit (slim jim, bump keys, folding lock pick)

— plastic sheeting, 6x8

— bleach, unscented

— change of clothes (donation bin special)

Each item is checked, double-checked, and rechecked. No improvisation. No emotion. Everything is part of the procedure.

Chapter Five

At home, I update the main log on my laptop, using a self-encrypting drive, print the relevant pages and file them in the red folder marked PHASE ONE. I burn the trash, grind the mechanical pencil shavings into the disposal, and wipe down the table with isopropyl alcohol. I do not eat dinner. I do not sleep. I go over the plan again, testing it for cracks, rerunning every scenario where she calls for help, or the neighbor comes home early, or the police cruise past on a random sweep.

By the time the sun rises, the plan is perfect. I review her social feeds one last time, catalog the day's posts, and for the first time in seventy-six hours, I allow myself to feel something: not anticipation, not nerves, but a quiet satisfaction that comes from a job completed to spec. I look in the mirror in the foyer, at the blue of my eyes and the even part in my hair, and I imagine what the world would see if they could see me now. They would see nothing at all.

The first rule of ingress is never go straight in, not even if you know the building is empty. Especially if you know. The second rule is: confirm. The target's parents are gone, documented on her feed, triangulated with a neighbor's Facebook post about "hitting the lake for the long weekend" and a tagged photo of the family at a rest stop four hours south. The little sister's away at a cheer retreat, judging from the group photo uploaded at 15:32, all identical ponytails and bared teeth, with the retreat center's sign visible in the background. For the next thirty-eight hours, the girl is home alone.

I note the data, cross-check it, and put a heavy black X over the days in the calendar. Tonight is optimal. I don't celebrate. Instead, I lay out the kit with the same focus I used to reassemble my grandfather's Browning after a cleaning, every pin, and spring in its precise groove.

The case is a nondescript black satchel, lined with cut foam, everything in its own slot. Gloves folded flat in sets of five. Shoe covers, Tyvek, size large, and disposable. Surgical masks and hair nets are not strictly necessary, but it's better to be fastidious. Next, the tools: a stainless scalpel with replaceable blades, a set of small forceps, and a curved boning knife that would look more at home in a butcher's freezer than a suburban bedroom. There's a compact folding lock pick, bump keys, a roll of transparent packing tape, and a pair of disposable booties for the ride home.

Plastic sheeting, 6x8, painter's grade, folds small. I cut it into two squares, rolling them tight. Bleach in a plain water bottle labeled Gatorade. Change of clothes, thrift store specials: jeans, gray hoodie, battered Nikes. No tags, no logos. Everything is disposable, except the satchel.

I run through the checklist one more time, gloves to bleach. Everything is present and correct, down to the frictionless pencils and the tiny evidence vacuum I built from an old Dustbuster. I zip the bag, placing it by the door. The time is 20:02. I set the kitchen timer for one hour. The target is probably watching TV, or on her phone, or maybe walking in circles, trying to bleed off the sense of being alone. She always gets restless after dark; there are three separate notations in the log of her standing in the backyard in her socks, shivering but refusing to go back inside. Tonight, I expect she'll last longer.

I kill the lights at 21:05 and stand in the living room, slowing my breathing, inventorying my senses. I can smell detergent on my shirt, the clean smell of nitrile from my hands, a faint trace of something sweet, possibly dryer sheets or a neighbor's lawn clippings. There is no fear. Not even a thrill but the same controlled anticipation I had before a decathlon event. At some level, I know my brain is flooding with adrenaline, sharpening edges, making time elastic. It's not like anything. I simply know more, perceive more, as if the world is rotating a little slower for me than it does for everyone else.

The drive takes eight minutes. I park on a side street, three blocks from the target's house. The bag is slung low across my back. The hoodie and hat are generic enough to pass as any other figure out at night, and the shoes, double-knotted, treads scuffed, make no noise on pavement. I time my walk to the intervals between passing cars, calculating how far the nearest porch lights reach and where the shadows fall. At one point, a dog barks two houses down. I slow my pace, flatten my steps, and wait for the owner to shout it quiet. The street is otherwise empty.

I take the alley, moving behind the privacy fences and trash bins. No motion sensors, no night-vision cameras, all checked in advance, confirmed by three dry runs last month. I pause at the Dwyers' yard and peer through the gaps in the fence. Her house is a blue rectangle in the dark, the porch light off, and all the windows black except for a faint glow in the living room. From the log, I know she watches TV at a volume of ten, low enough to hear footsteps if someone approaches.

I move silently around the house. The gate is latched with a spring hook, the same as every night, and I lift it without a sound. The sliding door to the patio is locked, but the side door, into the garage, has a Schlage deadbolt, easy to bump if you know the rhythm. I insert the key, wrap it in a strip of black microfiber, and tap gently with the palm of my hand. The lock turns. I step inside the garage, close the door behind me, and wait.

I listen. The world narrows to the sound of my breathing, the gentle tick of the engine cooling in the neighbor's driveway, the faint stutter of canned laughter from the TV inside.

Inside the garage, there are two doors, one to the kitchen, one to the backyard. I listen at the kitchen door for exactly fifteen seconds. No footsteps. The kitchen is dark, except for the open refrigerator spilling a rectangle of light onto the linoleum. I slip inside, scan the room, and close the door behind me. In the log, I had estimated eight seconds to cross the kitchen and enter the main hallway. I take seven.

I move into the living room, keeping to the wall, and peek around the corner. She's there on the couch, knees hugged to her chest, flicking through a show on Netflix, face flickering blue with every scene change. I stand perfectly still, watching for movement outside, listening for the telltale click of a neighbor's front door or a stray light coming on across the street. Nothing.

I watched her for a full minute, confirming the breathing pattern, the attention locked on the TV. When she shifts on the couch, I clock her movement at 0.7 meters per second, a slow, languid roll. She does not expect anyone. She is not afraid. The absence of fear in her posture is so total it's almost fake.

I retreat, step by measured step, back into the kitchen. I know the house's layout, down to the locations of creaky floorboards and the weird hollow knock under the dining table where her little sister once hid a dead gerbil for three days. I take the stairs to the second floor, heel-toe, never setting my full weight down until I'm sure of silence. At the top, I pause, count three full breaths, and let my eyes adjust. The light under her bedroom door is off. She will sleep here, as she always does, with the window cracked and the curtains open.

I slip out of her room and move into the master bedroom next door. I set the bag on the carpet and unzip it. The sound is so soft I can barely hear it. I check the gloves, tighten the mask, and arrange the implements on the plastic sheeting. I position myself to the left of the door, where I cannot be seen if she opens it suddenly. I wait.

Chapter Six

For six minutes, nothing happened. I hear the TV below, the laugh track rising and falling, and I hear the target moving on the couch, occasionally sighing, once speaking aloud, her voice higher and more uncertain than I expected. I memorize her footsteps as she crosses the floor, the way the light flickers as she passes the banister. She pauses in the kitchen, opens the fridge, takes something out, and climbs the stairs with slow, deliberate steps.

She walks past, not even glancing at the darkness where I stand. The mask makes my breath seem warm and contained. She enters her room and closes the door. I wait.

At 23:19, the house goes dark. The only sounds are the faint crackle of the heat kicking in and the whisper of the wind against the siding. I allow myself one deep breath. I listen. On the other side of the door, her breathing slows. I counted eighty heartbeats.

I moved into the hall and stopped outside her door. The door opened without a sound. I slide it open, and step into the darkness, my heart so still I almost laugh.

The room is exactly as I drew it in the notebook: the bed against the wall, the window cracked, and the laptop glowing faintly on the desk. She is curled under the covers, one arm outside, hand open and relaxed. I watch her for a full minute, standing perfectly still, letting the silence settle around me. She does not stir. She does not know I am here. I could be a shadow, or a memory, or nothing at all.

I position the plastic sheeting at the foot of the bed, careful to avoid the nightstand. I unroll the tape and place it next to the implements, and kneel beside the bed, watching the rise and fall of her back.

This is not anticipation, or excitement or anything so human. This is inevitability, a process completed by rote, as if my hands belong to someone else. I count her breaths: ten, twenty, thirty. I am ready.

She sleeps with her face toward the wall, back exposed, sheets tangled around her legs. The moonlight outlines every vertebra with surgical clarity, pale and blue as a clinical lamp. Her phone buzzes once and goes silent. I make a mental note of the vibration pattern, wonder if it will matter in the reconstruction.

I kneel beside the bed, waiting for the shift in her breathing, the telltale pause that signals a descent into a deeper sleep cycle. It comes at exactly 23:42. I adjust the mask, secure the gloves, and count down from thirty.

At zero, I move. The plastic sheeting unfolds with a practiced flick and settles soundlessly onto the carpet. I position it beneath the bed, reach across and pinch the duvet between gloved fingers, pulling it back enough to expose the target's torso. Her skin is luminous, unblemished except for a scatter of childhood scars. She stirs but does not wake up.

The first touch is always gentle. I place a gloved palm lightly on her shoulder, applying enough pressure to transmit intention, not enough to startle. She murmurs, frowns, and tries to roll away. I increase the force. Her eyes flutter open, unfocused, wide with confusion, and instantaneously flooded with adrenaline.

She tries to scream. I clamp her mouth with my left hand, flattening her to the mattress. The sounds that emerge are small, animal and muffled. I expect the kick, brace my weight so the motion dissipates into the bedding and not the frame. Her arm flails for the phone, but I've already swept it off the nightstand, out of reach.

Her fingers claw at my hand, nails scrabbling against the glove. I press harder, pinching the jaw shut, and bring my right hand up, blade ready. She thrashes, almost bucking me off, but I expected this and adjust my knees to anchor her hips. Her panic is efficient and tactical; if circumstances were reversed, I'd almost respect it.

The blade enters above the collarbone, in the soft triangle between muscle and artery. It severs the carotid cleanly, a shallow puncture, followed by a deeper slice as I withdraw and press the wound with gauze. The blood jets hot and bright at first. It slows as I keep pressure, using the body's own panic against itself. She's losing consciousness before she realizes she's dying.

I maintain the hold for seventeen seconds, counting aloud in my head. At twelve, her limbs go slack. At fifteen, the eyes glaze. At seventeen, she is still.

I lift her gently, lowering the body to the center of the plastic sheeting. I straighten her limbs with the respect of a museum preparator, not a killer. She's lighter than I calculated, and the smell of blood is less metallic than expected, more animal, like a dog's tongue after too much licking.

There is almost no mess. The incision is perfect. The sheets will show a faint stain, but I have already prepared a bleach solution for any residue. I check my gloves, immaculate, and peel them off, sliding on a fresh pair to complete the procedure.

I position the body as in the sketches: arms extended along the sides, legs straight, face tilted forty-five degrees toward the window. I smooth the hair across her shoulder and close her eyes with a light, two-finger touch. Her expression is not peaceful, but not grotesque either, like surprise, the sudden blankness of an interrupted sentence.

The last step is the signature. I retrieve the scalpel and slice open her nightshirt from hem to neck and fold it open. She has small breasts and is pretty. I make a single horizontal cut below the breastbone, not too deep, followed by a vertical incision from the sternum to the navel, intersecting the first. It forms a perfect cross. I extend the upper arm of the cross with a spiral, carved with slow, careful pressure, starting at the intersection and widening outward. Blood beads up along the spiral and dries quickly in the chill air. I wipe the blade on the plastic, and step back to admire the effect. I'm not sure why I chose this symbol. It's something that is rolling around in my mind, like someone planted it there for me to follow. I'm not religious, but the symbol makes me feel at peace.

Something compels me to take a black Sharpie from my bag and draw the same cross on her wrist. I finish, stand and look at it. I'm not sure why I did it, but somehow it feels right.

It is exactly as planned: the geometry, the scale, the contrast of clean lines against unmarred skin. I almost take a photo, but I have no use for trophies.

I bundle the plastic around the body and secure it with three strips of tape. The package is tidy, compact, and leakproof. I tuck the implements back into the case, swapping gloves after every step. I wipe down the nightstand, the bedframe, the window ledge. I collect the phone, the charger, a handful of stray hairs from the pillow, and bag them for disposal. The bleach erases any trace on the sheets, leaving the faintest ghost of a stain, visible to someone who knows where to look.

Before I leave, I scan the room once more, searching for anomalies. The laptop screen is dark, but the charger is still warm. The closet door is ajar, as it always is. I align the books on the desk to match the last photograph I took of the room. There is nothing out of place, not even the breath of air I leave behind.

I descend the stairs, my shoes muffled by the Tyvek covers. I wipe down the door handles and sweep the entryway with the hand-vac. I exit through the garage, reset the lock, and close the door behind me.

The night air is colder than before, and the stars are out, sharp and indifferent. I walked to the car the long way, keeping to the alleys. The silence is complete. No one sees me; no one suspects me.

At the car, I strip the Tyvek covers, mask, and gloves, and place them in a trash bag. I put on the backup clothes, rub my hair into a slightly messier configuration, and get behind the wheel. My hands do not shake.

On the drive home, I replay every step, noting timing, efficiency and cleanliness. There is little to improve, but I logged three minor corrections for next time: use coarser tape for the plastic wrap, swap the entry kit for a lighter pick set, and wear looser jeans for ease of movement. I make the notes in the red notebook, transcribing each detail in crisp black ink. This is how progress happens.

At home, I shred the gloves, bag the trash, and clean the implements in the downstairs sink. I put the satchel back on its shelf, next to the files for other cases. I sit in the dark, glass of water in my hand, and watch the minute hand of my father's Omega sweep past midnight. I wonder how the cops will interpret the scene: random, brutal, and senseless. They will not see the design, the order, the absolute absence of chaos. They will not see me at all.

In the morning, I put on a fresh shirt and jeans. I part my hair perfectly, the way my father used to. I get in the car, adjust the clock, and drive to church. I pass the target's house at exactly 07:16, and I make a note of the police tape on the door, the cluster of patrol cars, and the news vans already waiting. I observe, record, and move on.

There is always another project.

Chapter Seven

The air in the apartment complex's breezeway is laced with disinfectant and the damp smell of melting snow. Dirk Trainor steps through the puddled entrance, one hand clutching his backpack, the other braced against the wall as he navigates the slip hazard past the sign reading OCCUPIED: POLICE BUSINESS. His suit, dark blue, slim-cut, tailored out of necessity not vanity, sucks the chill straight to his skin. The strobing lights of two patrol units and a Denver coroner's van throw intermittent splashes of red and white up the pale stucco, illuminating the half-frozen mud that encases his shoes.

He pauses at the perimeter tape, below the battered mailboxes, and tilts his ID at the officer standing guard. The young cop's eyes, heavy-lidded and pink around the edges, hesitate for half a second before reading the badge. The standoff lasts exactly one beat longer than comfort allows.

"Special Agent Trainor. FBI. Scene log?" Dirk's voice is low, level, shaped by thousands of bureaucratic exchanges.

The cop fumbles a clipboard from beneath his parka and pivots it so Dirk can sign. Dirk notes the roster, two DPD homicide, three CSI techs, and a name he recognizes: SAIC Anthony Spinella, his superior and sometimes antagonist. He lets his thumb hover over the page. The latex glove crinkles.

"Elevator's broken," the cop says, gesturing toward the stairwell. "They're waiting for you on three."

Dirk nods, wiping his shoe on the mat out of reflex before ascending. Each step groans with the weight of boots, gear and last night's snowpack. The building is technically luxurious, but the stairwell's paint is already peeling, and the sensor lights are slow to wake. Dirk's mind sets itself to audit mode, mapping exits, memorizing the tilt of every security cam, cataloguing the apartments passed on the way.

Third floor, Unit 312. The door stands open at an angle, like a broken jaw. Inside, the living room is almost theatrical in its neatness. The carpet is new, probably less than a month since it was installed. The walls are white except for a single row of family photos. No partners, no kids, only the victim in a dozen different graduation robes, nursing uniforms, and one old snapshot of her posing with a volleyball team. Everything else is sterile: a Formica coffee table with nothing on it, a sectional that looks new, and an unlit candle.

Dirk stops inside the threshold, letting the temperature differential assault him. The heater is set for a tropical bloodbath.

He hears voices, subdued and professional, in the back half of the unit. He crosses into the kitchen. The path is obvious; CSU has marked the perimeter of the scene with blue tent cards. The kitchen is a monochrome of stainless steel and cheap laminate.

The body is laid out in the bedroom. Dirk's

approach slows, attention telescoping to every tread of the hall, every hint of movement. He registers the murmur of the forensic pathologist conferring with a CSI photographer. He registers the exact hue of the blood: arterial, fresh, still glossy in the center but already drying to rust at the edges.

The woman lies on her back on a heavy-duty contractor's plastic sheet; the kind used to protect floors during renovations. Dirk observes first the plastic: no rips, no gaps. The corners are folded under her feet, military-bed style. Her shoes are off, set neatly beside the body. The corpse is not posed, not exactly, but arranged. Her arms are folded over her chest, and her hands are palm-over-palm as if she were praying. The left sleeve of her Colorado Juvenile Authority sweatshirt is rolled up. Her throat is slashed in a single, deliberate line; the cut is so clean the edges are nearly flush together.

Dirk notes every detail in mental dictation:

— victim: White female, mid-40s, clothed, not bound

— blood loss: catastrophic; no evidence of a struggle

— hands: no defensive wounds visible

— face: calm, mouth closed, eyes closed

— scene: clean, no forced entry, no sign the house was ransacked

He steps closer. The forensic photographer pauses and waits for the okay. Dirk changes the angle of the body so that the incision at the neck is more visible.

The wound is precise, as if mapped in advance. Not a hack job, not a crime of passion.

He glances at the pathologist, a pale woman in an N95 and a CORONER windbreaker. "Victim identified yet?" he asks, still studying the hands.

The pathologist doesn't look up. "Cheryl Huxley. Leaseholder. She lived alone. She was found by building maintenance this morning after she missed a safety check-in at work. She's a counselor at the county juvenile hall. Or was."

Dirk looks for a response in the technician's eyes, but she's unreadable. "Any signs of sexual assault?"

"We're waiting on the kit, but the preliminaries are negative," the pathologist says. "No indications externally. I'll know more after the autopsy."

Dirk nods, not breaking his line of sight from the throat wound. "Anything left behind?" he asks.

The CSI lead, a heavyset guy with sweat stains under his lab coat, answers, "Not a hair. Whoever did this wore gloves and wiped the doorknobs. No footprints, plastic laid out from the entry to here. Partial palm print on the window, but that could be the vic's."

Dirk takes a step back and scans the room, narrowing in on the lack of clutter. "Any evidence this was a targeted attack?"

The photographer answers for him, his voice muffled behind his mask. "You don't kill like this by accident."

Dirk glances at the body again. The arms are locked

over the chest, fingertips overlapping precisely. The line of the neck wound is almost artistic, as if the killer wanted to display their skill. A faint, almost invisible bruise is developing under the right eye, but otherwise the face is untouched. He's seen this precision before.

Dirk's phone buzzes at his waist, but he ignores it. He kneels, one knee popping, and examines the left hand more closely. The victim's nails are short, clear, and scrubbed. Not a single jagged edge or hangnail, even though the skin of the knuckles is chapped from the cold. There is something unsettling about the carefulness of the pose, the way the body seems preserved rather than discarded.

He stands, brushing his hands on his trousers. "Any notes, letters, threats?" he asks the CSI chief.

"Not that we've found. Detectives talked to the neighbors. She kept to herself. Worked a lot. No stalkers, no exes with priors." The tech wipes his face with a sleeve. "It's just weird. Too neat."

Chapter Eight

Dirk surveys the room, looking for anything out of the pattern. He spots a single paperback novel on the nightstand, The Bell Jar, pages dog-eared to the final chapter. The clock radio is set to 5:45AM, matching her likely wake-up time for a day shift. The phone is on the charger, screen blank, but with a strip of lint stuck under the case. He makes a note to get it unlocked.

"Preserve everything," he says to the CSI chief. "We'll want to walk the scene again after the first pass."

The pathologist nods, already prepping a swab.

Dirk lingers a moment longer, letting the scene envelop him. The smell of blood and bleach and warm human residue forms a cloud in the cramped bedroom. His heart picks up a touch, thumping in his ears. He notices the prickling on his forearms, an old sensation, familiar, half dread, and half anticipation.

He steps back into the hall and pulls the phone from his belt. One missed call, three new messages, all from the Bureau. He reads the top preview line. **IS THE VICTIM SPIRAL CROSS COLORADO VICTIM #6?** He exhales slowly.

Down the hall, he hears the shuffle of foot traffic. The sense of the scene shifts, filling with a slow, building energy. Dirk pockets his phone, squares his shoulders, and reenters the main room, already mapping out the interview process in his head. He knows the drill. In his line of work, the way to avoid being swallowed by the horror is to ritualize it, turn the process itself into armor.

He glances once more at the bedroom, the tableau of careful violence, and files it away with all the others. There's a pattern, if he can make himself look at it straight.

Dirk stands in the kitchen, shoulder braced against the archway, replaying the last five minutes of the scene with forensic precision. Every detail is a thumbnail print: the single drop of blood on the baseboard, the silent body on plastic, the clock radio's mute LED. He runs the data through his internal sieve, hunting for the deviation that would unlock everything. The rhythm of the crime scene, the shuffle of CSI, and the static flicker of crime scene tape becomes a white noise buffer.

The forensic pathologist clears her throat. She is kneeling at the victim's side; her gloves are slicked with a thin sheen of blood. "You want to see the rest?" she says, words clipped to the bone. Dirk moves forward, watching her hands as she gently uncrosses the arms. A faint click of cartilage sounds as the elbows flex open.

The sweatshirt, navy, pilled at the sleeves, has been sliced vertically from the hem to the base of the throat. Beneath the sweatshirt, a hospital-green T-shirt soaked up most of the visible blood, but the cut underneath is what matters.

The pathologist pulls the fabric apart and exposes the chest. Dirk leans in, every nerve ending firing.

Directly over the sternum, someone has carved a cross, four precise incisions, intersecting at perfect right angles. There is no ragged edge, no hesitation in the stroke. The vertical slash runs from the dip of the throat to above the navel. A spiral, deep and symmetrical, radiates outward from the upper quadrant, extending the vertical line with a perfect coil. The wound is deep, more than cosmetic.

The sight of it hits Dirk harder than he expects. He's seen the same spiral cross five times before, in five different cities, each with its own murder board, each with its own set of composite sketches and suspect matrices. The signature is not a flourish; it's a demand to be recognized. Dirk's pulse stutters, his jaw clicking once as he grinds his teeth.

Dirk stands and leans on the kitchen table as his legs go weak. A scene flashes in his head radiating from behind his eyes. It's momentary, like a movie running in fast forward. He glimpses another kitchen. Another body on a floor and the flash of a similar symbol. The image disappears as fast as it appeared, and he leans into the counter to steady himself.

"Agent, are you okay?" asks the pathologist.

Dirk recovers. "Sorry. Please go on."

The pathologist glances up at him. "Does this match the others?"

Dirk nods. "It's identical. Even the spiral's direction, clockwise, with one and a half revolutions. Depth and placement, too. One saving grace is that the victims were all dead before the cutting began."

The CSI chief, standing a step behind, makes a low noise. "That means this wasn't random."

"Nothing about this is random," Dirk says, his voice flat.

He pulled a phone from his pocket, dialed into the FBI's case management system, and brought up a cluster of crime scene photos. He flicks through them, pausing on a close-up from the Greeley case: same pose, same symbol. In another case from Fort Collins, the victim, a retired special-ed teacher, had her throat cut, and her arms tucked neatly to her chest. The same image after the victims' arms were moved.

He angles the phone at the pathologist. "This is what you're looking at," he says. "Victim in the first was a youth pastor. Second, a group-home administrator. The spiral always sits at the top of the cross. The tool is probably a fillet knife, ultra-sharp, used by someone who knows anatomy."

The pathologist traces the spiral with her gloved fingertip, careful not to disturb the drying blood. "It's too clean. No hesitation marks at all. No second passes."

"First cut is the hardest," Dirk says, immediately regretting the phrasing.

Two Denver detectives step into the kitchen. One young, tall and athletic. The other, older, tired-looking, and slightly overweight. They stop short when they hear the conversation.

"That's why you guys are here. We've got a serial killer," said the younger detective.

Dirk looks at him. "It looks that way. We're getting our footing in these cases. We're looking for additional cases."

"Shit," said the older detective.

The kitchen fills with a moment of silence. Even the techs seem to back off, as if the wound has become its own gravity well. Dirk forces himself to inventory the room again, eyes darting for anything that might explain the signature's escalation. His own reaction irritates him, but he shoves it down, focusing instead on the geometry of the wounds, the careful way the plastic sheeting is folded, the brutal economy of the kill.

In the background, a CSI tech finishes sweeping for trace evidence. He holds up a lint roller, blank except for a few stray hairs. "All we're getting out of this is dog fur and a couple of split ends," the tech says. "No skin flakes, no fibers that don't belong."

Dirk taps the side of his phone, thinking. "The killer is forensically disciplined. It's possible the killer has military or medical training. There are no footprints or glove smears according to the other reports I've read so far. The killer uses disposable tools or cleans them on-site."

Chapter Nine

Heavy treads echo in the hallway. Dirk glances up, expecting a uniform, but the man who enters is square-shouldered, mid-forties, and in a rumpled FBI windbreaker. Anthony Spinella's hair is cut to a near-buzz, his jaw forever in five o'clock shadow. He walks straight into the epicenter of the scene, eyes skating over the body, the blood, the bruises, landing instead on Dirk with a pointed sense of ownership.

"Trainor. You look like hell," Spinella says. He turns to the pathologist. "What've we got?"

"Victim's name is Huxley. juvenile counselor, no dependents. Time of death was maybe ten hours ago. Single incised wound to the throat. The chest mutilation came after. No sexual assault, no sign of forced entry. Scene's cleaner than a surgical suite."

Spinella grunts. "Signature?"

Dirk lifts the victim's wrist gently, exposing the inside of the arm. There, above the pulse point, is another spiral cross. This one inked, not cut, but the lines are as deliberate as a tattoo.

Spinella's eyes flick to Dirk's, narrowing. "Just like the others?"

Dirk doesn't answer, but swipes the phone again, showing the pattern from the other cases. "So far, all the victims work with at-risk kids. They're all single, all mid-career, all women. The pose is the same; the cut is the same. In every case, no witnesses, and there was no forced entry."

Spinella rubs at the bridge of his nose. "Fuck. Serial killer. What's he telling us?"

Dirk studies the wounds, the scene, the arrangement. "That he can go anywhere, do anything. That he's untouchable and that the he you keep referring to could be a she."

Spinella breathes out through his teeth. "What kind of sick bastard are we dealing with here?"

Dirk hesitates. He thinks about the spiral, the cross, the way the wounds always get neater, more practiced. He thinks about how the victim was a counselor, how she'd given twenty years to keeping broken kids out of jail. He thinks about the way the body is arranged, like an exhibit, and something twists inside him.

"An artist," he says. "A technician. A true believer. Who knows?"

Spinella snorts. "That's the worst kind."

The pathologist sets the victim's arms back over her chest, and peels off her gloves. "We'll know more once we get inside," she says.

Dirk looks back at the body, tracing the perfect geometry of the cross and spiral. He catalogues every line, every angle, already building the next layer of the profile. But he's not sure if he wants to see what's coming next.

Spinella snaps a photo of the wound with his own phone. "Let's get ahead of this before the press puts these murders together," he says.

Dirk nods but doesn't answer. He keeps his eyes locked on the wound, as if by force of will he can pull meaning out of the gash. The scene presses in, clinical and stifling. He waits until the room is empty except for himself and the body. He studies the spiral cross again, memorizing its every nuance.

He lets his hands shake for a second before pressing them flat to his sides.

Dirk sets his jaw and slips a new pair of gloves over his hands, beginning the documentation. He works deliberately. First, a slow walk around the perimeter, dictating every stain and mark into the recorder on his phone. Next, he uses a laser pointer to confirm the angles of blood spray, testing the pathologist's time-of-death calculation. He logs the temperature, the humidity and the micro-patterns of dust on the heater vent. He kneels at the victim's side, ignoring the stick of blood on his slacks.

The spiral cross is less dramatic up close, but more disturbing for its exactness. The crosshatch is cut to sub-millimeter precision, and the spiral widens in a geometric progression, a golden ratio, if you were sick enough to apply mathematics to murder. Dirk reaches out and nudges the plastic sheet, testing how it absorbs the pooling blood. There are no tool marks on the plastic; the killer either cleaned up or was simply that good. His hands remain steady as he measures each cut, dictating length, depth and direction into the voice recorder on his phone.

Around him, the CSI team recedes into their routines. A tech shoots frame after frame with a Nikon, the shutter noise soft but relentless. Another brushes a swab along the doorjamb, careful not to smear the single droplet of blood suspended there. The tension is communal and stifling. Nobody jokes or complains. Each step is a choreography of despair.

Dirk stands, stretching the ache from his knees. He reviews his notes, pulling back the corner of the plastic sheet to examine the underside. He's not looking for anything, just hoping for a micro-flaw, a clue, a sign of imperfection. He finds none.

A drop of sweat slides down the side of his face, cold despite the room's oppressive heat. Dirk wipes it with the back of his wrist, as the latex catches against his skin. He pivots and steps out of the room, needing air that isn't loaded with blood vapor and defeat.

He walks to the window, lifts the sash an inch, and inhales the sting of winter. Below, police cars idle in a ragged line, headlights pooling in the runoff. On the far side of the parking lot, a news crew adjusts its gear, hands cupped to block the glare. Someone in uniform is handing out statement sheets to the building's residents. Dirk watches the world turn, slow and unhurried, as if nothing inside the apartment could disrupt it.

His phone vibrates against his hip. He pulls it out and reads the new message, subject line in all caps: **SIMILAR CASES IN AZ.**

It's from Special Agent Jill Quarters, his partner. The body of the message is terse:

— **Two cold case homicides in the Phoenix metro. Both females, both in-home, both carved with a spiral cross.**

— **Another one in Santa Fe, but MO not

confirmed.

— **Only common factor: throat slit, carved spiral cross.**

He leans against the window frame and closes his eyes for a count of five. When he opens them, the world outside is the same, but his pulse is doubled, a tremor under the skin. He reviews the files again, comparing the angle, the depth and the rhythm of each cut. None of these details were ever released, not even to local police. Whoever this is, they're working off a template. Or they're learning, adapting, and getting better.

Dirk pockets the phone, takes a breath and closes the window. He re-enters the scene, ready to recite his findings to the detectives and the pathologist, but for a moment he stands in the bedroom, looking at the clean line between horror and order. There is something about the pattern that's more than mere repetition. It's a message being sent, one that he hasn't yet decoded. He senses it in the arrangement of the body, in the golden ratio spiral, in the silence that follows the click of the camera shutter.

He pinches the bridge of his nose, shakes his head once, and tells himself to compartmentalize. There's no space for fear, or for awe, only the next step. The Bureau needs answers, not emotions. The world outside the window expects nothing less.

Dirk steps back to the center of the room. His investigation has grown into something ugly.

Chapter Ten

The FBI's Denver Field Office is a hive of synchronized movement under unsparing fluorescent lights. Walls vibrate with the undertones of ringing phones and the pulse of the building-wide HVAC. Rows of battered desks sprawl outward, each topped with screens flickering from case files to databases to interoffice memos. In the corner, a bank of printers deposits a steady ticker tape of legal sheets onto the tile floor. The air tastes of dust and coffee left too long on the burner.

Jill Quarters moves with purpose through the open bullpen, a slim manila folder in one hand, a stick of gum in the other. She is tall, almost Dirk's height, with her hair in a tight ponytail that amplifies the severe lines of her jaw. Her eyes are serious, dark green, and she does not smile at the jokes or small talk that tries to snag her as she passes. She heads straight for the war room, barely glancing at the men and women crowded in their bullpen silos.

Inside the war room, there's nothing but a cold wood table, four leather desk chairs, and several whiteboards pushed to one corner. Dirk sits at the table, sleeves rolled up past the watch, and his face is ashen above a cup of black coffee. He's looking through the photos he transferred from his phone to his laptop. When Jill enters, he nods and points to the chair next to him.

Jill slides the manila folder onto the table between them. She peels the gum wrapper with a thumbnail and crumples it before speaking.

"We have a pattern match," she says. "Arizona forwarded us a cold case out of Maricopa County. They want your eyes on it."

Dirk lifts the folder and sifts the contents onto the table. The first is a stack of glossy eight-by-tens: overhead shots, blood-wet tile, something surgical about the plastic and tape holding the victim's limbs apart. Next is a series of close-ups, the wounds limned by evidence markers and tight-edged ruler tape. Dirk leans in, chin almost touching the table, and sorts the photos into chronological order. He pauses once, his finger hovering over a raw image of a spiral cross carved into skin.

"You see it?" Jill asks, a hint of impatience at the corner of her mouth.

Dirk's eyes flick upward. "Identical. Even the tool marks look the same. No fraying on the margins, no double-cuts. It's a single stroke, the same as Greeley. What's the timeline?"

Jill plucks a document from the pile and flattens it on the table. "Three months ago. The victim was found at 0500 by a groundskeeper. No sign of forced entry and no sexual component. The picture looks like it could have been taken at your crime scene yesterday, except for the tape. Our guy didn't use tape on his victims, did he?"

Dirk's jaw tightens. He flips to the next set of photos. "No. There was no sign that he had had to subdue his victim before he killed her. Did they send us a victim profile?"

"She had worked for the past fifteen years as a data entry clerk at an accounting firm," Jill says. She taps the summary sheet. "Her husband works in the oil industry out of state. No children are listed in the profile. She lived alone while he was working in the fields. According to the police report, he is home one week out of every six."

Dirk lays a hand on the table. He reviews each image, organizing them by detail: entry wound, angle of attack, postmortem manipulation.

Jill watches him, arms crossed. "You look like you haven't slept."

"Didn't," Dirk says, not taking his eyes off the photos. "Neither did the killer."

For a minute, they sit silently. Jill fishes a pen from behind her ear and circles two points in the document margins: a note about the location of the wound on the sternal notch, and a notation about a missing segment of spiral at the base. Dirk traces the pattern with a pen cap, matching it against the Greeley and Fort Collins bodies. The symmetry is off by a degree, nothing a layperson would notice but glaring to Dirk.

"Why now?" Dirk murmurs. "What changed?"

"What do you mean, what changed?" she asked.

"Why move to Arizona and come back to Colorado?"

"Business travel?" asks Jill.

"I don't know," said Dirk. "Look at the crime scene photos. The five scenes we have are clean and meticulous. The Arizona scene is chaotic, more haphazard. It's like the scenes are the same but slightly different. The Arizona unsub tied his victim with tape to secure her; ours doesn't."

Jill pulls a chair and sits opposite him, chair legs screeching against the floor. "I think he's playing to the audience," she says. "We keep it out of the press, see if he gets louder. If he doesn't get any recognition, maybe the signature gets bigger."

Dirk snorts. "Ego."

"Or confidence," Jill says. "He's not worried about getting caught."

A printer kicks on in the hallway, ratcheting the noise up a notch. Dirk ignores it and holds two photos side-by-side, the wounds overlaying each other. He closes his eyes for a heartbeat, sets the photos down, and draws a quick, rough diagram in the notebook.

Jill leans forward, tapping the side of her pen against the table. "So, I heard you had an issue at the crime scene yesterday. You lost focus for a minute. Anything you want to tell me?"

Dirk says nothing, lips thinning as he considers. His skin seems to pale further, eyes drawn and faintly red. His fingers tap the tabletop, first in a slow rhythm, then faster.

Jill looks at him, at his hand, and says, "You know, you can talk to me, right? Whatever it is."

Dirk's leg has stopped bouncing. "I'm fine," he says, but the words land too quickly.

Jill watches him for another moment. "I ran the profile against the previous cases. We're looking for a white male, late twenties to early forties. Works with his hands, maybe a vet, someone in the medical field, or a butcher. No wife, probably no family. Grew up in the system, bounced around as a kid." She pauses. "And in my gut, I think he's local. These last two are close to each other geographically."

Dirk's eyes flick up, pupils dilated. "Back to the same question. Why kill in Arizona?"

Jill flips a few pages deeper in the file, uncapping a highlighter. "The victim in Arizona wasn't connected to the juvenile justice system like the Colorado victims. According to the police report, she left work at six p.m. like she did every night. She met a girlfriend for dinner at a plain-Jane restaurant close to her house. Left the restaurant and drove straight home."

Dirk digests that. "You think she was targeted?"

Jill nods. "I'm not sure. The vibe I get from the chaotic crime scene photos is that Arizona was a crime of opportunity, but our guy in Colorado doesn't do random. I get the sense that our guy targets his victims and follows them until he establishes a routine before he strikes."

Dirk licks his lips, staring at the table, and says, "Has to be someone with access to their backgrounds. Not someone googling names."

"Or he's inside the system. Case worker, tech, maybe even law enforcement," said Jill.

Dirk picks up one of the Arizona crime scene photos and stares at it. He closes his eyes. His breathing shallows. For a second, the room spins, and the buzzing light whines up a semitone. His hands grasp the table and his knuckles go white.

Jill notices and stands, moving to his side. She puts a hand on his forearm, not a comforting gesture. More like bracing him so he doesn't collapse.

"Dirk," she says, her tone flat and command-like. "Look at me."

He blinks, blinks again, and finally lifts his chin. Sweat beads along his temples.

"Are you having an episode of some kind?" she asks. "Because I can call Spinella in here right now and tell him to—"

"No." Dirk's voice is thin, but it holds. "I'm fine. Just moved too quickly."

She doesn't move her hand. "Dirk. You look like you're about to fall out of your chair."

Dirk forces a laugh. "I'll live. Sorry." He sits up straighter, and the color seeps back into his cheeks. He reaches for the coffee, sips, and sets it down with a trembling hand.

Jill retracts her grip and moves back to her seat. "Next time, tell me when you're about to go under."

"It's not a thing. Really. I probably need to eat something." But his eyes are darting, flicking from folder to photo.

Jill sighs, opens the next folder, and slides it across the table. "This is from Flagstaff. Last month, but it came through because the case was classified as a domestic. Spiral cross, identical MO. Only the vic was an adult male, a retired teacher, sixty-seven. He was found on the kitchen floor with a plastic sheet under him. The house looked as though there had been a violent confrontation. Chaotic."

"Why was this classified as a domestic abuse case?" he asked.

Jill pulls out the police report. "According to the detective on the case. The victim was at the start of Alzheimer's and had an adult son living with him. They had had some issues in the past, and the locals had been called to the house several times. They have been unable to locate the son."

"But the victim had the spiral cross carved into his chest, correct?" asked Dirk.

"According to the photos, that's correct. It looks like their focus was on finding the son and not in dealing with the cross."

Dirk steadies himself. He leans forward. "Could the son be our killer as well?"

Jill shrugs. "I don't see it. Why would he be meticulous up here and chaotic in Arizona?"

Dirk shakes his head. "Anything's possible. The cuts are similar, but not exact. If it's not the same guy in Colorado and Arizona, we could have two killers."

"Are they talking to each other?" she asked. "We've mentioned nothing about the spiral cross, and neither have the locals. We'll need to check with the Arizona office and see what they say."

Jill frowns. "What are you thinking?"

Dirk runs his hands through his hair, fingers combing the strands until they stand up at odd angles. He studies the spiral cross, every angle, every increment, and says, "We need to go to Arizona."

He stands abruptly, scraping his chair. The tremor is gone from his legs, but a hollow look lingers on his face.

Jill watches him, her face unreadable. "You sure you're okay?"

"Never better." He picks up the file. "I need to get some fresh air and some real food."

Jill gathers the files, her motions brisk and practiced. "Don't wander far," she says. "Spinella is expecting an update."

Dirk nods, already moving toward the door. He pushes through, letting the static air of the office chill his face.

Jill sits alone in the room for a moment, tracing the spiral in the photo with the end of her pen. She gathers her things and leaves.

In the hall, the phones ring, the printers spit out reams, and the lights burn on. Dirk walks the length of the corridor, his footsteps deliberate and slow, until the sounds of the field office dissolve into white noise behind him.

He finds a bank of windows, presses his palm to the glass, and looks out over the city. The sky is a bruised violet, dawn crawling slowly behind the skyline. Dirk inhales and lets the cold soak into his skin.

The images from Arizona persist behind his eyelids,

sharp as the first moment he saw them.

He opens his eyes again, steadies himself, and steps away from the glass.

Chapter Eleven

Morning at the field office: a knot of agents in the break room trade stories about last night's scores; someone microwaves oatmeal, someone else refills a vat of stale coffee. The smell of scorched grounds drifts into the hallway, pooling at the threshold of Dirk's office. He sits inside, half-immersed in a stack of case files, highlighter poised above a paragraph as if it might brand the answers into the paper itself.

The walls are beige, adorned with two blown-up prints: one a Colorado Rockies outfield shot, the other a seven-pointed graphic from the BAU's training modules. The desktop is scarred by years of bored penmanship, but every current case is arranged in perfect quadrants: active, cold, suspended, and personal research. Dirk's own handwriting covers the margins of every printout, tight and precise.

At 8:17, the desk phone rings, two short bursts that jar the silence. Dirk snatches it on reflex, wedging it between his shoulder and cheek.

"Trainor."

A voice on the other end, light and a little breathless: "Hey, uh, hi, Agent Trainor? My name is Carl Bunch. I'm an analyst at Headquarters. I hope this isn't a bad time?"

Dirk eyes the digital clock on his desk, sets the highlighter down and picks up the file on the latest Colorado Victim. "Not at all, Carl. What's up?"

Carl's voice is a staccato blend of excitement and

apology, the kind that can only be produced by a life spent double-checking facts. "So, um, I saw your request come through yesterday looking for similar cases with a carved cross in Colorado and Arizona. I'm kind of a nut about serial killer cases, and I work after hours sometimes to see if I can find anything new in the old files. Last night I ran a new search, and I found…well, something that didn't match before. A cold case. Two of them. Phoenix, 2002. Two Kids."

Dirk is reading the pathologist's preliminary autopsy report and is semi-focused on the call. "What kind of kids?"

"Teenagers. Girls. One was fifteen; the other sixteen. They were… uh, discovered in a ravine north of the city limits. The crime scene is all but textbook for your unsub. They went missing after a high school football game. The bodies were found the next morning. Both had that cross symbol, but the Phoenix ME called it an anomaly, and the detective handling the case saw them as some local kid trying to scare folks, and the file got tagged as possible cult activity. Nobody looped it in with any other cases. It never went beyond being a local case. The database… it, um, it never matched because the age bracket was off. I'm in the office, and we're running a new search for similar cases, but I wanted to get these to you asap."

Dirk keeps reading the coroner's report. "Were the wounds postmortem?" he asked.

"I checked the original coroner's notes," said Carl. "Yeah. Both girls' throats were cut, there was no sign of sexual assault, and according to the police report, the scene was chaotic. It looked like at least one of the girls fought back."

Dirk stopped reading and put the report down. "And the families? Did they have any overlap with the victims in the Colorado cases?"

"I cross-referenced, but didn't find any commonalities to your victims," said Carl.

Dirk taps his notepad; the noise is sharp and staccato. "Anything else in the file?"

Carl's breathing ramps up a notch. "Yeah. There's a detail in the evidence log. Uh, one of the crime scene photos shows a Sharpie spiral drawn on one girl."

Dirk sits up in his chair, shoulders rising. "The drawn spiral. Was it on the girl's wrist?"

"Yes, sir. Does that mean something?"

"Your name is Carl, right?" asked Dirk. "Can you send me the files on that case?"

"Yup. I digitized them already. I can send the link right now."

"Do that. All the raw photos, too. Not only the writeups," said Dirk.

"Already queued up. One thing, Agent Trainor," said Carl.

"Yes?"

"You think it's the same guy? I mean, the timeline is huge. Twenty years. Is that even… possible?" asked Carl.

Dirk studies the outfield photo, the clean lines of the chalk against the green. "Possible isn't the word. But it's not impossible. Sometimes the gap isn't a cooling-off; it could be a lot of things."

Carl is silent for a beat. "You want me to run it against anything else?"

Dirk's answer is immediate and clipped. "Every spiral cross in the system, no matter how sloppy. Flag every age, every location, every pattern. Include the ones classified as suicide or accidental, if the signature shows up. Expand to Canada if you have to and go back as far as 1990."

"Copy that. I'll, uh, get started right away."

Dirk kills the call. He stares at his screen. The spiral cross from Arizona is still up on the monitor, the lines ink-black and stark on skin.

He types a quick command, opens his email, and pulls up the link to the BAU files.

The photos load, first a police mugshot of the two girls in jeans and T-shirts, followed by a set of evidence photos: the wound pattern is unmistakable. The same spiral cross, but this one is shaky with rough edges and hesitation marks. Dirk's pulse quickens, but his fingers remain steady on the mouse.

He zooms in on the wrist. The spiral, even in shaky marker, is as deliberate as a tattoo.

Dirk makes a note: "Origination: Phoenix, 2002. Cut spiral rough, spiral hand drawn on wrist. Victims: minors. Could this be his first kill?"

The office outside his window surges to life, a ripple of voices, a fax shrilling, the intercom calling for a supervisor. But Dirk sits perfectly still, a single point of silence in the storm. He reads every word, looks at every photo, and every timestamp in the file, searching for something.

After a minute, he closes his eyes, letting the images drift behind his lids. He counts his breathing down from ten, exhaling slowly. He opens his eyes, clicks to the next folder, and keeps searching.

Chapter Twelve

Scottsdale PD sits squat and sun-bleached between a strip mall laundromat and a drive-thru pizza chain, but inside the station, the air hums with the same institutional pulse as every other cop shop in America. The front desk is a barricade of Lucite and faded protest flyers. Overhead, the lighting flattens skin and sharpens shadows; every surface wears a slick of sanitizer. Dirk and Jill step into the lobby as an officer in tactical gear bullhorns into the phone, her voice slicing through the reek of burned coffee. Even the potted snake plant looks stressed.

"Federal?" asks the desk sergeant, not looking up from his crossword.

Dirk flashes his badge. "Trainor and Quarters, FBI. Here to see Detective Veracruz."

"Third floor," says the sergeant, uncapping a fresh pen with his teeth. "Elevator is taped off. Use the stairs."

They hike three flights past a flotilla of blue-shirted officers, most too busy to acknowledge the suits weaving through their orbit. Dirk notes each surveillance camera, each junction box, and the lingering scent of a thousand microwaved burritos. On three, a man waits, late fifties, slab-chested, balding at the equator. His badge rides low on a belt of perpetual expansion, his face set in the world-weary resignation of a desk lifer.

"Special Agent Trainor?" The voice is gravelly dry,

but with the lingering musicality of Arizona. "Julio Veracruz. Homicide." He shakes hands with Jill and Dirk, the grip more ceremonial than committed.

Veracruz leads them down a corridor of windowless offices to a cubicle, claustrophobic even by precinct standards. The desktop is a minefield of paper, stacked in shifting pyramids. Framed photos, family, a marathon medal, a dog, battle for territory with battered reference books and two empty energy drink cans. On the wall, there's a sun-faded poster of the 2001 Diamondbacks. Julio gestures at the two plastic visitor chairs that groan under the insult of new weight.

He pops a file folder and shoves it across the desk. "You wanted to see the two-thousand-two double?"

"That's the one," says Dirk, voice brittle but polite. He thumbs the folder open. The first page is a ME's intake report, standardized to the point of abstraction. The second is a 35mm crime scene photo: day shot, two teenage girls splayed out in a grass clearing surrounded by trees, faces turned away. The flash reveals a smear of red, pooling under their chins. Arms crossed over their chests, no, Dirk corrects, folded in a strange, prayerful pose.

"Victims," says Julio, as if reading the photos for the thousandth time. "Kaitlin Suarez and Desiree Logan. Juniors at Mesquite High. Best friends vanished after a home football game. Search teams found them the following morning in the woods behind the school. Both throats were cut, and some kind of ritual carving on the chest. No drugs on the tox panel. No sexual assault."

Jill leans in, flipping the photo. "Any indication they knew the perpetrator?"

"Nothing in the initial interviews. No boyfriend overlap, no beef. Kaitlin did some youth church stuff; Desiree had two part-time jobs. They weren't even from the same side of town. No prints at the scene, but the ground was torn up pretty good and there were some broken shrubs. One of them put up a fight." Veracruz taps the side of his nose. "Rumor was cult initiation. Some shithead drew a pentagram on the sidewalk, and the media ran with it. After a month, it was a page ten story."

Dirk shuffles the stack. The next photo is a close-up, harsh, and overexposed. It shows Kaitlin's chest, skin incised with a cross, arms folded perfectly below the sternum. The spiral is cruder than the Denver victims, but unmistakable. He notes the hollow snap behind his ribcage; a faint echo of the first time he saw the pattern.

He places the photo on the desk. "Were the wounds postmortem?"

"That's what the ME said, yeah. He called it devotional mutilation. Not a phrase you forget. Like I said, the scene was a mess. They found a Sharpie spiral on Desiree's wrist, which was bizarre." Veracruz scratches his beard, eyes flicking to the wall. "It didn't stop the public from turning in every goth kid in a hundred-mile radius into a suspect."

Jill takes out her phone, cross-referencing dates and times. "Can we see the rest? Scene log, initial interviews?"

"Sure. You got a minute for paperwork, you've got a minute for me," says Julio. He reaches behind him and extracts another file, the tab labeled in violent neon. "This is everything I kept. The originals are in storage, but there's nothing you can't see here." He flicks a copy of the scene diagram onto the table: two stick figure bodies, shaded with red pencil, labeled Suarez and Logan. "See the spiral? Our crime scene guy called it a doodle. Now I'm hearing you have another case in Denver with the same design. Twenty-three years is a long time between murders, or you figure it for a copycat?"

Dirk nodded, shuffling through the case materials. "Our most recent case makes six. Once we got involved, we came up with five cold cases over the past ten years. We're still looking for more. All our victims were adults, all female, all with some kind of connection to kids, teachers, social workers, counselors. The signature matches, but the precision is getting sharper. Yours is rough by comparison."

Veracruz shrugs. "Means he was young, or it was his first time, right?"

"Or he had an accomplice," said Jill.

Julio's mouth twists into a frown. "What I don't get is why the Bureau's here now. This case went dry before YouTube even existed. You got a tip-off, or what?"

Dirk hesitated. "We're chasing the pattern, not a person. The current unsub may have ties to the old Phoenix case. Or he's been inspired by it."

Veracruz leans back, his hands splayed on his

knees. "You're saying we got a copycat? After twenty years?"

"Or a second subject," says Dirk, eyes pinned to the crime scene diagram. "If there were two, the apprentice might still be active. You ever get a sense from the scene that it was a two-person job?"

The detective's lips purse, but he doesn't answer right away. "I always thought the wounds looked the same. Like you said, rough. But the lab was too busy looking for DNA to care. We were lucky to get a full day on a murder before they shoved us onto the next one."

Jill scans the intake interview with Kaitlin's mother. "Did the families ever receive a threat? Any sign they were targeted in advance?"

Veracruz's expression darkens. "Kaitlin's mom got a call once. A blocked number. The caller said her daughter was a sheep led to slaughter. We pulled the phone record, traced it to a motel payphone on the 101. Nobody on the cameras. Desiree's people never got anything. They moved to Texas two years after."

Dirk pivots a photo under the harsh cubicle light. "Anything else?"

Julio glances over at the glass door. The bullpen outside is louder now, a wave of officers cycling through lunch and shift change. "There was a third girl with them, apparently. They walked to the stadium as a group, but the friend bailed at halftime. Her name was Vicky. She never came up as a suspect, said goodnight, and went home. Nobody bothered her after the funeral."

Jill: "We'll want to talk to her. Got a current contact?"

"Yeah. It's probably in the log. Hell, she might still be local."

Dirk lines up the three photos. He traces the wounds with a pencil eraser, mind running every overlap. "The killer improves with every attack. In Denver, the cut is surgical. Here, it's hesitant, like a rehearsal. My bet is we're looking for someone who's been in the system a while but got spooked and went dark for years."

"Prison," says Jill. "Or hospital."

Veracruz stands, palms on the Formica. "Or he left town. Hell, for all we know, he joined the Marines." He leans in. "You really think he's going to kill again?"

Dirk meets his gaze. "If he hasn't already."

The three of them sit in the crowded office, the case file now a living organism, breathing with the tension of the unknown. On the wall, the Diamondbacks poster grins, oblivious to the horror on the table.

Dirk's phone buzzes in his pocket, a double pulse, Bureau number. He answers on autopilot, "Trainor."

On the other end, a thin, nervous voice: "Agent Trainor? It's Carl Bunch. We met over the phone yesterday. I'm, uh, running a side channel on your spiral cross inquiry."

Dirk glanced at Jill, who was already poised, pen to paper. "Go ahead, Carl."

"Sorry to bother you, but there's a current case in

Arizona. Prescott PD flagged it. A woman in her thirties, found in the woods, same cross, and the same spiral. I, uh, didn't want to send you the photos over email, but I can if you need."

Dirk stiffens. "When was she killed?"

"Unknown, but the body is fresh. BAU received a request for similar cases from Detective Sandy Malloy."

Jill's eyes go wide; she grabs the phone from Dirk's hand. "Carl, send us a copy of the request."

"Yes, ma'am. You want me to keep running the old cases?"

Dirk takes the phone back, voice hard. "Full capacity, Carl. Go all the way back to the eighties if you have to. And cross-check for men. This guy might have changed his victimology."

"Copy that." Carl hesitates. "You think there are two of them, don't you?"

Dirk weighed the question. "I think we haven't seen everything yet." He hung up with a flick of a thumb.

Veracruz's eyebrows jump. "You've got another victim already?"

"In Prescott," said Dirk, gathering the photos into a neat stack. "We need to get up there now."

Jill stood, pocketing her notes. "We'll want copies of the file, Detective. And the Vicky contact, if possible." She hands him a card. "That's the address for the FBI lab. Please gather all the evidence, clothes, personal effects, and anything else you might have and send it to that address, asap, by secure courier. We'll pick up the cost."

Julio shrugged into his jacket and lumbered out of the office, already barking orders for a junior to pull the archive. He returned in under a minute, handing over a battered manila envelope and a printed page of numbers.

Dirk tucked the file into his satchel. "We'll keep you in the loop."

Veracruz waves a tired salute. "If you catch the bastard, call me. I owe those girls."

In the hallway, Jill steps in close and whispers. "How likely is it that there are two?"

Dirk runs his tongue along his teeth, thinking. "If it's two, they're competing. Or collaborating. Either way, it got a lot messier."

Jill nodded, her expression unreadable. "Better not keep the killer waiting."

They cross the parking lot, the sky so blue it's blinding, and slide into their rental car, pulling up the next address. As they pull out, the station's shadow recedes in the rearview mirror, leaving nothing but sun and the endless, empty highway.

Chapter Thirteen

They drive north with the air conditioning blasting and the windows closed tight against the heat of the Sonoran Desert. Dirk keeps his hands at ten and two, eyes fixed on the seam of blacktop slicing through scrub and saguaro. To the east, a billboard advertises discount cremations. To the south, the haze of Phoenix lingers on the horizon, always receding, but never disappearing.

Jill spent the first few minutes of the drive reviewing the Prescott request. She called Detective Mallory and set up a meeting at police headquarters. She read the case notes with the efficiency of a human scanner, lips pursed as she flipped through each printout. She marked the margins with a red pen, cross-hatching potential links between the Phoenix cold case and the fresh Prescott murder. For twenty minutes she said nothing, except the occasional "huh" or "interesting" as a detail surfaced.

"What stands out?" asked Dirk.

Jill flips a page. "The spiral motif is getting more refined. Phoenix was a shaky cartoon; Denver was a gold-leaf replica. Same design, but the technique is different. Whoever did Scottsdale has practiced, or it's a new hand."

Dirk's right foot twitches on the accelerator. "You think there are two?"

"Two, or one who has killing down to a science." Jill underlines a sentence with surgical precision. "Or someone else is copying. We won't know until we see the newest body."

The highway climbs. The desert gives way to brittle juniper and pine. The temperature drops ten degrees in half an hour. The rental shudders at every hairpin, its shocks never built for mountain roads. As they approach the outskirts of Prescott, the world shifts from barren to tentative green. In the valley below, the town huddles like a picture postcard: brick storefronts, a courthouse ringed by granite steps, and Victorian houses stubbornly bright against a backdrop of ponderosa and dusk.

They park in front of the Prescott PD, a blocky tan building with dark windows. Inside, the squad room is a fraction of Scottsdale's, but the nervous energy is the same. An officer at the front desk sizes them up, clocking the badges, and points them down a hallway.

In the corridor, a woman waits. She's in her mid-thirties, average height, with dark hair pulled back in a ponytail that doesn't tame the stray wisps. Her suit is neat, but not expensive. Her gaze has a precision Dirk immediately respects, every detail registered, nothing wasted.

"Detective Sandy Malloy," she says, shaking their hands. "Thanks for coming up so fast. It's not every day we get the Feds in town."

"Special Agents Trainor and Quarters," says Dirk. "We were in the neighborhood. You're the lead on the body?"

"Yeah," said Malloy. "I got the short straw. The show is up at Thumb Butte Trail." She hands over a single glossy photo, female, late twenties, or early thirties, laid out on a bed of pine needles. Throat slashed, arms folded at the chest. Dirk looks for the signature, finds it, and nods.

"You said it was unique enough to flag?" asks Jill.

"First time I've seen it, and I've worked plenty of weird murders." Malloy's eyes flick to the clock on the wall. "The medical examiner is out there already. Her name is Pauline. She's the best coroner north of Phoenix but doesn't take well to people walking through her scene."

"She'll take it from us," says Dirk.

Jill looks at him and answers. "We'll be respectful."

"Fair warning," says Mallory. "The press is sniffing around. Word gets out fast when a body's found near a hiking trail." She studies Dirk for a beat. "Do you two want to go see, or do you want the files first?"

"Let's go look at the scene. We'll get to the file later."

Jill tucks the photo into her notebook, clicks her pen shut. "Did you send any samples to the lab yet?"

Malloy shakes her head. "Not yet. We bagged everything, but I didn't want to jump the gun and miss something. I checked up on you guys with a friend in Denver. If this is a serial, I'm open to any suggestions you might offer."

There's a pause as they walk through the vestibule. On the walls, framed photos: police athletic league trophies, and a few memorial plaques. Malloy leads them to the lot and unlocks a battered gray Explorer with a police bar-coded sticker on the bumper.

They pile in, the inside still holding the ghost of someone else's cigarettes. Malloy drives. The roads coil through town, past the old courthouse with its bronze statue of Bucky O'Neill, up through neighborhoods where mailboxes lean on their posts like old men. They leave the residential grid and hit the fire road that serves the Thumb Butte trailhead.

Jill scans the forest as it scrolls by. "Any sign this was premeditated? Or did she get unlucky?"

Malloy doesn't look back but keeps her eyes on the road. "We don't have a name for her yet, but she was geared up for a day hike. Water bottle, some trail mix, phone fully charged. No indication she knew the killer. Someone took her by surprise."

"Any witnesses?" asks Dirk.

"None. The closest house is three hundred yards uphill. Hikers found her around six a.m." Malloy slows as the dirt road grows rough. "Sheriff's office pulled a few game camera images, but nothing useful. Whoever did this walked in and out, clean as a whistle."

"Did they move the body?" asks Jill.

"If they did, it was only a few feet," responds Mallory. "The ground was soft from the rain, but the body's initial position matched the drag marks. She was posed where she fell."

The car jounces into a clearing already lined with yellow tape and the buzzing of police radios. A forensic van sits to one side; the back doors open like jaws. Past the tape, the forest breathes deep, and cool sunlight filters to surgical blue through the dense canopy.

Dirk steps out, rolling his sleeves to the elbows. Jill follows, notebook and pen in hand.

They duck under the tape, and the world goes quiet, as if the woods itself is holding its breath.

Chapter Fourteen

The woods above Prescott are frozen with the anticipation of late fall. Shadows suture the trees together, light and cold holding their uneasy truce. Beyond the yellow tape, the forest floor is churned with evidence of a desperate fight: snapped twigs, a clawed pattern of disturbed needles, flecks of red on the leaves.

Dirk walks the perimeter, boots making no noise, counting footprints and imagining the attack in real time. He notes the way the rain has polished the rocks, the sticky web of sap on a broken pine limb. He records each outlier with a flick of his phone's camera: a granola bar wrapper, a lens cap, a shoelace ripped loose and left in the dirt.

The victim lies ten feet from the nearest trail marker, sprawled as if the ground refused to let her rest. She wears a teal windbreaker, muddy at the hem, and dark leggings streaked with old pine tar. The throat wound is surgical, more precise than any Dirk has seen so far. Her hands are crossed like the others, but her face is turned toward the sky.

The Medical Examiner crouches by the body. Her hair is silver and cut short, glasses on a chain bobbing with each movement. She's wrapped in a battered down vest, but her gloved hands work with the precision of a safecracker.

Dirk kneels beside her. "Time of death?"

The ME doesn't look up. "Body temp and liver

mortis suggest late Thursday, maybe between seven and nine p.m. The cold slowed everything down. Hikers found her at six this morning, but she was here at least thirty-six hours before that. I'll know more once I get her on the table." She shifts the jacket aside, exposing the chest wound and the cut T-shirt. "No blood under the jacket. She was cut after she was dead."

Dirk goes still as an image flashes through his subconscious. He sweats and places a hand on the ground to steady himself. The image flies by and disappears. Jill steps up and rests a hand on his shoulder as the ME looks up at him.

"You alright, Agent?" she asks.

Dirk shakes off the effect when a thought sneaks into his mind, taking the place left by the flashing image.

"Did you say Thursday evening?" he asks.

Jill looks at him. "Shit," she says louder than she expected.

The ME and the detective look at each other. "Something wrong, Agent?" asks Mallory.

Dirk looks at Jill, and she nods. "That's the same date and time range as our Denver murder."

Mallory looks surprised. "The killer can't be in two places at the same time. What are we dealing with?"

Dirk stands. "Doc, we're gonna need the TOD as soon as possible."

Jill trains her camera on the scene. She circles the

body, photographing the position of the feet, the way the arms are folded. Her expression never shifts, but her eyes flick to Dirk's every few seconds, tracking his reactions.

Malloy stands off to one side, watching the investigators with a poker player's detachment. She doesn't intrude, but her foot taps an irregular pattern in the dirt.

The ME moves the hands to the side of the body. The incision is perfect: a cross scored onto the skin, a single spiral radiating from the intersection. There's no smudge, no wasted motion. The lines are so exact they almost look like they were made with a compass and straightedge.

"This matches the Colorado case down to the last millimeter," says Dirk. He shifts, eyes narrowing. "Anything on the wrists?"

The ME rolls up the victim's sleeve. On the left wrist, faint but visible, is a marker-drawn spiral cross. It looks rushed, almost like a stamp or a brand. The ME takes a photo with her own phone. Dirk does the same.

Jill is scribbling notes, her handwriting a tight line of code. She never glances up.

Malloy moves in, squatting beside the ME. "Her phone was found, powered down. No texts after four p.m. yesterday. I checked the cell logs, nothing suspicious, but we're waiting on the subpoena for her social feeds. If this were random, it's a hell of a risk for the unsub. If it hadn't rained soon after she was killed, she would have been found before today. This trail is very popular."

"The victim was random. The kill isn't. No drag marks, no hair pulled out. The pose is intentional." He gestures to the cross. "This spiral cross is more precise than the one in Denver."

The ME sits back on her heels, pulling off her gloves with a snap. "Can I finish my post? There's not much else I can tell you until I get her on a table."

Dirk stands and walks ten yards up the trail. Jill follows, keeping her notebook tucked against her ribs.

"What are you thinking?" she whispers.

"She died within hours of our Denver vic. That's not copycatting, that's coordination." He turns to face Jill, eyes hard. "There's two. Or more."

Jill processes this, eyes narrowing. "We need to let Spinella know."

Dirk pulls out his phone and calls the Denver field office, patching through to Spinella's direct line. It rings once before picking up.

"Trainor. What have you got?" says Spinella. His voice is a buzz saw.

"We're on site in Prescott," says Dirk. "Identical MO, simultaneous timeline with Denver. The signature matches down to the pose."

"I thought you were in Scottsdale. What are you doing in Prescott?"

"Long story. I'll fill you in when we get back."

A pause. "Fuck. You think it's a cell?"

"Not a cell, but at least two operators," says Dirk.

"The signatures are getting more polished. They're communicating, maybe competing."

Spinella's breathing sharpens. "You want backup? I can get the local field office on it."

"We need to set up a task force. We may be looking at multiple serial killers. Can you put a hold on the big conference room and put together a team? Also, call headquarters in Washington and see if you can get them to transfer Carl Bunch to Denver ASAP. Everything he's found, every cold case, every shred of evidence. If there's a pattern, he'll see it." He glances back at the scene. "And have the BAU run a profile on spiral crosses. We're missing something."

"Done. Anything else?" asks Spinella.

"Lock down the press. Don't leak the signature. If this is about recognition, we don't want to feed it."

"Roger. Keep me posted."

Dirk hangs up. He and Jill stand silently, the pine needles crackling under their boots. Somewhere deeper in the woods, a crow calls, harsh, repetitive, like an alarm.

"How do you want to handle this?" Jill asks.

"We treat it as a double. Two unsubs, or one pulling the strings from somewhere. Either way, the next move is already in play."

Jill closes her notebook. "Detective can you run the plates on her car and let's get an ID. I'll need you to notify her relatives. Keep the cause of death to yourself. Keep it simple. Get me the ID as soon as possible so I can get our people to do a deep background check on her."

Mallory looked serious. "Already in the works. Do we have anything to worry about? It sounds like you think this is not the work of your guy in Denver, but someone communicating with him."

Dirk nods. "That's a strong possibility, Detective. We'll let your chief know that we'll be taking over this case, but we'll also ask if you can continue to work the case at the local level."

Mallory is not happy, but she understands that this case is bigger than Prescott.

"Detective, please keep what we have discussed today as quiet as possible. Also, once you can collect the clothes and personal effects from the victim, please call Jill, and she'll direct you how to get them to the FBI forensic lab."

The day fades to blue, and the woods draw in on itself. Dirk turns away from the spiral, already reconstructing the next steps, the next scene, the next impossible move. But the echo of the pattern stays with him, burned behind his eyes, relentless as the cold.

Chapter Fifteen

2010 Calvin Walker

Tucson after dark doesn't so much cool down as relax its grip, a child's hand uncoiling from a dog's throat, not letting go, but changing strategy. The air outside pushes in through the warped window glass in waves. Inside, I have the booth by the front, where the lights are dim enough to make anyone interesting look dangerous, and the Formica is clean enough that no one will ask if you're waiting for company.

My water glass sweats harder than I do. I kill it in two pulls and roll the ice cubes along my tongue one at a time, experiencing the slow melt against my molars. The diner is half-lit and half-alive. There's a couple at a corner table, faces lost in their phones, sharing silence and a side of battered zucchini. Behind the counter, a girl with heavy eyeliner and neck tattoos watches the clock with murder in her eyes, wishing every second would catch up and finish her. If you could bottle the mood in here, you'd call it Clerk Suicidal.

My leg jumps under the table, heel jack hammering out Morse code on the cracked vinyl. Fingers trace a groove in the glass rim. There's a kind of thirst that isn't for water or alcohol or sugar, a hunger you can't name in polite company. If you let it build, it flays the inside of your chest until everything else is white noise, heat, fatigue and the flavorless crunch of ice. Two months since my last, and my body is done pretending patience.

Through the window, dusk gives up the ghost in stages. The sky turns orange; the orange dribbles down to gray, and the street outside is a fading rumor. On this block, there's nothing but bank towers, a couple of lofts, and this diner, the last stop before you hit the warehouse desert. Even the panhandlers give this side of Congress a miss in summer. It's triple digits at 7 p.m., and the street is as empty as a church on a Tuesday.

I watch the bank building across the street, counting lights as they switch off, cataloging the exit order of the cubicle rats. Most of the staff bailed by six, but I caught the tail end of a department party, girls in flats and business-casual guys with limp handshakes, faking end-of-week cheer before they scatter to vape shops and Subaru hatchbacks.

Half an hour later, the doors open and out comes a girl in a sleeveless, flowered dress, heels biting the pavement like they want to taste blood. I clock her from across the avenue: twenty-four or twenty-five, too thin for her face, hair in a sharp-angled bob, arms sunburned at the shoulder. She's with another girl, sweater, chinos, tortoiseshell glasses, but it's the flowered one I zero in on. She carries her purse tucked high under her ribs, a habit of the wary. Her right hand fidgets with the phone in her pocket, even as she tries to look relaxed, like the city is an old friend with harmless intentions.

They stop a few feet from the door, talking with the lazy body language of people who'd rather be anywhere else. The friend keys the lock, double-checks the knob, and walks away in the opposite direction with a half-hearted wave. The girl in the dress hesitates at the curb, checks her reflection in the glass, a glance, nothing narcissistic, more like she wants to confirm she's still there. She pulls a fine-knit sweater from her bag, drapes it over her shoulders like a shield, and immediately regrets it. The heat swallows her in seconds. I can see sweat on her collarbones from fifty yards.

She checks her phone again, scrolling, before she jams a pair of cheap wireless earbuds into her ears. The way she thumbs at the screen, there's music for every block she walks, some playlist that promises company but never delivers. Her stride lengthens as she heads east, away from the daylight, away from me. For now.

I watch her go, counting each step until she's almost lost in the pink shimmer from the Circle K up the block. I drag my gaze back inside, forcing myself to observe the ordinary: the eggshell paint puckered by humidity, the cracked pepper shaker left behind by someone who overestimated their taste for spice, and the faint echo of a TV game show from the kitchen. My body wants to move, to get up and follow, but I force myself to stay put. No sense in looking eager. The predator that gets caught is the one who acts like one.

The server sees me eyeing the street and glides over, refilling my water with the precision of someone who's been told off for spilling it once too often. Her perfume is sweet and heavy, a futile cover for the industrial dish soap smell that sticks to her skin.

"Anything else?" she says, her tone flat but not unfriendly.

I shake my head. "The check, please."

She rips the ticket from the pad and slides it across the table, her thumb grazing the condensation on my glass. "You wanna box that up?" she asks, nodding at my untouched club sandwich.

"No," I say, "but thanks." She gives me a look like I'm supposed to tip extra for declining styrofoam.

I take my time peeling out two twenties and a five, fan them on the check, pinning them under my empty glass. Always cash, never a card. It's not about traceability. I enjoy watching people pretend not to notice how much you leave behind. It changes how they remember you. Big tips make you invisible. No one suspects the patron who covers two meals for the price of one.

I pause at the door and let my eyes linger on the street. The sky is in that colorless in-between phase, and the sodium lights on the crosswalk flicker, coughing up an orange glow. The flowered dress is a quarter block up now, walking faster, sweater abandoned and balled up in her hand. She doesn't check over her shoulder, not once. That's how I know I've already picked right.

The bell above the door chimes when I push out, releasing me into the stifling dark. The air slaps me with a wet sock of heat and sidewalk silt, plus the smell of exhaust from an idling delivery truck. My shirt sticks to my ribs in an instant, but I keep my pace casual, hands in pockets, and face slack. I've been here long enough to know which way the wind moves. People in Tucson walk like they're melting, no sudden gestures, no fast talk. Only tourists or cops hustle. I fall in, set a rhythm, and close the distance.

I'm half a block behind her. The anticipation is a narcotic that makes my fingers tingle, makes the hair on my arms stand up. The hunger that gnawed at me an hour ago is gone, replaced by a crisp, bright focus. No more doubt, no more anxiety. The clean hum of purpose and the cool, sweet promise of the kill ahead.

I pace her from across the street, letting the sodium bulbs cut me into and out of existence every hundred feet. She walks with purpose, but it's the purpose you get from a memorized routine. Her steps are too even and her head too rigid. I mirror her rhythm, drifting between the walls and ducking when a car's headlights flatten the world to a comic strip. The few cars that do pass are tinted, windows up, air inside probably forty degrees colder than this hell, and not one of them sees me.

My shirt is glued to my back now. Sweat slicks down from my hairline, pooling at my neck, and, I think about the stories they'll invent after the fact, how some nutcase stalked her for weeks, how he plotted every move with military precision. They never guess how much is improvisation. How close it comes to falling apart at any second. I'm three paces ahead of disaster, and five behind her, and that's where I live.

The knife handle taps my ankle, the old comfort. The blade is small, three inches, polished so bright it could shave the black off a shadow. I'd cleaned and oiled it this morning, not knowing for sure I'd use it, but hoping.

Chapter Sixteen

She crosses at the intersection, jaywalking because she can, no cars, no witnesses, no one to judge. She cuts through the parking lot of a shuttered thrift store before taking a sharp right onto a residential side street. Here, the houses crowd in on themselves, all Spanish tile and mesh screens, the front yards a mix of dead grass and plastic flamingos. There's no sign of life. The TV is on inside, but nobody is on the stoops, and no barking dogs. The few windows that aren't blacked out reflect her movement, so for a second, it's like watching three versions of her at once.

I move to the sidewalk on her side now, closing the gap to maybe half a block. My breath comes in fast, shallow pulls. Not panic, not quite excitement, but the way you feel on a roller coaster, gravity waiting to catch you. The knife bumps against my ankle every step, telling me: not yet.

The park is huge, a rip in the grid where developers gave up and let the city have its wild space. From the street, it looks like a cluster of orange trees and a kid's playground, but past the first layer of soccer fields it drops into a gully thick with eucalyptus and weed-choked brush. You can lose a body in there, and no one will find it until a monsoon or a hiker's dog does the work.

She enters the park through a break in the cyclone fence, and I ghost after her, keeping to the blue-tarped shade under the maintenance shed. The path here is a foot-wide ribbon of trampled dirt, the only light coming from the dying sun and the sallow spill of the city. Her steps grow softer. She's not on alert, not thinking anyone's behind her. Her earbuds are so loud I catch the bass line of some Top 40 track; the volume is shy of self-destruction.

There are no witnesses. No one comes to this park after seven, not even the homeless. I watch her veer off the path, cutting across the brown grass to a little rise where a ruined bench sits under a scraggly Palo Verde. She's heading for the shortcut to the back gate, the one that spits you out onto her street on the back side of the park.

My heart kicks hard. Now. I slide the knife from its sheath, hold it tight against my thigh as I close in. Ten feet behind her, five. She doesn't see me, doesn't turn around. The first step off the trail is a hazard, tree roots, broken concrete under the grass, but I know the park's geography by heart. At the bench, she stops and checks her phone again, scrolling, probably texting the boyfriend or mom or killing time before the last push home.

I cover the last five feet in silence, a single breath. She senses something, the shift in the air, or nothing at all, and turns, but I'm already there. I grabbed her head, clamping my hand over her mouth and jaw. I yank her backward off balance. She jerks, her knees buckling, phone flying from her hand. I'm stronger than I look, or she's too light, but either way, she never gets a sound out.

The knife draws across her throat in one smooth pull, like slicing an apple at the stem. Warm blood erupts, spraying across the front of her dress. I've done this so many times that I know how to avoid getting blood on me. It's never as much as they say on TV. Most of it pours out, hot and dark, over her collarbone, into the V between her breasts. She claws at my hand. The look on her face is confusion, not pain. The song keeps playing in her ears, and for a second, I think about what the last thing she'll ever hear is.

I drag her behind the bench, into the tangle of fallen branches and weeds, and lay her out on the ground. She twitches once, legs jerking in a final spasm, and goes completely slack. The air smells like iron and rain and the sharp, oily sweetness of eucalyptus. I crouch over her, breathing in short, hard bursts, the hunger gone and replaced by the slow flood of something deeper.

Her blood soaks into the earth, making a dark, spreading stain. I count to thirty, making sure she's done. The grass soaks up most of it. I check the path. No one. Not even a stray cat. I squat there for a moment, letting the adrenaline back off, and watch the last sliver of sunlight bounce off the silver of my knife.

There's a calm that follows. I hold the blade in my hand, stand, and look down at my work. The world seems empty and perfect, like the moment after a thunderclap, when all you hear is your own heartbeat and the promise that nothing can touch you. Not for a while, anyway.

I kneel beside her, still breathing hard, and rearrange the arms so they don't sprawl in that clumsy, puppet-wrecked way bodies want to fall. Hands crossed on the chest, always the classic pose. There's dignity in it, or it's the only way I ever learned. Her head tips back, mouth open in a question that no one will answer.

The blood pools around her, slow and sticky, like spilled paint on cracked clay. I watch it soak into the soil, darkening the dirt to a weird, purplish black. The heat of the day gives way to the heat of oncoming night, and there's nothing but the cicadas and the rush of cars a mile away.

I roll her gently and use the knife to slit the dress from navel to neck. The blade parts fabric with no resistance; even in death, there's less to her than you'd expect. The bra takes more effort, nylon, padded, bought for show. I cut it in the middle, spreading the cups apart like opening the pages of a cheap paperback. Her chest is flat, ribs showing the way they do in old anatomy books, and the skin translucent under the park lights.

I steady my hands, gripping the knife the way Dad showed me when we used to clean trout. It's muscle memory by now: push through, up, a little twist, and let the edge do its work. The first cut goes horizontally, right below the collarbones, shallow enough not to sever anything important. The blood beads, a red line, running down the sternum. The second cut is vertical, intersecting the first. I press in deeper, finding the midpoint, and carve the spiral, tight at the origin, widening out as I follow the natural grain of the skin.

I work slowly. The spiral cross needs to look intentional, not frantic. There's magic in how skin resists at first, before surrendering. The knife flashes as it catches the last light, the steel almost gold-edged for a second. I look up and realize her eyes are open, staring up into the tree branches above. I wonder if it's the first time she's ever really seen the stars.

My breath calms. The frenzy is gone, replaced by a clarity I get nowhere else. I finish the spiral, clean the lines with the tip of the blade, and use my thumb to press the skin smooth. I step back and admire the pattern, the neatness, the way the edges stay open long enough to show I did it right.

After a minute, I pull the black Sharpie from my pocket, fat, chisel tip, brand new, and kneel beside her wrist. I wipe the blood away, draw the spiral cross again, centering it over the blue vein like a badge. The ink goes on glossy, before it settles into the skin as if it were always supposed to be there. I flex her hand, tuck it over her other, and press them together on her chest. It looks peaceful. Like something out of a painting.

I close her eyes with two fingers, gently. The face relaxes. There's no pain in it. I have the urge to say something, an apology, or a thank you, or a quiet prayer that nobody else will ever understand. Instead, I breathe out and let it all go.

I wipe the blade clean on the inside of her dress, snapping it back into the sheath at my ankle. My hands are sweaty, and I notice a couple of spots of blood, so I rub them clean on the grass. They seem tacky, but it won't last long. I sweep the area for anything I left behind, no hair, no prints, no footprints that matter. The phone she dropped is cracked but still lit. I pop the battery and bury it in the mulch a few feet away.

No panic. No hurry. I move slowly, letting the calm wrap around me like armor. By the time I stand, my body's already thinking about the next step, what to do with his night, how good the world seems when you're in it, and no one else knows.

I walk out the same way I came in, hands loose, stride even, not a care in the universe. The city is still hot, but my skin prickles in the breeze. Sirens start up a mile away, probably some idiot drunk driving or a domestic. It has nothing to do with me.

I cross the main road, duck into a convenience store, and buy a bottled water and a bag of chips. The clerk doesn't even look up. I toss a five onto the counter and leave the change. Always cash, always generous. Let them remember the tip, not the face.

When I get back to Phoenix, I'll take a shower and scrub my hands raw. I'll watch a movie; something stupid with car chases and gunfights. In the morning, I'll scan the news, watch for any mention of a body in the park. There won't be, not yet. They won't find her until the light is right, until the world needs a reason to be afraid again.

For now, I walk under the streetlights more alive than anyone else. The pattern is perfect; the hunger is gone. I blend into the city, another shadow among many. No one will ever see me coming.

Chapter Seventeen

2015…James Freemont

The room is dark, but not to me. In the blank half-light of Alison Greer's bedroom, I see the subtle green tint of the blackout curtains, the swollen lines of stucco on the ceiling, the silver skein of dust lit by the city's ambient haze. She lies in the middle of a queen-size mattress, arms outstretched, one calf cocked over the other in what I know from research is her preferred sleeping posture. Her breathing is even, shallow. REM phase, most likely.

I stand exactly one meter from the left side of the bed, close enough to hear the soft click of her uvula when she inhales, far enough that she would need to lunge to reach me if she woke. I wear a full Tyvek ensemble, booties, hood and mask. The suit crinkles when I flex my shoulder, so I do not flex unless absolutely required. The knife in my hand is a Henckels 7 boning blade, new enough not to have yet taken a set to my wrist. Its edge flashes once in the diffuse light, vanishing as I hold it parallel to the mattress.

The cliché is that time slows before an act of violence, but for me, it's the opposite. My vision speeds up, reviewing a thousand potential outcomes, all mapped in advance and catalogued for risk. I can see the cut, the spatter, the precise vector of arterial spray; I can also see when Alison's arm snags my sleeve, the moment she screams loud enough to draw attention from the next apartment, the moment she fights back and damages the entire choreography. But I do not freeze. I run through the procedure one last time, as if defending a thesis before an unfriendly board.

She exhales. Her left hand curls into a loose fist, pulling at the duvet.

I take two slow steps forward and position myself over her. The knife hovers six inches above the jugular. In another life, this would be a medical demonstration.

It's the same knife I used to trim my children's steaks. The symmetry is not lost on me.

***

The first time I saw Alison was at a client event, a tech firm in the process of building a new data center. My firm is designing the mechanical systems, and I had been invited to attend the event at the Petroleum Club downtown by the CEO of the company, an old friend from college. My wife didn't want to go. She was never fond of going to these kinds of rubber chicken events, although this one was very elegant. I arrived solo and circulated like a ghost among the black suits and statement jewelry. Alison was the CEO's executive secretary and, as such, handled the event. She was there to smile, to organize, and to smooth every uneven patch of social interaction. She did it with the efficiency of a military press-gang. When she smiled, you could see the ridge of tension at the corner of her mouth. She wore her hair in tight braids; all pulled back into a single knot. Her skin was luminous and dark, and her blue blouse was crisp under the stylish suit she wore.

I watched her for twenty-four minutes. Every ten minutes she rotated to a new position: lobby, main room, the catering crew, and the bar, making sure every guest had what they wanted. You could tell from the looks on some men in the room that what they wanted was her. At no point did she stop moving, except to check the time on her phone. She wore a cheap fitness tracker, never once glanced at it.

I made a note in my field notebook: "Observes with intent. Corrects deviations immediately. Overcompensates for male expectations."

As the crowd thins I approached her, standing next to the bar, watching the festivities wind down. "Long night," I said, smiling the way I'd practiced in a hundred mirrors.

She did not meet my gaze. "Not as long as some," she said, rechecking her phone.

Her voice was perfectly neutral, an octave lower than most women's, the effect both formal and oddly intimate.

She noticed my Omega and nodded at it. "You're James Freemont, with Freemont Mechanical Engineers, correct?"

I said yes, but she had already shifted focus. I admired the way she could disengage from a conversation and make it feel you'd ended it on your own. I went home and wrote her name three times in the notebook, underlining it with a mechanical pencil so faint it didn't indent the page. That was five weeks ago.

***

I followed Alison for exactly twenty-nine days. It was not surveillance, not really, more like a controlled study. I built the schedule in layers: first her office hours, her gym routine (Tuesdays and Thursdays, Equinox on 16th), her grocery runs (always on Sundays, never Whole Foods, always Trader Joe's). I track her weekend rituals; her boyfriend, Brian, joined her every Friday for dinner at the same Mediterranean café. He always stayed the night. I documented this. On weekends when Brian was gone, she drank exactly one glass of red wine before bed and watched, invariably, one episode of a reality dating show on her phone.

The notebook entries filled half a volume. Every detail was cross-referenced to a digital copy on my home machine, and every night, after my children went to sleep, I would scan the day's observations and build the probability trees: when she'd be alone, when she'd be most vulnerable, when she'd be least likely to attract witnesses.

Two weeks in, I ordered a second notebook and devoted it entirely to risk assessment.

A month in, I learned Brian would be away for a week, a trip to San Diego, confirmed by the passive check-in on his Instagram account. I circled the week in the notebook with a bright red marker.

***

On her last night, Alison met two girlfriends for drinks at a local bar. They sat at a patio table, ignored the men who tried to buy them shots, split a plate of nachos, and left together at 22:14. I followed at a safe distance, black Civic again, nothing notable in the mirrors. The three women split up at the street corner; Alison hugged her friends and walked away solo, never looking over her shoulder. Her apartment building was one of the new construction jobs, with high ceilings, thin walls, a secure entry at the front, but a side gate with a defective latch. I'd checked it out a week prior.

She entered, locked the door behind her, and turned the lights on. I counted the windows that illuminated: living room, bedroom and kitchen. She left the bedroom light on the longest. I observed the sequence through a gap in the hedges. I marked the time.

I waited in the car, watching the apartment for another hour. At 23:40 the lights went out. I let another forty minutes pass, enough for even the most anxious mind to unclench. I reviewed the checklist, tools, gloves, Tyvek, knife, tape, and mask. I pulled the kit from the Civic's trunk, slung the backpack over my shoulder, and set out for the building's side entrance.

The gate opened with no resistance. I slipped in, pressed myself flat against the stucco wall, and took three slow breaths.

Her unit was on the third floor, corner left. I found the stairwell, checked for cameras (there were two, one inoperative), and ascended. I reached her door at 00:22 according to the digital timer on my phone. I withdrew the lock-pick set from the front pocket of the suit, selected a Bogota triple, and worked the lock. The deadbolt turned in less than five seconds.

I waited, my hand on the latch, counting down from ten. At zero, I opened the door and entered the apartment. Inside, the air was cool and over-filtered, the scent of cheap air freshener fighting with the acrid baseline of ozone from the building's HVAC. I stepped into the kitchen and set my backpack on the table. I pulled the new Tyvek suit from its bag and slipped it on, followed by the booties, mask, hood and finally the blue nitrile gloves. I moved to the bedroom, closing the doors behind me as I went, minimizing the chance of noise travel.

Alison slept on her back, arms spread wide like a swimmer in freefall. She wore a pale blue tank top that had trouble containing her ample breasts and shorts; the duvet bunched at her feet. I took another slow breath and confirmed my pulse: steady and unhurried.

I unsheathed the knife, clicked the timer on my phone, and closed the last distance between us.

They say a man is never more honest than in the moment before violence. That is not my experience. I am most honest after the part where the blood pools on the sheets, the part where I wipe the blade clean on a torn piece of T-shirt, the part where I arrange the body for display and mark the signature with a careful, unwavering hand.

But that is for later. Now is the moment before. I raise the knife. She exhales, turns her face toward the wall, and mutters something half-formed. I exhale, too. My hand is steady. The blade catches the faint green of the curtains. I count down from five. And I act.

Chapter Eighteen

2015… James Freemont

The knife enters at the notch of her clavicle. There is resistance, as always, skin, followed by a tense grid of muscle. The hollow of the airway, and finally, nothing. Alison's eyes flick open, a single frame of panic and confusion, mouth yawning for a scream that never escapes. I clamp my left hand over her lips and jaw, compressing with the practiced pressure that collapses sound and movement into a muffled tremor. The blade arcs downward, severing the carotid, the blood warm against the webbing of my glove.

She bucks once, her knees banging against the footboard. Her hands slap weakly at my arm, nails scratching Tyvek but leaving no mark on me. I ride out the motion, pinning her shoulder with my forearm, letting the body's chemistry burn itself out. Her heart hammers against my palm, slows, then stops.

I hold the position for thirty seconds, counting the pulse as it fades to zero. Her eyes are wide, pupils fixed in the far corner of the room, searching for the pattern that will let her make sense of this. There is none. I relax my grip, watch the color change in her cheeks, watch the rhythm drain from her neck and chest.

I slide her off the mattress, supporting her head as I lower her onto the plastic sheeting I placed before the kill. The blood sheets onto the plastic, pooling in a perfect ellipse. The sound it makes is soft, like the drip of rain from a balcony.

I lay the knife on the bedside table and survey the scene. No spatter on the wall, no stains on the duvet, only a thin red line creeping toward the baseboard. I unroll the tape from my wrist and tear off two strips, using them to hold the plastic tight under her shoulders. I check the wound, clean, no ragged edges and the cut is sharp as if done by a surgical resident.

I pause. In the silence, I hear nothing but the slow, evaporating hiss of the city outside. I remove the hood and mask, letting the air settle over my scalp.

The next step is the signature. I slit the tank top from hem to neck, folding back the cotton to reveal her chest. The skin is smooth, almost flawless, and I admire the contrast of blood against the subtle, luminous brown. I take the scalpel from the kit, score a horizontal line just below the sternum, and a vertical line from the xiphoid to the navel, intersecting at a right angle. I deepen the cuts just enough for the cross to stand out in shallow relief.

With the point of the blade, I inscribe a spiral, starting at the top left quadrant of the cross and winding outward in a single, continuous stroke. The spiral is the most important part. It's not decoration, or a flourish. It's a statement. A way to mark the completion of a cycle, to warn anyone who finds her that this is not chaos, but a pattern.

I clean the blade on her shirt and take out the black Sharpie from my kit. I kneel beside her and draw the spiral cross on her left wrist, just above the pulse point. The skin is already cooling, but the ink goes on bright and permanent.

I cross her hands over her chest, arranging them in the classic prayer pose. I step back and observe the tableau, adjusting the angles until they match the sketches in my notebook. I correct for symmetry, align her legs, and close her eyes. She looks at peace, if peace can be engineered.

I begin the cleanup. First, the gloves; I peel them off inside out and drop them into the biohazard bag. I pull out a new pair and put them on. I roll up the plastic sheeting, folding it tight to the body, taping the bundle shut with three more strips. No blood escapes. The bed is a mess, covered in blood splatter and a pool of blood under where her neck had been. I hate leaving it for someone else to clean up but so be it.

I collect every tool, every scrap, every disposable from the kit. The Tyvek suit, hood, mask and booties go into a second bag, sealed and double knotted. I wipe down the bedside table, the doorknob and the light switch. I retrace every step from entry to exit, running my gloved hand over every touch point.

Before I leave, I review the checklist. There are no witnesses, no cameras. Her phone is on the charger by the bed, untouched. Her laptop is open, screen dark, but I know she was logged out. I pocket the lock-pick set and the timer. I put the bags of bloody clothes into the backpack, and I check the room one last time.

At the door, I check the hall. It's empty, as I predicted. I step out and descend the stairs in silence. I do not look back.

In the car, I sit for a moment, letting my breath settle. My hands do not shake. I check the rearview mirror, adjust the tie, and brush a stray hair from my forehead. In the city, a siren starts up, distant but growing. I watch the red and blue flicker in the side-view as it fades in the distance. Another poor soul in need of help.

I drive home, the body of Alison Greer arranged and waiting, the pattern complete. At the next intersection, I roll down the window and let the air rush in, washing away the chemical trace of bleach and latex. By the time I reach my street, the scent of death is gone. Only the memory remains.

When I pull into the driveway, the clock on the dash reads 01:18. The house is dark, only the exterior sconce by the garage casting a soft corona onto the drive. I cut the engine, enter through the garage, and key the door shut behind me. There's a comfort to the sequence. The predictable click of each deadbolt, the staccato warning chirp of the alarm before I kill it at the panel. I set the Tyvek bundle in the bin under the workbench, cover it with a trash bag, and make my way into the main house.

I walk the halls in bare feet, making no sound. The air inside is forty percent humidity; the thermostat is locked to 70; not a molecule is out of place. I pass through the kitchen and pour a glass of water, rinsing my mouth with the first swallow. It takes a full minute for my body to accept I am home, the pulse, and blood from earlier now just a chemical echo in my veins.

In the master bedroom, my wife sleeps on her side, arms folded under the pillow, and her hair fanned across the sheets like a question in the dark. I change in the walk-in closet, slide the clothes into a dedicated garment bag, and stand under the shower for fifteen minutes, letting the hot water strip away any memory of the night. I scrub until my skin tingles, until there is no trace left to be found. The soap is unscented, the shampoo a plain drugstore label; anything else would register as deviant, a signal to her subconscious that something is off.

When I emerge, towel around my waist, she stirs. Her face is blurred with sleep, but beautiful. Her eyes were deep and black in the low light.

"Hey," she whispers. "You're late."

I slide into bed. "Had a last-minute drink with a client. The West Valley project."

She mumbles something about, "You work too hard." She slides one cold foot between my legs and drifts back to sleep. I lie on my back, breathing in time with her, heart slowing to the domestic average.

After a few minutes, I rise again, silent, and pad down the hall to the children's rooms.

In the first, my daughters, age eight, sleep in a cocoon of purple sheets, their arms splayed above their heads. My daughters are twins, identical in every way except one wears glasses. A pair of glasses is on the nightstand; the lenses fogged from her palm. I tuck them in, pulling their blankets over their shoulders, and press my lips to the crowns of their heads. Neither one wakes.

The third child is sixteen months old, and she sleeps in a crib in the corner of the nursery. Her breathing is irregular. I stand at the rail and watch her, counting each in and out, until the urge to smooth her hair overwhelms me. I do gently, with the back of my knuckle.

I close the doors, one after another, and return to the bedroom. My wife is half-awake, propped on an elbow.

"Did you check the thermostat?" she asks.

"It's fine," I say. "Everyone's asleep."

She watches me for a moment, and for a split second, I think she will ask me something else, something closer to the bone. But she exhales, sets her face back into the pillow, and tucks her hands underneath. She is asleep in seconds.

I glance at the ceiling, replaying the night's work in the abstract. Edges, vectors, pressure points and the arc of the blade as it opened the skin. I let it dissolve; the memory receding like a tide, replaced by the neat order of the house around me, the silent proof I am exactly where I am supposed to be.

I turn on my side, pull the blanket to my chin, and let myself drift under. I am asleep before I am even aware of it.

In the morning, I will rise before anyone else. I'll brew the coffee, make the children's lunches, lay out my daughter's glasses and the baby's favorite spoon. I will dress in another suit, a different tie, a different face and drive to the office, where my calendar is already stacked for the day. There will be meetings and site visits and performance reviews, all mapped in advance. There will be laughter and handshakes and, later, the same curated quiet at home, the same certainty that this life is mine, built brick by brick and never in danger of collapse.

No one will ever see the other half of me, the side that moves through the world at night, collecting its pattern, completing the cycle. There will be news of Alison Greer, of course. The city will mourn. Her friends will recall her smile and the way she hated inefficiency. The detectives will circle for a while before drifting away, never once suspecting the shape of the man who did it, never once looking in my direction.

The only trace will be in my notebook, one page added to the record, the spiral cross precise and flawless.

Tomorrow, I will help one daughter with her math homework and listen to my other daughter recite dinosaur facts. I will hold my wife's hand and remember for a moment how it was to see her for the first time, and how it is to see her every day since. And when the next cycle begins, I will be ready. I will always be ready.

Chapter Nineteen

It's just after 6:00 a.m. when Dirk Trainor slips his badge through the Denver field office security reader and steps into a world that's not supposed to exist this early in the morning. The air is church quiet, lit by a third of the overheads, the buzz of the fluorescent tubes amplifying every echo in the atrium. At this hour, even the janitorial staff are gone, their bins lined up like soldiers against the wall, with the night's garbage bagged and awaiting removal.

Dirk walks the perimeter, feeling the press of cold against the windows and the vacuum of absence in the cubes and bullpen. The rhythm of empty offices is always the same: unwashed mugs, chairs left mid-swivel, the faint aftertaste of burned coffee and artificial lemon. He drags his fingers along the wall, index to the seams, and times his footsteps to the exact microsecond between each security camera pan. Old habits, impossible to quit.

He stops at his office and pushes through, drops his jacket and backpack onto the nearest chair, and stands for a moment in the half-light. The window offers a glimpse of the parking lot, a patchwork of black asphalt and dirty snow. He unlocks his desk drawer, takes out a new legal pad, and flips open to a blank page. He doesn't write anything. Instead, he sits, presses his palms to the desk, and listens to the silence. It hums louder the longer he waits.

Somewhere down the hall, a voice cracks the void. It's faint, nearly a mutter, but persistent. Dirk follows it, pausing every few feet to check for other signs of life. None. The noise leads him past the elevators, one of which stutters briefly alive before lapsing again. Around the bend, the main conference room glows behind a wall of frosted glass, the light so harsh it knives through even the etched federal seal. The floor is a canyon of dimness, the only movement a swirl of dust in a distant updraft.

Dirk watches from the doorway. Inside, a kid, barely out of college by the look of him, stands on tiptoes at the long whiteboard, taping photographs into tight, overlapping rows. The kid is pale, almost sickly, with hair that's forgotten how to lie flat and a rumpled button-down that looks two days old. He moves with the frenetic energy of someone halfway between a panic attack and a manic episode. Every few seconds, he swipes his sleeve at the bridge of his nose, which is already red and raw from constant abuse.

The whiteboard is a graveyard. Faces stare out in regimented lines: some young, some old, but all dead. There are so many of them that the kid has doubled up, pasting two to a card, and tacking those cards with small, round magnets in every unused inch. The logic of the board is unclear; clusters and constellations, not chronology. Dirk recognizes two of the Denver victims from last week, and at least one from the Flagstaff file, but the rest are strangers. A hundred eyes, frozen in time.

Dirk knocks once, his knuckles against the metal doorframe. The kid flinches and drops the sheaf of photos he was holding; they scatter like poker cards across the table.

"Sorry," Dirk says, holding up both hands. "Didn't mean to scare you."

"It's okay! Sorry," The kid's voice cracks, but he bends to gather up the photos. His hands shake, and Dirk wonders if it's caffeine, exhaustion, or both.

Dirk enters and closes the door behind him. The conference table is stacked with files and manila folders, most still banded shut, but several are open, spilling their contents across the laminate. There's a laptop, three different color highlighters, and a bottle of supermarket-brand energy drink sweating onto the table. A notepad is filled with what looks like time codes and cryptic initials.

The kid collects the fallen photos and stands almost at attention, like this is an inspection. "Special Agent Trainor, right?" He says it the way you'd recite a geometry theorem: careful, memorized, unsure if it's relevant.

Dirk nods, waves the kid to sit down. "And you're Bunch. Carl Bunch."

The kid, Carl, gives a nervous half-laugh and jams his hands under his thighs to stop them from trembling. "Sorry about the mess," he says. "The flight from Dulles was delayed three hours, and I got in, like, at one a.m. I went to check into the Residence Inn, but I remembered you said you wanted to hit the ground running, so I came straight here. I didn't wake anybody up, did I?"

"No. It's just us. No one else until eight." Dirk studies him. Carl has the haggard look of a data analyst who's been eating stress for breakfast since puberty, but there's a keenness behind the glasses, an intensity corralled by professional awkwardness.

Dirk points at the wall. "You did all that last night?"

Carl's face flushes. "I, um… yeah? There's a copy in my files, but it's easier for me to see the faces. Pattern recognition. It's what I'm… you know… good at."

Dirk stands at the head of the table, takes it all in. Some of the victims' eyes are X'd out in Sharpie, some have colored stickers in the corners: red, blue and yellow. The spiral cross from the case files is drawn repeatedly, sometimes on the photos themselves, sometimes on index cards tacked above clusters of victims.

"How many?" Dirk asks, voice lower than he intends.

"Confirmed spiral crosses? Or everything with a mark that matches within two points of deviation?" Carl scrubs his nose again, eyes darting between the wall and Dirk. "If we include Arizona, Colorado, New Mexico, Utah and parts of Nevada, I found… uh, two hundred thirty-seven. And counting. But not all of those are for sure. I color-coded for probability. Red is confirmed, blue is probable, yellow is a little fuzzy but possible."

Dirk cuts him off. "Two hundred thirty-seven?"

"Yeah. Most of them are cold or misclassified. A lot of local PDs called it cult stuff or gang initiation and didn't pursue linkage. But once I started cross-referencing the wound patterns, and the postmortem positioning, the clustering." Carl stops, looks embarrassed by his own excitement. "Sorry. You probably already know all this."

Dirk moves closer to the whiteboard, hands in his pockets. He reads the names, the captions and the spirals. It's not what he expected. He stares, saying nothing, for almost a full minute.

Carl clears his throat softly. "Sorry about the mess. I'll have it sorted by the team meeting."

Dirk glances at the board. "Don't. Leave it as is."

Carl blinks. "Okay."

They both stand there, the silence stretching. On the table, the bottle of energy drink gives a single, lonely crackle as the plastic cools. The wall of faces blinks back at them, unsleeping.

"You should sit," Dirk says. "We'll go over what you've got."

He watches as Carl sits down, fidgets, and pulls the notepad in front of him. Dirk stands unwilling to break the spell of the board. "When you say pattern recognition, how did you find these?" He keeps his voice gentle, a teacher coaxing a shy kid to talk.

Carl launches into it. "I built a custom search tool using the NIST's VICAP API, but the public portal is useless, so I wrote a scraper that grabs PDFs from state and local agency sites. I did a word-vector search for anything with 'carved', 'incised', or 'engraved' in the ME's notes, then set it to scan for geometry in the wound description. Like 'cross', 'spiral', 'X', 'swirl', and that kind of thing. Once I had the dataset, I filtered for post-1990, then for women, then for the victim pose. Then I… you know… did this."

He gestures helplessly at the board, as if the word "this" means "months of relentless, pathological sorting of horror."

"When did you start?" asks Dirk.

Carl flushes deeper. "I… uh… started before the Bureau asked me. I mean, I read about the Colorado case and got interested. Just like on my time."

Dirk can't help but smile. "Don't apologize. It's better than anyone else has done so far."

They fall quiet again, a sense of shared exhaustion settling in. Dirk approaches the table, sits at the long edge. He studies Carl. "How much sleep have you had since you landed?"

Carl checks his watch, a battered digital Timex. "I napped on the plane. Then here, maybe an hour and a half."

Dirk gestures to the pile of files. "Go to your hotel, shower, and come back at nine. If you keep going at this pace, you'll burn out by tomorrow."

Carl protests, "But you said we needed to," but Dirk cuts him off, holding up a hand.

"We need you. Not a walking corpse."

Carl hesitates. "Yeah. Okay."

Chapter Twenty

Dirk stands, crosses to the window, and looks out. The sunrise is a smear of orange against the dirty snow. He wonders how many of the people driving in for work this morning would believe that their lives overlapped with a tally this big. He wonders how many more there are.

He turns back. Carl is already packing up his laptop, still glancing at the board as if afraid it will vanish the second he leaves.

"Thanks for coming in early," Dirk says. "You just changed the game."

Carl smiles, a nervous twitch at the corner of his mouth. "It's what I'm good at."

Dirk waits until he's gone, then stands alone in the middle of the room. The board seems bigger now, heavier. He examines the spirals, the faces, the tiny human horror behind every snapshot.

He sits and lets himself feel the fatigue, and then does what he always does: reaches for a blank sheet, starts a new column, and builds the next step. The faces on the wall don't care about sleep or hope or fear. They're just waiting for the pattern to be solved. Dirk sits with them, silent, until the lights in the office flicker on.

At 8:59, a full minute before the hour, Jill Quarters steps into the Denver office wearing the tailored charcoal suit that looks expensive but moves like athletic gear. Her hair is pulled back so tight it gives her eyes an extra jolt of severity, and the badge on her hip rides at the perfect tilt to be visible and intimidating. She walks the main corridor with the momentum of a person who's spent a decade plowing through crowds, indifferent to the possibility that anyone would dare slow her down. Even the most self-important desk agents edge out of her way.

At the conference room door, she hesitates for a microsecond at the glass. Her profile silhouette is backlit by the bright, inhuman light. She opens the door. The hinges issue a polite squeal.

Dirk looks up from his seat, rubs his eyes, and sets down a cup of coffee that's gone cold and oily at the top. "Jill. You beat the clock."

She glances at her watch, then the board. Her eyes scan the photos, the color-coding, the unbroken rows of faces. "This is new."

Dirk stands and gestures to the far end of the table, where a lean, sleep-starved man sits re-stapling the corners of a pile of case files. "Meet Carl Bunch, our analyst from D.C. He's running the statistical side of the pattern."

Carl stands, nearly knocking over his chair, and wipes both palms down the sides of his slacks before extending his hand. "Special Agent Quarters. I've read a lot of your case files. Your work on the Inglewood Strangler was, uh, next level."

Jill looks at the hand, then at Dirk, then takes it. One pump, brisk. "You're the spiral guy."

"Not the spiral guy, just the one who found the

links," Carl says, then immediately seems to regret the clarification.

Jill turns to the board. "How many victims so far?"

Carl blinks. "Red dots are ninety-seven confirmed, but there's about sixty-three more with at least two elements matching the pattern. That's before culling false positives."

Jill pulls out the chair and sits, crossing one leg over the other and leaning forward so her spine forms a perfect right angle with the chair back. She studies the arrangement, following the arc of victims across states, then squints at a huddle of faces in the lower right. "What's the cluster in Colorado Springs?"

Carl snaps to attention, scoots in. "Five incidents over seven years, but three overlap with the tenure of a traveling nurse. She was cleared, but two victims were found within a mile of her old address, and both had a cross carved in the same direction."

Jill considers. "Any overlap on weekends or holidays?"

"Almost all are weekend events. There's a spike at Memorial Day, which doesn't mean much, but…" Carl scans his notes, then flips to a pre-highlighted page. "It was Memorial Day when the Phoenix double happened, too."

Dirk paces the window, arms folded. He's watching both, but mostly Jill, waiting for her to find the crack in the logic. "You think there's more than one unsub?" he asks.

Jill leans back, tilts her head so the tight ponytail

pulls her skin taut. "It looks like the same hand, but there are a few anomalies, like he's learning from himself. Or copying from someone else." She flicks her eyes to Carl. "You have a timeline spreadsheet?"

"Yeah. Two versions, one by kill date, one by case number. I can share the link." Carl's fingers jump to his laptop. He types with speed but not accuracy, each typo corrected with a physical recoil. "I color-coded the columns for sequence, but there's so much noise I had to cross-reference with autopsy reports."

"Show me," says Jill.

Carl turns the screen. "See here." He points to the three highlighted rows. "Denver 2018, Pueblo 2014, Greeley 2011. Same spiral orientation, but the depth and length of the incisions increase over time, like he's refining the technique. Also, the postmortem interval is shrinking. In the first five, they were staged hours after death. Now it's happening almost immediately."

Jill taps her pen on the screen, then snaps the pen shut with her thumb. "That suggests confidence. Or compulsion."

Dirk steps closer, leans on the table. "What about the Arizona outliers?"

Carl brightens, nervous energy back. "I dug deep on those. The 2002 double is unique. Two victims, same night, same MO, but the spiral crosses are rough. The wounds are ragged, like the killer didn't know what he was doing. It reads as a test run."

Dirk pulls out the file they got from the detective on the Arizona double. "I think this was his first.

Everything is rough, spontaneous, no planning." He sets the file aside and looks at several of the other Arizona possibles. He scratches his chin. "If this is the same unsub, the quality of the kill got much better, but the attacks still look spontaneous. The Colorado ones we know about are precise, calculated."

The table is quiet, the only sound being the thrum of the building's HVAC system. Outside, the morning sun slants in sharply across the parking lot, strobing through the window blinds and casting the board in alternating bands of white and shadow. The faces stare out, unmoved.

"Let's eliminate the noise," said Jill. "We go through every file, every victim, and cut anything that doesn't fit the emerging pattern. If there's an anomaly, we mark it, but don't ditch it. Even mistakes can be informative."

Dirk nods. "I'll take Arizona and Utah. You take Colorado and New Mexico."

Carl says, "I can sort Nevada and anything that's a statistical outlier. I have the highest-confidence ones flagged red."

They get to work. The table becomes a hive: files spread like a blackjack dealer's bad day, coffee rings and thumb-smudged Post-its migrating across every surface. The next hour vanishes in the tactile, deeply bureaucratic joy of forensic auditing. Jill moves with clinical grace; her handwriting is as small and perfect as a printer's. Dirk is more aggressive, tearing open file jackets, sifting for the single line that will kill or confirm a case. Carl operates on the edge of entropy, four screens open, tapping at keys and highlighting in quick, convulsive bursts.

"Hey, Bunch," says Dirk. "Do you have a heat map for body disposal?"

Carl, without looking up: "It's in the secondary tab on the Google Sheet. I'm updating it as we talk." He gestures with a pen at the row of faces. "Most of the Colorado victims have been found inside a house or apartment. In Arizona, many of the victims were found outdoors. They were also found all around the state in both cases. There's little location overlap."

"That fits the profile," says Jill. "He likes the ease of movement but doesn't want to be seen. He's not showy, but he's not risk-averse, either. He plans but improvises."

Dirk's phone chirps with a calendar alert. He ignores it, scanning a set of autopsy reports. He sets aside one file, then another, building a discard pile three inches thick. "Our guy likes women between eighteen and fifty, but if some of these files are right, he also kills men."

Jill looks up. "Almost all the victims are professionals. Educators, health care workers, and state employees. There are no prostitutes or hitchhikers."

"That's why I flagged this one yellow," says Carl. He points at a file. "This victim was a home health nurse, killed in a rural hospice facility. It was dismissed as a murder-suicide, but look." He pushes the photo forward. "Cross and spiral. Perfect."

Jill inspects it, then nods, impressed.

Dirk, tired, sits and rubs his temples. "We're going to need another pot of coffee."

"Get a carafe from the break room. I'll keep pushing here," says Jill.

Carl jumps up, nervous to be helpful. "I'll get it. I need to stretch anyway."

Chapter Twenty-One

He hustles out, leaving Dirk and Jill at the table, both hunched, both focused. For a few minutes they work in silence, the room defined by nothing but paper and tension.

Jill breaks it. "Dirk. What's your read on Bunch?"

Dirk, not looking up: "He's weird, but brilliant. Doesn't know how to manage his own energy, but he'll burn for the case."

"Do you trust him?" she asked.

"I don't know him well enough to make a call, but since the first time I ever spoke to him was two days ago and in that time, he's put all this together. I think he has what it takes."

"Good," says Jill. "We need someone willing to go crazy."

Carl returns, breathless, hands full with a coffee carafe, three donuts, and an entire sleeve of Styrofoam cups. He deposits the lot on the table, pours for everyone, then resumes his seat, jittering with purpose.

Dirk starts back in. "Let's mark any overlap. If you see any case that's a true outlier — different age, gender or location, flag it, but don't waste time trying to rationalize it. We focus on what's clear."

For the next three hours, the conference room is an engine: noise, data, sweat and coffee. They speak in clipped phrases, grunts and code. Jill's ponytail frays at the edges; the top button on Dirk's shirt is undone and forgotten. Carl's hands shake so badly he spills his coffee on the sleeve of his sweater but doesn't even notice. Cases fall away, leaving only the hard, bright core.

By 2:00 p.m., they're down to 160. The board is a horror show: every face is a tiny, mute witness, and every string of red yarn a clue to an unsolvable puzzle. There are clusters, urban, rural, and suburban, connected by nothing but the spiral and the meticulousness of the hands that made it. No obvious motive, no signature victim, just the relentless perfection of the work.

Carl leans back in his chair, eyes glazed and triumphant. "That's it. Everything left on the board is a hit. The oldest is from 2002; the most recent is the one three days ago in Prescott." He gestures at the faces, the clusters and the strings. "This is the biggest contiguous serial case I've ever seen. It could be the biggest in American history."

Jill leans forward, both elbows on the table, hands laced. "He's out there, and he's been working for twenty-three years, and no one even knows he exists. How the fuck did we miss this, and by we I mean the law enforcement community?" she asks.

Dirk looks at the whiteboard, then at his partners. "We have the pattern. Now we need to find the man."

Jill looks at Carl, who's suddenly very pale. "You, okay?"

He swallows hard, nods. "Yeah. It's just... I've never done this in real life. Just on screens."

"Welcome to the field," she says. "It's always worse than you think."

The three of them sit in silence, regarding the board like priests before a bloodstained altar. Outside, the day is already dying, the sun a bright smear against the glass.

Dirk dials Spinella's internal line after 3:15, pressing the keys slowly, knuckle by knuckle, as if each digit requires confirmation. He puts the call on speaker, lets the low rattle of the ring set the room's tempo.

Spinella answers before the third ring. His voice sounds like it was run through a cheese grater and dunked in whiskey. "Spinella."

Dirk glances at the board, then at Jill and Carl. "We're ready for you, sir. Conference room three."

Spinella: "I'll be there in five."

The line clicks off. Dirk looks at the others, arches a brow. "Final bets?"

Jill smirks, but her eyes are still wired into the evidence wall. "He'll stare for ten seconds, then ask for coffee. That's how he handles a shock."

Carl pushes his glasses up and starts straightening his notes, his hands so jittery he drops his pen. "Should I, um, stand? Or…"

"Breathe, Bunch," says Dirk. "Let the work talk."

Spinella arrives like a squall with a long stride, his tie at half-mast, and a face two days past a shave. He walks in, stops cold at the threshold, and lets his gaze glide from the leftmost corner of the whiteboard to the farthest string of victims. He doesn't speak for a long, full measure. The only sounds are the faint tick of the clock on the wall and Carl's ragged inhale.

"Jesus Christ," says Spinella. It's not a curse, but a diagnostic.

Dirk stands. "Special Agent in Charge Anthony Spinella, meet Carl Bunch, the analyst from HQ. He built the board."

Spinella sticks out a hand, and Carl nearly misses it before remembering to stand. "Good to meet you, sir. Big fan of your testimony on the Wayne County case," Carl blurts. He flushes and sits again.

Spinella ignores the awkwardness, his eyes locked on the wall. "Give me the ten-cent tour."

Dirk gestures at Carl, who squeaks out a nervous "Yes, sir," and finds his footing. He flips his notepad open to the first page. "We've confirmed one hundred sixty victims with the spiral cross signature or a tight deviation. Almost all are women, mid-career or older, professionals in public service, caregiving or business. No hookers or drug addicts. The earliest is Arizona, 2002, but the pattern goes wide after the 2002 Phoenix double." He points to the cluster on the far right. "That's the hinge point. After that, the pace increases. He moves north, but bounces back and forth between Arizona and Colorado, with spikes in Nevada and Utah."

Jill takes over. "All the murders have the same ritualistic element. The wounds get more precise over time; the staging gets bolder. He's learning and refining. The one oddity is that the kills in Colorado appear to be very detailed: they're not spontaneous kills. The ones in Arizona look spontaneous. Other than the symbol detail, the scenes are messy and hurried."

Spinella grunts, walks up to the board, and picks a photo at random. He studies it and sets it back on the magnet. "What's the link? Why these folks?"

"They're all what the unsub would see as professionals. Teachers, counselors, nurses, secretaries and corporate executives. Some have a connection to at-risk youth. Some do not. There's no obvious sexual component, no rape and no ransom demands. It's about the kill and the statement."

"What's the statement?" asks Spinella.

Jill looked at him. "We're going to need someone from the BAU to help us with that. If you're looking for an opinion right now, I'd say perfection. Every cut, every victim and every signature. He wants to be seen, but only as a ghost. The spiral cross is his fingerprint, but it's also his brand. This is not a guy looking to get caught."

Carl, now into his rhythm, adds: "He never repeats locations. Lots of small communities with small police departments. The timeline is all over the place. There's no pattern we have been able to discern. The time between kills varies, and we believe the victims are killed immediately. No kidnapping. He has never contacted the media, and there have been no taunts to local law enforcement. It appears he hits, kills and moves on."

Spinella nods slowly. He points at the board. "What's your play, Trainor?"

"We need to assemble the task force," says Dirk. "We need a profiler from the BAU. If we can get him, Dan Cole in L.A. is one of the best. We need a dozen agents to sift through the data Carl has put together. We need to talk to every agency that has an unsolved case that meets the profile. Those can be in person or over the phone, but we need first-hand accounts, and we need to know if any of the agencies had a suspect or suspects. We need to anticipate the next kill in either Arizona or Colorado, and for right now, we need to keep this out of the press. We've done nothing to alert the unsub that there's an investigation going on. We need to keep it that way for a while, if we can."

"We also don't want to feed his ego," says Jill.

Spinella looks at each of them and returns to the board. He lets the silence do the work for a few seconds. "You have an ops plan?"

"It's in draft," says Dirk. "Jill has the outline. I'd also like to keep Carl to run analysis as more information comes in. Refine the data points."

Spinella walks the full length of the whiteboard, studies the clusters, and turns. "You know what this means, right? If you're right, we're looking at the biggest serial killer in the lower forty-eight."

"That's why we needed you to see it first," says Dirk.

"I need to call headquarters," says Spinella. "Shut the blinds on the window and cover the glass in the door. No one gets in or out of this room until I say so. Keep everything locked down. No leaks."

"Understood," says Dirk.

Spinella leaves the conference room, the door hissing closed behind him. The room seems for a moment like the inside of a bomb shelter. Jill relaxes by a centimeter, but only a centimeter. Carl exhales.

"You did good, Bunch. You held your own," says Jill.

Carl, sheepish but proud: "Thanks. I've never met a real field team before."

"Welcome to the deep end," said Dirk. "Don't drown."

They sit. They drink the dregs of their coffee, stone cold and bitter. The fluorescent lights overhead flicker, just for an instant, but then hold steady.

Outside, dusk is creeping in, flattening the world to gray and blue. Inside, the war room is just warming up.

Dirk, Jill and Carl lean forward, eyes pinned to the faces on the board, the spiral cross their only map. They are alone but no longer outnumbered. The monster on the wall is real, but so are they. The manhunt at last has begun.

Chapter Twenty-Two

The FBI conference room on the top floor of the Denver field office is lit by a single overhead fixture, the space draped in sullen twilight. The cold from the night before still lingers on the glass windows, and the air tastes faintly of stale coffee and the electrostatic grit of recycled HVAC. Dirk Trainor enters at 6:45, drops his bag by the side of the table, and inspects the whiteboard. Nothing has been erased since last night.

He gazes at the crime scene table, where a row of glossy prints has been arrayed in near-military order. He takes a seat at the end, settles his hands palm down, and counts his breathing to four, the way Dr. Whitman suggested the last time the nightmares got bad. In the silence, the whir of the mini-fridge and the faint rattle from the ice machine in the hallway are the only evidence of life.

At 6:53, the door opens. Dr. Rachel Whitman enters the room with a soft, predatory precision, like someone who has never once in her life stumbled. She wears a slate-gray blazer over black slacks, a thin chain at her throat, and a watch Dirk recognizes as a 1960s Bulova. No ostentation, just surgical utility. Her hair is parted neatly and pulled into a high, disciplined twist, the color in the overhead light a variegated dark brown. She pauses in the doorway, taking a full inventory of the room before letting the door close behind her.

Dirk stands halfway, then reconsiders. Whitman cocks an eyebrow, not at him, but at the whiteboard, as if the clues arrayed there are insufficient.

"Agent Trainor," she says, voice smooth and modulated for indoor acoustics. "You beat me here."

Dirk gestures at the table, the two chairs at either end. "I couldn't sleep. And we rarely get the BAU's best in our conference room."

She slides into the seat opposite, sets her legal pad and tablet to the side, and immediately scans the crime scene photos. Dirk watches her eyes; how they pause and flick, and how she sorts and reshuffles images as if shuffling a deck of cards.

Whitman picks up a pair of images, one in each hand, and holds them under the light. "These two," she says, voice dipping into a near-whisper. "They're the same design. The spiral cross at the sternum, shallow postmortem incisions and the victim's arms folded exactly at thirty degrees. But look here." She points to the leftmost photo, then to the second. "The entry wound is different. This one is clean and clinical. The other is…" She pauses, her lips forming a tight bracket. "Messy. Unstable."

Dirk shifts in his chair, fighting the urge to take notes on her diction. "You see it as two different offenders?"

"I see it as two different events in the same offender's life." She taps her nail on the shinier of the photos. "This is textbook organization. He staged the scene and cleaned up after himself. He even repositioned the body to minimize blood spatter on the carpet. Here?" She slides the second photo over. "This one is impulsive. The crime scene is sloppy, disorganized, spur of the moment, but the symbols is carved with precision."

Dirk leans forward, locking eyes. "The sloppier crime scenes are in Arizona, and the more precise crime scenes are in Colorado. That's what leads me to believe we are dealing with two individuals. Jill isn't sure."

"Exactly," says Whitman, drawing the two images together until their lower margins overlap. "This isn't escalation. It's regression. If it's the same subject, then he's unraveling," she draws a horizontal line in the air between them. "Or we're looking at a shared MO."

Dirk nods, steeples his fingers. "These murders have been happening for twenty-three years. I don't see it as his unraveling. Could it be a Copycat?"

"It's possible," Whitman says. "There's another possibility." She reaches for the autopsy file, opens it to a page of hand-sketched diagrams. "Have you ever seen a signature so precisely duplicated, not in appearance, but in dimension, even down to the spacing between the spiral arms?"

Dirk looks at the photo, at the diagram, and at the photo again. The spiral in both is the same width at every interval; the lines are parallel to less than a millimeter. "It's uncanny," he says, "because the word uncanny is less alarming than impossible."

Whitman's mouth tightens in what might be a smile. "It is. And that's why I wanted to see you before the rest of your team arrived." She leans in, voice lowering to a hush. "What do you know about dissociative identity disorder?"

Dirk blinks. "You think he's a split personality?"

"I don't think anything yet," she says, holding up a hand. "But if I did, I'd say that the best way to maintain two divergent MOs while keeping the signature identical is to have the same hand doing both, only at different points in a psychological cycle. The skill doesn't disappear, but the intention, the emotion behind the kills, can shift dramatically."

Dirk's mind races. "You're saying our unsub has an alter ego."

"I'm saying the clinical literature allows for compartmentalization of violence in ways we're only beginning to understand." She slides the pad closer, pulls a pen from her blazer, and begins sketching two overlapping ovals. "Look at the case from Greeley, and the one from Phoenix. The violence is different, but the 'handwriting' of the mutilation is identical. This isn't a signature. It's a mnemonic, a self-reminder, or a handshake between the two selves."

Dirk senses a chill despite the room's manufactured heat. He scans the whiteboard, at the phrase he scrawled last night, and wonders if the spiral cross is less a message to law enforcement than a private signal. One that means nothing to anyone but the killer or the killer's other half.

Whitman continues, voice taking on a more measured rhythm. "In the clean cases, the subject displays mastery. No evidence was left behind, not even DNA. In the chaotic cases, the scene is in turmoil, but there is still no usable DNA or prints. My theory is the subject enters a fugue state, loses some discipline, and becomes what you described as 'unsubtle.' But the spiral cross is always there, always perfect. That is the true self."

"But there are now two events on the same night, in two different states. Simultaneous murders. How does that fit?" asks Dirk.

Whitman frowns. "It doesn't unless we're dealing with a dyad. Two subjects intimately linked, one teacher and one disciple."

Dirk leans back. "The killings are six hundred miles apart, and there's evidence the subject was at the scene in Prescott within hours of the Denver murder."

Whitman's smile vanishes. She picks up a file folder, thumbs through it until she finds the map printout, and spreads it on the table. "Driving would take, what, ten, twelve hours?" she asks, not expecting an answer. "It could be a flight, but it would have to be private to make the times work."

"It's not possible," says Dirk. "Our timelines are solid. Unless the subject can be in two places at once."

He stops, the words echoing the raw terror in the back of his own mind. For a second, he sees the spiral not as a symbol but as a fingerprint: a whorl that means nothing, or everything, if you know where to look.

Whitman's face softens, a rare break in her academic armor. "It's not possible, of course. But there may be something in the signature. A method of training, or even a cultic aspect, that allows two unrelated subjects to duplicate it so precisely." She closes the folder and folds her hands on the table. "The

BAU sees a lot of copycats. But I've never seen this."

Dirk rubs his chin, feeling the static from the air. "So, what do we do?"

"We build a profile for both: one for the professional, one for the chaotic. And we search for overlap. Not only in the method but also in the emotional state at the time of the crime. There will be tells. What they take from the scene, and what they leave behind. Victimology is your best hope. There's always a pattern."

Dirk considers. "In the Phoenix case, there were two victims, both minors. In the others, they were all professional women. Do you see a link?"

Whitman is already scribbling notes in shorthand that Dirk can't read from across the table. "The link isn't the victim; it's the kill. All the victims are professionals. There are no street people, and no sex workers. Those are usually the easiest groups to target. This is different. This is not about sex or power. Until we can get the profiles, we will have a hard time figuring out the why. Who do you have working on the profile?"

"Dan Cole," says Dirk. "We were able to pull him out of L.A. for a couple of days."

Whitman smiled. "Dan is one of the best we have. Let's see what he comes back with."

Dirk notices some hesitation in her voice. "What?" he asks.

"With what we know so far, I fear we are dealing with a killer whose sole motivation is that he likes to kill. Those are rare and incredibly dangerous."

Dirk watches her for a long moment. The silence in the room is now thick, the kind that is both comforting and threatening. It is the silence of insight, but also of horror.

He reaches for the legal pad she left in the center of the table, flips it to a blank sheet. "Okay," he says. "Let's find the pattern."

He writes the word SYMMETRY in block letters, then underlines it twice. The case is less like a chase and more like a chess game.

Whitman clears her throat, her expression returning to baseline. "I'll need all the original files from Arizona and Colorado. If there's a common thread, it'll be in the details. The language of violence is always on the margins."

Dirk slides a card across the table, about the size of a business card, with the file location printed on it. "You have everything we have. Except the sense of dread."

She almost smiles again. "I have plenty of that, Agent Trainor. But thank you."

They sit in the strange half-dark, the only light pooling over the symbols on the table. Dirk fights the urge to open a window, to shatter the climate-controlled stasis of the room, but he pulls out his phone and begins compiling the timeline.

It is a quiet, furious race to see who will get there first: the investigators, or the killer's next cycle. Outside the city is still mostly dark. But on the other side of the glass, the first pink line of dawn is bleeding into the black. Dirk sees it, notes the time, and waits for the world to catch up.

Chapter Twenty-Three

The world outside the conference room advances in slow increments. Security badge whines in the elevator, a rising tone from the coffee machine in the break area, and the measured thud of foot traffic along the vinyl corridor. Inside, dawn has thickened the shadows on the walls, and the projector screen's glow has grown from a gray rectangle to a searchlight.

At seven sharp, Jill enters. She moves in a straight line from door to board, her hair still damp at the nape from a too-short shower, face marked by a sleeplessness she refuses to acknowledge. She sets her phone and field notebook at her seat, then stands just behind Dirk's left shoulder, silent but unmistakably present. She eyes Dr. Whitman and offers a crisp, "Morning, Doc."

"Special Agent Quarters," says Whitman, her voice registering the formality of rank but softened at the edges by respect.

"Jill's fine. We met at the domestic violence conference in D.C. three years ago." Jill leans in, her gaze falling to the photos arrayed in front of Whitman. "You're still using the color-coded sticky tabs?" She smiles at the sight of neon Post-its bordering the open case files.

"I do," Whitman says, "though the Bureau's switch to digital has made me a minority of one."

Dirk resists the urge to smile. Instead, he draws Jill's attention to the sequence of crime scene prints, sliding the most recent set to her. "These are the ones from Prescott. Tell me if you see what I see."

Jill runs her finger along the first photo, then the second, her eyes flicking up twice, almost involuntarily, at Dirk. "It's the same signature, but look at the spacing on the spiral. This one's less controlled, a little wild." She traces the lines, then says, "And this cut isn't as deep. Is that deliberate, or just a rush job?"

Whitman nods. "Very good. We were just talking about that."

Before they can discuss further, a trickle of agents enters. Two, then three, until the conference room is a hive of shifting dark suits and battered briefcases. Carl Bunch, the analyst from headquarters, stands awkwardly in the doorway for a full ten seconds before Dirk waves him to the table. Carl's face is pale, his hair rumpled from a morning spent pulling out handfuls in stress. He clutches his phone like a lifeline.

The field team slides in, every seat occupied but one. The chatter is low and urgent, but all eyes dart back to the whiteboard, to the wall of names and wounds and maps pinned in surgical grids.

At 7:14, the last member arrives. Dan Cole is taller than Dirk remembers, just over six feet and athletic, with a shaved head that makes him look both ageless and weirdly boyish. He wears glasses, jeans, and a leather jacket over a black T-shirt. He carries a backpack, which he sets next to the door before moving to his place at the table.

"Sorry I'm late," he announces, but his voice is

more an apology for his own existence than any real tardiness. "Flight from L.A. got in at six, so I came straight here."

Dirk nods him toward an open chair. "Glad you made it, Dan."

Dan pulls a notebook and a MacBook from his backpack, flips open both with a single practiced gesture, and scans the room. His eyes settle on Jill, then Whitman, then back to the whiteboard, and Dirk gets the sense that nothing in the room has escaped his notice.

Seconds later, Anthony Spinella enters. The effect is immediate as the noise level drops and every head turns towards him. Spinella's suit is navy, conservative, with the Bureau pin sharp on the lapel. His hair, always a point of pride, is perfectly in place, but there's a new red tinge at the edges of his eyes, a fatigue that's worked its way into the marrow. He walks to the front, sets a tablet on the podium, and fixes the room with his gaze.

"I want everyone's full attention," he says, the familiar baritone threading through the air. "Thank you all for showing up early and on short notice. We have a situation that is." He glances at the whiteboard. "Unprecedented, even for the Bureau. As of midnight, we have confirmed a series of connected murders stretching from Denver to Phoenix, with at least six cases and potentially as many as one hundred and sixty if the pattern holds."

The room's silence thickens.

Spinella lets that number hover, then gestures at

Dirk. "Agent Trainor will run the task force, and I expect everyone here to report directly to him, unless I say otherwise. There's no space for ego on this one. No territory, no internal turf wars. Anyone with a better idea than the one on the table is expected to speak up. We're all working together until this bastard is stopped."

He turns to the whiteboard, and with a quick motion, underlines a row of victim names. "The oldest confirmed case is from 2002 in Arizona. Most recent was yesterday, here and in Prescott. The killer or killers are using a signature." He points at the photos, the spiral cross. "It's never been released to the press or to local law enforcement. That's how we know the connection is real. We have BAU, forensics and regional teams working round the clock, but the scope is too large for standard protocol. That's why you're here. I need you all to familiarize yourselves with every detail, every case file, every timestamp and every grainy crime scene photo. The answer is in there somewhere. It's up to us to find it, and to do it before anyone else dies."

He lets the weight settle. A few agents, all veterans, nod in the silent way of men who have seen the worst and still believe they can fix it.

Spinella glances down at his tablet, then up. "I'm not one for speeches. Trainor, it's yours."

Dirk stands, ignoring the micro-tremor in his knees. "Thank you, Special Agent in Charge." He gives the room a moment to adjust, then says, "Most of you know me, but for those who don't, I'm Dirk Trainor. This is my partner, Jill Quarters, and this is Dr. Rachel

Whitman from Quantico. Carl Bunch on loan from D.C. is our analyst, and Dan Cole," he gestures. "Is our profiler on loan from Los Angeles. This team is handpicked, and every one of you brings something the others don't."

Dirk cues up the projector, and the screen lights up with the timeline of deaths, each one color-coded by geography and victim profile.

"I'll get right to it. We have possibly two serial killers. They share the same signature, but not the same method. Some murders are surgical, perfectly executed, with no forensic trace. Others are chaotic, almost impulsive, with sloppy clean-up and evidence left behind. The link is the spiral cross, carved or drawn at the same anatomical location, with exact precision. We have two theories. One: we're dealing with a copycat. Two: the unsubs are working together, or they share a common origin, possibly even a split personality or a cultic connection. We feel confident that we can rule out a single killer, since the Prescott killing and the Denver killing happened within a few hours of each other."

He turns to Whitman. "Dr. Whitman, I'd like you to brief the team on your findings, and then we'll field questions. After that, Jill will pass out the files. I want everyone to go over every detail and then reach out to the local officers who handled these cases. We need any eyewitness testimony, what the police didn't put in the reports, and if the locals ever keyed in on any suspects."

Whitman stands instantly in command of the room's attention. She pulls her tablet closer and flips to a page of diagrams. "Thank you, Agent Trainor. I'll be concise, as most of you have already read the preliminary brief."

She uses the laser pointer to draw two bright dots on the screen. "We have two primary MOs. In the first, the victim is incapacitated quickly, with a minimum of physical trauma. The throat is cut, followed by a signature cross and spiral at the chest. These scenes are almost sterile, suggesting not just expertise, but detachment. In the second, the scenes are often chaotic, rushed, but the spiral cross is precise. There are minute differences in the crosses, but they are both so close that it would take an expert to see the differences. The crosses are surgical. The killer leaves no physical evidence, and in the case of the Colorado killer, it appears he even tidies up the location before he leaves. There is also no sexual or other criminal motive to the cases."

She clicks, flipping the slide. "The key detail is that the spiral cross is identical, not just in appearance but in execution. We're talking about sub-millimeter precision in the width of the spiral arms. This is not learned overnight, nor is it easy to duplicate without training. My professional opinion is that the killers are connected at a psychological level. Either through mentorship, shared trauma, or a formalized ritual."

A hand goes up, a senior agent with a mustache and a voice like gravel. "You said the deviation in the spiral cross is identical, yet not quite perfect. That would suggest the same person in both locations. Are you sure about the timeline of the most recent cases?"

"We are," says Whitman. "Two killers using the

same symbol is statistically rare. Serial offenders coordinating with each other are rare. Until yesterday, when agents Trainor and Quarters confirmed the timelines in both Denver and Prescott, we were working on the assumption that we had one killer using multiple locations. The timeline confirmation changes that thinking. That's why I suspect two."

Carl Bunch shifts in his seat, voice tight. "You mentioned mentoring. What about the possibility that the killers are related. Brothers, sisters or some other family arrangement?"

Dirk glances at Jill, who says, "We are looking at that. It's an even rarer scenario, but at this point nothing is off the table."

A ripple of nods around the table. The room is alive with the small, granular hope that always follows the whiff of an actionable lead.

Dirk resumes. "We're going to have you work in teams of two. Jill has the breakdown. She'll give each group several case files. Follow up with the locals, police, forensics and medical examiner. Find out what's not in the file and like I mentioned a few minutes ago, see if they had any suspects or any evidence that can be sent to the lab. Some of these cases are old, and as you are all aware, DNA retrieval has improved dramatically, but memories may not be so good. Treat each of these cases as if this were a new crime. Since this is a top priority for the Bureau, we will have a direct link and address to a forensic lab to process our evidence in a timely manner. The lab info is on a card in the case file. Jill has also created a short cheat sheet of questions to get you started with each local agency. This will help you cut through the crap and get to the meat. Our priority is confirming which of these one-hundred-sixty cases fits within our criteria. After that, you can go back and do a deeper dive. Set up interviews and, if it's needed, set up site visits. Any site visits, clear them with Jill."

Dirk looks around the table. "Dan, meet with Dr. Whitman after the briefing. Carl will continue to scour the database for similar cases that you can use to update your profile as we go. Review the files and create your profile. I'd like to have a first go on the profile by tomorrow morning."

He looked around the table. "This is going to be a lot of grunt work for the next couple of days. Don't burn yourselves out to get through your case files. We need this to be by the numbers. Once we get through all this paperwork, then the manhunt can begin."

Spinella steps in. "Last thing. The press doesn't have the signature, and I want to keep it that way. If a local tries to leak, you let me know before you return fire. We keep the circle tight, or we risk giving the unsub exactly what he wants."

He surveys the room. "Go do your jobs. And watch your sixes."

The room comes alive as folders are passed, laptops are booted up, and the agents pair off with military efficiency. Jill moves among them, whispering directives, answering questions before they can be voiced. Whitman stands with Dan and Carl, sketching a spiral on a sheet of legal paper.

Dirk stands at the board, watching the agents

deploy, and he senses the full, brutal scale of what they're up against. He imagines the next kill, and the next, and the sense of failure that will accompany each one. He looks at Jill, who catches his eye, and they both remember why they do this job: because the alternative is to let the world go dark.

Jill moves to his side; her voice pitched for his ears only. "You, okay?"

Dirk smiles. "Not even close. We've opened a twenty-year can of worms, and we have no idea where this is going to lead."

She smiles, and this is the first time it looks real.

Chapter Twenty-Four

Dirk leaves the field office at 10:18 p.m., his face washed out by the sodium spill of the parking lot lights. He unlocks his car, slides in, and sits a moment in the driver's seat with his palms on the wheel. The silence outside is absolute; the windows bead with the exhaust of a dying winter, fogged in from breath and temperature differentials. He starts the engine and clicks on the defrost.

For ten seconds, he sits with the car idling, knuckles whitening, then backs out slowly, one hand steering, his eyes clocking the empty stalls and the single security vehicle patrolling the perimeter. At the traffic light, he checks his reflection in the glass. The lines have deepened since morning. His phone chirps once with an update from Jill, but he ignores it. The night is a blank, stretched flat from here to the city's western edge.

He turns west, merging onto the arterial. The city is quiet, stripped down for the late shift. Through the windshield, he sees strip malls sleeping in neon, a dozen gas stations, and a liquor store fronted by three dead pines. His hands drift to the radio and then back. There's nothing he wants to hear.

When he reaches the corner of Federal and 80th, he takes the exit and cuts into a Mexican fast-food drive-through. The parking lot is empty but for a single red Corolla with a crumpled rear fender, its taillights dull as a dying insect. The building itself hums with the constant, insectile blue of a bug zapper over the back door. Dirk pulls into the drive lane, orders a number three (beef burrito, no sour cream, extra red sauce) and a large Coke, and then idles at the window with his badge on the dash, in case someone in line has a question.

The teenager manning the window is bored but polite. He hands over the bag and Coke and says, "Stay warm out there, sir." Dirk nods, drops a folded five in the tip jar, and pulls into a corner slot to eat.

Inside the car, the smell of lard and cumin is overpowering. He unwraps the burrito, balances it on the lid of the takeout box, and eats in even mechanical bites. He sips the Coke after every third swallow, as if it's protocol. The food is hot and flavorless, the nourishment that passes directly through the body's inspection. He wipes his mouth with a napkin, folds the trash, and deposits it in the passenger floor well. He breathes through his nose, slowly and controlled. He's not hungry, but hunger is not the point.

Fifteen minutes later, he pulls out, heads north to the subdivision that used to be a farm but now contains thirty-two identical two-story homes along the cul-de-sac. He pulls into the driveway of the eighth house, keys the garage, and waits for the door to slide open before he kills the lights. He sits in the dark a moment, engine off, then steps out, closes the door with the barest click.

Inside the mudroom, he finds what he always finds: Lego blocks in the entryway, a drift of schoolwork on the shoe bench, one of his daughter's plush toys half buried in a boot. The house is asleep but not peaceful; every surface speaks of activity arrested by exhaustion.

He places his badge and keys on the metal tray by the wall, then bends to pick up the scattered Legos, pinching them one by one until his palm is full.

The kitchen is dim but not unlit. The glow from the fridge's water dispenser bathes the tile in blue-white light. Dirk opens the pantry, slides his service pistol from the holster, and places it into a small lockbox bolted at eye level behind the oatmeal. He works the dial slowly, eyes half-lidded, and listens for the satisfying click of tumblers dropping into place. The routine is the only thing that guarantees him sleep.

He pours the Legos into a canvas bin, then takes a slow circuit of the main floor, scooping up a plush yellow duck, a sippy cup and a pair of pink sneakers. Everything goes into its designated basket or bin or shelf, a silent act of contrition for the mess he makes by not being home.

He climbs the stairs, stepping over a tangle of rubber dinosaurs and a crumpled Elsa dress. The house is quieter here; the air carries the trace of lavender and low-watt nightlights. At the top landing, he pauses, listening. The heater ticks and sighs. The twins' door is open four inches, according to the house rules.

Dirk enters and stands just inside. The twins are side-by-side in their bunks, one upside-down and clutching a Minecraft plushie, the other cocooned in a Star Wars comforter. He watches them for three full breaths. Both snore, but only a little; it is the most perfect sound in the world. He steps to the foot of the bed and gently rotates the one whose foot dangles off the edge, tucks the blanket up. He listens to the rise and fall, confirms it, then backs out, careful to leave the door ajar.

The nursery is next. He enters on silent feet, adjusting to the gloom. The baby is in the crib, half-sprawled, one hand clutching the edge of a knit blanket. She is not technically a baby, but he cannot bring himself to call her a toddler yet. He approaches the crib, bends over, and holds his palm half an inch from her mouth. Her breath is shallow but warm. He counts five slow exhalations, then gently tugs the blanket up to her chin. He does not kiss her, not tonight; some superstitions are too deep to break.

He leaves the nursery, closing the door with a pressure only learned through years of practice. He moves down the hall to the master bedroom. The door is ajar, and the faint sound of a podcast drifts from his wife's phone on the nightstand.

Inside, the room is chilly and dim. His wife lies on her side, head propped on a forearm, eyes closed but not sleeping. She doesn't move as he enters, just emits a low, wordless noise of acknowledgment. Dirk crosses to the bathroom, strips in the dark, and steps into the shower. He lets the water go hot, scalding, and scrubs the day's residue from his skin. The shower is brief but thorough; he shaves, even though he doesn't need to.

When he returns to the bedroom, his wife has turned away, the comforter pulled up to her chin. He dresses in a clean T-shirt and gym shorts, then sets the alarm for 5:30 a.m., double-checks it, and sets the phone face down on his nightstand. He stands for a moment, staring at the ceiling, then climbs into bed, trying not to disturb the mattress.

She reaches a hand back and places it on his thigh, palm flat, neither invitation nor rejection. They say nothing. He listens to her breathing, slow and steady, and lets the weight of the day drop off his shoulders. In the morning, he'll make coffee and breakfast. He'll pack the lunches and double-check the shoes. For now, he sleeps, anchored by her hand and the certainty that nothing in the house will change before the sun returns.

Dirk dreams in bleeding color. The world in the dream is distorted, as if viewed through the wrong end of a telescope, but everything close at hand is hyper-real: the whir of the Xerox, the sickly fluorescence above, the way the heels of the woman's shoes bite into the industrial carpet. She is alone in the office. Too late for the building to make sense as anything but a stage for something terrible. She hums to herself off-key, fingers tapping a careless rhythm on the copier lid. He wants to warn her, but in the dream, he has no voice, no body. He floats formless, a passenger in someone else's skull.

The woman reaches to the side tray, shakes loose a jammed printout, then sighs and bends low to clear the feed. The back of her neck is a pale crescent, lit blue-white, and delicate as a peeled grape. The sound of the copier drowns out the soft pad of footsteps behind her. He knows the sound is there, knows the pattern, but cannot make it audible to her. He is an observer, cursed to watch.

A gloved hand appears in his field of view. Someone's field? The flash of metal is perfect, surgical. He sees the blade before she does. He wants to shout, to warn, but the words come out as static. The knife enters just above the curve of her collarbone, slides in so smoothly it is a second before the blood follows. She stiffens, tries to scream, and the sound is a gurgle. The attacker's grip is perfect, the hand steady. He recognizes the angle, the pressure, the choreography. The body slumps to the floor, and the hand lets go.

He wakes with the sheet tangled around his chest, wet with sweat. His breath scrapes in and out like a runner finishing a race. His wife sits up, her hair a black corona in the dark, one arm wrapping around his shoulders before he has fully re-entered himself.

"What's wrong?" Her voice is soft, and she is reaching for comfort.

Dirk wipes his face with a trembling hand and tries to laugh. The sound is brittle, but it does the job. "Probably shouldn't have had that burrito after a full day of crime scene photos." He gestures vaguely at his own stomach. "Hell of a combo."

She pulls him close anyway, tucking his head beneath her chin. Neither of them moves. The only sounds are the tick of the bedside clock and the movement of forced air in the vent above the closet. Eventually she drifts back down, pulling the comforter with her, leaving him above the surface, blinking at the ceiling.

He tries to slow his breathing. He counts the rhythm of the clock, the four and seven and eight of the in-breath, the long, careful out. He recites the case numbers in order, then the names, then the locations. The images from the dream refuse to go away. They surface with each flicker of the digital display: the wet, cartoon red of the woman's neck; thc feel of paralysis; the hand with the blade, entering from the margin.

Dirk rolls to his side, faces the wall, and lets his eyes adjust to the faintest gray seep from the street outside. He listens to the house. In the hallway, something creaks. One twin mutters in her sleep. The night seems thinner than usual, less able to hold the weight of what it's supposed to protect.

He lies awake until the alarm, not quite ready for the next day, but unable to call back the dream to finish it. There's work waiting, and his mind drifts back to it, looping through the sequence until, at last, the sun reaches through the window, and the world is bright enough to pretend nothing happened at all.

Chapter Twenty-Five

Dirk arrives at the Denver field office a full hour before the building hums. The dawn is slow, ash gray, and limps past the frost that sheets the glass. He sits in his car for six minutes, finishing the rest of last night's Coke, and makes his way inside. The lobby is empty. The lights are set to minimum. The badge reader sticks: he waits for the buzzer and then shoulders through.

On the top floor, the conference room is already occupied. Jill sits at the table, her hair coiled into a tighter, meaner knot than usual, a stack of folders set at 90-degree angles. She has a yellow legal pad and a fresh mug of coffee, which she cradles in both hands. The room smells faintly of bleach.

Dirk enters. He slides his laptop from his bag, sets it on the table, and begins a slow, deliberate boot-up. He does not meet Jill's eyes.

She watches him for a moment, then says, "You look like you fell asleep in a garbage truck."

Dirk smiles. "Couldn't sleep."

Jill sips her coffee, then sets it down. "Nightmares?"

He shrugs, still not looking up. "Just didn't sleep well."

Dirk flips open the top folder, scanning the first two pages without processing. The words stutter and float; the residue of dream clinging to the back of his skull, stubborn as mold. He pulls a pen from his pocket, underlines a sentence, then immediately forgets why.

Jill studies him, her eyes fixed and bright. "Did you have another attack?"

Dirk flinches, then forces his hand to still. "Nothing to worry about," he says. "Just tired."

"Dirk." She speaks his name as if pronouncing a technical term. "If you're getting more of those spells, we need to deal with it before Spinella notices."

He keeps his eyes on the folder. "It's not a problem."

Jill sighs, loud enough to be heard but not loud enough to be a challenge. She picks up her coffee, turns a page on her own stack, and begins annotating in the margins. "Bunch is in early," she says. "He's down the hall prepping the next round of data for the board. Wants to go over his pattern logic with you before the morning meeting."

Dirk nods, eyes on the printout, but the words still won't settle into meaning.

Jill makes a note in her pad, then closes it. She studies Dirk as if he's an evidence bag, something to be cataloged and stored. "Let's get through the pile of daily reports from the team before he gets here," she says. "You take Colorado, and I'll take Arizona. We'll meet in the middle if there's anything urgent."

For twenty minutes they work in silence. Every click of the keyboard, every snap of the paper, is amplified by the isolation. When Dirk finally glances up, Jill is still watching him, her gaze unblinking.

"Anything?" he asks.

She tears a page from her pad and slides it to his side of the table. "The Arizona team found another one. A cold case in Mesa, Arizona, in 2003 that was misclassified," she says. "It fits the pattern, but there's a deviation on the cross. Shallow cut, almost looks like hesitation."

He reads the printout, then looks at her. "You think it's a copycat?"

"I think it's the same guy, but he's still learning."

Dirk turns the idea over in his head, lets it sit. "I had a dream about one last night," he says. "I saw it as it was happening. From inside." The words sound foreign, like reciting someone else's lines.

Jill nods, as if she had expected this. "You ever get dreams like that before?"

He hesitates. "A few times over the years. But never like this."

She writes something on her pad, then tears it out and crumples it in her fist. "Tell me if you get another one. Or if the dreams match a case we're working."

He nods. "Will do."

Jill sets her jaw and goes back to the files. She makes no mention of the hand shaking as she marks her next case. Dirk notices but says nothing. The partnership has always been built on the architecture of mutual denial; both know when to let things slide and when to escalate.

The sun finally breaches the window, painting the folders in harsh orange. The building wakes up, doors opening and closing, the murmur of voices creeping down the hall. The day is about to begin.

Jill stands, gathers the prioritized printouts, and hands half to Dirk. "Let's see what Bunch has before Spinella arrives," she says. "He'll want to see these."

Dirk stacks the pages, stands, and follows her out. The war room seems lighter in the morning, but the board is heavier than ever.

The two of them move as one, rehearsed, ready for whatever waits at the other end of the corridor.

Chapter Twenty-Six

Present day…Calvin Walker

I lurch out of sleep so hard I tear my shoulder. I feel searing heat, not from a muscle but the space behind it. The way nerves catch fire and make you forget which world is the real one. My throat snaps open for air, and I'm already halfway off the mattress, both hands up like I'm catching the fall, or warding off a punch I saw coming in my sleep.

The walls of the room are running. It takes a minute to remember the fan's broken and the night air outside is swampy, sucked through the mesh of my window and slow to fade. Everything on me is slick. My T-shirt is pasted to my chest, and there's a salty sting in my eyes before I even rub them. The stink of old sweat and plastic mattress pad is familiar, but what gets me is the new, stranger note underneath it. A sharp, medical smell, like latex gloves and bleach. My brain keeps tripping over it, even after I remember I live alone and there's nothing here but my rot and a month's worth of laundry.

For a second, I don't know what woke me. Not the traffic. At this hour, nothing is moving outside. Not a siren, though there's always at least one orbiting out there, Doppler up and gone. It's my heart, going hard against the ribs, way too fast for someone lying in bed. It's like the nightmare left a hole behind, and all my blood is trying to leak through it.

Then it comes back in jagged flashes. The woman.

I don't know her face, just the angle of the neck, the soft hinge where jaw meets throat. She's standing in the dark. No, not standing, but floating. No feet. Just torso and bare arms. Not a hint of what she'd sound like if she screamed. But that's not the worst of it. The knife isn't mine. The cut isn't mine either. When it goes in, there's none of the smooth edge, none of the feel of flesh resisting, or the little catch when you hit cartilage. It just… opens. A line of red as sharp as a fucking laser. And there, right where the blood wells, someone draws the spiral cross, slow, neat, almost tender. Like they've practiced it a thousand times.

It's the wrong spiral. Not the one I do with the shake in the wrist, the stutter when the adrenaline hits. This one is perfect. Tight lines, clean symmetry, the kind that would get you an A in geometry if your teacher didn't know you were carving it on the inside of your own arm.

My stomach flips, and for half a second, I taste bile and cheap whiskey in my mouth. My tongue is furry. The night sweats have done their thing, but now I'm ice cold, gooseflesh all down my legs. My right foot thumps the side table, and something falls. There's a glassy thunk and then the slow, glugging roll of an empty bottle under the bed.

I'm out of the sheets before I can stop myself, one hand braced on the paint-chipped dresser. My nails dig in. The world tilts, and I have to steady the fuck up before I black out. I breathe once, twice, counting the inhale because it's the only way to prove I'm awake. My pulse is a red alert, but the rest of me is shutting down. My hands are numb, my toes are tingling, and my eyes are tracking nothing.

I look at the floor, but all I see is the woman's throat, the perfect cut, the spiral cross left behind. It's not my kill, but it's been sewn into my head so tight it's like a scar that opened again.

I take three steps and nearly slip on the spilled whiskey: the bottle knocking against my heel. My T-shirt, plastered to my ribs, reeks of last night's sweat and old cigarettes, but I leave it on. I want the punishment. The burn, the itch, the knowledge that I'm still here, still real, still me.

I reach down for the bottle. The floor's sticky. I wipe my hand on the shirt, not that it does any good. I'm awake now, sure, but the images aren't fading. There's a voice in my skull that keeps whispering not you. But the worst part is, it could be. If you ever learned how to keep your hands steady.

I stand in the dark, the ceiling fan dead above, the window pulling in nothing but wet heat and the sigh of cars on wet pavement. My breathing slows, but my hands still shake. The cut, the spiral, the woman, whoever she is, they're all waiting for me behind the eyes. Like a message, or a dare.

I set the bottle upright on the dresser; the glass leaves a ring in the dust. The smell lingers, sweet and bitter and burned. I've had dreams about my kills before, but this one's got teeth. It doesn't let go, not even when I force my brain to replay something, anything, from real life.

I glance at the clock. It's 3:24 a.m., but the red digits are swimming. I blink, rub my face, and blink again.

There's no point trying to sleep. Not now. Not when I know someone out there is doing my work better than me. Cleaner. Meaner. With a purpose I can't even guess at.

I lean my head against the window, my forehead cold on the glass. Outside, the city's barely breathing, but somewhere a couple of blocks away, or halfway across the country, someone else is up and thinking about the next time they'll carve the spiral. I'm afraid I might not be the only one.

There's a moment after a panic spike where you have to keep moving, or else you drown. I'm not in the business of drowning, so I pace the apartment like a tiger in a zoo, never letting my skin cool down, never letting my brain settle on any one thing for longer than a second. The floorboards in this shithole are worn and warped, probably water-damaged under the carpet, and the squeak is more noticeable this morning. My feet slap and sting. I do a circuit from the window to the fridge and back until the pattern seems like something I'm carving into the building's memory.

Every pass I make, I catch myself in the cracked glass of the oven door. Eyes gone wide, bloodshot, hair stuck up on one side and matted on the other. It's not a look that wins points at work or anywhere else, but I don't go out much anymore. I don't have to.

I'm muttering. I know I am, but the words are half thought, half static. "Not my kill. Not my kill." I shake my head hard enough to hurt. "I saw it. It wasn't me. It was like I was watching it happen from the outside. No, not outside. Behind." I grab a chunk of hair and yank. The pain helps. I keep muttering.

The lamp in the corner is a cheap torchiere from Walmart, the last bulb on its last leg. It flickers in time with my steps. Sometimes when I pace, I get the idea that my shadow's moving a fraction of a second before I do, leading the way, pulling me toward something I'm supposed to see.

There's only one piece of furniture in the room that matters. It's a battered coffee table made of pressed board, with a cigarette burn shaped like Florida right in the middle. I keep a single mug there, always half full of something that used to be hot and is now a film on the inside. I walk a lap, then slam my palm into the table's edge. The pain jumps to my elbow, not quite numb. The lamp shudders, then steadies.

The cut in my head, the one from the dream, was nothing like mine. It was surgical. Not just precise but made by someone who had a plan before they ever held the blade. I want to be mad about it, offended, but all I feel is this gross envy. It's like I saw a painting that made mine look like shit. Like there's a real artist out there, and I'm just a guy who can fake it with enough time and sweat.

I press both palms to my forehead, mashing the hair against my skull. The headache is coming back, high and tight, right above the eyes. I close them and see the woman from the dream. Her face is vivid. I can see every detail. I see her mouth open, but not in a scream, but a question. Why me? Why this?

I hyperventilate, but not on purpose. It's how my body reacts when the walls close in. There's a noise in my chest, a little animal whimper I'd be embarrassed about if anyone could hear it. I get up too fast, slam my knee into the table, and almost tip the whole thing.

"Not my kill," I repeat out loud. "Not my work." I slap the side of my head three times. "You saw it, but you didn't do it. Who did?"

The lamp buzzes, throwing a weird yellow stripe across the room. My spiral, rough but proud. The dream spiral mocks me from memory. I feel like I'm in a test I didn't study for, and someone else is feeding me the answers. But they're all in code, and every time I try to translate, I lose something.

I rest my forehead against the corkboard and close my eyes. There's a silence in my head now, like the calm after a thunderstorm. But underneath it, a slow pulse: the promise that this isn't over. That somewhere, the person from the dream is watching, too. They're as freaked out as I am. Or they're waiting for me to catch up.

I sit there until my legs go numb, just tracing the lines, the curves and the history of my obsession. The cut is in the memory now, permanent as any scar. And I know, even if I wanted to stop, it wouldn't let me.

I stand up too fast, and the head rush almost drops me. I need to get control. I need data, proof, and I need to see if I'm losing it for real or if the world's changed the locks again without telling me.

The kitchen is ten feet from the living room, separated by a strip of counter and a tile floor sticky from something that spilled. The fridge buzzes like a dying wasp. I open the top drawer by the sink and jam my hand inside, pushing past takeout napkins, dried-out pens, old rubber bands, until my fingers close on the black notebook. It's got a fake Moleskin cover, corners gone white with wear, and the pages so stuffed the binding's warped. I slam the drawer with my hip, using the motion to keep my knees from giving out.

On the way back to the table, I step over a pair of sneakers I forgot I owned and nearly trip. I kick them out of the way, leaving a dark smear on the tile from whatever's still on my heel. The lamp is still going, but the flicker is faster now, like a strobe at a club, or a warning signal.

I sit at the table and pull the notebook onto my lap. The cover seems warm, but I know it's not. I just ran that hot in the dream, I guess. The first few pages are a mess of block letters, addresses, dates. I thumb through fast, looking for the old photos glued inside. Some are clipped from newspapers, some printed from library computers, and some just scrawled out in my hand. A stick figure diagram to remember what was important.

Page by page, I flip. I'm looking for her, the woman from the dream, but all I see are the ones I already know. One victim, a girl I followed into a dark alleyway in Tucson. The mark is a mess, but I had to rush because I heard footsteps coming towards us. Another, an old teacher in Bisbee. I got the angle wrong, and it looks like a fishhook, but I had to keep moving her huge, sagging tits out of the way. After that, they got good. Efficient. I know my work by the way the skin pulls at the ends, the minor hiccup in the line. I look at each victim. A few of them smile from grainy yearbook photos; others don't have names just photos. I flip faster, and my hands shake again.

I hit the section at the back where the recent ones

are, the ones I did myself. I pause there. Some photos are Polaroid; others are from an old Instax I got off eBay. The film was expensive but worth it for the lack of a digital trace. They're tucked into a paper sleeve, never more than one or two per page. I slide them out, line them up, and study the spiral crosses with my thumb over the edge. Each is mine; I know it. They're not clean, not like in the dream. The skin bunches and pulls, and blood soaks into the outline. Sometimes the wound closes up before the spiral's done. That's how I know it's real: nothing is ever perfect.

But the dream cut, that was nearly perfect. I close the photos, press the entire stack flat, and rub my hands over my face. The notebook smells of ink and finger oil.

Through the window, the city's waking up. There's the wail of a siren. Not the fast kind, more like the slow, warning one when they want you to know someone's coming. I hear a car horn, sharp, then a laugh from across the street. A garbage truck roars down the block and rattles the glass in my window. It's all normal, all routine, but the sound makes the apartment feel even smaller. Like the world is moving on and I'm trapped behind, stuck in a night that won't quit just because the sun came up.

I push the notebook aside, knocking it to the floor. The urge is there, in my fingers now, not just in my head. I shove aside a stack of old takeout containers: lo mein leaking grease, a pizza box with the phone number circled in Sharpie, and grab the laptop from underneath. I open the lid, hit the power, and wait for the sickly blue glow to fill the room.

The password is just six digits. I type it one-handed, eyes on the loading icon spinning slowly. The computer is as old as the apartment, missing two key caps, and the battery is so weak that it only works if it's plugged in. The desktop background is the default. I don't need a picture to remind me of anything.

First thing I do is hit the local news. There's a story on the front page about a highway accident, three dead. Not my kind of kill, so I ignore it. Next is a shooting on the south side, a robbery. Skip. I dig deeper, going through the obits, the police logs, scrolling until my finger cramps. Every new body gets a second look. If it matches the dream, a woman killed by a knife with a spiral cross, I should see it. But there's nothing. Just overdoses, old age and a few car wrecks.

I try three different news sites, then a true crime blog, then one of those crowdsourced forums where amateurs pretend they know how the police work. Someone posted about a possible serial killer in the Mountain West, linking to a Denver story. The photo is blurry, but the cut is close to mine. Not the same, but close. I stare at it. The spiral is sharp. Clean. I run a fingernail over the screen and shiver. This isn't right. I haven't been to Colorado since I was three years old.

I back out and close the window. My hands won't stop moving. I open an old bookmark, the police database I cracked a while back, the one that lets you see the first line of every incident report before it locks you out. It's risky, I know. If they're tracking IPs, I could get flagged. But the urge is bigger than fear now.

I click the link. Enter the old login. It still works. The menu opens, and I search for key terms: knife, cross, spiral, ritual, woman. Hundreds of hits, most useless. I sort by date, then skim for the last week. There, three days ago, in Colorado, a woman was found dead in her apartment. No details, just a note about an unusual wound pattern. My breath hitches. I click again. The full report is locked behind another login, one I don't have.

I peruse the line of text, the blinking cursor, the space where the story should be. My skin crawls. There's a sense of being watched, even though I know I'm alone. I lean back, press my knuckles into my eyes, and try to remember the dream again. The spiral was clean; the cut was perfect, but the hands in the dream weren't mine. The nails were trimmed. The wrist was pale, almost white. The knife had a wooden handle.

I look at my own hands. My nails are jagged, a scab on the middle finger, and my cuticles are stained. My wrists are thin, but they're not pale. Not like that.

For a second, I want to laugh. This is crazy, even for me. I should be out in the real world, not haunting the corpse of a city at dawn. But the need is back. The sense that whatever I am, someone else out there is, too. And they're not just copying. They're improving. Like they know the rules, I'm just learning to play.

The room is brightening, but it doesn't feel like morning. It's more like the end of something, or maybe the beginning. I close the laptop, but the screen stays black, a faint ghost of my face reflected in it. The eyes looking back at me aren't mine. Not quite. There's something off in the angle, the way the light hits. A stranger or a brother. I can't tell which.

I sit not moving until the garbage truck makes another pass, and the sound shakes me loose. I pick up the notebook, place it back in the drawer, and then close it gently. I make a list in my head of what I have to do next, but I already know the first thing: find the spiral. Find the other. See who finishes the line.

Chapter Twenty-Seven

Present Day…James Freemont

I snap awake, and for a few seconds it seems like someone else's room. The ceiling overhead registers first. Smooth, perfect knockdown texture, repainted last summer because the old stains made Rebecca crazy, but the geometry of the space is wrong; everything is misaligned. I think I'm standing, but I'm not. I'm in bed. Twisted so hard, the fitted sheet has pulled loose on my side. Every muscle in my back is clenched, like I'm about to throw up or punch through a wall.

The red glare from the digital clock says 3:17 AM. There's enough ambient city light bleeding through the blackout curtains to put a green edge on every shadow. The bedroom is a boxed-in ocean of silence. Rebecca is on her side, facing me, her hand curled in the gap between the pillows. She breathes in tight, measured cycles, never snores, and never drools, the paragon of self-control even in REM. But tonight, the rhythm is off. She's awake or close to it, and my panic spike is the stone that finally breaks her surface.

She makes a soft noise, and I catch the flutter of her eyelids, one eye opening in a slit, then both widening as she sees me twisted up and bug-eyed. My hands jammed under the pillow like I'm palming a gun.

Her hand lands on my wrist. The grip is gentle but sure, a reminder that I'm not floating. "What's wrong?" she whispers, and her voice is husky with sleep, a sexier register than she'll allow herself at any other time of day.

"Sorry," I say. The word barely makes it past my teeth. "Just a dream. Go back to sleep."

She lifts her head off the pillow enough to put her eyes level with mine. In this light, her irises are near-black, and her hair is a cloud on the pillow, fanned wide and mussed with sweat. She studies my face for a long beat. "Your heart's going a hundred miles an hour."

She's right. I can feel it in my chest, my throat and my fucking wrists. I force myself to breathe slowly, and the act of doing it brings back the dream. Sharper than a memory, wired into my sense of self, and impossible to ignore.

I see a woman's face, not quite resolved, a nose too prominent, lips parted in surprise or mid-sentence. The cut is precise, more so than most of mine; the bloodline traces a neat path under her jaw, pooling perfectly. The hands that do it are mine, but not mine. Someone else's skin, gloves and a blade I'd never use. Then the mark: then the spiral cross, cut between her breasts that are not familiar, not anyone I've ever seen or imagined. Not anyone I've ever killed.

Rebecca's hand moves from my wrist to the back of my neck, massaging the skin with her thumb. "Was it the twins?" she asks.

"No. Just work," I say. A lie, but the only one that matters.

She exhales and drops her hand, rolling back to her

side. "You should call the therapist," she says, already fading into the comfort of sleep. "You know what they say; the job will eat you alive."

I watch her body settle, her breathing elongate. She's always been able to go back under, no matter what. It's a talent I both resent and admire. When she's out, I let myself exhale all the way. My arms and legs are still buzzing with adrenaline, and my heart rate is down.

I roll out of bed and stand on the balls of my feet for a count of three. The cold air of the room is bracing, and my briefs are already damp with sweat. I don't bother with a shirt; the effort would feel performative, like dressing for a role I've already been fired from.

I leave the bedroom and step into the hall. Every fifth floorboard in this house creaks, but I know which ones to avoid. The twins' door is closed. The nursery is dark, its nightlight a soft blue halo on the carpet. I pass them both, my feet making almost no sound.

The stairs are steeper than code allows today because back in the day; the code was less strict, and I use the rail like a rappel line. On the main floor, the air is denser, heavy with the aroma of yesterday's dinner and the lingering ozone from the HVAC cycling on and off. I pad through the kitchen, past the laptop blinking on the island, past the ghostly blue clock of the microwave. I reach the basement door, run my palm over the deadbolt, and then stand there for a long minute, trying to decide if I'm awake.

In the dream, the woman's face blurs at the margins, like an old JPEG. The only thing that stands out is the mark: the spiral cross, drawn with such intent, it's almost holy. I can see the blood seeping under the curve, the ink running into the skin, the signature as precise as any I have done, but the face is not one of mine. I shake my head and try to re-seal the image. No use. It's carved into the back of my eyelids.

I take the basement key from its hiding place, wedged behind the framed schematic of the Peterson Tower, my one professional trophy Rebecca has not relegated to a drawer. I unlock the door, turn the knob, and descend into the dark.

The air here is cooler, less forgiving. The light switch is at the bottom of the stairs, not the top, and I navigate by memory, counting the risers. Eleven, twelve, thirteen, then the slight lip at the landing. I flick the switch, and the fluorescent bulbs pop and buzz to life.

My workspace is a shrine to myself. The left side holds tools: screwdrivers, pliers, blades, each hung on a pegboard with monastic precision. On the right side are boxes, family stuff, tax returns, baby clothes and Christmas ornaments in brittle Tupperware. Front and center is the old drafting table, still ink stained and cracked from the years when I first ran my business from home.

I open the closet under the stairs. The lock is cheap, unnecessary, but the ritual matters. Inside, there's only one box that matters: battered cardboard, once used to ship college textbooks, now the repository for every record that matters. I set it on the drafting table and slit the packing tape with a utility knife.

The box is heavier than I remember, the cardboard gone soft at the corners, held together by layers of clear packing tape and whatever nostalgia I have for the days when "College Textbooks" seemed like a future instead of a cover story. I set it down on the drafting table and stare at it for a few heartbeats, feeling the soft rush of old dust and the acidic sting of nerves under my fingernails.

The basement light is cheap fluorescent, installed by the house's previous owner, who believed every utility space should be bathed in the color of a morgue. The tube hums, a steady 60-cycle whine that sits just above my hearing, vibrating the enamel on my teeth. The shadows it throws are stark, binary, the contrast you get in a police lineup or a crime lab. I prefer it. The world makes more sense in black and white.

The key to the closet is still warm from my palm. I set it on the bench, next to the black marker I use for labels. I pop the lid on the box, peel back the tape, careful not to let it tear, and fold the flaps open like a magician about to reveal the prestige. Inside, the journals are stacked in order, spines outward, each labeled in neat block print with a date range and a city or state abbreviation. I take them out one by one, setting them in a row on the table. Each notebook is unmarked but unmistakable. Black leatherette, rounded corners and an elastic band holding it shut. They are heavier than they look, packed with years of entries, sketches, photos and the private taxonomy of a man who has outlived his usefulness as both engineer and killer.

I open each one, flipping through the pages as if

cramming for a final I already know I'll ace.

Each kill is catalogued: date, location, target profile, method, spiral type, aftermath. The early ones are messy, equal parts panic and calculation. As the years progressed, the handwriting got smaller and neater, and the entries more factual, less emotional. I know each one by heart, but I check anyway.

I open the oldest one. My hands are shaking, which pisses me off; I pride myself on manual steadiness, a trait I inherited from my grandfather, who could build model trains at a scale that required tweezers and a jeweler's loupe. The first entry is from Aurora, Colorado, 2002, a warm-up kill, more of an experiment than art, but even then, the lines of the spiral are tight, deliberate, and measured in centimeters. I flip forward; the pages flicker by in a blur of blue ink, dry glue residue and the faint scent of old glue and rubbing alcohol.

I go through every notebook, front to back, scanning each line, each sketch, searching for the face from the dream. Nothing. No entry for a woman with a nose like that, or a spiral that clean. None of the victims has the same wound geometry or wrist circumference. I double back, check again, this time slower, mouthing the names as I go: Lynette, Arlene, Cassandra, Vanessa. Nothing matches. The memory from the dream has already warped; the face is fading, and I'm terrified I'll lose the details before I can get them on paper.

I grab the most recent notebook, the one with a torn elastic and a gouge down the cover from when it fell off the workbench and landed, corner-first, on a screwdriver. The dream woman is not here. There is no record. No entry, no sketch, and no off-the-books deviation. I check again, slower this time. Nothing.

I slam the last notebook shut; the sound echoes off cinderblock and HVAC ducting. I sit, breathing through my teeth, willing the tremor out of my hands. It's not a panic attack, but it's close. The image from the dream pulses under my skin, a residue I can't wash out.

I rifle the box again, to make sure. I might have missed a loose sheet, a Polaroid or some evidence I misfiled. There's nothing. My entire history is in these books, and the only kill I can't place is the one in my dreams. I set the latest notebook on the drafting table.

For a moment, I am tempted to throw the box. The urge is physical. One swift motion, and it's airborne, papers and ink confetti in the harsh white light. Instead, I press the box closed and set it under the bench. I do not trust my hands not to break something important.

I flip to the next blank page, my thumb scraping at the edge to force the paper open. The pen I use for these is a rollerball, German, weighty in the hand. I'm not an artist, but the act of putting it on paper helps. I draw the woman from my dream.

First, the head shape: oval, thin at the jaw, the kind that used to mean aristocracy before everyone started marrying for bone structure. I rough in the hair, parted at the center, long enough to touch the shoulders, a blunt cut. The nose is prominent, but not comical; the lips are wide and set in a line of confusion, as if the woman isn't sure what's happening until it's already too late. I give her the eyes, almond-shaped, set deep. The irises are dark, the kind you see in paintings of Renaissance martyrs.

I draw the wound, careful to angle it just so, a single smooth arc under the left jaw. The spiral cross goes on the inside of her left wrist, drawn with almost erotic precision. I get the details down before the image dissolves, which it already has. The pressure in my skull tells me I'll lose the face in minutes if I don't finish.

When I'm done, I sit back and look at the sketch. It's not a perfect likeness; it never is, but the basics are all there. A woman in her late twenties, possibly early thirties, with dark hair and pale skin, the wound exact. The mark is, for lack of a better word, beautiful. It makes me angry. Someone out there is mimicking the mark, using my method, copying it down to the millimeter. The idea is at once horrifying and exhilarating.

"Who are you?" I mutter. The sound bounces off the cinderblock and comes back at half-volume, an accusation, and a dare. I press the heel of my palm into my left eye, hard enough to see white stars. I let the pain settle me.

I set the pen down. My hands are steady now. The next step is clear. If there's a copycat, or a competitor, or some freak from the dark web who's learned the signature, I must find out. I have to know before the FBI or some hack local detective connects the dots and pulls my name from the aether.

I glance at the sketch again. The more I look, the

less I remember. The face is shifting already, the context bleeding out. I hate not knowing. It's the one thing in life I promised myself never to allow: the loss of control, the unanticipated variable. I keep my world in balance by making sure every equation has only one unknown, and tonight I have two.

I take out my phone, open the notes app, and type a single line: "Possible copycat, location unknown, signature exact. Run news scan." Then I lock the screen and set the phone face down.

Upstairs, the house is perfectly still. I imagine Rebecca's chest rising and falling, the kids' tangled hair on their pillows. I picture myself not as a father, or a husband, or an engineer, but as the thing I am: a predator among predators, soon to be hunted by another version of myself. A presence in the dream that isn't me. A victim I didn't choose.

I look at the ceiling, where a faint brown water stain runs in a perfect arc, and count the beats of the light's hum. I force myself to think like an engineer, not a killer. If there's an error in the design, you trace the fault to its source. I know what comes next. I'll have to search the networks, the news, maybe reach out to some of the old contacts, the ones who lived for the thrill of reading about their own handiwork in the crime columns. I'll have to see if anyone out there is sending a message.

My hands stop shaking. I take the sketch, fold it in half, and slide it into the notebook. I shut it and put it in the box with the others. I am scared. Not of getting caught, or of failing, but of being outclassed, of being obsolete.

Above me, the house creaks. I picture Rebecca padding to the bathroom, maybe checking on the kids, and then returning to bed. The girls are probably dreaming, their bodies still and peaceful, their minds untouched by any of this. I envy them.

I gather up the keys, the marker, the pen, and return everything to its place. I flick the basement light off, let the darkness fill in, and stand there until my eyes adjust. The sketch is burned into my retina, but I know it will not last.

I go upstairs two steps at a time. The main floor is dark and silent, the only noise being the hum of the fridge and the tick of the wall clock. I pour a glass of water from the tap, sip it, and let the cold settle my stomach.

In the hallway, I pause outside the twins' door. I press an ear to the wood, listen for their breathing. The sound is soft, even, perfectly regular. I check the nursery, just to be sure, and find the baby asleep, one arm above her head, mouth open in a small perfect O. I stand there for a minute, just watching her. I wonder what she will remember about me when I'm gone.

Back in the master bedroom, I slide under the comforter as carefully as I left it. Rebecca stirs but does not wake. I close my eyes and try to match her breathing, slow and controlled. It's harder than it should be, but after a few cycles I get the rhythm.

I know I won't sleep. The image is waiting for me, just outside the field of vision, ready to invade again.

But when it does, I'll get another look at the face. I'll learn something about who's drawing the line this time. I lie in the dark, hands flat on the sheets, counting the seconds between the beats of my heart. I am not calm, not safe, but for now I am contained. That will have to do. Tomorrow, I'll start the search. Tonight, I will not let go of the spiral. Not yet.

Chapter Twenty-Eight

The FBI war room, technically Conference Room 4D, but no one's called it that since the murders started stacking up, hasn't seen a quiet moment in sixteen hours. Fluorescent light pounds the tables, erasing shadows except where they're darkest: under the board, under the eyes of the agents, and in the broad map of the western United States pinned along the back wall.

Dirk stands in the middle of the churn; sleeves shoved past the elbow and his tie abandoned to the conference room table hours ago. On the wall behind him, a patchwork of victim portraits fans out like a migration chart. Red string links faces, names, towns, and printouts bracket the edges in crisp rectangles of bureaucracy. The air smells of old pizza, dry-erase markers, and recycled tension.

"Let's start from the top," Dirk says, voice cutting through the low hum. He points at the board with a laser pointer, the beam carving a straight line from Denver to Prescott. "We have one-hundred-sixty bodies, in two states, and a signature that should be impossible to copy. Where are we?"

The agents in the room, eight this time, two more dialed in via Zoom, and one who hovers in the doorway like a student waiting to be called on, shift in their seats. Jill Quarters, her auburn ponytail snapped tight, has her legal pad braced against her forearm. Her pen moves with the quiet ferocity of someone who doesn't miss words.

A hand goes up from a junior agent with an Arizona assignment. "I met with the Scottsdale detectives, sir. They agreed that the signature matches, but they flagged a variance in the cuts. The Arizona killer starts with the throat, as does Colorado, but the Arizona victims were cut with a left-to-right slash, and the Colorado victims were slashed right to left. The victimology matches."

"Any trace evidence?" asks Dirk.

"None that isn't environmental. Dust, pet hair, a single fiber from what the local ME thinks is a disposable painter's suit. No prints, no DNA. The scene was wiped cleaner than a hospital room."

Dirk glances at Jill. She underlines something on the pad, then, without looking up, says, "The Colorado state coroner called. She's overnighting a sliver of blood-tape from the latest body to Dr. Chen's lab."

Jill's voice is low, but the room listens. Dr. Sarah Chen's forensic lab has the best DNA turnaround in the Bureau and a reputation for confirming or upending every working theory.

"Good," says Dirk. "Update the chain of custody for the evidence run. Next?"

Another agent, older, his voice rasped by three decades of cigarettes, leans in. "I talked to the Prescott PD myself. Their chief detective is convinced it's one guy. He says the wounds are too consistent for a team. No way a copycat keeps the signature this tight after twenty years," he said.

Dirk resumes pacing. "I disagree. The cuts in

Arizona show a slight difference, and now we know that the direction of the throat cuts is opposite. That's two different methodologies."

An agent at the back, bored, with a buzz cut and an FBI jacket a size too tight, leans in. "Perhaps he's using, then sobering up. Coked to the gills in Arizona, clean in Colorado?"

Dirk raises a finger. "Could be, but to use your vernacular. Someone who is coked up doesn't change from left to right-handed."

A younger agent with curly hair and intense eyes raises his hand and speaks. "What about the gap years, sir? According to our timeline, there is a five-year gap in killings in Arizona. Did he go dark, or were there no discovered bodies?"

"Prison," mutters the older field agent. "Or in the hospital."

Dirk stops, eyes boring a hole in the whiteboard. "That's one option. But the lack of drift in the signature is what's eating at me. These lines." He taps a photo, and the next. "They're like blueprints. Our unsub either never stopped practicing, or he's been documenting every detail for decades."

Jill scribbles and looks up, tapping her pen. "Or there's two killers. Teacher and apprentice, like Dr. Whitman said."

"You really think someone trains for this? Like a trade?" asks the buzz cut agent.

"You're in this room, Agent Mills, because you know how rare this pattern is," says Dirk. "Six hundred cases in Arizona since the millennium, zero repeats except these. Same in Colorado. Either the unsub is a savant, or he's got a shadow."

"Dr. Whitman thinks the spiral cross is a mnemonic, maybe a code," says Jill. "It could be a tribute to the actual killer if it's an apprentice."

Dirk's phone buzzes against the table. He ignores it, eyes flicking to the timeline. "Every time we get closer, it slips sideways. We need something the killer doesn't expect. Surveillance, maybe. Has anyone pulled the neighborhood cams from the Prescott scene?"

An agent in the back, blue blazer, stacks her papers. "Prescott PD says the trailhead had motion sensors but no active video. I called the Parks Department; they're checking for any footage from nearby wildlife cams. It's a stretch, but who knows."

"Keep pushing," Dirk says. He returns to the board, traces the red string from Phoenix to Greeley. "Okay. Walk me through the ritual."

Jill looks up from her pad. "Throat cut first, then the cross incision. Spiral is always at the intersection, carved post-mortem. Hands posed over the chest; right thumb tucked under left. In every scene, the unsub leaves a marker. Usually, a spiral cross drawn in Sharpie on the left wrist."

"A signature so deliberate, he wants it found," says Agent Mills.

"That's right," says Dirk. "But why does the unsub add the spiral cross on the wrist after he cuts it into the victim's chest?"

Carl Bunch chimes in. "What if it's communication? One symbol for the original, one for the copy?"

"What, like a tribute?" asks Jill. "The cut is his, but the drawn cross is to honor his counterpart."

Dirk nods, a flicker of satisfaction. "Exactly. If these are moves, we need to figure out what the endgame is. Jill, can you get me a chronological lineup of the last ten, with any deviation flagged?"

She's already writing. "Will do. Anything from Dr. Chen's lab?"

"She's still running the samples," says Dirk. "But last I heard, the touch DNA from the Denver kill had a partial profile. No match yet."

The phone buzzes again. Dirk sets his jaw and ignores it. On the board, he arranges the victim portraits by date, then by geography. The string tangles almost beautifully if you forget what the faces mean.

Someone cracks a can of Monster, the hiss echoing down the table.

"This is all performative," says another agent. "If there are two, they're one-upping each other."

"Or showing off for us," says Agent Maddox, a tall, Black woman with long hair tied in tight cornrows. "The unsub might know we're watching."

Dirk runs a hand through his hair, which stands up in odd spikes. "Fine. If it's a show, then what's next?"

No one answers.

He looks at Jill, who stares back, unblinking. "Jill, take everyone through victimology. Is there anything we missed?"

Jill clicks her pen, then speaks in a measured cadence. "All the victims in both states are professionals. First responders, educators, office workers and professionals. We have six lawyers, seven doctors, five architects, and seven engineers. We also have four plumbers, a mechanic, and three electricians. No sex workers, no randoms. Most are single or living alone for extended periods."

Carl interrupted. "There's another methodology difference. In Colorado, the unsub appears to follow his victim for a period before the kill. In Arizona, the attacks seem to be blitz attacks. This shows a pattern of control. I don't think the posing is as important as the kill."

"There are no trophies taken," says Jill. "Nothing is removed from the scene except the victim's voice."

A pause. Dirk closes his eyes, and when he opens them, the tension in his jaw is a physical presence. "Okay," he says, quiet but with force. "Keep reviewing the victim files and see if anything jumps out. Jill, keep in close touch with Dr. Chen's lab. If we get DNA, I want to be the first to know."

Dirk pushes his chair back and stands. "I know we're tired. I know the odds. But we're going to catch this son of a bitch, even if it takes all night. Dismissed."

The room erupts in controlled chaos: agents grabbing phones, laptops, evidence binders; and someone opens the window to let out the lingering scent of cold pizza and sweat. The Zoom call ends with a hollow click.

Jill remains by the board, a legal pad to her chest. "You okay?" she asks, voice low so only Dirk can hear.

He glances at his phone, still buzzing, then at the board. "I'll be fine when we have something that makes sense."

She hesitates. "If there's two, it's not your fault."

He almost smiles, then reverts. "Yeah. Tell that to the next body."

She watches him arrange the red strings, her eyes tracking his every move.

As the agents leave the war room, Dirk remains. He faces the wall of faces, the knots of red, the timeline that refuses to resolve. He is so close he can smell the ink on the photographs. The phone buzzes again, more insistent this time. He doesn't answer.

Outside, the world dims to blue, and the only light left is the one over the war room, and the certainty that time is running out.

Chapter Twenty-Nine

Under the blinding fluorescent lights of the Quantico forensics annex, Dr. Sarah Chen has not blinked in at least five minutes. Her eyes burn, not from the retina-bleaching white of the lab, but from the line of digits marching relentlessly across her screen, each confirming the same impossible thing.

The lab is dead quiet except for the cooling fans in the DNA sequencer and the faint slosh of someone's two-day-old Mountain Dew. Chen herself is hunched over a rolling bench, her lab coat wrinkled beyond hope, and her dark hair pulled back with a pencil and a broken pipette tip. On the counter behind her, six empty coffee cups stand in rigid formation. Four of them are hers; she swears by tea, but she's resorted to whatever's left as the hours stack up.

At the center of her attention are three computer monitors, each with a different window open, and all echoing the same mutation index and allelic repeat sequence. The labels flash: ARIZONA VICTIM 2002, COLORADO VICTIM 2014. Run after run, the graph spits out a curve so tight, it can only belong to one person.

Her hands, usually as steady as the robotic pipettor she favors, are trembling. She sets them on the bench and stares at the readout, daring it to change. It does not.

Across the room, one of her techs, a heavyset man with a chinstrap beard, peers into the void of the fridge. "You want anything, Doc? I'm getting a protein bar.

You look like you could use something."

She cuts him off. "No, thank you, Darren. Please prep the next aliquot and run the negative controls, per protocol."

He shrugs and shuffles off, still chewing. She waits until he's clear, then mutters under her breath. "Replicate and verify."

Her own internal checklist reboots: Sanger confirmation, restriction digest, even a legacy STR test for old time's sake. Each run takes hours, but she is relentless. Nothing in her professional experience has prepared her for an identical DNA profile to show up in two victims murdered hundreds of miles and mere hours apart, much less when the living timeline puts any suspect at only one of the two scenes.

She drags up the personnel database, runs the match against known felons, then against law enforcement, then, in a moment of exhausted paranoia, against the FBI's own background checks.

She gets a partial hit on one line: TRAINOR, DIRK. The alleles at five loci line up too closely for coincidence. She checks again, cursing the software, then herself. There is no error. Even adjusting for sample degradation, the probability is astronomical.

By the time the final replication run is done, Chen is talking to herself, voice trembling as much as her hands. "It's not possible." But the graph stays unchanged.

She calls over the tech. "Darren, look at this," she says, pointing to the match report.

He leans in, squints. "Shit. He's one of ours."

"That's not supposed to happen," she finishes for him. "Rerun the sample. Full chain of custody, fresh tubes, triple-check the PCR prep. And get me an unbroken bottle of Tris buffer from the lockup, not the open one on the bench." He nods but can't stop staring at the screen.

"I don't know," says Chen. "Get the team to rerun the tests and let's confirm this again before it gets out."

Six hours later, Dr. Chen is sitting at her desk staring at her monitors. Standing behind her are Darren and two members of her team. She leans back and sips her cold coffee. She pulls off her glasses and squeezes the bridge of her nose.

"Looks like there's no doubt," says Darren. "We've gotten the same results on all three runs. The results tell us we are dealing with one killer. We found no DNA matches in CODIS or in the private sector, but there is also no doubt that Special Agent Dirk Trainor is related to the killer."

Chen doesn't answer. Her team moves as one and steps out of her office, closing the door behind them. She takes a deep, calming breath, picks up her desk phone, and dials the office of Anthony Spinella, the Denver field SAIC.

On the second ring, the line picks up. Spinella's voice is tight and formal. "Spinella."

"Sir, it's Dr. Chen," she says. "We have a problem with the DNA from the Arizona and Colorado victims."

He grunts, his voice all caffeine and zero patience. "If it's contamination, fix it and don't waste my time. If it's not."

"It's not," she says, her voice breaking on the first consonant. "There's a match, and it's inside the Bureau. Partial, but close enough. I've replicated it three times."

The line is dead for a long second.

"You're sure?" asks Spinella.

"Three times, sir. I'll share the screen. Agent Dirk Trainor is a partial match."

She sets up the Zoom, hands no steadier than before, and pulls up the allelic run. The security camera over her monitor blinks green, and she sees Spinella's face fill the little square, his eyes bloodshot and suit rumpled.

"Talk me through it," he orders.

Chen launches into it, scientific jargon now weaponized to shield herself from the implications. "Colorado and Arizona victims. STR and mitochondrial profiles are identical, except for one microsatellite variation likely due to PCR stutter. Sanger sequencing confirmed no cross-sample contamination."

"And the match is to Trainor?" asks Spinella.

"It's partial," says Chen, "but enough that it suggests parentage. Not a sibling. Not a close cousin. Parent or child, but with some allelic dropout in the older sample, possibly because of sample degradation. Also, the blood types are different."

Spinella swears, then leans back in his chair, face going several shades paler. "Does Dirk know?"

"No, sir. I wanted to be sure before alerting anyone. I'll keep running until you tell me to stop, but."

"I'll set up a secure call with you when I have Dirk and Quarters in my office. You're going to walk us through this on the record."

"Yes, sir."

She ends the call, exhales once, then again, this time louder.

Darren pushes open her door. "Doc, are you okay?"

She forces a smile. "Never better," she says. "Just another day at the office."

But her eyes never leave the screen, and the match stays lit, red and relentless, on the monitor.

Anthony Spinella stands and opens his door. "Trainor, Quarters, my office, please."

Dirk and Jill look at each other, and Jill picks up her notebook and pen from the desk. They head into Spinella's office and close the door behind them. Spinella is sitting behind his desk, jaw clenched, with his hand hovering over the connect button for the secure Zoom call.

He hits the connect call button and waits. The moment Dr. Chen answers, Spinella's voice is low.

"Doctor, I've got Trainor and Quarters in my office. Please start over. Tell us what you found," he says, his eyes never leaving the spiral cross crime scene photo pinned to the divider behind his screen.

Chen speaks, her voice tight but even. "The Colorado and Arizona samples, sir. DNA profiles are indistinguishable. The only explanation is a direct biological relationship. I ran the STRs and mitochondrial markers. There's zero variance, not even in the stutter regions."

"So, you're telling us that despite a timeline that can't possibly work, that this is the work of one killer?" asks Spinella.

Jill looks at Dirk, who tips his head.

"Were you able to find a match in CODIS?" asks Spinella.

"No direct match in CODIS or any of the military or private genealogy sites we have access to, but we came up with a partial match," says Chen.

"Do you have a name for us, Dr. Chen?" asks Spinella.

Chen inhales. "The match is Dirk Trainor. I pulled Bureau HR, criminal and familial databases. Agent Trainor matches the partial at five loci. Statistically, that's parent to child, sir."

Dirk and Jill looked stunned. Dirk opens his mouth, but Spinella holds up his hand.

Spinella swears, a controlled exhalation. "Thank you, Dr. Chen. Please continue searching for a match to the unsub."

He clicks off the call and spins his monitor so they can see the screen with the DNA results highlighted in yellow.

Spinella looks at Dirk. "You want to explain this?"

Across the desk, Dirk's head snaps up from viewing the monitor. He glances once at Jill, who shrugs, helpless.

Dirk leans in, reads the summary notes again, then blinks once. "That can't be right," he says.

"It's right," says Spinella. "Dr. Chen ran it three times. Arizona and Colorado samples are genetically identical. The only partial match in Bureau records is to you."

Dirk processes, eyes darting. "That's not possible. I've never been to Arizona except for training, and you can check my travel history."

Spinella cuts him off. "This is not about an alibi. It's about the killer's DNA being so close to yours that it triggered a parental match flag in the database. How do you explain that?"

Dirk sits, then stands, then sits again. "I can't. There must be a mistake."

"Chen doesn't make mistakes," says Spinella, voice climbing in pitch. "And you know it."

Dirk rubs his hands over his face. His voice is muffled. "Is this a joke? Some prank out of headquarters?"

"Not a chance," says Spinella. "And I don't think it's a joke when two women wind up dead with your DNA in their wounds." He leans forward, elbows on the desk. "Who's in your biological family, Dirk?"

Dirk doesn't answer. The pause lengthens.

"You want to keep your badge, you tell me right now," says Spinella.

"My mother lives in the house I grew up in here in Colorado. My father was a Denver detective and was killed on the job. You know all this."

"And that's it?" asks Spinella. "No siblings?"

"You know me, sir," says Dirk. "You know I'm an only child. There has to be another explanation."

Spinella processes this, then pushes the laptop closer. "Then explain how your genetic signature ended up in two murder victims killed six hundred miles and twelve years apart."

"I don't know," says Dirk.

Spinella's patience cracks. He stands, voice now too loud for the walls. "You'd better figure it out. If this goes outside the Bureau, you're done. You're not just off the case, you're in cuffs." His voice is loud enough that the bullpen gets quiet, and everyone is focused on his office.

Jill leans forward. "Sir, there's got to be a mistake. We've worked together for years. Dirk is no killer, and his family is the salt of the earth."

Spinella slams the laptop closed. "There is no fucking mistake. This could destroy our entire case once we catch this prick. A defense attorney will have a field day with this. And now we have to deal with the fact that the DNA says we have one killer, so now we have to figure out how he can kill two people at the same time. Worst of all, there's now a question whether you should be anywhere near this case."

Dirk stands, pulse visible in his jaw. "You think I'm the killer?"

"I think you're compromised. And until you prove otherwise, you're off lead," says Spinella.

A stunned silence. "What do you want us to do?" asks Jill.

"Figure out what the fuck is going on," he yells. "Have someone run a full background check on Dirk and his family. I want to know everything, and I want it yesterday. Dirk, go home and think about what the hell this is all about. Jill, you keep him on a short leash and away from any evidence we collect. Shift the focus of the investigation to one unsub."

Dirk, drained, nods once and leaves without a word. Jill Lingers, looking at the SAIC. "You really think Dirk's involved?"

"No," he says. "But I don't believe in magic. Figure it out."

He sits back, lets the silence expand, then opens the laptop again and stares at the spiral cross, burned in color on the screen.

Chapter Thirty

The moment Dirk emerges from Spinella's office, the entire task force becomes suddenly and profoundly interested in whatever's directly in front of them. Fingers dance on keyboards, heads cluster over screens, but in the glass-walled bullpen, there's no hiding the shift in air pressure. Dirk stands in the doorway a full ten seconds, face hollowed, tie hanging limp from his collar like an apology.

Jill waits for him in the corridor. She doesn't touch him; Dirk isn't built for that, but her stance is unmistakable: one shoulder turned towards the agents, her body a small dam against the undertow of gossip. She nods towards a small room and leads the way. Dirk follows two steps behind.

They end up in a supply alcove behind the copy machines, an improvised fortress where even the overheads flicker with defeat.

"Do you want to talk about it, or do you want to sit until the spinning slows?" she asks.

Dirk nods. "There's nothing to talk about. The DNA says I'm related to the killer. That's all anyone will see."

Jill's lips purse, fighting for composure. "You know it's not you. Spinella knows it's not you. The lab knows it. The goddamn janitor knows it. But right now, we can't have you actively participate in the investigation, at least on paper."

Dirk slumps back against the cinder block, the pain

of it grounding him. "Did he really yank me off the case?"

"He did. For optics. But he still wants you to dig. You just have to do it from the outside. Make some calls. Let us handle the fieldwork until we clear you."

Dirk nods and looks up, his eyes red-rimmed but clear. "He thinks I'm dirty."

"No," says Jill. "Right now, he doesn't know what to think. None of us do. But he's right. With this hanging over your head, any evidence you touch becomes tainted. If you had a secret identity, you'd be the first to know."

Dirk almost laughs, but the sound comes out wrong. "Would I?"

Jill softens, the professional mask sliding just a little. "Go home and take a day to clear your head. I'll keep you posted. If I get any static, I'll call."

"What if this is all true?" asks Dirk. "What if I'm the reason all those women died?"

Jill leans against the copier, dropping her voice so low he has to lean in. "If you were, you'd be the first one to put yourself in cuffs. But you're not. And if it makes you feel better, I'll double-check your trash every week until the end of time."

A silence, not as heavy as before. Dirk stands, straightens the tie, then lets it go slack. "Thank you," he says, and means it.

Jill steps into the hall first and squares her shoulders. Dirk follows, and the agents on the floor pretend not to notice, but every screen reflects him as he passes.

At his office, Dirk stuffs a few files into a canvas bag, grabs his coat, and heads for the exit. He pauses at the elevator as if expecting a last-minute reprieve, but none comes. He hits the down button and waits.

Jill returns to the war room. She finds the agents huddled around the evidence wall, Spinella at the center, barking orders. The theory has shifted; the talk now is Dirk's involvement with the unsub, and the reality that they are dealing with one killer. Every mind in the room races to adapt, and already, the red string on the board is being rearranged to reflect the new directive.

Dirk rides the elevator to the ground level, the noise of the building fading behind him. Outside, Denver is thick with dusk, the city bleeding neon under a sky that won't decide if it's night yet. He walks three blocks before he realizes he's forgotten his car.

He keeps walking, head down and hands in his pockets. The only thing that matters is finding the origin point, his, the killer's, maybe both.

Behind him, the lights of the FBI office burn late, a hive of motion and theory, while in front, the world opens into silence and the unlit space of possibility.

Chapter Thirty-One

Dirk's home office looks like it's been hit by a high-yield paper bomb. The entire desktop is nothing but DNA printouts, torn legal pads, and case folders, all spread at tangents like a conspiracy theorist's idea of organization. It's six a.m., but the darkness outside his window is punctuated by Denver's sodium afterglow. In here, only the monitor is alive, flooding the room with enough blue light to make the veins in Dirk's hands look surgical, translucent as x-rays. He sits motionless in a straight-backed chair, elbows on the table, eyes dry and raw from hours of recursive failure. Soon his family will wake up, and he will need to pull himself away from his fruitless searching.

He's not sure how long he's been staring at the screen. The tabs run in two rows across the browser: FBI genetics division, medical abstracts and blood type charts. The coffee at his elbow has gone cold, the rim ringed with oily residue. A half-eaten protein bar is melting into the edge of an evidence envelope.

He scrolls up and down mindlessly. The DNA report is the same as it was two hours ago, and the red-flagged text haunts him like a migraine: "Possible familial match. Second-degree relation. Anomalous at 19 loci." The numbers mean nothing to anyone but a few hundred gene jockeys in the country, but they have become Dirk's white whale.

He drags a spreadsheet into view and starts lining up the alleles. His own, the unsubs, and the one from the 2002 Phoenix case Bunch color-coded yellow. It's not a perfect overlap, but the noise is too regular to be an accident. He glances at the blood type summary, taps the row with his index finger. His own is O negative; the unsub's is AB. He can't shake the feeling that this, too, is a message, but one he can't read.

His eyes drift to the only picture left tacked above his monitor: an elementary school class photo, faded to the color palette of an old department store. He is front row, center, a pale, pinched face surrounded by the indistinct sea of children. His own name, printed in crooked letters, is the only one he remembers.

He presses the base of his palm to his temple. There is a ghost of a headache in there, the kind that won't resolve unless he gets up and walks, or throws something, or passes out. He sits back, closes his eyes. The room is chilly, but he does not shiver. His mind is a pinball table, the problem ricocheting in tight, pointless loops.

Is it possible, he thinks, for siblings to have the same parents but radically different blood? The DNA match is too close for a stranger, too distant for a full brother. He remembers reading years ago about twins that aren't really twins. Two embryos with two sets of DNA, sometimes born years apart. Or, more horrifyingly, not born at all. The idea blooms in his mind, unwelcome but irresistible: What if he's not tracking a killer? What if he's tracking himself?

A memory surfaces unbidden. It's not his own but the dream, always the dream. The woman's face, the surgical cross, the sudden flood of red on white. He's seeing it more clearly now, as if the act has been burned into his brain by repetition. He flexes his fingers, trying to push the sensation away.

He opens a new window and searches "twin telepathy." The results are exactly as idiotic as he expects. Superstition, tabloid fodder and clickbait on miracle births. But among the dross is a research paper from a Dutch university, something about "monozygotic resonance." He scans it, frowning. The case describes twins separated at birth, communicating in code as children, then manifesting identical symptoms years later without ever meeting. Dirk reads the summary three times, looking for the catch.

The screen blurs. His hands shake with an energy that is not fatigue, but something closer to the adrenaline high of a new clue. The pieces are all there, scattered across a decade and several million years of evolution, but they have not snapped into place.

He gazes at the spiral cross on the evidence photo from Prescott. The wound is nearly perfect; the lines so clean you could lay graph paper over them and find the axis. He overlays it digitally onto the 2002 Phoenix case. The match is close. Closer than chance. He lets the files flicker on the screen, one over the other, like an afterimage.

The air grows thicker. He understands with the gut certainty of a profiler that this is not random. Someone is making a point. Someone who knows him intimately, perhaps better than he knows himself.

His wife taps him on the shoulder. "Can you get the girls ready while I take care of the baby?" she asks.

Dirt closes his laptop and heads up the stairs. His two little angels are sitting up in bed, and they are reading a story. Dirks stops and stares. They are each reading the same story, and they are on the same page. His brain goes into overdrive, and suddenly everything he studied during the wee hours of the morning rushes into his head. Is it possible that his twins communicate with each other on a different level?

He gets the girls dressed and cooks breakfast for the family. Today, his wife is taking the kids to the library, and he'll have the house all to himself. After they leave, he sits at his computer and rereads the information he pulled up during the night. He reads it a third time, and his brain locks up.

He needs help. Not from Jill or Bunch, and not from Spinella. Not even from the Bureau. He needs to go outside the pattern.

He picks up his phone and scrolls to the contact labeled "Lang, M." The call rings twice before a woman's voice answers, low and even with a slight catch, as if she's pulled away from a microscope mid-sentence.

"Dr. Lang," she says.

Dirk keeps it tight. "Mira, it's Trainor. I need to ask you about some DNA irregularities."

"I'm in the middle of a project, Dirk." Her tone is neutral, but he can hear the curiosity sharpening at the edges. "Are you the irregularity, or is this another Bureau screwup?"

"Both," says Dirk, and immediately feels the room tilt a little further. "It's important. You have ten minutes for me, or can I bribe you with artisanal donuts?"

She pauses as she decides. "Ten minutes now and you can bring me donuts tomorrow. Make it quick."

Dirk opens his laptop camera and lines up the window to share. "I'm sending you three case files. Ignore the context; just look at the blood work and the short-tandem repeat analysis. The unsub's DNA doesn't line up with mine, but it pings on familial markers. Except that the blood type is all wrong. How does that happen?"

Mira's keystrokes are audible; she's already running the numbers before he can finish the sentence. "It's rare. The most likely answer is a mutation in the H antigen pathway, but that wouldn't explain this gap at Locus 21. Are you sure these aren't just cousins?"

Dirk thinks. "No extended family on file. One parent is alive, and one is deceased. No siblings."

Mira hums, noncommittal. "I see what you're talking about. Sometimes you get a blood type switch if the marrow is replaced, like in a bone marrow transplant. Or vanishing twin syndrome. Happens in utero. Second embryo absorbed by the first."

Dirk's vision tunnels. The room is suddenly too small, too cold.

"Let's say, hypothetically, someone had a fraternal twin they didn't know about. Could they share enough genetic markers for this kind of match, even with different blood types?"

"Hypothetically? Sure." Mira's voice is crisp, the way it always is when she's onto something real.

"Especially if the mother's prenatal environment was a mess. Or if one twin had had a bone marrow graft. But, Dirk, this is real edge-case stuff. There's only a handful of documented incidents. Are you telling me your killer might be a sibling you don't know about?"

Dirk's hands are cold, but his face feels sunburned. "I'm telling you I don't know."

He notes the class photo on the wall. He tries to remember if anyone ever mentioned a brother, or even a friend who looked like him. He comes up blank.

Mira says, "You want to come in for a real panel? We can pull a sample and run it deeper than the FBI lab can."

Dirk is already up, shoving files into a messenger bag. His computer is powered off before he's at the front door. "I'll be there in twenty," he says, and he kills the call.

He stands in the entryway, keys in hand, the silence of the house pressing on his eardrums. He feels watched, but not by anything in this house. He wonders, as he locks the door behind him, whether the ghost in his blood will feel the sting of the needle when Mira draws it, or if that, too, will be left to the dreams.

He's in the car and halfway to the genetics lab before he remembers to breathe.

Chapter Thirty-Two

The genetics center is a steel and glass ribcage. The lights inside are industrially bright. As white as the inside of a chest freezer, humming with the faint undercurrent of compressed air and refrigeration. Dirk enters the lobby, passes through security, and walks down the long hall to the lab. Each footfall lands with a small, forensic echo.

Inside, the main floor is an open expanse. Every surface is chromed, every counter cleared, and every instrument docked in its cradle. There are people in lab coats working at several stations. Across the room, Dr. Mira Lang moves among the centrifuges and PCR cyclers with an economy that belongs to an entirely different species. She wears her lab coat unbuttoned, sleeves rolled up to the elbows, and a pair of blue nitrile gloves already in place. Her hair, glossy black and swept into a loose twist, is held together with a plastic pipette. She does not look up when Dirk enters; instead; she types a note into her tablet, with one finger flying, then stabs the save icon with unnecessary force.

She gestures him over with a casual flick of the wrist, then slides a fresh vacutainer and a tourniquet out from a drawer. "Sit," she says. "Left arm."

Dirk complies, rolling up his sleeve. The inside of his elbow is mapped with a network of fine blue veins; Mira studies them for exactly one second before snapping the tourniquet into place.

"You want to tell me what this is really about?" she asks, swabbing the skin with an alcohol pad. Dirk can smell the isopropyl, sharp and clean.

"Just a hunch," he says. "And a weird dream."

"You and every cop I know." Mira lines up the needle, her eyes narrowed. "Make a fist, then relax." The draw is fast and nearly painless, the tube filling with a bright, arterial red that looks more artificial under the LEDs than real.

Dirk watches the blood run, feeling the familiar vertigo of having his insides extracted. He's never been squeamish about blood, but today what leaves his body is not entirely his own.

Mira caps the tube, scribbles a barcode on it, and immediately slots it into the bench-top analyzer. It whirs to life, a small green diode pulsing like a heartbeat.

He hands her the case file, DNA profiles, the timeline and the full dossier on the spiral cross signatures.

She reads as she moves, flipping pages with the back of her glove, eyes darting across columns and rows. "You know," she says, "if this is a case of an unknown sibling, you're looking for a needle in a haystack of other, equally sharp needles."

Dirk leans forward, hands steepled, elbows planted. "Run it anyway. If there's a chance, I need to know."

Mira shrugs, a half smile creeping into the corner of her mouth. "You're the boss." She heads to the workstation and enters a string of commands. The analyzer spits out a first pass panel, which she scans, then sends into a waiting queue for a full breakdown.

"Results in twenty," she says. "We can do the regular song and dance, or you can tell me what's keeping you up at night? You look like hell. Your call."

Dirk is quiet for a moment. "Have you ever heard about twins, identical or not, communicating over long distances? Sensing things at the same time?"

Mira laughs, short and bright. "Every twin pair says they have it. But peer review doesn't give a shit about feelings. There's some evidence of shared gestures, or learning, but nothing at the genome level." She looks at him, squints. "Why?"

Dirk laces his fingers, palms damp. "Two of the spiral cross murders happened hours and hundreds of miles apart. The MO was identical. The wounds are… too similar for chance. But the DNA." He taps the file. "The unsub's DNA is almost a match for mine. Not full siblings, but close. Except the blood types are off, and the markers don't add up for an ordinary relationship."

Mira sets the tablet down, all pretense of casualness gone. "And your dream?"

Dirk exhales through his teeth. "It doesn't show up on a schedule. I don't know if I'm seeing something from the past or something current. I see the wounds, the place, and sometimes even the knife. I'm seeing the crime through someone else's eyes. I didn't think it was anything, but lately when it happens, it knocks the crap out of me."

Mira looks at the printouts he pulled from the internet. "You pulled up a lot of crap here, Dirk, but you could be on to something. Most of this information is garbage, but here are the facts. There have been several studies done that show that twins can communicate psychically." She taps the keys on her laptop, opens a file, and asks Dirk to step behind the table.

Dirk stands behind her and reads over her shoulder. He sees two case studies:

•   Silberstein & Bigelow Study (2024): In a rigorously controlled experiment, five pairs of identical twins were tested for telepathic responses. One twin (the "sender") was shown emotionally charged images while the other (the "receiver"), in a separate room, viewed a static screen. In 14 instances, the receiver's brain activity changed in ways that correlated with the sender's experience. The statistical likelihood of this happening by chance was calculated at 1 in 20 million. *Documented in Frontiers in Human Neuroscience (2024): Brain functional connectivity correlates of anomalous interaction between sensorily isolated monozygotic twins. Also reported by the Frontier Journalists' Network (April 2024).*

•   IONS Discovery Lab (2024): A broader study is underway by the Institute of Noetic Sciences (IONS), recruiting twins and emotionally bonded pairs who report telepathic experiences. The study uses psychological scales and psi tests to identify candidates for deeper analysis. While still in progress, it reflects growing interest in scientifically exploring these phenomena. *Officially described by the Institute of Noetic Sciences (IONS) in their blog Exploring the Mystery of Telepathy: A Groundbreaking Study (June 2024).*

The studies raised questions about mechanisms and theories:

•	Genetic and Environmental Synchrony: Identical twins share nearly 100% of their DNA and often grow up in nearly identical environments. This may lead to deeply ingrained emotional mirroring, which could explain some "telepathic" experiences without invoking paranormal mechanisms.

•	Filter Theory (William James): Some researchers speculate that the brain may act as a filter, normally blocking out subtle signals. In rare cases, such as between twins, this filter might be "loosened," allowing for anomalous perception.

Dirk leans back, and Mira continues. "There is also a lot of anecdotal evidence, but most of that has not been verified by science. Despite the intriguing results, mainstream neuroscience remains cautious. The sample sizes in these studies are small, and replication is essential. Researchers like Silberstein emphasize that their findings are preliminary and call for independent replication to confirm any anomalous twin communication effects. Bottom line, yes, communication is possible, but now we would be talking about you having a twin, not just a sibling. Has your family ever indicated that you might be a twin?"

Dirk looks confused. "No. And I've seen nothing that would lead me to that conclusion. So, I could have been a twin?"

Dirk flexes his hand, inspects his own wrist as if the proof is written there. "Would that explain why the killer's DNA is close to mine?"

"Could be. Or, if there were two or more embryos, you might all be out there, running around, with slightly different fingerprints. Since you weren't a full match, you could have a fraternal twin. Those are twins that are not identical. You could have different blood types, DNA and fingerprints." Mira types a note, pauses, and grins, suddenly energized. "I'd love to see your stem cell profile. I can run it if you want to lose a little more blood."

He tries to smile, but it lands crooked. "Take what you need."

The second draw is slower, the tube filling with a richer, deeper red. Mira labels it, then snaps off her gloves and drops them into the trash. She hands the vial to a technician who disappears through a double door. She pulls up a rolling stool and sits almost at eye level.

The analyzer beeps. Mira glances at the screen, and her professional mask slips; she is positively gleeful. She pulls up the rapid DNA test from the earlier blood draw. She leans back in her chair. She reads through the report and looks at Dirk. "Your unsub is not only a sibling. You share enough DNA that I am positive that you have a fraternal twin. You are not identical, but you are definitely twins.

Mira's assistant walks up and whispers in her ear. She looks up at him. "Are you sure? Did you run the test twice to confirm?"

Her assistant nods. "We're positive. Have you ever seen or heard of anything like this?"

Before Mira can answer, Dirk interrupts. "What's going on?"

"You're not going to believe this," she says. "You have two blood types. O-positive and AB. Running the STR markers now. You also have two distinct DNA strains. Two distinct sets. One is dominant; the other is about thirty percent. It's patchy, but it's there. You probably absorbed a twin early, or the cells mixed at the blastocyst stage. Either way, besides being a twin, you're a chimera."

"What the hell is a chimera?" he asks. "It sounds like something from a sci-fi movie."

Mira laughs. "You're not that far off. Let me try to make this as unscientific as I can. In the early stage of your life as an embryo, you were a fraternal twin, which is not uncommon. At some point and for reasons we don't fully understand, one embryo was absorbed by the other, transferring its DNA to the other embryo, which grew into you. Now, if that's not enough to freak you out. The DNA tests the FBI indicated you have another sibling. Our test gets way more detailed, and not only do you have a sibling, but that sibling is also your fraternal twin. Meaning you share DNA traits but are not identical."

Dirk pulls up a rolling chair and plops down. He glances at the laptop screen. "There were three of us?"

Mira's eyes light up. She leans in, fingers dancing on the desktop. "That's the interesting part. There was a vanished twin, and you absorbed part of its genome, so you have a subset of its DNA, right alongside yours. Sometimes, in the right tissue, it can take over. They've documented women giving birth to children with their non-dominant DNA. Technically, the mother is the 'aunt' at the genome level."

Dirk processes this. The idea is as beautiful as it is horrifying. "So, I'm carrying two sets of DNA. Mine, and…" He trails off.

Mira nods. "In rare cases, it shows up in the blood. That's called mosaicism. If you had a bone marrow transplant as an embryo, or even a microchimerism event, you could have it throughout your body. It doesn't always affect phenotype, but the markers will show."

Dirk stands and walks around the counter. Mira could see that his mind was racing.

"I'll be honest, Dirk. If this pans out, it's probably a world first. I've read of triple chimeras in lab animals, but not in a human. It would explain your match with the killer, but the twin thing—" She shakes her head, half in wonder. "It's bananas."

Dirk's mind is already running ahead. "If I have two sets of DNA, could that explain why I'm?" He stops, unsure how to phrase it. "Why I'm dreaming of the murders? Like I'm tuned into the same frequency?"

Mira tilts her head, thinking. "Hard to say. But the psychology is interesting. If you shared prenatal space with a sibling, you could have fragments of their brain chemistry in yours. At the cellular level, anyway."

Dirk lets that land. The chill of the lab is now inside him, rooted in his chest. Dirk can't move. His hands are ice.

Mira pushes off the stool and walks over to the printer, which is already spitting out a summary of the test. She hands him the first page: "You're a statistical miracle, Dirk. If you weren't so uptight, I'd say you should celebrate."

He does not smile. He is counting backward from ten, steadying his breath. He looks at the results, the columns of numbers, the strange beauty of two selves mapped in a single body.

"What about the killer?" he asks, voice low. "Is it possible there are more like me? Out there?"

Mira's eyes shine. "With this profile? It's more than possible. If you had two fraternal siblings, and both survived…" She trails off, letting him finish the math.

Three.

She looks up from her laptop. "Here's something else to add to all of this. Based on your evidence, the timeline, and the match of DNA from Arizona and Colorado, you could also have another sibling, who is identical to your unsub."

Dirk feels the world tilt under him, a sharp drop, as if the floor has just given way. His legs tingle, unsteady. "Keep it simple doc."

"I've heard this is possible, never seen it, but your mother could have been pregnant with one set of maternal twins, identical, and one set of fraternal twins. Quadruplets, until you absorbed your twin, who was your fraternal twin."

Dirks loses his balance and grabs the table to support himself. "I could have two brothers out there who are identical, and they're both killing people in the same manner hundreds of miles apart. How the fuck?"

He paces then stops at the wall of glass that divides

the main floor from the empty corridor. His reflection stares back at him, a split image, double-shadowed by the hard lights. He is unsure which one is the real him.

Mira's phone buzzes, a low hum on the counter. She answers without breaking stride. "Lang."

A beat, then: "Yeah, I can run it. Send the swab, and we'll match the loci." She ends the call, her eyes on Dirk.

"I'll need more samples, but I'll help you find them. All of them," she says.

Dirk nods, mind running parallel tracks: the murder board, the spiral crosses, the impossible odds of a killer with his blood in its veins.

He tries to picture himself as an infant or before. He wonders which parts of him are original, and which are borrowed, or stolen, or left behind. He wonders whether the nightmares will stop or if they are only the beginning. His thoughts turn to a dark corner of his mind. Did he murder his twin while still in the womb, and if his brothers are killers, what about him?

In the glass, his face splits into two, then three. He waits to see which one will blink first.

Chapter Thirty-Three

Dirk parks two houses down from the Trainor home, ignoring the open spot in the driveway. He sits behind the wheel for a full minute, hand tapping out an arrhythmic Morse code on the steering wheel, before he grabs his backpack and walks up the walkway. The overnight rain has pooled in the cracks of the old concrete, flowing into jagged little mirrors that reflect the sagging eaves of the house. He trips on the third step, catches himself, and makes a mental note of the maintenance lapse. Something he'll have to make time to come back and fix.

Inside, the lights are on in every room, as if Maggie's warding off some encroaching evil. She answers the door in a peach cardigan over a nurse's blouse; her hair pulled back in a way that signals she gave up on fashion a long time ago. Her smile is instant but too taut, the kind designed for bad hospital news.

"You didn't have to ring the bell," she says, ushering him in. "It's not locked."

"I wanted to give you a heads up," Dirk says. "I know it's late."

She closes the door behind him, but not all the way. "It's never too late for you."

The living room is a museum of memories. There's a couch that looks new but isn't, a glass coffee table covered in magazines even though she doesn't read any of them, and three end tables cluttered with framed photos. Maggie gestures toward the couch. Dirk doesn't sit. He surveys the room, eyes grazing over each photo in sequence. First the baby pictures, then the elementary school class shots, and finally the obligatory senior photo with Dirk in an ill-fitting tux. He notices he doesn't resemble his mother or his father.

"Want tea? Or coffee?" Maggie asks, moving to the kitchen. She opens and closes a cupboard before he answers, as if it's scripted.

"No thanks," Dirk says. He stands perfectly still, arms crossed, scanning every inch of the room. "This won't take long."

Maggie fills the kettle anyway, her back to him. "You sounded urgent on the phone."

Dirk watches the kitchen light halo her head. "I want to talk about my birth certificate."

Maggie's hand stops on the kettle. There's a quiet hiss as it overflows a bit, then she sets it down and dries her palm on a dish towel. "What about it?"

"I want to see the original," Dirk says. He doesn't blink. "Not the copy you sent in for the background check. The real one."

She's quiet for a second, then comes back to the living room, the towel bunched in her hands like a stress toy. "You know I don't keep that out in the open. I gave you what the county clerk sent. You're a federal agent, Dirk. I'd think you'd trust your own paperwork."

Dirk's jaw flexes, a muscle in his temple pulsing like a fuse burning down. "That copy was certified by the county six months after I was born. There's no attending doctor's signature, just a notary stamp. I ran the chain of custody through the FBI. It came up…weird."

"Weird?" She folds the towel, then unfolds it, then sits on the couch. Her posture is ramrod straight, as if bracing for a car crash.

"There's no hospital record," Dirk says. He keeps his hands in his pockets, so she doesn't see them shaking. "No blood type logged, no APGAR, no vaccination schedule. I ran it against the city's database. Nothing. Like I just appeared."

Maggie looks at her hands, rubs the base of her left thumb with her right. "That was a long time ago," she says. "You know record keeping wasn't digital back then. Sometimes things get lost."

Dirk moves around the coffee table, so he's directly in her line of sight. "Not everything," he says. "You kept these." He lifts one of the framed photos, Maggie in nurse's whites, holding a baby, but the child is blurred, out of focus, as if the camera couldn't decide where to aim. "Who took this?"

Maggie's eyes go to the floor. "A friend from work."

Dirk sets the photo face down on the table. "Which hospital were you working at when I was born?"

Maggie looks up at him. "Dirk, please."

"Which hospital?"

She closes her eyes. "Denver General. Right here."

Dirk waits, lets the silence stretch until it's almost unbearable. "I called Denver General. They have you on the payroll, but you took a leave of absence the month after I was born, and there's no record of you ever being a maternity patient."

"That's normal after the birth of a baby," she responds.

She presses the dishtowel to her mouth, as if to keep the words from escaping.

"So," Dirk continues, voice flattening to monotone. "If you didn't give birth at DG, and you were on leave and there's no birth record…where did I come from?"

The kettle in the kitchen screams. Maggie ignores it. Her hands clench in her lap, the knuckles whitening.

"I want the truth," Dirk says, each word a hammer. "Now."

Maggie stands and crosses to the bookshelf, where a row of albums leans at a dangerous angle. She pulls one, opens it to the middle and extracts a single loose photograph and a folded piece of paper, slipping it from between the pages as if it might shatter. She holds it to her chest, arms crossed over it protectively.

"You were so wanted," she says. "More than anything in the world."

Dirk doesn't move. "But?"

Maggie looks at the photo, then at him, then away again. "But I couldn't have children," she says. "And you, you were a miracle. There was a lawyer, an adoption, and you were mine from the first second they put you in my arms. That's what mattered to me."

Dirk's eyes narrow. "So, you're saying I was adopted?"

Maggie shakes her head. "Not in the normal way. It was a private adoption. Understand, your biological mother couldn't keep you. She was. She had her own problems. But I loved you as much as if."

"As if what?" Dirk snaps, stepping forward. "As if I were a secret you had to hide? As if I'd break if I ever found out?"

Maggie's lips tremble. She grips the photo tighter. "I did what I thought was right. You were my son, Dirk. That's all I ever wanted."

He stops a foot away from her, the space between them crowded by decades of omission. "Who is she? My birth mother?"

Maggie's shoulders slump. "Her name was Stephanie; that's all I know. She was…young and alone. She didn't want you to go into foster care."

Dirk's nostrils flare as he absorbs this. "You lied to me my entire life."

"No," Maggie says, and then, more softly, "I tried to protect you. I tried to give you a normal life."

"You have no idea what normal is," replies Dirk.

Maggie finally lets go of the photo, offering it to him at arm's length. Dirk takes it with two fingers, not looking at her. The image is of Maggie holding an infant swaddled in blue; her face half-shadowed by the hospital curtain behind her. The paper is a birth certificate issued by the court after the adoption was completed. Dirk notices a case number in the lower left corner, pulls out his phone, takes a picture of the certificate and hands it back to Maggie.

"Why are you telling me now?" Dirk asks. His voice is flat, the edges sanded off by exhaustion.

"Because you asked," Maggie whispers. "Because you won't let it go. I thought if you knew how much I loved you, it would be enough."

Dirk tucks the photo into his jacket, never breaking eye contact. "It's not."

She opens her mouth to respond, but he cuts her off. "I'm leaving," Dirk says, already moving for the door. He hears her say something, maybe his name, or an apology, but he doesn't stop.

He closes the door with hard, deliberate force. The sound carries down the block, ricocheting off the faded siding and out into the street.

Dirk stands on the porch, breathing in the dry air, eyes locked on the trembling lights of the city in the distance. For a moment, he didn't know which direction to go. But then his hands stop shaking, and he walks back to his car, the photo burning cold against his chest pocket.

***

The county records building looms in the flat afternoon light, a squat bunker ringed with mostly dead hedges and a flag flapping listlessly on a creaking pole. Dirk enters through a vestibule that smells of mud and copier toner and signs the visitors' log with a borrowed ballpoint pen whose barrel is held together with tape. At the checkpoint, he flashes his Bureau credentials, though it's not strictly necessary, and walks past a pair of county clerks bickering in low voices about misplaced property taxes.

The research room is bigger than he remembers. Ten rows of file cabinets, each tagged with a strip of color-coded plastic, and a bank of ancient computers blinking in the back. Most of the desks are empty except for the one closest to the microfilm archive, where a woman in a Denver Broncos hoodie pecks at the keyboard with two fingers. Her eyes never leave Dirk as he moves through the aisles.

Dirk sits at the end table, pulling up a box of birth records from January through March 1984. The box's contents are in rough order, but the logs are hand-typed, some with smudged carbon duplicates, others with names and numbers crossed out and rewritten in thick blue pen. He flips through each page methodically, scanning first for his name, Dirk Aaron Trainor, then for anything resembling the name Stephanie, or for entries flagged as adoption. He is slow and meticulous, logging each anomaly in his notebook, then referencing the entry in the cross-list of city hospitals.

Thirty minutes in, the repetition becomes narcotic: rows of names, dates, parents and signatures. Then, on a page near the back of the box, his finger stops on a line with a smear of faded red ink: TRIPLETS—SEE ADOPTION RECORD. The names are blacked out by the official marker, but the birthdate matches Dirk's own. He feels his pulse trip.

He shuffles forward and finds a second document, stamped FILED LATE, which includes a scrawled note in the margin: **all three adopted separately, per maternal request, see attached**. The attachment is a photocopy of a form letter; the lines are darkened with age. Near the bottom, there's a signature in a careful, upright hand: Stephanie. The last name has been redacted.

Dirk's vision tightens, the edges of the page going gray. He sets the crate down and rubs at his face, suddenly aware of how cold his hands are. His mouth tastes of iron and burned coffee.

He turns to the next page and finds the adoption log. He finds the information he had taken from the birth certificate provided by the court. Case number 317198417 BABY BOY A-adopted March 20, 1984. Above his case number are two case numbers, but both those numbers refer to baby girls. He reads the case numbers below his number. Case number 317198418 BABY BOY B- adopted March 31, 1984. The third note is different. Case number 317198419 BABY BOY C- adopted July 17, 1992. All with identical notations about closed adoption records.

Dirk examines the names for a long minute, unmoving. The woman in the Broncos hoodie is openly watching him now, curiosity writ large. He pays her no mind. He flips back to the first page, checks the birthweights, the times, 8:23, 8:25, and 8:27, and the hospital: Denver General. His hands tremble so much that when he reaches for the pen, his grip slips, and the pen clatters across the desk. He leans back in the chair, breathing slowly. The fluorescent hum overhead is suddenly oppressive.

He rakes through the box again, finds the last

relevant page; a blurred carbon with the word CONSENT circled, and there, in a block of text near the bottom, is the confirmation: "Separated at the express request of biological mother. No contact allowed between adoptive families."

He reads the line four times, the text vibrating, until it sinks in.

When he stands, his knees lock, and he clutches the table for balance. His left hand is numb. He gathers the files, tucks them under his arm, and steps over to the copy counter. The woman in the hoodie intercepts him.

"Need help?" she asks, but her tone makes it clear she already knows the answer.

"No. I'm good. Thanks," says Dirk.

He pays for the copies in cash, leaving the change on the counter. He pushes through the doors into the parking lot, the cold air slapping him awake. He staggers to his car, drops the file on the passenger seat, and sits with the door open, breathing in short bursts. His heart pounds so hard it rattles his vision.

For a moment, he does nothing but stare at the dashboard; the wipers work pointlessly against the rain on the windshield.

After a long time, he reaches for his phone and scrolls to Carl Bunch's number. He hesitates, then dials. The call connects after two rings.

"Carl Bunch," says a clipped, precise voice.

Dirk steadies himself. "Carl, it's Dirk," he says. "I need you to run a search for me. It's urgent."

Carl is silent for a moment. "Go ahead."

"I'm texting you a page from the county birth record. All the names have been left out. The birth date is March 17, 1984. All three babies were adopted out of Denver, Colorado, and were born at Denver General Hospital. We need to find out which attorney handled the adoptions and try to find the birth mother's name. All I have to go on is Stephanie."

He pauses as he writes. "Relationship?"

"Siblings," Dirk says. "Triplets. They are possibly my brothers. Stephanie is the mother."

Another pause, this one longer. "Does this have something to do with the loud meeting in Spinella's office yesterday?"

Dirk's voice is as flat as concrete. "It might. I need you to put together a package for each family and see if you can find out the boy's names. I know they are not in CODIS or any private DNA databases, but I need to know if either of them shows up in a criminal database."

He can almost hear him frowning through the line. "Dirk, that will take some time. And you know, with adoptions, there will be privacy issues. Did you run this by Jill or Spinella?"

"I will as soon as I'm certain of the facts, but I'd like to get ahead of this," he says. "Please."

A beat. "Alright. I'll see what I can find out."

Dirk ends the call. He stares at the cracked vinyl of the passenger seat, then picks up the folder. The word TRIPLET, stamped in faded red, repeats in his mind.

He sets the page down and looks at his own hands, as if he might see something written in the lines of his palms.

He doesn't drive away. He rolls down the window and lets the cool morning air flush through until he can breathe again.

Chapter Thirty-Four

Jill Quarters' apartment is a still-life painting. There's a bottle of Malbec breathing on the Formica counter, her Glock 19 locked in a biometric case on the hall table, and a half-empty bowl of grapes and cheese cubes sweating under the blue tint of the kitchen bulb. The living room is orderly, surfaces scrubbed clean of any memory except the row of Le Creuset mugs on the windowsill. The only mess is the threadbare blanket balled up on the couch, where she sits, feet up, eyes on a rerun of some British baking show streaming in perpetual loop. It is eleven-forty-seven, and the world is dead silent except for the giggle-squeal of contestants piped through her flatscreen and the hiss of the AC vent rattling.

Jill is on her second glass. She has let the wine warm almost to room temperature, which she considers a personal failing but not enough to get up and fix. She sits motionless, right hand palming the remote, left cradling the glass, every inch of her body in a state of calibrated off-duty slack. Her phone is face down on the coffee table. She stares at the show, but her mind replays the wound photos from the case: the spiral cross, the plastic sheeting and the look on Trainor's face when he touched the victim's wrist.

At the fifty-minute mark, the doorbell rings. It is a crisp, mechanical bing-bong, not the wet slap of knuckles, and it shakes her out of her slouch with a spasm of dread. She glances at her phone, no texts, no missed calls, no Bureau email, but something in her gut says this is work.

She kills the TV with her thumb, slides the glass to the coaster, and stands. Her first move is to the biometric lockbox; the mechanism reads her print with a tiny stutter, and the slide snicks back, offering the familiar weight. She thumbs the safety and heads to the door, bare feet whispering across the laminate, and every sense alert.

Through the peephole, the lens blurs the hallway into a warped funhouse tunnel. There, rocking back and forth, hands jammed in the pockets of his suit, is Dirk Trainor. His shoulders are bunched up, jaw clenched, hair a disaster. He isn't even trying to smooth it down or act like a human. Jill feels her body loosen, then tighten.

She tucks the Glock behind her waistband, clicks the deadbolt, and opens the door. "Dirk?"

He doesn't move. He is breathing hard; his cheeks are flushed with more than the cold. For a moment, he stares past her, through her, into a room only he can see.

"Can I come in?" he asks.

She steps back, leaving the door wide. "Yeah. Of course." She notes he doesn't bring a jacket, just the navy suit and the backpack hanging loose from one hand. "Do you want?"

"Anything," he says, voice hoarse. "Just please."

She guides him to the couch, where he sits and then immediately leans forward, elbows on knees, head down. She watches the muscles jump in his back, the fine trembling of his hands, and she thinks he's about to puke.

She returns to the kitchen and pours a tumbler of bourbon. No ice, two fingers, the way she knows he takes it. When she returns, he hasn't moved.

"Dirk, how much have you had to drink tonight?" she asks.

"Just a couple after I left the courthouse."

"Dirk. The courthouse closed hours ago. Where have you been?"

"Some bar on Broadway, down from the hospital. It was only a couple to calm my nerves."

She sits next to him and waits for him to breathe. After half a minute, he raises his head, stares at the floor, and says, "I'm going to lose my job."

Jill sets the glass on the table. "You're not. What happened?"

Dirk picks up the bourbon with both hands, takes a long sip, and then laughs, one dry, brittle bark. "What do you know about chimerism?" He slurs his words, and Jill listens closer.

Jill's eyebrows climb half a centimeter. "Human chimerism? Like two sets of DNA?"

Dirk nods, knuckles bone-white around the glass. "Turns out it's a thing. More than a thing. It's me."

Jill sits still. The air in the room feels viscous, as if she has to push the words out through Jell-O. "Dirk, what did you do?"

"I went to see Mira Lang," he says. "I needed answers. She ran her tests three times to confirm." He looks up at her, and his eyes are the color of cobalt in an autopsy room. "They all match. They all say the same thing."

She leans back, letting the new gravity settle. "Is this about the case? The DNA at the scene?"

"No, it's worse." He sets the glass down with a clatter, but not before draining half. "I went to see my mother. Then I went to Denver General Hospital and then to the courthouse. All roads lead to the same answer. I'm not who I thought I was."

He explains it, voice steadier now, falling into the rhythm of a procedural briefing. The sealed adoption records. The late-filed birth certificate. That he is one of three brothers, all split at birth, all with their names blacked out by some pen-wielding bureaucrat. The possibility that the killings, the ritual carving, the entire sick pattern, are connected not by chance but by something in their blood.

Jill listens, every micro expression chiseled away, her face blank. She interrupts only to clarify a detail, to pin down a date or a name, or a timeline. "Do you know the others' names?" she asks at last.

"No," Dirk says. "Carl is looking. I have a list of adoption attorneys and agencies, but all the files are locked. None of the logs lists the adopting families, only case numbers. I found the case number that was on my birth certificate, and there are two more in sequence following mine. They have to be my brothers. But it's me, Jill. It's my DNA at the scene."

Jill stands, paces once to the kitchen and back. She refills his glass. When she speaks again, her voice is lower, pitched for the room, not the case file. "Are you saying you could have done this and not remember?"

Dirk looks at her, the edge of a smile twisted with something like pain. "No. But that's the problem, isn't it? I could be anyone. If someone wanted to set me up, or make it look like I'm a step ahead on this case."

"You're not that guy, Dirk."

He laughs louder this time; the sound rising and then guttering out. "I hope not."

She sits again, close this time, her knee brushing his thigh. "You're scared," she says. It's not a question.

"Terrified," he responds. "It was about the dreams."

Jill stares at him. "What dreams?"

Dirk finishes the bourbon and pours another glass. This time it's more than two fingers, and he downs it in one gulp. He reaches for the bottle, and Jill grabs it and sets it alongside the couch, out of reach.

"What dreams, Dirk?"

"I've been seeing the murders, but it's like I'm seeing them through someone else's eyes. Old cases and recent cases. The victims are always fuzzy, but I see the cuts and the blood. It's so real, it freaks me out."

"Dirk. Is that what happened at the crime scene in Prescott, when you looked like you were going to pass out?"

Dirk nods his head. "It's happened several times."

"Dirk. Those happen while you are awake. They're not dreams. They're visions."

"I know," he says. "After we got the results of the tests, Mira and I discussed twins' telepathy, that's what some sites on the internet call it. It's a special bond twins have, where they communicate on a different level than anyone else. It's like a code."

Jill stands and walks to the window. She turns and faces him. "And you think our unsubs are communicating using this telepathy thing and now suddenly you're plugged into them?"

"Yeah. And it's freaking me out. Suppose deep inside, I'm also a serial killer. Suppose it runs in my family. My daughters are twins. Suppose they grow up to be killers?"

Jill walks to the couch. "Slow down, Dirk. Is there any proof that this telepathy thing is real?"

Dirk nods. "Mira found a couple of studies, but the results are controversial, and no one has ever tested the premise with twins separated by long distances. Jill, what am I going to do? I feel like I'm losing my mind."

"Tomorrow morning, we'll go to Spinella. Bring him what you have and see if Carl has anything we can use?"

"No. Not yet. Not until I know," says Dirk.

Jill watches him for a long moment, then says, "What do you want me to do?"

He lifts his hands, then lets them fall, boneless. "Tell me what to do, Jill. Please. I don't have the perspective right now."

She closes her eyes. The wine is thick in her head, but the sense of duty is sharper. She marshals her thoughts, runs through every Bureau policy, every worst-case scenario. "We can go in tomorrow and present it together. Get ahead of it. If you're right, you need backup. If you're wrong, we solve the case."

Dirk nods, but he doesn't speak. He drinks the bourbon and sets the glass down as if it might shatter if he lets go too quickly.

Jill watches him for another minute, stands, and heads to the linen closet in the hall. She returns with a heavy wool blanket, shakes it out, and drapes it over his shoulders. He looks at her, startled, and she grins, slow and sardonic. "You're not leaving tonight. I'm not letting you drive like this."

She turns and walks to the kitchen, stopping at the door.

"Have you eaten anything?" she asks.

He shakes his head and wipes the tears from his eyes, and she walks into the kitchen.

He opens his mouth to protest, but she holds up a hand. "No. Food first, then we'll call your wife and tell her you're on a case. She'll understand."

Jill leaves and returns a few minutes later with a couple of slices of pizza. Dirk is sound asleep on the couch; the blanket is tucked around his neck, and his breathing is slow and regular. Jill stands over him for a moment, watching the way his face unknots, and the way sleep erases the last of the panic. She picks up her phone and goes into the bedroom, closing the door behind her before dialing.

The phone rings twice before it's answered. Jill keeps her voice low and warm. "Hi, Connie, it's Jill. Sorry to call so late, but Dirk had kind of a bad day and a little too much to drink. He showed up on my doorstep, and he's now sound asleep on the couch. He asked me to let you know he's okay. The case is just… it's a lot right now. He's safe. I'm going to let him crash on the couch tonight, just to be sure he gets some sleep."

The voice on the other end is sleepy, but grateful. Jill promises to check in again tomorrow.

She hangs up, returns to the living room, and flicks the TV back on at low volume. The British bakers are still at it, making souffles or meringues or something. Dirk doesn't stir.

Jill sits beside him, wineglass in hand, and watches the world's most perfect sponge cakes rise in silence. She tries not to think about what the morning will bring, but she keeps her Glock close, just in case.

Chapter Thirty-Five

The next morning, the FBI field office is a buzz of activity. The overheads burn white in the cubicle maze, illuminating pale faces, stacks of manila, and the perpetual churn of agents moving from point A to B with coffee in hand and stories in their eyes. The caffeine buzz and hum of logistics echoes from floor to ceiling, but two people move through the tide like sleepwalkers: Quarters and Trainor, the visible residue of whatever hit them the night before clinging to their skin. Neither speaks on the way in; both set on a vector for Anthony Spinella's glass-walled office.

Spinella is at his desk before sunrise, already reviewing something on his laptop when they tap the door. He waves them in, doesn't rise, doesn't do the small talk. Just gestures for them to sit.

"You said you needed the first slot," he says, no inflection, scanning the wall clock behind their heads. "Make it count."

Dirk starts, voice stripped down to its essential parts. "There is an issue with the case. With me. I need you to hear me out all the way before you make a call."

Spinella's face is a granite mask, but the eyes are alert, triangulating every nuance. "Go ahead." He leans back in his chair and focuses on Dirk.

Dirk starts from the beginning with the visions since this case started, and the discovery of the chimerism. He talks about the three DNA tests, the hospital, the county records, his twin brothers and his own adoption.

Jill chimes in with the details as needed, her sentences clipped, each fact a building block she slams onto the table. They talk about the secret language of twins and the findings of Dr. Lang, which once again casts serious doubt on the one-killer theory.

Spinella doesn't blink but listens in silence. He doesn't look at Dirk or Jill.

At the end, Spinella folds his hands on the desk, glances up at the glass wall as if expecting the building itself to weigh in, and says: "This all sounds like science fiction. Do you think you're being set up?"

Dirk doesn't hesitate. "Not set up. I think I'm tapped into their communication stream. It's like I interrupted their internet stream and I'm watching what they're doing, either in the past or live. I can't really explain it, but I'm not doing it consciously."

He looks at Jill. "Are you buying this?"

Jill hesitates for a minute. "Sir. Dirk and I have worked together for a long time, and he is one of the most stable people I've ever met. He has never tried to deceive me or hide anything from me until this case. I can't explain any of this, but if Dirk says he is tied into his twin brothers telepathically, who are killing people, and he can see it happening sometimes. I believe him."

Spinella sits back. For a moment, he's silent, chewing on a thumbnail, then says: "Let's get Dr. Lang on the horn. See if this holds up."

He pivots his laptop and dials. The speaker rings twice, then connects to the clinical efficiency of Mira Lang, still in the lab, voice filtered through the morning's second or third coffee.

"Lang," she answers.

"Doctor. It's Spinella. I'm here with Trainor and Quarters. We need you to talk us through everything you and Dirk spoke about yesterday. And skip all the science mumbo jumbo and talk to us in plain English."

Lang responds. "What has Dirk told you?"

Spinella gives her a summary of the conversation and then sits back.

She explains. "What Dirk told you is all true, and we did the test three times to be sure. To keep it simple. Dirk's mother originally carried four fetuses. Two maternal or identical twins and two fraternal twins, individuals but not copies. For some reason, the fetus we'll call Dirk absorbed his twin and took on some of its blood and DNA characteristics. This is called chimerism. The maternal twins share everything. Blood type, DNA, and they are identical in every fashion. Your own timeline for at least two of the murders bears this out, which I know puts you back to square one and dealing with two killers. As far as the telepathy thing. I sent you the studies, Dirk and I discussed. These were small localized studies and are controversial, and Dirk is correct that long-distance telepathy has never been studied, nor has the connection of maternal twins connecting with fraternal twins. Whatever is going on it's fascinating from a scientific standpoint."

Spinella's face doesn't move, but the set of his jaw changes. "Doc, this all sounds like science fiction, especially this chimera stuff. Is this for real?"

Mira laughed. "It's a scientific fact, Tony. To keep it simple and non-scientific, I'll read you something off the internet. According to Wikipedia, human chimerism is not speculative; it is a rare but well-documented genetic reality. Verified through peer-reviewed medical reports, DNA testing and legal cases, it has reshaped our understanding of identity, genetics, and even the justice system. I'm texting you a list of four cases mentioned in the article that have proven the existence of human chimerism. You can look them up for yourself on Wikipedia if you want more information."

His phone sounded with a text alert. He opened his phone and read the message.

- 1953 British Medical Journal Case: A woman was found to have two different blood types, traced to cells from her twin brother living in her body.

- Karen Keegan (2002, New England Journal of Medicine): Genetic testing revealed she had two sets of DNA, which initially made it appear she wasn't the biological mother of her children.

- Lydia Fairchild (2002, Washington State): DNA tests suggested she wasn't the mother of her children until further analysis showed she was a chimera. Her case became a landmark in legal debates over DNA evidence.

- Taylor Muhl (2009): A singer diagnosed with chimerism after doctors linked her large torso birthmark to two genetic lineages.

Spinella read the summaries and scratched his head.

"So, you're saying that Dirk's DNA can be a match for these twin killers even though he's had no contact with them?"

"With everything Dirk and I discussed, I'd say that's likely."

"Anything else?" Spinella asks, pen poised.

"Yes. After Dirk left, I spoke with the author of one of the telepathy studies. To say the least, he was fascinated, but to the point. It is possible that your two killers, separated by a long distance, may have never met or known about each other. They could be communicating with each other and have no idea they are doing it."

Spinella thought for a minute. "Doc, is Dirk a danger to himself or others?"

There was silence for a few seconds before Mira spoke. "Now you are getting into another severely understudied area, nature versus nurture. Could Dirk be dangerous because his brothers are serial killers? It's certainly possible, but there have never been any indications so far in his work. It's possible that because of his upbringing, those tendencies never developed. We have no way of knowing."

Spinella thanks her, ends the call, and sits in silence for another five seconds. He looks at Dirk, really looks at him, like he's trying to find the difference between the man he knows and the man who might exist on a forensic spreadsheet.

"You're to stay away from any evidence," Spinella

says. "You and Quarters work on the people backgrounds. Full cooperation, all channels open. You make a single move outside the lines, I pull you, and I mean it. Understood?"

Dirk nods, voice flat. "Understood."

"Follow up with Carl on the list of adoption lawyers and let's find the families. See if anyone can shake loose a name or two of these supposed siblings. Quarters, you're lead on this."

Jill nods, already scrolling through her phone, drafting the taskers.

Spinella stands, pulling on his jacket, and beckons them into the war room with a jerk of his chin. "Let's brief the team. I want everybody in sync before this goes viral."

They march down the corridor. The war room is a blast of light and motion, agents at every surface, and the board crawling with names and maps. Spinella calls for quiet, then lays out the facts: the potential triplet scenario, the evidence DNA misdirection, the new protocols for processing future crime scenes and the fact that they are back to two killers possibly operating independently. "We need to find out who else is in play, and where the fuck they are now. Focus on the adoption trail. Lean hard on any lawyer that handled these cases, even if they're dead."

He paces as he speaks, hands laced behind his back. "Anything that comes in, I want it flagged and in my hands. Quarters will be the lead. Everything goes through her and then me. Nobody goes directly to the media unless I say so. Dirk will work with Carl in locating his brothers. He is not to touch a single piece of evidence until I say so. Got it?"

Dirk nods again. He feels his ears burning and wonders how many people in the room are recalculating their opinions of him on the fly.

Spinella dismisses them with a chop of his hand. "Get it done. Now."

Jill heads to the bullpen with Dirk close behind. They set up at twin computers; the monitors facing outward so everyone can watch. The silence is tight, but in a good way, focused, no chatter. Jill's fingers fly, shooting out FOIA requests and cross-referencing the state bar for every adoption lawyer in play from 1984 to 85. Dirk works the crime scene database, searching for anything that matches their new parameters.

After fifteen minutes, the silence is broken by a shout from across the room. "Hey! You've gotta see this!"

One agent working on some of the old Arizona cases waves a USB drive in the air. "I just received this from a retired Phoenix detective. It's surveillance footage from the mini-mart next to the second murder. It was never entered into evidence because it was too grainy, but I had our tech guys take a look to see if they could clean it up."

The agent plugs it into the boardroom display. The team crowds around as a jittery black and white video comes up. There's a person, hooded, maybe a man, maybe not, walking out of the store with a duffel bag at their side. The timestamp is fifteen minutes before the estimated TOD. The figure lingers in the parking lot, seems to stare directly into the camera, then flicks their hand as if waving. The face is blurred, but there is something haunting in the set of the shoulders, the way they turn and move with the stiff efficiency that matches Dirk's walking style.

Nobody says it at first. Several agents glance at Dirk, then at the screen, then back at Dirk.

"Looks like a younger version of you, Dirk," says Jill.

Dirk looks at the screen, unable to look away, as if he could bring the pixels into focus and prove it's not him.

"Shit," Dirk whispers.

Jill lays a hand on his arm, but keeps her voice loud, authoritative. "We already have the DNA. Check for partials and look at the gait. That could be anybody."

Spinella, watching from the doorway, barks: "Run it through gait analysis. Run it through every damn system we've got. And make sure that video stays in this building. I don't want Dirk getting snatched up by a bunch of local yahoos looking to make names for themselves."

Another shout, this time from the far corner of the room. Carl Bunch, wild-eyed, jogs in clutching a folder.

"I got it!" he says, voice cracking. "The adoption attorney on Dirk's case. He's still alive. Practicing in Cherry Creek."

Jill is already up, jacket in hand. "Let's go."

Dirk follows, adrenaline surging, the edges of the world a little too sharp. They don't look back at the war room, but both know every eye is on them as they head out.

In the elevator, neither speaks. Jill checks the address again, then looks up. Her eyes are clear and dangerous.

Outside, the day is full of sun, but it feels like interrogation light. The air bites clean and cold as they cross the parking lot to Jill's car.

Inside, the engine idling, Dirk glances at the mirror and sees his own face reflected, split between shadow and sun.

"We'll find them," Jill says.

Dirk looks at her, then the mirror, then straight ahead.

"I hope so," he says.

Jill throws the car into gear and punches it onto the street, the Bureau building shrinking behind them. They drive east, toward Cherry Creek, and the unknown.

Chapter Thirty-Six

The doors to Turner, Baxter, and Fellows are double slabs of black walnut, tall enough to require a sidelong angle to see the etched gold letters at eye level. They move on hinges made for swinging open on verdict day, not for casual drop-ins. Dirk and Jill stand side-by-side before the threshold. Dirk puts both hands into the task, muscles bunched along his forearm as he shoves the right-hand door wide. It opens a patch of darkness and air-conditioned chill, then Jill follows, forcing the left with her shoulder. Inside, every inch is curated for intimidation: plush runner underfoot, abstract sculptures like blunted weapons on pedestals, and a scent that's equal parts toner and rich people's aftershave.

At the reception desk, a woman with the face and posture of a syndicated anchor sits behind a mahogany counter gleaming to a high sheen. Her smile is bright and predatory. Her black blazer shows zero lint, and her hair, mid-length and ironed flat, frames her face with the crispness of a geometry diagram.

"Good morning," she says, voice pitched at the same frequency as the climate control. "How may I help you?"

Dirk flashes his Bureau credentials before he even finishes crossing the Persian rug, and Jill does the same. The receptionist's gaze flickers across them both, recalibrating.

"Special Agents Quarters and Trainor. We're here to speak with Lloyd Fellows. It's regarding a criminal matter."

"Mr. Fellows has a full calendar today," the receptionist says, defaulting to the script. Then she notices the tiny gold badge crest above the words "Federal Bureau of Investigation." The smile stutters. "May I ask the nature of your business with Mr. Fellows?"

Dirk glances at the wall clock, then at Jill. He leans into the counter's dead zone. "It's about an ongoing homicide investigation with direct ties to his firm's casework. We'd prefer to speak with him in private."

"Please let him know it's urgent. Several people may be in danger," says Jill.

The receptionist's eyes dart to a pale blue phone perched on the desk. She lifts the receiver, punching a code with polished nails. Her voice is smooth, but the syllables lag half a beat. "Mr. Fellows? You have two FBI agents requesting an unscheduled conference. They say it's regarding a homicide investigation." A pause. "No, both are here now." She glances at Dirk and Jill, and her left hand flutters over a logbook. "Very well. I'll have them wait."

She returns the receiver, her face back in formation. "Mr. Fellows will be available in just a moment. Please have a seat." She gestures at a horseshoe of leather chairs, arranged like a tribunal beneath a wall of law school diplomas.

Dirk sits first, spreading his arms over the chair back and fixing his stare on a framed document labeled "Supreme Court Bar Admissions, 1987." The waiting area is over-lit, every light bulb's color temperature slightly at odds with the next. Jill sits one over, foot already jiggling with metronome regularity. Neither of them speaks. The receptionist types, audible clicks from nails that look more like they should sign affidavits than type, and glances over her screen at the two agents, as if they might try to run.

Five minutes pass, then ten. Dirk's mind maps the room, labeling exits, shadowed corners and anything out of the normal. He counts the seconds between the receptionist's glances, always nine or ten, and matches her breathing rate to the shifting pitch of the ventilation.

At the seventeen-minute mark, a young man in a tailored but slightly off-kilter suit approaches from the inner hallway. His hair is combed with military neatness, but the cowlick above his right temple has launched a minor rebellion. His shoes squeak with newness. He carries a single legal pad, clasped to his chest.

"Special Agents?" he asks, voice too thin for the gravity of the firm.

Dirk and Jill both stand.

"I'm Bryce. Mr. Fellows' assistant. If you'll come with me, please?" He says this with the forced cheer of someone who got a C in acting class. He pivots on his heels and begins leading them down a corridor whose walls are hung with impressionist landscapes and old, color-faded photographs of city dignitaries. The air cools as they move deeper, sound dropping away until even Bryce's shoes seem to quiet in respect.

Bryce stops in front of a closed door with a brass

nameplate: "Lloyd Fellows, Esq." The name is engraved in all caps, and the corners of the plate are smoothed from years of fingerprints.

Bryce knocks once, waits for the muffled reply, then opens the door wide. "Mr. Fellows? The agents are here."

Dirk enters first, followed by Jill, both moving with the restrained energy of people expecting either a handshake or a lawsuit. The room swallows them, heavy with dark paneled walls and the redolence of old book glue. From the far side of a walnut desk, Lloyd Fellows, overweight and balding, with a face like an angry tomato, sits in a throne-like office chair. He does not rise, merely gesturing to two guest chairs as if inviting them to trespass on a sacred ritual.

Jill says, "Thank you for meeting with us," as they sit, voice as flat as a judge's gavel.

Dirk's knuckles whiten against the armrests. He has already seen enough. The show is about to begin.

The room is a vault. Floor-to-ceiling bookshelves line the walls, filled with leather-spined books, more ornamental than read. Dark panels drink the ambient light, and a double-paned window filters out the city's motion until even the sky outside looks clinical. The desk in the middle could double as a medieval fortress wall, and behind it, Lloyd Fellows leans back with his hands folded over the shelf of his stomach, thumbs twiddling like he's playing a fugue only he can hear.

Fellows sizes them up: Dirk, face a study in professional homicide, and Jill, upright and motionless. He lets them wait an extra beat, establishing the geometry of power. Only after that does he speak; his voice is more breath than bass.

"Special Agents, what can Turner, Baxter, and Fellows do for the federal government today?"

Jill fields the open. "We're investigating a series of violent crimes with potential ties to a group of adoptions your office handled in the mid-eighties. We're hoping you can clarify some details."

She sets a folded sheet of paper on the desk with the typed list of case numbers, each underlined in blue marker.

Fellows doesn't touch the paper, only cocks his head. "You know those files are sealed by the court? I can't unseal them without a judge's order, and I assure you I'm in no rush to violate client privilege."

Dirk stays silent, watching the way the sweat beads just behind the rim of Fellows' glasses. Jill maintains eye contact. "We're not looking for a violation. Just context. It's a matter of public safety. The adoptees are linked by DNA to a suspect in an ongoing serial case."

"DNA?" Fellows interrupts. "I'm no biologist, but isn't the whole point of sealed adoption that everyone walks away clean?"

Dirk's mouth hardens. "There are three subjects. All male. Same maternal DNA, split among different adoptive families."

Fellows snorts, a nasal buzz. "Sounds like a modern miracle, but again, I can't help you. I'm in the business of discretion, not exposure. Even if I wanted to, I couldn't just go into the records room and hand you those files. It's illegal."

Jill opens the paper, presses it flat with a fingernail. "Mr. Fellows, we don't need the full file. We only need the names of the adoptive families for these three case numbers. That information could prevent more violence. If you'd be willing to—"

He cuts her off. "I'd be willing to offer you a phone number for our general counsel. Beyond that, there's nothing I can do unless you bring a signed order from the bench."

Dirk leans forward, voice gaining volume by millimeters. "We're not here to litigate. People are dying, Mr. Fellows. Children. If you don't help us, you could be an accessory to a homicide by omission."

Fellows smiles, thin and reedy. "That's not how the law works, Agent. And I don't respond well to threats. Now, if there's nothing else."

Dirk stays put, shifting his weight in the chair. His hands splayed on the walnut desktop, fingers bracing as if to push the whole structure aside.

"I grew up in Denver," he says, eyes locked on Fellows. "I was adopted through your office. I tracked my birth, read the microfiche at the courthouse, and found the trail you left behind. There were three of us, all boys, born on the same day. We're connected by DNA."

The silence is taut enough to twang. For a moment, even the HVAC seems to pause.

Fellows looks from Dirk to Jill and back. His tongue wets the line between lip and mustache, and his next words are calculated for maximum deniability.

"Again, Agent, if you are who you say you are, then you already know the process. If you want access to those records, you get a subpoena. You can knock on every door in this building, and you'll get the same answer. Client confidentiality is absolute. You have no idea the cases I deal with. If I cave in to you, the entire system crumbles."

Jill speaks, ice in her tone. "We understand your position, but you need to understand ours. We are attempting to prevent two serial killers from killing more innocent people. All we are looking for are the names of the adopting families. We will follow up with them, and your responsibility ends."

Fellows blinks. This is not his script. "The adoptions were handled by me, start to finish, but I'm telling you, that's not unusual. Turner, Baxter, and Fellows handled the majority of private adoptions in the state for over four decades."

Dirk's fingers drum on the desk, faster now. "So, you refuse to even look up the case numbers and tell us the last names of the families involved?"

The hesitation is fractional, but there. "All adoptions are different," Fellows says. "Some people want a child. Some people want a secret. That's all I'm at liberty to say."

"Doesn't it bother you," says Jill, "that these two young boys you placed may be serial killers?"

Fellows laughs, the kind that bounces off hard surfaces. "I don't track what happens to my clients after the ink dries. But if you're suggesting I ran some kind of baby mill for future criminals, that's a new one."

Dirk's eyes are flat. "We're suggesting you had a hand in separating a set of siblings, and that separation is now at the root of a string of violent deaths."

The color drains from Fellows' cheeks. He shifts back in the chair, as if the desk might lose its magic. "If you're done accusing me of conspiracy, I have appointments waiting."

Dirk's frustration cracks the veneer. "We're not done. Give us the names or at least point us to the agency that finalized the records."

Fellows glances at Jill, then back at Dirk. "That information is sealed and is under lock and key. Code changes every day. Only the partners can authorize access to the sealed files, and my partners will not violate the seal either."

Dirk stands, chair protesting against the antique rug. "We'll be back," he says, his voice like a closing argument.

Jill rises too, her eyes lingering on Fellows a beat longer. "You could save lives by doing the right thing."

Fellows' smile is ugly. "You want to save lives, Agent? Try focusing on the ones you can reach."

He leans over, opens a leather-bound planner, and begins writing, as if they are no longer in the room.

Dirk and Jill exit, their silence a bunker against the cheap finality of the exchange. They make it halfway to the lobby before Jill murmurs, "You were about to jump that desk."

"I was about to break his nose," Dirk responds.

"Let's see if Spinella and the U.S. Attorney have had better luck with a judge," says Jill.

At the reception, the perfectly coiffed receptionist smiles again, but this time the whites of her eyes are wider, and she doesn't ask if they'll be needing another appointment.

They walk out together into the hall, both blinking against the real world after the shadowbox of law.

Chapter Thirty-Seven

They are almost to the elevator when a man in a starched button-down, his tie a little too wide, his smile laminated, cuts them off with a digital clipboard.

"Sorry, Agents," he says, "but Mr. Fellows' office asks for contact cards for all visitors. For the record." His eyes dart from Jill's badge to Dirk's face and back, cataloguing and cross-referencing.

Jill slides her Bureau ID card from her pocket and flips it with a practiced snap. "Special Agent Quarters. My card is electronic." She taps the badge on the clipboard, which pings and logs her data.

Dirk does the same, but when the clipboard's screen glitches, he simply takes the pen and signs his name on the blank. The secretary looks offended but accepts the gesture. "Thank you, Agents. Please let us know if we can be of further assistance."

They push past him, through the wide lobby, and out the black walnut doors. Outside, the day is dazzling, the wind slicing their faces like a warning. Dirk heads directly for the Bureau-issued SUV, clicks the unlock, and slides into the passenger seat, letting the air inside push the last of the law-office stench out of his nose.

Jill starts the engine, turns the heater to low, and says, "That was a total waste."

"Possibly," he replies

He pulls out his phone, thumbs through his

messages, and frowns. There in his inbox is a new email, time-stamped two minutes ago, the sender unknown. The subject line is "You Need These." No text, just a PDF attachment: "Gormley_Adoptions.pdf."

He opens the file. Jill's eyes are on the road, but her voice is sharp. "What's wrong?"

Dirk's jaw flexes. "We just got a break." He holds the phone so she can see the first page, two names, both highlighted: Freemont, Grand Junction, Colorado. Walker, Aurora, Colorado. Below is the birth mother's full name: Stephanie Gormley.

"Someone just gave us the answers," says Dirk.

Jill's expression goes from exasperated to electric. "Do you trust it?"

"I trust what I see," Dirk says. "And I trust Fellows is an asshole, but not a fool. Someone in that office just saved us a month of subpoenas."

Dirk quickly forwards the email to Carl with a note: **Carl, this is all we got. Have the team track the names and see if we can find these people.**

He turns to Jill. "Head to the field office. We need to mobilize everyone on this now."

"Already on it." She puts the SUV into gear, wheels squealing as she carves a hard right out of the lot.

On the drive, Dirk keeps the phone in his palm like a lucky token. He rereads the note. His head buzzes with the beat of adrenaline and the certainty that every second lost is another victim.

At the FBI field office, they barely park before Dirk is out of the car and inside, badge already out for the front desk. Jill follows, cutting through the cubicles to where the case team is already assembling around the war room's whiteboard.

Carl is at the front, hair even more chaotic than usual, fingers tapping a caffeine-rattled rhythm on his iPad. He looks up as Dirk and Jill enter.

"Got your email," Carl says. "We found a Freemont Family in Grand Junction. William and Elizabeth, six kids. We don't know if they are the right Freemonts, but you didn't give us a lot to work with. Walker is a little harder. There are several Walker families in Aurora, and we have no idea if they still live there. This is going to take some time."

"Run a criminal background check on the Freemonts and see what clicks," says Dirk.

A few minutes later, Carl steps into Dirk's office. "I ran the Freemonts. Clean as they come. Nothing criminal or civil, and no parking tickets. Nothing controversial on social media. She's the PTA president; they own their home, and go to church every Sunday. He coaches youth basketball. And they are very active in the adoption community."

"Any history of violence?" asks Jill.

"None on paper," says Carl.

Dirk's knuckles pop as he fists his hands. "Let's plan to go see the Freemonts?"

Jill nods and heads for her office; Carl heads back to the bullpen.

It's late in the afternoon when Carl steps into Jill's office. "We might have a line on Walker."

Jill looks up from her computer.

"We've been calling every Walker we can find in Aurora. One agent spoke with an elderly woman who told him that her daughter has an adopted son. Her daughter's name is Lyndsey Walker, and her son's name is Calvin."

"Do the daughter or the son still live in the area?" asks Jill.

"The lady hasn't heard from her adopted grandson in twenty-five years. The daughter is serving a nickel at the Colorado State Women's prison."

Jill stands and indicates to Carl to follow her. She heads for Dirk's office, where Dirk is talking with Spinella. They stop talking when she enters, and she has Carl repeat the information.

"We need to get someone to talk to her. She might know where her son is," says Spinella. He looks at Dirk and Jill. "Since you already planned to take the FBI jet to Grand Junction, you guys follow up with the Freemonts. I'll send another team down to the prison to talk to Walker."

Spinella steps out of the office and heads for the bullpen. Jill heads for her office to grab her go-bag and meets Dirk at the elevator. They head for Centennial Airport, outside Denver. Jill parks the SUV, and they walk into the Fixed Base Operator (FBO), badge their way through security, and walk towards the FBI jet sitting on the tarmac.

They board the jet. The engines throb, and within minutes they're slicing west toward Grand Junction, the setting sun flashing off the wings. Dirk holds the case folder, but his mind is elsewhere. He sees the crosshatch scars, the spiral signatures, the moments where the past and present blur into one another.

Jill watches him from across the aisle. "We'll get them."

Dirk nods but doesn't answer.

Chapter Thirty-Eight

The subdivision rises in a series of right-angled crescents, each one mapped to the horizon with uncanny precision. Grand Junction does not do grandeur; its houses squat low and square, hedges pruned to precise geometry, and driveways so spotless they echo with the memory of a thousand power-washings. At 9:01 a.m., the air smells of rain and juniper mulch. Dirk guides the rental, an off-white Toyota that still off-gasses new plastic, past a gauntlet of minivans before sliding it up to the curb in front of the Freemont home.

He kills the engine and glances sidelong at Jill. "You ready?"

Jill already has her badge in hand. "You're the one with the existential investment," she says. "Just follow my lead and don't overreact. I want to keep this low-key in case they are in contact with their son."

Dirk feigns a smile, but his eyes go to the house. Single-story, river-rock trim, with a roof so recent it hasn't faded from its manufactured blue. The front yard is terraced with railroad ties, spring flowers poking their green heads through the mulch. Nearest the porch, a holly bush is trimmed to a sphere, flanking a blue-and-gold sign that reads As For Me and My House, We Will Serve the Lord. Joshua 24:15.

The front door is painted red, no chips or fade. Above the knocker hangs a wooden plaque: THE FREEMONT FAMILY. Dirk takes this in and notes the slight leftward tilt, the sign of a recent re-hanging.

They cross the sidewalk and mount the steps. Jill hits the bell twice, sharply, and the echo is swallowed by a shuffle.

It opens less than two inches at first; the chain is engaged. A woman's face, cheeks pale as typing paper, peers through the gap. Her hair is a storm of tight brown curls, streaked gray but not unkempt. Her eyes land on Jill's badge, then flick to Dirk's.

"Elizabeth Freemont?" Jill asks.

The woman opens the door wider; the chain falls with a practiced motion. For half a second, she says nothing, only gapes at Dirk, mouth twitching as if prepping for a scream or a laugh.

"Good morning," Jill says, extending her hand. "Special Agent Quarters, this is my partner, Special Agent Trainor, FBI."

Dirk watches the muscles of the woman's face tense as a tremor starts at the jawline and works down her neck. For a split second, her gaze fixes on Dirk and does not let go.

Elizabeth's hands hover uncertainly, then she wipes her palm on the hem of her sweater and offers it to Jill. "Of course. You're here about…" She seems to lose the sentence, eyes flicking again to Dirk's face.

Jill glances at her partner, then back to Elizabeth. "We're following up on a cold case with possible connections to your son. Is your husband available to join us?"

Elizabeth's voice is thin, the Colorado edge erased by decades of vigilance. "May I ask?" The question fades, replaced by a look so soft it seems rehearsed for funerals or hospital beds. She turns to Dirk, and now the words land: "Have we met?"

"I don't think so, ma'am."

Elizabeth let the door open wider, her left hand going to the edge for support. She's maybe sixty, her body still holding onto its former speed, but her posture is brittle. She does not look away from Dirk.

Behind her, a man appears in the hallway. He's older, tall, his hair combed flat and neat, and his shirt is pressed into perfect tucks. He surveys the visitors with confidence so manufactured it almost squeaks.

"Bill," she says, voice wavering. "It's the FBI. They want to talk to us."

Bill gives a single, precise nod, as if every federal agent is a Jehovah's Witness who needs polite but absolute managing. "Of course," he says. "Please come in."

He takes his wife's elbow gently, guiding her back a half step, then motions Dirk and Jill through the entry. The inside is a time capsule of a different, more careful decade. The hallway walls are lined with 5x7s in mismatched frames, kids in various stages of toothlessness, graduation photos, church pageants, and two wedding portraits, all shot under the same relentless mall studio lighting. A brass cross hangs on the wall, so polished it casts rainbow blurs on the opposite wall.

Elizabeth floats ahead of them, her walk a practiced hover that keeps a foot of buffer between her body and any fixed object. She leads them past the family photo wall, slowing only to glance at a particular frame: a grainy image of six children, three girls, three boys, clustered in front of a forest green minivan. The entire family mid-laugh, eyes crinkled and wild with sun. Dirk watches her, notes the little recoil every time she looks at him.

The living room is staged for guests. There's a gas fireplace flickering under a white stone mantel, upon which rest seven photo frames (one with a crack in the glass, but the photo undisturbed), three porcelain angels, and a stylized wooden cross painted in gold leaf. On the wall above is a sampler stitched with Bless This Home And All Who Enter. The furniture is beige, the rug a cream-and-slate grid, every magazine on the coffee table squared up to the edges. Yet for all its order, the place feels lived in; there is a stack of crossword puzzle books by the armchair and an afghan half-crocheted over the couch's arm.

William directs the agents to the couch with a palm-down gesture, then takes the armchair across, leaving Elizabeth to stand behind his shoulder, hands clasped so tight her knuckles are translucent.

"Thank you for your time," Jill says. She sits first, a legal pad open on her lap, a pen uncapped and at the ready.

Dirk follows suit, perching at the couch's edge, elbows braced on knees. He takes in the details, the layered scent of citrus furniture polish and cheap incense, the way the morning sun catches the gold leaf of the cross and reflects onto the wall in trembling bands.

"You adopted a baby boy on March 31, 1984. Is that correct?" asks Jill.

Elizabeth looks at William. "That adoption was private. How do you know about that?" asks William.

"You said this was about a crime. Has James done something wrong?" asks Elizabeth.

Jill smiles. "Ma'am, this will go better if I ask the questions first. Your son's name is James?"

Elizabeth looks like she's been slapped. "Yes, James. James Aaron Freemont. He was our second adoption."

Jill nods as she writes. "And what does your son do for a living?"

"The last we heard," says William. "He was working as a junior engineer. We have no idea whether he still does that. We don't hear from James as much as we'd like. He worked for an architecture firm in Denver, but that was right after he graduated from UCLA. We haven't seen him in twenty years." He says this as if it is both a badge of pride and an ache he dare not show.

Elizabeth tucks a stray curl behind her ear, the hand trembling so hard it grazes her cheek. "Is James in some kind of trouble?"

"We are early in this investigation," Jill says. "Right now, it's just a routine background check. We wanted to get a sense of the man from the people who raised him." She lets the line hang, inviting them to fill the vacuum.

William smiles, but the eyes stay cool. "You'll find

James is as solid as they come. Never even got a parking ticket."

Jill glances at Dirk, then returns her focus to the Freemonts. "If you don't mind, we'd like to look at some photos of James through the years. It helps us build the timeline."

Elizabeth moves quickly, almost tripping over the rug as she goes to the bookshelf and brings back a single, worn photo album. She offers it to Jill, but her eyes stay on Dirk.

"You look just like him," she says suddenly, her voice a whisper. "It's the chin and the eyes."

Dirk blinks once, twice, then forces a smile. "People say that to me a lot. I must have one of those faces."

Jill opens the album. Every page is carefully assembled, each photo backed by themed paper and annotated in looping cursive. There are photos of James as a child, a sullen tween, and a letter-jacketed teenager with a shock of brown hair and an easy smile. The eyes are indeed blue, but the set of the jaw and the intensity of the gaze are Dirk's own, reflected and refracted through decades and DNA.

"Do you have any recent photos?" Jill asks.

Elizabeth bites her lip. "No, I'm sorry." She retrieves a picture from the mantel, a family portrait in front of a heavy pine tree, six children now grown and scattered across the country, four of them present, James standing on the edge, his hand touching the shoulder of a younger brother. He wears a button-down shirt, jeans and a smile that never quite reaches the corners of his mouth.

William explains, "Our other son lives in Portland; one daughter is in Chicago. The holidays are the only time we're all together."

Dirk studies the photo, noting the body language, James apart, stiff, with eyes a thousand miles away.

Jill sets the photo back on the mantel, careful to keep it at the same angle. "And your relationship with James is?" She lets the sentence fragment, inviting truth or fiction.

Elizabeth's hands twist the hem of her sweater. "He's a good son. Very smart. Never gave us any real trouble. He was a National Merit Scholar, you know. Got a full ride to UCLA." She hesitates, eyes going to Dirk again. "He was a little quiet after college, but we chalked it up to the stress of starting a career."

William's tone shifts, a touch defensive. "We did everything by the book. He never wanted for anything. If there was a problem, it didn't start here."

Dirk's voice is steady, neutral. "Did you ever notice anything…unusual? Any changes in his personality?"

Elizabeth shakes her head instantly, but William answers with a shade less conviction. "He became more private. Moved to the city, took a job we didn't understand, but that's how kids are now."

The conversation stills for a moment. Dirk studies the bookshelf. Besides family photo albums, there's a cluster of Bibles, two volumes of Reader's Digest Condensed Books, and a row of scrapbooks with neatly printed spine labels. Above them, a single hand-carved angel is suspended from the ceiling, wings outspread, frozen in the moment before flight.

Elizabeth finally moves to the couch, sitting at the farthest end from Dirk, hands still trembling. "Is he okay?"

Jill leans forward, softening her posture. "We believe so, ma'am. We're just being thorough. The government requires it."

William relaxes. "That's a relief."

Dirk watches Elizabeth watching him, and for a brief instant, it feels as if he's looking at a future that might have been, if his life had twisted just a degree left or right. He catalogues the tremor in her hands, the haunted pride in William's voice, and files them away for later.

"Is there anything else we can help you with?" William asks.

Jill raises her pen. "Just a few more details, and then we'll be out of your hair."

The fireplace ticks as it cycles, and in the silence, the cross above the mantel seems to catch more of the morning sun than it should.

Chapter Thirty-Nine

Elizabeth's composure disintegrates in increments, each new question eroding the careful layer she's lacquered onto her face. After a silence too long to pass for mere pause, she snaps her fingers once and says, "Oh! Would you like some tea?" as if they've come for a book club and not for an investigation.

She leaves the room, the hem of her skirt flapping around her calves. The rattle of cups and the tinkle of a spoon carry in from the kitchen. William sits rigid in his armchair, legs crossed, and forearms pressed tight to the arms of the chair. He looks at the table's edge, as if the next move belongs to him and not the visitors.

Jill fills the space with a soft "lovely home," and William nods like a man forced to listen to compliments he doesn't need.

Dirk's eyes roam to the mantel, the albums and the spectrum of children on the walls. There's a whiplash sense of continuity and fracture in the family photos. First, the baby portraits, none alike, and no two with the same features. Next, the lineup at Disney, kids with the same last name but not the same skin, all beaming in the anesthetic sun. By the time you hit the senior portraits, the unity comes in the clothes: the same photographer, the same background, and the same practiced hope in each smile.

Elizabeth returns with a tray, a pot, four cups, a sugar bowl and a half-sleeve of store-bought butter cookies. She sets it on the glass-topped coffee table with both hands, then stands behind the tray, unsure whether to serve or to let them. William saves her by lifting his own cup, pouring for himself, then nodding to Jill to go ahead. The rhythm of hospitality is its own kind of script.

Elizabeth sits between William and the guests. Her cup clinks twice against the saucer before she dares speak again.

"It's strange," she says, looking not at Dirk but past him. "How people from the same family end up looking so much alike. Even when there's no blood."

Dirk stirs a sugar cube into his tea. "I wouldn't know. I was adopted, too."

"Oh!" Elizabeth's face softens, the nerves massaged by instant commonality. "Isn't that funny? James never met anyone with his history, either. Not really. It was always a story we had to explain repeatedly." She sips, lips trembling. "But that's what families do, isn't it? They rewrite you in."

Jill lets the words settle, then steers back to the case. "How would you describe James as a child?"

William answers first, the words clipped as if pre-drafted. "Driven. Meticulous. Never lost his temper, even when the other kids got into it. Sometimes a little solitary. But always…present."

Elizabeth picks up: "He was gifted. He could draw and build. He took apart our coffee maker when he was five and put it back together with no leftover parts. School was easy for him. Social things, less so."

Dirk's voice, measured: "Did he ever mention his birth parents?"

"No," Elizabeth says. "No, the records were sealed at the request of the birth mother."

"Any idea why she wanted them sealed?" asked Jill.

"No," says William. "We asked the attorney once, but he wouldn't say much."

"Did James ever try to find his birth mother?" Jill asks.

William's gaze sharpens on his wife, but she pushes forward. "He tried in college. I know he called the agency, maybe even went back to Denver General, but nothing ever came of it. It's all closed, you know. By law."

"How was he during college?" asks Jill.

"He went to UCLA," says Elizabeth. "He was a double major, Mechanical Engineering and Architecture. He said he liked the lines of the old buildings, said they made more sense than people did." She stops, as if she's said too much.

William uncrosses and re-crosses his legs, the movement loud in the small room. "James worked hard. Paid his way with scholarships. He never visited home much after freshman year, but we figured that was normal for his age."

"Did he have any close friends?" asks Jill.

"He had a girlfriend for a while. A lovely girl from his freshman writing seminar. They were inseparable," replies Elizabeth.

William's jaw clenches. "Until she wasn't."

The room cools perceptibly. Even the fireplace

seems to hush. Jill lets the silence stretch, then asks, "Was there an incident?"

Elizabeth's voice thins to a filament. "She was murdered, you see, during their second year. They called it a cult thing. The papers said it had satanic overtones. Her parents went on the news. It was…horrible."

Jill writes a note, head dipped. "Do you remember her name?"

"Rachel. Rachel Ruther," says Elizabeth. "I'm not sure if the last name is right, but—" She snaps her fingers. "She wanted to be a poet."

Dirk's pen freezes on his pad. He doesn't look up.

William's voice is the voice of a man who has practiced keeping emotion at bay. "It nearly broke him. I'd never seen him that way. He was quieter, but also harder. If he didn't have school, I think he might have…" He doesn't finish.

Elizabeth jumps in: "We tried to get him counseling. He wouldn't go."

Jill's question is gentle: "Did he ever mention wanting revenge? Was he angry with anyone?"

Elizabeth looks at William, then at the cross above the mantel. "Never. He just disappeared after graduation. Started over. Occasionally, he'd send a Christmas card. Never with a return address."

Dirk waits for the opening, then stands and moves to the mantel. He picks up the family portrait, six children arrayed before the blue-and-silver church background. James stands, one foot slightly ahead of the other, his hands balled into fists and held behind his back. The eyes in the photo are nearly the same shade as Dirk's, but the mouth is set in a line with no give.

Dirk studies the picture, then slides his phone from his jacket and, under the cover of his body, snaps a photo of the portrait.

Jill watches him, then asks, "So you don't have a current address for James? We'll need to meet him in person for the background check."

Elizabeth hesitates; her face is caught in a vice between pride and dread. "No. Just the old one, but that must be twenty years old," she says.

Elizabeth stands again, this time heading for a roll-top desk near the dining room. She rifles through a drawer, producing a notepad and pen. Her handwriting is small and spidery, each loop forced to stay between the lines. She writes out the address, hesitates, then tears off the page and brings it to Jill.

"It was an apartment complex in Littleton."

Jill takes the note, folding it carefully. "Thank you. This will help a lot."

Elizabeth lingers, hands shaking so much that she presses the notepad to her chest to keep it from showing. "Will you…will you tell us if there's anything wrong? With James?"

Dirk meets her gaze for the first time. "We will. I promise."

William nods, as if a transaction has been completed.

Elizabeth sits again, this time not on the edge but collapsed into the cushions. Her cup is empty. She stares at the blue rim of the China and says, "You look so much like him."

"So, you've said," Dirk replies.

Quiet falls over the room, thick and oddly peaceful. In the silence, Jill closes her notebook and stands. "Thank you for the tea, Mrs. Freemont, Mr. Freemont. We appreciate your help."

William rises, extending his hand. Dirk shakes it; his grip is bone-hard. William says nothing further. Elizabeth only watches. He walks them to the door and steps outside, out of earshot of Elizabeth.

"He's in some kind of serious trouble, isn't he?" asks William

Dirk looks at Jill, then at William. "Thank you for your time, sir. If we need anything else, we will let you know."

The agents exit, guided by the fragrance of holly and the glint of the Joshua plaque.

Outside, the air is sharper. Jill tucks the notepaper into her coat, then looks sidelong at Dirk.

"Are you okay?"

He shrugs. "Not my weirdest family reunion."

She cracks the barest smile. "You ready to meet the last of the triplets?"

Dirk looks at his phone, at the photo he's just taken, at the line of the jaw and the light in the eyes.

"Let's go find out," he says.

They walk down the drive, past the coldly precise hedges, neither looking back.

They don't talk until they're in the rental, doors closed, the world outside glassed off by weatherstripping and the whisper of the car's heater. For a long minute, neither speaks. Jill unlocks her phone and scrolls for the Bureau's encrypted line.

She's the first to break: "We need Carl to run that address." Her thumbs move with sniper accuracy, typing in the digits from Elizabeth's note.

Dirk pulls out his own phone, clicks into the photo gallery, and brings up the mantel shot. He zooms in on James, one finger dragging the face to maximum size. He studies every millimeter: the way the smile is calibrated, the way the hair is parted so perfectly that it could be drawn on with a marker, and the angle of the ears. But mostly, he stares at the eyes, which catch even the low-wattage light and bounces it back like a warning.

Jill dials a number, puts her phone on speaker, and holds up a finger. "Carl. It's us. I just texted you an old address. I need you to check it out. The suspect's name is James, James Aaron Freemont. That was confirmed by his parents, who hadn't seen him in years. He's a mechanical engineer, so you might find him through some professional organizations and licensing authorities. See what the team can find out about him. Let's also make sure we don't do anything that might spook him."

Dirk leans into the centerline, drops his phone to his

lap, and says, "Carl. Can you also pull any police reports from UCLA between 2000 and 2005? I want everything you can find on the murder of Rachel Ruther. Not sure of the last name, but start there. James's mother said something about a satanic cult angle."

A hesitation on the line, then: "Copy that. Whoa, you think this is linked?"

Dirk shrugs, though Carl can't see it. "It's a pattern. I want to see how it fits."

Carl's chair squeals over the phone line. "I'll see what I can find before you get back."

Jill pockets her phone and stares ahead, hands still on the wheel though they haven't moved. "You don't really buy the satanic angle, do you?"

"Not sure," he says. "But if the trauma was real, it's a vector. If the trauma was staged, it's a signature."

Jill looks over. "You ever get the feeling people like the Freemonts are one heartbreak away from living in the dark?"

"I get the feeling they already are. They just don't look at it," says Dirk.

Jill shakes her head, amusement, and sadness tangled. "What do you see in that photo?"

Dirk taps the phone screen, where James stands so precisely, so separated from the rest. "He's isolated in every shot, always one step off the family axis. Look at the posture. His left foot pointed away, left shoulder pulled back. Classic exit body language. Even as a child, he's scanning for the escape route."

"And the parents?"

"Blind to it. Or in denial," he answers. "Either way, they stopped reaching him long before he left."

They fall silent as Jill pulls away from the curb. The houses blur by, then the highway, the clouds scudding low and fat with threat. It's not until they pass the turnoff for the airport that Dirk speaks again.

"You think the Freemonts ever guessed what their son might become?" His voice is softer than before.

"I think the father knows something is up, but is afraid to say," answers Jill.

Dirk nods, more to himself than to her. He flicks through the next photo, the one Elizabeth said looked just like him. He brings it close, inspects the line of the jaw, the symmetry of the cheekbones, and the slant of the eyes. It's a close match, a funhouse mirror running straight through thirty years and several hundred miles.

He puts the phone down and folds his hands together, knuckles interlaced so tight the bones pop.

Chapter Forty

The Colorado State Women's Prison is visible a mile before you reach the actual turnoff, even in the morning sun. The compound sprawls across a featureless valley, ringed by double chain-link fences and a haze of razor wire that glitters like wet tinsel above the perimeter. The main building, blocky and windowless, hunches behind a parade of blue-and-white Department of Corrections pickups. At this hour, the parking lot is three-quarters empty, as if the architecture itself repels visitors.

Special Agent Tom Lawson drives the Bureau SUV slowly, scanning every sign and traffic mirror on the approach. He's in his late forties, squared off at the shoulders, with hair cut to strict Bureau regulations and a face that seems both alert and exhausted. His partner, Tanya Delgado, rides shotgun with a legal pad already balanced on her knee. She's a decade younger, short dark bob, and eyes that take in everything but give nothing back. She does not fidget or chew pens, but her jaw twitches every time the vehicle goes over a pothole.

They park near the main gate, directly under a surveillance camera dome. Lawson kills the engine and surveys the security arrangement.

"Zero sightlines," he observes, nodding toward the entrance. "You'd need a tank to get in or out."

Delgado doesn't look up from her pad. "Or a visitor pass and some charm."

They collect their credentials, pass through the visitor's entrance and make their way to the security kiosk. The man in the glass booth, face scarred with what looks like acne and boredom, checks their badges before buzzing them into the foyer.

First, the security theater. They each surrender their sidearms, Glock for him, SIG for her, and place their phones and wallets in separate metal lockboxes. Next, a female guard with the build of a linebacker puts them through a standard pat-down, efficient but thorough, then waves them through the metal detector. The detector pings on Lawson's belt, and again on the clasp of Delgado's watch, but nothing triggers a pause. The guard hands them clear plastic visitor badges.

"You're here for the Walker interview?" she asks.

"That's right. We called in the notice yesterday. Any issues?" asks Lawson.

The guard grunts. "She's expecting you, but she's not happy about it."

"Was she ever?"

The guard almost smiles, then gestures at the next door. "Follow me. No sudden moves, and keep your hands visible at all times."

They pass through two more layers of electronically controlled gates, each with its own industrial buzz and heavy-thud closure. The corridor between checkpoints is painted the same pastel institutional green, but the cinderblock and fluorescent glare make it feel like a walk through the world's longest urinal. At each corner, another camera or mirrored bubble tracks their passage.

On the left, a series of visitation pods, glass-fronted, with bench seating and hard-wired telephones. A pair of visitors in street clothes (old woman, young man) are hunched over phones, faces pressed to the glass. The woman on the other side wears orange and white. Her hair is pulled tight to her skull, and her eyes range from dead to defiant.

They reach the administrative hallway, which is slightly warmer and smells faintly of disinfectant and floor wax. The guard ushers them into a waiting room with a vending machine and a row of battered plastic chairs, then leaves them with a final, "Someone will bring her down in ten."

Lawson stands. Delgado sits and crosses her ankles, her hands folded over the legal pad.

He leans against the wall and lets his eyes close. "How do you want to play it?"

Delgado smiles. "I'm good cop and you're bored cop. That usually gets them talking."

He opens one eye. "She's a career manipulator. You saw the notes?"

"Five priors, four for fraud or property, one for 'malicious communications, whatever that is. Also, grand theft and prostitution. The woman gets around."

Lawson nods. "She's going to try to play us."

"Let her," says Delgado. "We need her scared enough to cough up what she knows."

The door opens. A different guard, a woman in her

twenties, with a red ponytail and a sleeve tattoo, waves them out. "The interview is set up in D-3. Leave your bags."

They follow, past admin offices and a rec room where a dozen inmates watch TV under the disinterested gaze of two armed guards. Every sound, every footstep, every scrape of plastic, bounces off the concrete. The air is always a little too cold.

At the far end, another set of gates. Beyond them, a smaller, windowless chamber with only a steel table bolted to the floor and three lightweight plastic chairs. No cushions, nothing that could be weaponized. On the wall, a single two-way mirror, rimed with grime.

The guard gestures at the chairs. "She'll be here in two. Don't touch her, don't hand her anything, don't let her out of your sight."

Lawson nods and takes the chair with a view of the door. Delgado sits opposite, legal pad at the ready.

The door swings shut. The lock hums and then thunks.

They wait in silence. The only sounds are the fluorescent buzz overhead, and the echo of a distant door closing. The room smells of bleach, old sweat and something faintly metallic.

Lawson surveys the table. Someone has scratched "CUNT" into the steel with a pen or a key. He traces the word with a finger, then looks up at Delgado.

She says, "Ready to meet the mother?"

"She'd better not smoke," says Lawson.

Delgado laughs. "They don't allow it anymore. Too many fires."

He grins, but it's a dry, joyless thing.

She shifts in her seat. "I want to get her on the timeline first. If she's protecting him, she'll slip up."

"We'll see," says Lawson.

Outside, footsteps approach, slow and irregular. Through the crack under the door, a pair of green flip-flops, prison-issue, thin-soled, stained, pause, shuffle, then square up to enter.

Delgado's fingers flex on the legal pad.

Lawson folds his hands and stares at the two-way mirror, seeing only the faintest outline of his own jaw, ghosted over the green paint. A key rattles and the lock disengages.

"Showtime," he says.

The door swings open. Lyndsey Walker steps in, escorted by a corrections officer with a mullet and a smoker's mustache. Walker is a slab-shouldered woman in her late fifties or early sixties, though her skin is tight and pocked in the way of someone who never saw moisturizer or sunscreen. Her hair is stringy and gray, plastered behind her ears. The jumpsuit is regulation orange, short-sleeved, with a patch above the left breast: WALKER, L.

She sizes up the room instantly, one, two, three, and snorts. "You got smokes?"

"No smoking in the interview room," says Delgado.

She shrugs like this is just another morning and

plops into the chair, planting her forearms on the table and spreading her fingers wide. The guard locks the handcuffs to a bolt welded to the table. Lyndsey's arms are a horror show of old and new tattoos: snakes, barbed wire, crossed-out names, and a faded horseshoe. Her hands are gnarled and pale, a checkerboard of healed and recent scars. Her nails are bitten to the quick, stained yellow.

She leans forward. "Let's make it fast. I've got a class after this, and if I miss it, they take my TV time for a week."

The corrections officer lingers in the doorway until Lawson nods her off.

Delgado flips her legal pad open and studies Lyndsey for a full three seconds before speaking. "We're not with the State PD, Ms. Walker. We're with the FBI. You know why we're here?"

Lyndsey shrugs, but her eyes narrow just enough to show the game is on. "I assume it's about something else I did wrong, but federal. That's heavy."

"It's not about you. We're here about your son," says Delgado.

"What the fuck did he do now?" asks Lyndsey. "He's old enough to handle his own shit."

"We're interested in your relationship with your son," says Lawson. "Start at the beginning."

Lyndsey barks a laugh so abruptly it bounces off the cinderblock. "I knew it. I fucking knew it. What's he done now, kill a congressman or something?"

Delgado ignores the bait. "Let's stick to basics.

What is your son's name?"

"Calvin Randolph Walker," says Lyndsey. "He was born March 17, 1984, and I adopted him while I was living in Denver, Colorado."

"You were the sole guardian?" asks Delgado.

"Damn straight. Back then, you could get a baby with less paperwork than it takes to rent a car. My dad paid for it. I was twenty-four. I had a good job, a place of my own, and no husband. He was older than the other kids I visited with, and he had been shuffled through a bunch of foster homes. I guess I felt sorry for the little shit."

"Did you ever have any contact with the birth mother?" asks Delgado.

Lyndsey picks at her thumbnail. "Never. I wasn't interested in meeting her, and besides, she was long gone."

"What kind of job did you have?" asks Lawson.

She shifts, leans back, relishing the question. "I was an executive secretary at my dad's law firm. Three years later, my old man retires, and I got fired. After that, things went sideways."

"What was Calvin like as a child?" asks Delgado.

"Hyper as hell. Couldn't sit still, wouldn't sleep unless I put him in the swing or drove him around the block forty times. Smart, too. Smarter than me, by a mile. I used to hide the remote, and he'd find it every time."

"Did he have behavioral problems?" asks Delgado.

Lyndsey laughs, not kindly. "Who didn't in my family?"

Delgado: "You lost your job. What happened next?"

Her shoulders rise, then fall. "We bounced around. I started drinking, got into it with the neighbors, the landlords, whoever pissed me off that day. I had boyfriends. Most of them were assholes, but Calvin needed a man in the house. Or that's what I thought."

"You're saying the boyfriends abused him?" asks Delgado.

She nods, staring at her own hands. "They hit me, too. Sometimes more. After a while, Calvin just… stopped talking. He wouldn't answer the door, wouldn't go to school. Started breaking things on purpose."

"When did you notice he was… different?"

Lyndsey chews her lip, thinking. "He was always different. But after the last one, his name was Mark; he was a drywaller and Calvin was thirteen, I think. One day, I found him in the kitchen with the cat. He was petting her gently, but the look in his eyes showed he was gone somewhere else. And the cat knew it, too. She peed on the linoleum."

"Did Calvin ever hurt animals?" asks Lawson.

"Never," says Lyndsey, quick and defensive. "That's not what I'm saying. He just had that…look. Like he saw things nobody else did."

Delgado scribbles a note, then sets her pen down. "Why did you leave Denver?"

Lyndsey grins, a dry, dead thing. "Too many bad memories. I scraped together enough to move us to Arizona. Phoenix, then Tempe, and then Peoria."

"You brought Calvin with you each time?"

She fixes him with a gaze that is half challenge, half warning. "He was my son. I never let him out of my sight. Not until he turned eighteen and told me to fuck off."

"What happened then?" asks Delgado.

She shrugs, but the edges are sharper now. "He quit school. Moved in with some friends. I heard he went to trade school to become an electrician."

"You ever hear from him after he left?"

Lyndsey shakes her head, this time genuinely sad. "Not really. He'd call sometimes, say he was fine, then hang up. Last I heard he was working in Arizona."

"You never saw him again?" asks Delgado.

"Nope," she says. "Not since the day he left the apartment. What's this all about? Did he do something stupid?"

Chapter Forty-One

Delgado glances at her notes, then fixes Lyndsey with a stare. "We believe Calvin is connected to a series of homicides in both Colorado and Arizona. Does that surprise you?"

Lyndsey's mouth opens, then shuts. She snorts. "No. Not really."

Lawson's brows rise, and he lets the silence draw out.

Lyndsey finally cracks. "I mean, look. I love the kid, but he had a mean streak. He always did. He didn't start fights, but he finished them. Once a girl came to our door, bleeding from the nose. I asked her what happened. She said Calvin did it because she told him his shoes were ugly."

"He was violent?" asks Delgado.

"Sometimes. Never to me, but sometimes."

"Did he ever threaten you?" asks Lawson.

"No," she says again, almost indignant. "He was my son."

"What about your parents? Your family?" asks Delgado.

Lyndsey's jaw grinds. "Dead or lost. I was an only child. Dad drank himself to death after he retired, and Mom ran off with a yoga teacher. I raised myself."

Delgado shifts tactics, softens her tone. "It couldn't have been easy."

Lyndsey's face crumples, then hardens again. "Life is never easy, Agent. You get used to it or you die."

Lawson watches her, calculating. "Did you ever meet Calvin's birth family?"

"Hell no," says Lyndsey, a mix of pride and disdain. "It was a closed adoption. Money under the table. All I got was a name, Stephanie. Never even met her. Just signed the papers, and that was that."

Delgado jots this down, then glances at Lawson, who tilts his chin in the universal sign for go further.

"You mentioned boyfriends. Was there ever anyone who took a special interest in Calvin?"

Lyndsey blinks, then snorts. "Not like you're thinking. If anyone had tried, I'd have killed them myself. The guys would just beat him up sometimes. Nothing serious."

"Did he ever run with gangs, do drugs, anything like that?" asks Delgado.

Lyndsey barks a bitter laugh. "No, he thought gangs were for idiots. Plus, he was kind of antisocial. He didn't like most people. And he hated drugs. Hated them. Because of me, I guess."

"Because of you?" asks Lawson.

She stares at the green cinder block, seeing something far away. "I started using after we moved to Phoenix. Meth, mostly. A little heroin when I could get it. Calvin never touched the stuff. He hated the smell and hated the people I hung out with. I'd wake up, and he'd be gone for days, come back and not talk about it."

"Did you ever get clean?" asks Delgado.

Lyndsey rolls up the sleeve of her jumpsuit, shows the inside of her arm. It's a highway of collapsed veins and healed over tracks. "Four years now, thanks to these nice people," she says with an irony that could cut glass.

"Did he ever mention anyone from his past? Old friends, enemies?" asks Delgado.

"He wasn't a social kid. Not really," she says.

"You said Calvin got in fights, finished them. Any actual charges?"

She purses her lips, thinking. "Juvenile stuff. Shoplifting, mostly. Got caught a few times, but I talked them down to probation. He was too clever for the system, knew how to work the angles."

"But still in and out of trouble?" asks Delgado.

"Always. Once, I woke up in the middle of the night and he was gone. The next morning, cops bring him home. They caught him breaking into a neighbor's garage. He was eleven." She grins, the memory warm. "When the cops asked why, he said he wanted to see how their tools worked."

"Was that typical?" asks Lawson.

She shrugs. "Calvin's mind ran circles around most adults. But he couldn't hold a thought for long. He was always on to the next thing. Drove his teachers crazy, drove me crazy."

"Why did he quit school?" asks Lawson.

Lyndsey was quiet for a minute. "Kids thought he

did something bad. You know how cruel kids can be. He didn't want to deal with it."

"What didn't he want to deal with?" asks Lawson.

A couple of girls in his class were murdered in the woods behind the school following a football game. The kids said Cal was involved. They only said it because he was kind of strange and didn't hang with the cool kids. Cops looked at him, but nothing ever happened; but, the kids in school kept being cruel. He finally gave up."

"Did you believe he was capable of something like that?" asks Lawson.

She opens her mouth, then closes it, the truth churning for a full five seconds. "I could see it in him," she says finally, a hoarse whisper. "He had it. The thing. But he never let it show. Not to me, anyway."

"The thing?" asks Delgado.

Lyndsey looks up, meets her eye dead on. "He didn't have feelings the way you or I do. He understood what they were, but he didn't catch them. Like he was behind a sheet of glass."

"When did you see him last?" asks Lawson.

Lyndsey's tongue dabs at a split lip. "Twenty years ago. I moved back to Denver. He stayed in Arizona, or maybe California. On his last call, he told me he was working as an electrician. Union job, good pay. But it never lasted with him. I got arrested, did time, and by the time I got out, there was nothing. No letters, no calls. Like he dropped off the planet."

"Any history of mental illness?" asks Lawson.

She flashes a grin. "Who didn't in our neighborhood? No, not officially. Never got him diagnosed. I couldn't afford doctors."

"Any idea where he is now?" asks Delgado.

Lyndsey barks a laugh, ugly and dry. "If I knew, you'd owe me more than a cigarette. You can trade me a few days off this dump if I guess right."

Delgado doesn't blink. "We can't make deals, Ms. Walker."

She leans back, folding her arms. "I got nothing. Last I heard, he was in Arizona working construction. Or he's dead."

Lawson: "What would you do if you saw him again?"

The bravado cracks. Lyndsey folds into herself, her breathing sudden and ragged. She wipes her nose on her sleeve.

"I'd probably hug him," she says, voice nearly inaudible. "Or run."

"You think he could hurt you?" asks Delgado.

"Not unless he had to," she says.

There's a silence in the room, broken only by the fluorescent whine and the faint click of Delgado's pen.

Delgado looked at Lawson who nodded.

"Anything else you think we should know?" asks Delgado.

Lyndsey smiles, a slow, feral thing. "You're the Feds. You tell me."

Delgado and Lawson both sit in silence for a moment, as if measuring the distance between truth and performance.

Finally, Delgado says, "Thank you for your time, Ms. Walker."

Lawson bangs on the steel door and waits.

The guard unlocks the door and unlocks the cuffs from the bolt. He cuffs her hands behind her. Lyndsey stands, gives a theatrical bow. She turns at the door, looks back at the two agents.

"Hey," she says. "If you find him, tell him his mother is still alive. That'll piss him off."

The guard leads her away.

Lawson sits back, rubbing his eyes. "That was something."

"Yeah," says Delgado. "But we have his name and the info about his high school is verification that he was there."

He nods, and they wait for the all-clear to leave. The fluorescent buzz is louder than ever. The word "CUNT" seems to glow from the metal table.

They're out of the facility in under five minutes. The sun is still bright, but the air has cooled, and the parking lot is empty except for their black SUV. Lawson unlocks the doors, climbs in, and starts the engine, staring straight ahead. Delgado buckles up, sets her legal pad on the dash, and watches her partner.

Lawson exhales, long and hard. "You believe her?"

"Most of it."

He shifts the car into reverse. "If Calvin Walker is as smart as she says, he's already gone."

"Or he's waiting." says Delgado.

They drive in silence for the first few miles; the prison receding into the haze behind them. Just before the turnoff for the interstate, he taps Delgado on her arm.

"Call Carl. Tell him to run everything he can on Calvin Randolph Walker, last known in Arizona. Pull the entire work history, travel, credit, utilities, whatever he can shake out."

Delgado dials. The phone is answered on the first ring.

"Bunch here."

"Carl, it's Delgado. We need a full deep dive on Calvin Randolph Walker. Last known address was in Arizona, but he could be anywhere. We think he's operating solo but could have connections to construction or electrical contracting."

"Got it," says Carl. "Anything else?"

Delgado ends the call. Lawson drives with both hands on the wheel, his eyes fixed on the highway.

Delgado waits until they're at cruising speed, then says. "You think he's the one?"

"He checks all the boxes, and I think the issue at his high school with the dead girls is a clincher. We'll see what Trainor and Quarters think, but I think we've got some good info."

They drove in silence.

Chapter Forty-Two

The conference room in the Denver field office is a concrete tomb disguised as government efficiency. Fluorescent lights cast a blue haze over the table, flattening every face and document to the same dull shade. Case files sprawl across the Formica, loose photographs interleaved with forensics summaries, spreadsheets, annotated printouts, a diagram of the Grand Junction subdivision, and a trio of spiral cross crime scene blowups pinned to a warped whiteboard.

It's not even 7:00 a.m., and every chair is full. Lawson sits nearest the window, legs spread, one hand cupped over his phone like he's ready to leap up and respond to a raid call at any second. Delgado slouches next to him, her legal pad splayed and three pens arranged in color-coded order. Two Bureau analysts cradle mugs of instant coffee, trying to look as if they belong.

The war room's windows are blacked out with hastily tacked-up charts, incident maps and cell phone tower overlays. Carl Bunch sits at the conference table, his shirt sleeves rolled above the elbows, necktie stained by at least two different meals. He hunches over his laptop, fingers an indistinct blur on the keyboard, eyes darting between three open windows and a scrolling command line.

Dirk and Jill stand together. Dirk's suit is rumpled at the back from too many hours in a car; his tie is off-center and he's pale enough that the blue lighting makes his skin look waxy. Jill radiates kinetic energy.

Her hair is up and perfect. She has one hand on the folder and the other planted on her leg, a deliberate anchor.

At the center of it all, Anthony Spinella. He is a human tuning fork: arms crossed, tie loosened to the second button, and half-crescent lines stamped under both eyes. He doesn't waste words or energy, but there is a tension in his posture that suggests every cell is listening.

Jill breaks the standoff first.

"We interviewed the Freemonts in Grand Junction," she says. "Elizabeth and William, late fifties. They have six kids, all of whom are adopted. The subject of interest is their second son, James Aaron Freemont. Born March 1984, adopted at three weeks through a private agency."

She gestures to Dirk, who picks up the thread.

"James was a model student. National Merit Scholar and a UCLA-trained engineer. He lived at home until he was eighteen, then left for college and barely returned. Last known to be employed at Westward Structures, a boutique engineering firm in Denver. According to the parents, he severed contact years ago. The family is deeply religious, but James was not notably attached to the faith."

Dirk lays down the bio sheet with the photo of the Freemont living room visible underneath. "No known criminal activity. Nothing in the juvie records, nothing in local PD. There is, however, a suspicious link to a cold case in California." He waits for the click of pen on paper to subside. "James' girlfriend, Rachel Ruther, was murdered during their sophomore year. The crime scene had ritual elements, with alleged satanic overtones, as per local reporting. The file's been reclassified twice, but I suspect it's relevant. Carl is working on getting us a copy."

He stops. The room is silent except for a muffled cough from one analyst.

Spinella looks at Jill, then at Dirk, then says, "Any evidence James had contact with the other twin."

"None," says Jill. "No shared schools, no social overlaps. The adoptions were airtight. The only connection is the DNA."

Carl clicks a key on his laptop, and the wall monitor comes alive. The first image to appear is a color photo of James Freemont, cropped tight from a professional headshot. The resemblance to Dirk is chilling, though Freemont's jaw is wider and his smile practiced, less vulnerable. Dirk cringes. The caption reads: JAMES FREEMONT, PRINCIPAL ENGINEER, WESTWARD STRUCTURES.

"He owns the company now," Carl says, voice shaky with adrenaline. "Started as a junior, worked up to project lead in three years, bought out the senior partner's share last year. Lives in the Highlands and commutes to downtown Denver."

He taps again, bringing up a satellite map showing a street view of the neighborhood. The exterior of a stately brick house with neat hedges and a fire-red door is visible on the monitor. "He has a strong social media presence and is involved with several charities. He has no criminal record, nor has he been involved in any investigations."

Spinella enters quietly, seating himself at the mid-table with a low grunt. He doesn't ask for a summary; he just scans the screen, then shifts his gaze to Dirk, who stands half a pace behind Jill. Dirk's posture is a study in fixed calm, but his hands are in fists at his sides.

Carl, noting the tension, continues. "Now, the Walker side is trickier. Calvin has almost no social media presence. He has a checking and savings account at a local bank but has never taken out a loan. He has two credit cards in his name. I have another analyst checking the purchase history to see if we can connect him to any of the cold cases. His address is an apartment in Peoria, Arizona where he lived for the past ten years."

He clicks another button, and the screen now shows a mugshot-style photo of Calvin. The picture looks exactly like James Freemont except that his hair is cut short and he has a tattoo just visible under his left earlobe. "He's currently working as a foreman for a commercial electrical outfit. Current job is at a mall expansion in Scottsdale, where he started three months ago. No police record and a clean work history after graduating from the tech school."

Spinella makes a note, then tilts his chin toward Lawson.

"Walker interview," he says.

Lawson sits forward, elbows on the table, the skin at his temples tight. "We met Lyndsey Walker at the women's correctional facility in Florence. Early sixties, five-time repeat offender, tattoos up to her jawline. Raised Calvin solo, no father listed on any documents. She claims he was a handful from day one: behavioral issues, violent outbursts, problems with authority. He dropped out of school at eighteen and moved out at the same time. He worked odd jobs in the Phoenix area. Walker told us she had heard he went to trade school and became an electrician."

Delgado picks up seamlessly. "There was no warmth and no affection when she spoke about him. It was clear Lyndsey didn't care for Calvin much, except as a project or a grudge. She mentioned, unprompted, that the boy had a mean streak, her words, and that he acted spontaneously. Also, he was unusually smart, and never fit in. There were hints of trauma at home, abusive boyfriends, drugs, and the like, but nothing on record for institutionalization or therapy."

She glances at Dirk, then the room. "She said she always expected Calvin to turn up dead or in prison and didn't seem surprised we were asking. She told us he left school because some kids accused him of being involved in the murder of two high school girls in the woods after a football game. Sound familiar. She said the cops cleared him, but the kids still teased him. He couldn't deal with it and quit six months before graduation."

The room grew silent, and everyone looked at the crime scene photos on the board of the first Arizona kill. A soft murmur grew until Spinella slapped his hand on the table. Spinella leans forward, elbows on the table, and there's a ripple along the edge as the agents adjust in unison.

"So, we've got two adults, same birthdate, both with fractured early attachments and a probable capacity for violence," he says. "What about travel? Any sign the timelines overlap?"

Carl Bunch, silent until now, pipes up from the back corner, his voice small but urgent. "I've been running background on both. Freemont's engineering career put him in Denver. At the same time, Calvin Walker was working a construction job in Tempe, Arizona. There is no overlap I could find. I'm waiting for the file for the Rachel Ruther murder. Should have it this afternoon."

Chapter Forty-Three

The buzz of the lights grows louder for a second, like the office itself is listening.

"We need to account for the possibility of communications between them," says Jill. "Whether they're aware of each other. There could be something deeper, some shared compulsion, some kind of programmed behavior."

"Twins telepathy," says an agent with a smirk.

"Don't count that out as a possibility. Your info packet from Dr. Lang has several case studies about twins being able to communicate silently. There's another possibility. They could be playing us," says Dirk. "Acting as mirrors. The pattern might be less about compulsion and more about taunting the system."

"Well, you're one of them," says the agent with a scowl. "Why don't you send them a brainwave and tell them to surrender?"

No one says anything, but a few agents stare at their notebooks, and one shakes his head slowly, in disbelief that the agent said it out loud, although a lot of them were thinking about Dirk's connection to the killers.

Spinella stands and glares at the agent who slinks deeper into his chair. He looks around the table. "You are all professionals. I expect you to act like it. If I ever hear another comment like that from this group or anyone else in the building, I will come down so hard, your heads will swim and you'll find yourselves working out of a one man office along the Canadian border in Montana. Do I make myself clear?"

The room grows silent, and everyone nods.

"If these guys are coordinating," replies Lawson. "It's the cleanest I've seen. Zero digital footprints. No shared bank records, no mutual contacts. Nothing."

"Which brings us to the core question," says Spinella, his voice as flat as a legal pad. "How do you catch two men who don't exist anywhere except in the blood and the crime scenes?" Right now, we have nothing actionable. We have DNA from two crime scenes, one old case in Arizona and one recent case in Colorado. The DNA is a match to our suspects, but to which one. Do we arrest both men and let the system sort it out? That would be a losing proposition since we have no other evidence and no witnesses. Nothing that puts either suspect in the crosshairs."

"We need more than circumstantial to take action," says one agent.

Jill asks, "Any sign they know we are looking?"

Carl shakes his head. "I pinged every darknet alert I could. Nothing, but then, these guys are in a different class than most criminals we deal with."

The war room is quiet. Even the analysts stop pretending to multitask.

"What about the mother?" asks Dirk.

Carl perks up, as if waiting for this cue. "I got into a database that cross-references sealed adoptions with census records. There's a match. Stephanie Gormley, age sixty-three, lives in Leadville, Colorado. No phone, no social, but she's had the same address since 1998. I can't find anything to show that she owns the property. It's title to a corporation. Blue Sky Investments. I'm drawing a blank so far."

He projects a grainy scan from the county assessor's office: a weathered bungalow, dead grass, nothing out of the ordinary except for the handwritten mailbox and the fact that Gormley has not, according to public record, ever held a job. "It could be an alias, or she could be a shut-in, but it's a live lead."

Jill looks at Carl, who has already bent back to his laptop, jaw working a loose thread of skin on his lower lip. "Can you send us everything you have on Gormley, including any health or psych records?"

"Already in your inbox," he replies.

Finally, Spinella looks at Dirk. "Thoughts?"

Dirk glances at Jill, then says, "We have to get ahead of them. We could interview each one and see if we get any reaction, or we can surveil them and see if we can catch one or both in the act."

Spinella nods, scribbles something, then stares at the table. "Everyone is to go through the travel records, construction projects, building permits, anything that puts either man within a hundred-mile radius of a victim. Work it backwards and forwards. I want a timeline for every month since 2003. Use flagged credit reports, lease agreements, anything. Don't wait for a subpoena; if you hit a wall, bring it to me."

He stands, shuffles his own files into a stack. "We have two unknowns, and the Bureau is about to make them famous. If you have a direct hit, you call me."

Spinella stops and looks at the board. "Dirk, coordinate with the Phoenix office and have them set up surveillance on Walker, job, home, anywhere he goes twenty-four seven. Jill, same thing on Freemont. Keep it tight, but I don't want them to know they are being followed. Use whatever resources you need. The rest of you have your assignments. Let's get cracking."

"What should we do about the birth mother?" asked Jill.

Spinella thought for a minute. "I doubt she knows anything, but let's leave her for now. If we need to, we can always circle back around and pay her a visit. Doesn't sound like she's going anywhere."

The agents murmur their assent, collecting pens and notebooks, their eyes brighter than at the start.

As they filter out, Dirk stays at the front of the room, fingers splayed on the table. Jill stays beside him, close enough that their shoulders touch when they lean.

Spinella waits until it's almost empty, then walks over, lowering his voice.

"That comment was uncalled for," he says. "Unfortunately, that's not the first time I've heard something like it. If at any point this becomes too much for you and you want off the task force, you say the word and it's done. No recrimination."

Dirk meets his gaze. "I appreciate that, but I'm in this to the end."

Spinella nods, a sharp, one-degree tilt. "Then make it count."

He leaves, closing the glass door behind him. The room is empty except for Dirk, Jill and the ghost trails of what they're up against.

Jill exhales, slow. "You didn't flinch once. Even when you talked about your brothers."

Dirk says nothing, just keeps looking at the whiteboard. The spirals cross, lined up like targets. The faces of the suspects staring back through the light.

He runs a finger over the crime scene photo, tracing the line between victim and killer.

"Do you think we're hunting them, or are they hunting us?" he asks, voice a whisper.

"Let's not find out the hard way," she says.

The conference room is left in a kind of postmortem stillness. Only the sound of the projector and the tick of the wall clock remain, underscored by the Doppler of the elevator bells. The evidence board, scabbed with mugshots and forensics printouts, seems larger in the silence. It dominates one wall; the suspect's faces arrayed in uneven columns: James, Calvin, and now an old photo of Stephanie Gormley.

Dirk stands three feet from the board, one hand balled in the pocket of his trousers, the other cupping his chin. He scans the photos, but his gaze slips, skating from the eyes of James Freemont to those of Calvin, then to his own Bureau ID, propped on the table edge. His reflection in the window overlays all three faces, blending and fracturing the lines until he cannot tell one from the next.

Jill is a presence beside him, her shoulder brushing

his as she scans the evidence, searching for the connective tissue between clues. When she speaks, her voice is pitched low just for the two of them.

"Now that we know where your birth mother is, I'll bet you'd like to run up there and talk to her, but you heard Spinella. Let's deal with the surveillance first."

Dirk nods, but he keeps his eyes on the suspects' grid. After a beat, he says, "Thank you. For not… making it weird. With the adoption stuff."

Jill's smile is slight, but her voice is soft and certain. "I figured you'd rather I didn't psychoanalyze you."

He almost smiles back. "That's your job, isn't it?"

She nudges him, gentle as a shoulder bump in a crowded bar. "No. My job is to keep you from making stupid decisions."

He lets that settle, then uncoils his arms, flexing his scarred forearm as if trying to relieve a phantom cramp. "You think she'll recognize me? The birth mother?"

Jill thinks for a second, then: "I think she'll see what I see, someone who is an honest, capable man." She points to the photo of Stephanie Gormley, her face thin, hair flat, and a dark smile worn ragged.

She slides the last of the files into her bag, then gives him a look that's half challenge, half comfort.

"Come on," she says. "We have work to do."

They step into the corridor, leaving the blue-lit room behind them, and vanish into the buzz of the office.

Chapter Forty-Four

The Bureau van is a rolling crypt, its cabin perfumed by cheap styrofoam coffee and the accumulated sweat of three men who haven't opened a window in days. Dirk sits in the passenger seat, right knee jiggling, binoculars braced to his brow like a sniper's scope. Down the street, the target house is a museum display. The porch light timed to sunrise, the mailbox battered by the same weekly junk mail, and a flag that never falls below half-mast. In seven days, Dirk's team has seen every permutation of the neighborhood's life cycle, including joggers, kids on bikes, garbage men and mothers with strollers.

James Freemont is a human metronome. At exactly 6:56 every morning, the front porch light dies, and within four minutes the man emerges. Punctual. His routine is the sort you can set a pacemaker by: his dress shoes shine like a mirror, his tie is knotted in a perfect Windsor knot, and he always wears the same charcoal overcoat unless it's raining (then navy). He walks to the Audi with a stack of blueprint tubes under one arm and a travel mug in his other hand, never fumbling, and never glancing back at the house. Freemont starts the car at 7:01 sharp, backs out with surgical precision, and moves down the street like his car is robotic.

"Bet he shits at exactly the same time every day, too," mutters the driver, a field agent with a sunburned scalp and a nervous habit of unscrewing and re-screwing the rearview mirror.

The third agent, in the back seat with a laptop

perched on his knees, snickers and logs the data point into the tracking spreadsheet. Dirk doesn't dignify the commentary; he follows Freemont's exit through the Zeiss lenses, lips pressed thin, then flips the binoculars to rest against his breastbone.

After a week, surveillance is less about observing the target and more about being marinated in your own thoughts. Dirk spends most of the hours scanning the printouts Carl Bunch prepped for the task force, or simply staring at the sidewalk cracks, seeing how they spiderweb all the way to the curb. He is a professional at monotony, but even he is not immune to the seep of boredom turning into irritation and then into a species of mild paranoia.

He opens the accordion folder on his lap and thumbs to the back. Here, inside a blue cover sheet stamped PERSONAL, is the Gormley file. He doesn't know why he keeps coming back to it. The urge to review the case is compulsive, but the urge to analyze it is something else. He tells himself it's a professional interest, but each pass through the documents raises more heat in his chest than the last.

Carl's summary is clinical. "Stephanie Gormley, born in 1967 into a prominent religious family in Cherry Creek. She attended two years of private high school before being transferred to the Jefferson County public school system. No academic honors and no extracurriculars. At 17, she was allegedly raped after a post-prom party. The pregnancy was concealed from her classmates. She was supposedly studying in Europe. The triplets were born at Denver General Hospital. Each child adopted to separate families at birth, facilitated by Turner, Baxter, and Fellows, LLP. Stephanie was sent to boarding school in Lake County, later confirmed as the old St. Jude's Sanatorium for Women, now defunct. In 1998, she moved to a remote property outside Leadville that was purchased by her parents. No employment, no further education. All public contact ends there."

Dirk reads it three times. On the fourth, he stops at the photo Carl included at the end: a blurry, out-of-focus shot of the Leadville property. It's small, gray and half hidden by pines. The cabin is so deep in the trees that it looks more like the home of an animal than a human. The only visible sign of civilization is a blackened, hand-built mailbox, no number, just GORMLEY stenciled in faded paint. Dirk traces the line of the roof with his finger, then flips the photo over to find nothing on the back.

The backseat agent glances up from his screen. "Any new action on the mother?"

Dirk ignores him, tucks the Gormley folder away. The less said the better. The last thing he wants is to have this obsession on record.

He checks the clock on the van's dashboard. 7:11 AM. Freemont is four city blocks away, but the follow team is on him, ready to turn him over once he hits his office.

Dirk slips silently out of the van and stretches. He walks around the block to his SUV, slides in and heads for the office. He'll come back tonight for a little while after James gets home.

As he drives, he lets his mind wander. What if

James Freemont is the sort who needs nothing but a perfect schedule? He's built himself a fortress so airtight that nothing can get in, nothing can seep out. It's an idea that rankles.

He unrolls the window an inch, listens to the wind blow through the crack, and tries to imagine what Freemont is thinking at this moment. Is he planning another perfect day, another flawless set of blueprints? Or is he, even now, cataloging the eyes watching him and the car two blocks behind?

Dirk pulls into the parking structure, slides out of the SUV and heads to the elevator. He rides to his floor lost in thought until the doors open and he steps into a hive of activity. For the next several hours, he sits with Jill as they review the surveillance logs. Their frustration builds. Dirk calls for a break, and he stands, walks to the kitchen and pours another coffee. He walks back to his office and picks up the Gormley file and opens the cover.

He can't help it. He digs up the cabin photo again, studies the angles of the porch and the sag in the front steps. The mailbox is still the thing that sticks. He tries to remember his own childhood mailbox: was it black, or green? Did it have their family name on it, or just the house number? He has a memory of standing at the curb, hand deep in the mailbox, pulling out a fistful of bills and catalogs.

He wonders what Stephanie might think about him. It's been a long time. He looks at the photo of the cabin again, but this time, instead of tracing the lines of the roof, he looks at the darkness behind the window. He wonders if anyone is in there now, staring back. If

Stephanie, or some part of her, has spent the last thirty years waiting for someone to come home.

Chapter Forty-Five

At midnight, the Denver field office is all hum and ghost-light. The bullpen's ceiling fluorescents hum with relentless blue intensity, washing the cubes and desks into a smear of gray-on-gray. The only movement is the night janitor's cart, gliding past cubicle rows with the slow gravitas of a tugboat. Jill sits alone at her desk, surrounded by stacks of printouts and the slow, steady heartbeat of her muted computer.

She's been here for four hours straight, but it could have been ten. Her lower back aches, her eyes burn, and she's finished the same cup of coffee three times, the last inch topped off repeatedly, each refill colder than the last.

Spread edge-to-edge across the desk is the week's full run of surveillance reports on Calvin Walker. She's gone over each sheet with three colors of highlighter and a fine-point Sharpie, cross-referencing time stamps and jotting notes in her own jagged shorthand. At a distance, the desk would look like the aftermath of a bureaucratic bloodbath. Up close, it's a monument to futility.

Calvin's pattern is an echo of Freemont's. He leaves the apartment each morning at 5:55 and drives his old pickup truck to the construction site. He works nine hours, sometimes outside, sometimes in a trailer office, and leaves promptly at five. Never late, never early. Stops at the same Circle K every day for a Red Man and a Gatorade. Back at the apartment by 5:38, lights off by 10:15, no visitors, no calls, no digital trail at all.

There is nothing. Nothing but the grind of hours and the slow death of hope that he'll slip up, deviate, even blink out of sequence.

Jill rubs her eyes hard, blurring the world into streaks. She digs the heels of her palms into her brow and waits for the fiery ache behind her eyeballs to recede.

She shuffles the stack: Wednesday, Thursday, Friday. Each page is a near-identical log, broken only by the color of Walker's shirt or the variety of his lunch bag. There is no emergent pattern unless you count the pattern of perfect repetition.

She flips open her laptop and keys up the email threads with the Phoenix office. The last half-dozen messages are polite despair, the local agents unable to believe the Bureau is spending this kind of money to watch a man water his dying potted plant every morning at 5:20. The most recent message ends: "He's a ghost, Jill. Are you sure he's not dead already?"

She wants to laugh, but it comes out as a sigh.

She pings the Denver team's folder, hoping for some revelation from Dirk or the van crew. But it's all the same, the color of Freemont's tie, and the brand of his coffee. The sameness is galling, even in a profession that builds itself on the hope that boredom cracks into violence.

Jill opens her notebook and, almost without thinking, draws two columns. She heads one FREEMONT, the other WALKER. Then she fills in the lines. Wake. Dress. Depart. Commute. Work. Lunch. Return. Sleep. She draws lines connecting each corresponding hour. It's a lattice of nothing, but she keeps going, as if she can force a hole to appear.

The janitor passes again. This time, he stops at her desk, checks the trash bin, and quietly replaces the bag. He glances at the stack of printouts but doesn't comment, only gives her a solemn nod and moves on.

The clock ticks past 12:30. Jill's phone glows once, before it dies. She leaves it dark.

She considers calling Dirk. He may have seen something she hasn't, some blip in the code. She pulls up his number and lets her thumb hover above the call icon. She can picture him in the van, jaw locked, eyes hollow from too much time at the glass.

Instead, she closes the phone, shoves it deep into her bag, and flips to a blank page of her notebook. She uncaps the Sharpie and writes, in huge block letters, ADJUST STRATEGY.

She opens a new email to Spinella, the subject line: Walker/Freemont Surveillance Update. She keeps the message tight. No meaningful deviation or evidence of external coordination. Both subjects maintain rigid, near-identical routines, and the cost/benefit of continued static surveillance is negative. Recommend a pivot to active engagement, or controlled contact. Open to suggestions for escalation.

She hovers over the SEND button, her finger shaking just enough to rattle her.

For a long minute, she doesn't move.

Then she clicks SEND and watches the email vanish into the night.

She leans back, lets the air escape her lungs, and studies the glowing blue cube-farm around her. Every screen is dark now, every office door closed. She sees her reflection in the monitor, hollow-eyed, hair escaping its bun, and her face mapped with exhaustion.

She wonders what the point is sometimes. If all they do is document the routines of the damned until the cycle breaks and someone dies. If maybe they're not the hunters, but just a better breed of prey.

She stacks the surveillance logs into a single pile, aligns the edges, and slides them into her outbox.

She stays at her desk another hour, just breathing, listening to the soft thrum of the building's circulatory system. It's the only sound in the world.

At 2:03 AM, she finally gathers her bag and heads for the exit. The lobby is dark, the glass doors reflecting her back in duplicate. She scans her badge, steps into the night, and stands on the empty sidewalk for a moment, her arms crossed against the cold.

She looks up at the building, dozens of windows, most already black, and a handful still glowing with the last fever of overtime.

She thinks about Dirk, about the two men they're hunting, about the woman at the center of it all, out in the trees and the cold. She wonders if this is how it ends: not in violence, but in slow erosion. She walks to her car, starts the engine, and sits for a while with the headlights off. Then she drives home, watching for patterns in the empty streets.

Chapter Forty-Six

James Freemont's basement is a palace of uniformity. He has set every surface in order: walls painted bone-white, shelving measured to the millimeter, a grid of halogen spots embedded in the ceiling so that the room is never anything less than a surgical theater. His desk is at the exact midpoint of the far wall, positioned under a bronze architect's lamp that casts an immaculate circle of light over the mat, the pens, the blueprints and the solitary mug of black coffee. Every night he returns here after dinner, and every night he tries, and fails, to lose himself in the crystalline logic of lines and forms.

Tonight, he is not working on blueprints. Tonight, he is writing in the journal. The dreams are the worst they have ever been. For a week now, each night has brought another memory, raw, relentless, and impossible to shake. He sees an old woman, face cut from bone and angles, standing by a frozen window, mouthing something he can never hear. Sometimes he looks at her from the outside, pressing his face to the cold glass. Sometimes he is inside, and she is close, so close he can see the network of veins under her eyelids, the angry pinprick of blood in the crease of her nose. She always looks right at him.

Tonight as he scribbles, he draws her again. He can never quite get the face right. It flickers between old and young; the skin pulls taut and then loosens; the eyes shift from blue to gray to nothing. He presses harder; the graphite shatters until the line tears the page and smears the portrait.

He curses and rips out the sheet. It hangs from the journal by a single thread. He tries again, this time slower, hand shaking with something more than fatigue. This time, the face comes together. The woman's mouth is set in a narrow grimace, the lips almost gone to parchment, but there's a flash in the eyes, anger, accusation or something that looks like forgiveness but isn't.

James stares at the drawing, sweat prickling at the base of his neck. Then, as always, he catalogs this. This is the third instance of the woman this week. He numbers the sketches, time stamps them, then flips to the next page and writes, "Stephanie Gormley. Birth mother." The name is not his own, but it's familiar now, printed with the authority of a court transcript.

He doesn't know where the name comes from. Three nights ago, he saw it in a dream, in a government file, held by a man whose face he couldn't see. The page said, birth mother. It's been echoing in his head ever since, and he's written it at the top of every page for three days, like an invocation.

He is sweating now, but his hands are steady. He closes the journal, locks it in the metal box and stashes the box under the stairs. He then takes a clean sheet of graph paper and draws the house from his dreams: a gabled roof, sagging porch, and blackened windows. He is surprised at how he can remember it; the orientation of the steps, the angle of the mailbox, even the lopsided pine that seems to hold up the eastern wall. He shades the trees in last, then writes the address at the bottom, careful and blocky:

GORMLEY/LEADVILLE.

He sits back, breathing hard. His shirt is damp at the collar, and his pulse is a hammer behind his eyes. He peruses the address, then at the clock. It is 1:03 a.m.

He stands and stretches, the movement abrupt, almost violent. He paces the length of the basement twice, arms folded tight. Then he stops at the wall opposite his desk, where the sketches are tacked in perfect order. He scans them, seeking evidence of intrusion. Has any image changed since last night?

He turns to the narrow window set high in the cinderblock wall. The streetlight is dimmed by a mesh of dirty snow, but he can just make out the roofline of the neighbor's house, the van that hasn't moved in a week, and the glimmer of the street sign at the corner. He knows, with the iron certainty of the condemned, that someone is watching. He's seen them, two men, once a woman, always in pairs, sometimes walking, and sometimes idling in the vehicle. He's catalogued their routines but has not yet caught their eye. That will come in time.

He moves to the laptop. He doesn't use his work machine. He keeps an old notebook, an air-gapped brick, for the files and maps that belong to the other half of his life. He keys in the address from the dream. GORMLEY/LEADVILLE. A quick search from earlier, and he brings up a grainy photo from a real estate site, a cabin so close to the one in his head that the breath leaves his lungs in a rush.

He clicks through to the satellite view. The house is a speck in a sea of trees, but the orientation matches his drawing exactly. He feels a slow, chilly thrill as he zooms in, matching lines to lines. It is real. She is real.

He closes the laptop and goes to the far end of the room. Beneath the bottom step is a locked space. He bends, keys in the combination, and swings it open. Inside is a black medical bag, leather, and double-zipped, the kind used by doctors in old movies. He removes it, sets it on the desk, and unzips it with a surgeon's care.

Inside: two pairs of nitrile gloves, three scalpels wrapped in gauze, two rolls of tape, his favorite knife and a folded plastic sheet. The kit is old, but every tool is clean and perfectly arranged.

He adds a coil of rope from the workbench, a box of alcohol wipes, and a compact first aid kit. He pauses, considering, then adds a single folded photo of the Leadville house, printed from the screen, cut and trimmed to fit the inner pocket of the bag.

He zips the bag and sets it at the foot of the stairs.

He stands there for a moment, letting the reality settle in. His hands are at his sides. He feels a ringing in his ears, the kind that comes after too much silence. He looks back at the desk. The drawing of the old woman stares at him, eyes blank and unforgiving. He picks up the page, folds it in half, then half again, and tucks it into the pocket of his jacket.

He turns off the lamp and climbs the stairs in darkness; the bag bumping against his knee. At the top, he unlocks the door, slips into the tiled hallway, and listens for the sound of breathing from the rest of the house. He strolls to the kitchen, pours a glass of water, and drinks it in three long gulps. He rinses the glass, wipes it dry, and returns it to the exact spot on the counter.

He checks the window. The van is still there, lights off, dark behind the glass. He allows himself a smile. He wonders if they are watching him right now.

He takes the bag and walks to the back door. He stands on the threshold, breathing in the cold. He opens the door, steps onto the porch, and closes it silently behind him. He is calm now. The world outside is vast and empty, the last of the snow reflecting the faintest light from the city.

He walks down the steps, bag in hand, his feet making no sound at all.

He heads towards the address he has never been to but knows better than his own. Three blocks from the house he calls for a car pick up and gives the driver the address of a parking garage downtown where he keeps his alternate vehicle. He climbs in and heads for the mountains and to whatever the fates have in store for him.

Chapter Forty-Seven

Calvin Walker doesn't move for hours, except to breathe.

He's planted at the window of his third-floor unit, all the lights off, a cooling slice of pizza untouched at his elbow. He watches the black SUV parked just beyond the streetlamp, eyes pinched against the darkness. Every so often, a shadow shifts behind the windshield, and Calvin marks the interval in a spiral-bound notebook. He's filled half a page with the numbers already: minute, second, movement and pattern.

He's not afraid of them. If anything, he's flattered. No one ever cared enough to watch him before.

His apartment is a sunken cave, carpet thin and buckling in the corners, but it's clean. Calvin likes it clean. All his life, he's been told he can't control himself, but he can control this. The plates are stacked, the silverware sorted, and even the torn takeout menu on the counter is folded along its crease. Above the couch, the wall is a tapestry of taped-up sketches, dozens of them: faces, hands, trees and a house repeated so many times the graphite ghosts layer into a blur.

Tonight, he flips through the newest stack, mind working over the details. The house is always the same. Front steps bowed, mailbox eaten by rust, windows blank and black. He's never been there, but it feels as real to him as the skin on his own arm. The way the woods crowd in, the way the snow slumps off the roof. He can draw it from memory, in the dark, left-handed.

The face is harder. A woman, older, her hair thin and wild, and her face drawn into a mask of worry.

The face makes him angry. He's surprised he can be this angry at someone he's never met, but he knows this woman. This is the woman who abandoned him. She didn't care enough about him to take care of him. She is the one who turned him into the thing he is today. She is his next victim.

Calvin turns the page and finds the words again, written in the thick, ugly marker he only uses when the voices in his head are louder than the sound of the TV. "Stephanie Gormley. Birth mother. Leadville, Colorado." He doesn't know where he learned this, but it's been crawling across his brain for days. He thinks it was a dream. He's never been to Leadville, but the name tastes right.

He flips back, finds the sketch of the old woman. Her eyes follow him, no matter the angle. He tears the page free, crumples it, and shoves it into the mouth of the empty pizza box. His hands are shaking. He likes that. The feeling reminds him he's alive.

He stands, muscles singing with static, and paces the apartment. He checks the window: the van is still there, still watching in the dark. Good. He likes the dark.

Calvin moves to his bedroom closet, pulls out a duffel bag. He throws it open on the bed, starts shoving things in: a flashlight, a set of insulated gloves, three pairs of socks. He drops in two hunting knives, sheathed but sharp, and a coil of rope. He checks the contents, shakes the bag, then adds a folded change of clothes and a single pack of peanut butter crackers.

Last, he goes to the desk and finds the sketch of the house. He folds it into quarters, slips it into the front pocket of his jeans. The address is printed in his own blocky hand, beneath the picture.

He moves through the apartment with quick, clean efficiency, turning off every trace of light or movement. He stands at the door for a long moment, listening to the apartment breathe. The next-door neighbor snores, loud and wet. Downstairs, the washing machine thumps in time with his pulse.

He waits for the right moment, when a car drives by from the opposite direction, then slips out the back stairwell, the duffel slung loose at his hip. He knows how to move quietly. He grew up needing to be invisible.

At the alley, he pauses and looks up at the sky. There are no stars, but the cloud cover glows faint, almost purple. He wonders if the old woman ever stands outside at night, if she knows what's coming for her.

He grins, slips into his pickup truck and drives onto the street behind the apartment with his lights off until he's clear of the street. Calvin Walker has a place to go and something to do. He keeps driving into the cold, into the dark, and into the night that will never end.

Chapter Forty-Eight

Dirk dreams in frames. They come not as memories but as hard overlays, each one layered with the precision and brutality of real time. In this one, he walks a path he's never seen before, except he knows it with the sick certainty of déjà vu. Pine trees hunch overhead, their black branches raking the night. Moonlight leaks through the clouds in quivering pools. Every footfall is muffled by old, granular snow and the cold is so deep it bites through the sole of his boot and chews at the marrow.

He doesn't realize it's a dream, not at first, because all the details are too sharp. The air is wired with the scent of burning pitch; the wind lashes his face, wet and needled with ice. Ahead, a house materializes from the trees. It squats low, as if pressed into the earth by the weight of the night. No porch light, but from one window glows a yellow smear, a single lamp burning behind a lopsided curtain. The glass is frosted at the corners, but in the glow's warmth, something moves.

He steps closer. There is an animal logic to the approach. He sees how the snow is trampled from the woods up to the porch, how someone has made this journey before, repeatedly. The steps are warped, two inches off level, and the first plank bows under his weight with a creak that fires down the joists and into the hollows below. Dirk does not flinch, though in the dream he can feel his heart pounding so hard it feels like someone else's.

The front door is painted the color of dried blood,

but years of storms have stripped it down to bare wood in streaks. His hand closes over the knob. He smells, beneath the sharper tang of snow and smoke, something softer: old paper, a sour note of dust, and underneath that the slow, rich scent of something cooking.

He turns the knob.

Inside is the sound of nothing. Just the rattle of the wind against the glass. The room is one open space: to the left, a table scattered with envelopes and the husks of peeled oranges; to the right, a battered recliner facing a wood stove blackened by decades of fires. The walls are pine paneling, yellowed and knotted, nailed up in uneven lengths.

There is a woman at the stove. Her back is to him, shoulders wrapped in a hand-knit shawl the color of bruised plum. She stirs the pot in slow circles, the wooden spoon scraping the sides. Her hair is gray, pulled back in a severe knot, and her posture says she is old, but not fragile. On the counter next to her is a single mug of tea, steam rising in tight spirals.

Dirk is close enough to see her hands, knobby and blue-veined, but steady. The spoon stops. The woman sets it down, lifts the lid off the pot, and inhales. She turns as if hearing his breathing and faces him. Her eyes are black with shock. The mouth goes slack. The spoon clatters to the floor, but neither of them moves.

Dirk tries to speak, but nothing comes. His lips shape a warning, don't, but no air comes out, and the silence gets harder. He sees through the eyes of the other, a hand rising at the edge of his vision. The hand is gloved in blue nitrile. It holds a knife.

The cold metal flashes in the lamplight. The woman's mouth opens, soundless and wide. Her eyes flicker left and right, as if looking for a face she recognizes behind the mask. Her left hand gropes for the edge of the stove. Her right goes up, not in defense, but in recognition.

"Please," she says, but in the dream her voice is silent.

Dirk is screaming at himself, inside the dream, to stop, to move, but the arm is not his. The blade arcs in a clean line, slicing through the glow of the lamp, and as it swings down, he feels the cold of it like a second pulse against his wrist. The sound of it, metal on bone, is the last thing before the dream tears itself open and drops him through the floor.

He wakes in his own bed, lungs flooded, heart slamming against his ribs. It takes three full breaths for the room to settle around him, and even then, the afterimage lingers, the eyes, the knife, the scent of pine and old tea. He sits up, shaking, and for a wild moment he wonders if he has blood on his hands.

He sits hunched over the edge of the bed, the cold sweat on his back already drying in the cool air, chest heaving as if he's just run full tilt through the woods. His hands keep flexing as if trying to release a memory that's stuck in the tendons. The room is black except for the faint shimmer of city sodium through the curtains, and in that light, he is a man made of cuts and shadow.

His wife wakes up instantly. Her hand finds his arm,

her body shifting so she can gather him up. "Dirk, what is it?" she asks, voice ragged with the panic that comes only from the edge of dreams.

He can't speak at first. His tongue is dry, and his heart will not slow, so he sits and breathes and tries to focus on the here and now: the groan of the heater, the distant horn two streets over, and the tremor in her palm as she clutches his wrist. She smells like sleep and coconut shampoo and a whiff of fear.

"You were yelling," she says, louder. "You said no, over and over."

He draws a breath and says, "It's nothing. Just a dream. Sorry." But his voice is sandpaper, and it fools no one.

"Dirk," she says, moving in front of him now, squatting so she can see his eyes. "You're scaring me."

He looks at her, and he almost tells her everything, but the dream is still riding him hard, not letting go. He stands abruptly, sheets twisting around his shins, and shuffles into the closet. The urge to move is animal, and he lets it carry him.

She follows, barefoot on the wood floor, trailing his name in a whisper. He's already into jeans, tugging them up with hands that will not quite obey him. Shirt over his head, arms into sleeves, then he's at the top dresser drawer, pulling the badge from its holder and clipping it to his belt. Next comes the gun, checked, loaded, slipped into the holster in three movements, like muscle memory.

She leans against the closet frame. "Dirk, stop.

What are you doing?"

He's tying his shoes now, jaw clenched. "Someone's in trouble," he says, not looking at her.

"It's almost midnight," she says, and the concern in her voice is edged with something like anger. "You had a bad dream."

He straightens, and this time his eyes are cold and clear. "I have to go," he says. "Someone's going to kill an innocent woman, and I need to stop it."

She answers, but his hands are already on her shoulders. He kisses her fast, and mechanically, but real, and says, "I'm sorry," into her hair. Then he's out, down the hallway, pulling a jacket off the peg and shoving his feet into boots by the door.

He hesitates at the threshold for just the blink of a second, hearing her voice behind him, pleading, "Dirk, talk to me." But the vision of the woman in the cabin, the horror on her face, has lodged behind his eyes. He has to move. He has to fix it.

The night is clear and hard and endless. The cold burns his lungs as he jogs to the SUV, and as he slams the door behind him, the world narrows to a point, then the ignition catches and the engine rumbles to life. He glances back once, sees her silhouette in the window, arms wrapped around her torso. She looks impossibly small.

He pulls out fast, tires biting the wet pavement, the city receding behind him. Every nerve is tuned to the image in his head, and he lets it drive him, lets it blot out everything else. Even the thought of what she must be feeling now. He turns onto the highway and flips on the red and blue flashers and stomps on the gas pedal.

The bedroom is silent again. His wife stands at the window for a while after the car is gone, the cold creeping through the glass and into her bones.

Sleep doesn't come back. Not for a minute, not for a second. The house groans and shifts, and the ticking clock on the dresser counts off each new failure to find calm. She rolls onto her side, stares into the dark, and tries to thread some sense from the tangle Dirk left behind. The sheets still smell of him, and something about that makes it worse.

She turns the pillow, presses her face to the cold, and lies perfectly still. The window stays blank, and the heater keeps up its background hiss, but every time she closes her eyes, she sees him again, his face lit by the streetlight shining through the bedroom window, his jaw set like stone, and some terror chewing through him from the inside.

She lasts like this for an hour. At 12:30 she gives up, sits up, and swings her legs over the side. She considers texting him, but the phone isn't where it should be, on his belt. Instead, it's on the nightstand, where he left it in his hurry. That chills her.

She picks it up, checks the screen. Four missed calls, one from the Bureau, three from a number she recognizes as his partner, Jill. The notifications make her throat tighten.

The next logical step is Jill. She grabs her phone, finds Jill's number, and hits the call button. It's late, and she feels a twinge of guilt, but as soon as Jill picks up, her voice is thick but ready, and the guilt is gone.

"Quarters."

"Hi, Jill, it's Connie. I'm sorry to call this late," she says, "but Dirk. Something's wrong."

Jill's tone sharpens. "What happened?"

"He had a nightmare, or something, but he said he had to go. Said an innocent woman was going to be killed, and he needed to stop it. He just left, and his phone is here on the nightstand."

There's a quick, muffled sound on Jill's end, paper rustling, a lamp switching on, the gearshift of a mind dropping into high. "How long ago?"

She glances at the digital clock; the red digits mock her. "Just after eleven thirty."

"Thank you for calling me. I'll find him. You did the right thing," says Jill, all trace of sleep gone.

"Can you?" She hates the pleading note but can't stop it. "Can you let me know he's okay?"

"Of course. I'll call when I have him."

The line goes dead. She stares at the phone until the screen blacks out.

Jill is already out of bed before the call is over. She moves with the violence of someone whose body has been trained to react, to shift from zero to one hundred in the space between syllables. She dresses in the dark: black jeans, a field shirt, and heavy boots. She clips her badge to the belt, checks her weapon, and loads two extra mags. In the bathroom mirror, her eyes are bloodshot but focused, the rest of her expression blank and smooth. This is what she is made for.

Downstairs, she takes her go bag from the hall closet and slings it over one shoulder. The keys are on the table, the Bureau tag heavy in her fist. She checks her phone for new intel, finds nothing, then heads out into the parking lot.

The SUV is cold, but the engine turns over first try. She drives out of the apartment complex with the headlights on full; the beams slicing the empty dark. The city is asleep, the roads emptier than they ever are in the daytime. She moves fast, almost recklessly, but never quite losing control.

Jill doesn't need to check the map. She already knows where Dirk is going. It's the Leadville cabin, the Gormley woman, the last line in his family tree. Every neuron in her brain says she's too late, but she has to be sure.

Out on the highway, she flips on her flashers, passes three trucks and a single patrol cruiser. She doesn't slow down.

The mountains are a black shadow against the night. Every few miles she checks her phone for a call or text, hoping for a miracle, or a message, or just a clue. There is nothing.

Back at the house, Dirk's wife puts his phone back on the nightstand, screen down. She gets under the covers, lies still, and waits for the headlights to return.

Chapter Forty-Nine

The unmarked SUV crawls up the last switchback, headlights brushing the gnarled pines, and idles to a stop where the Forest Service road spits gravel onto the shoulder. At 10,000 feet, the air is thinner than Dirk expects. Every breath comes with a fractional delay, like the mountain itself wants you to reconsider. He kills the engine and sits in the dark for a minute, surveying the perimeter. Above, a blacked-out sky, no stars, just the weird bounce of the town's distant sodium vapor against the cloud deck. In front of him, a hundred feet of nothing and then the outline of a cabin: small, ancient, sinking into the ground like it's being reabsorbed.

He waits, eyes adjusting, cataloguing the details. The window glow is a sickly yellow, no porch light and no visible motion inside. Someone has salted the steps to prevent ice. The mailbox is missing; the post leans right. There are tracks in the snow leading to the door, deep and single file, as if the occupant never expects company. He checks the side mirror. Nothing but trees and his own fear, stitched tight across the back of his skull.

Dirk exhales, then wipes the condensation from the steering wheel. He looks at his hands, fingers pale, with one nail bitten to the quick. He flexes, stretches, and opens the car door slowly. The night is so cold it dry-shaves his cheeks. His shoes crunch the old crust of snow as he picks his way to the path. He leaves the vehicle unlocked. If he needs to run, he wants no obstacles.

The first five steps are normal. The next five are performed knowing that someone is watching. Dirk feels the lens of the world on him, anxious and expectant, like the moment before a riot breaks loose.

Twenty feet from the door, everything stops. The porch light snaps on, a harsh, institutional LED, blue-white and buzzing. The cabin door swings open before Dirk can blink. A woman fills the threshold, left hand clutching the jamb, right hand already at the business end of a twelve-gauge pump shotgun. The barrel wavers not at all. She's older than her file photo, but her posture is straight as rebar. Her face is gaunt, the bones ridged and sharp, eyes a flat, seawater gray.

"Another step and I drop you right there." Her voice is dry, crackling, each word a command. "Hands where I can see 'em."

Dirk's profiler brain kicks in: left index slightly lighter on the grip, a hunter familiar with the gun; a smudge of blood on her apron, evidence of something recently cleaned, or killed. Her nose is straight, unbroken, but her upper lip bears a white, lightning-shaped scar. In this instant, Dirk has never seen anything more awake than the woman pointing this shotgun.

He raises his hands, palms up, deliberate. "I'm not here to hurt you, ma'am. My name is Dirk Trainor. I'm with the FBI." He moves one hand slowly toward his jacket, exposing the badge on his belt, and lets the light catch it.

The woman does not blink, but she sees the badge.

The safety stays off. "Get your ID out and do it slowly. Move fast and you'll die where you stand."

Dirk swallows. "I'm here because your life is in danger."

She barks a laugh, clipped and mean. "My whole life's been in danger. What's changed?"

He stands still, the air burning through his suit. "Two men are coming here to kill you. They're your sons." The line is insane even as he says it, but it's the only move.

Her mouth twists as if the words taste rotten. "My sons are dead. They died at birth."

Dirk suddenly realizes why the adoption was private, and she was stashed away in the woods. She had no idea her children lived. "No, they're not. I can explain, but you need to let me in before they get here."

The woman's jaw works the information, grinding it between her teeth. The gun does not move. "Explain from there."

Dirk lowers his hands an inch. "You gave birth to triplets in 1984. All boys. You were the mother, but they split us up." He keeps his voice low, not pleading. "The other two are killers, and I believe they are coming for you. To get closure. Or revenge. I don't know which yet."

"My babies died. Daddy told me and what do you mean they split us up? Who are you?"

Dirks looks at her. "I'm one of your sons." This gets her. The barrel drops a degree, just enough to suggest doubt. She stares at him for a full three seconds, then steps forward, careful, boots squeaking against the icy plank. "Let me see your face."

He takes a half-step, just enough into the light that she can study him. He knows what she sees, the thin nose, the cut of the cheek, and the eyes that won't settle. Her own eyes go glassy for a second, as if memory is flooding her vision.

"You look like my grandfather," she says, the words coming from somewhere below the surface. "But he was a better liar."

Dirk can only nod. "I'm not lying."

The shotgun sags, not in fatigue, but in the controlled way a gunfighter would lower it to the ready. "What the hell do you want?"

"To keep you alive," he says. "And figure out what this all means."

She studies him another beat, then jerks her chin at the door. "Get inside. Now." Her finger is still on the trigger, her aim unwavering. "And don't think for a second that you're welcome."

He walks up the steps, feeling her gaze crawl down his spine. At the top, he opens the door, steps inside, and feels the barrel of the shotgun graze the small of his back as she follows.

Chapter Fifty

The inside of the cabin is warmer than the air outside, a fact Dirk registers first as he crosses the threshold, the barrel of the shotgun brushing his shoulder blade. The entry room is nothing but a plywood floor and four walls patched in a confusion of old pine, insulation foam and hardware store paint. Above the door, a hand-stitched cross hangs crooked; beside it, a yellowed prayer card taped to the log wall. The furniture is minimal: a folding table littered with unopened mail, two mismatched chairs, and a futon with a threadbare army blanket. On the floor near the stove, a heap of split logs is stacked in military order, ends painted blue to keep the rot out. There's no TV, no radio. Only the slow heartbeat of the woodstove ticking as it fights the night.

Stephanie closes the door with a heel, the gun never wavering. She gestures Dirk toward the center of the room, then circles wide, flicking on a lamp that throws every shadow into stark, surgical relief. Her eyes never leave him as she sets the shotgun down, but even then she keeps one hand close to the stock, fingers tight on the trigger guard.

Dirk moves to the table, keeping his hands clear, and waits. He can see that the doorframe is reinforced with an extra steel plate and the windows are barred. A blackout curtain blocks the outside line of sight. All of it says: siege mentality.

Stephanie circles him once. "You've got ninety seconds to explain why I shouldn't blow your head off."

Dirk sets both palms on the tabletop. He sees the scuffs in the veneer, the dark flecks of cigarette ash ground into the corners. The badge glints at his waist; he leaves it visible.

"Start at the beginning," Stephanie says, her voice flat, "and don't skip anything."

Dirk begins, forcing his voice to a calm he doesn't feel. "You gave birth to three boys in March 1984. You never got to see us before they took us and split us up. You don't know where we ended up, or what became of us."

Stephanie's eyes twitch at the date, then freeze. "I remember. Daddy told me the babies were too small to survive, and they died at birth. After that, we never spoke of my pregnancy again."

He nods but keeps his eyes on the shotgun. "One of us was adopted by a family in Denver. Another went to Grand Junction. The third moved out of state. We never knew each other. I know them only from crime scene photos of their victims."

Stephanie's posture softens for half a heartbeat, but she hides it with a shrug. "So? Life's a bitch. If you think you're the first hard-luck bastard to get traded off for a better future, you're wrong. Why now?"

Dirk breathes once, in and out. "There's something else. The other two are identical twins; I'm not. My DNA says I'm a chimera. You originally had two sets of twins inside. One set was maternal, and one set was fraternal. I carry the DNA of my sibling who didn't make it. There's a lot of scientific explanation involved, but instead of four babies you delivered three."

She laughs, but it comes out broken. "So, you're here to save me? You? The man with the badge?"

Dirk straightens. "I'm here because I had the same dreams they did, but I didn't want to see you dead. I want to stop them."

Stephanie grabs the shotgun and levels it again, but her hands are shaking now. "You want me to believe that? What are you, a genetic experiment? I don't even know if you're real."

Dirk lets the next words fall hard. "You can shoot me. But if you do, one of them will come for you next, and you won't see him until it's too late."

Stephanie's lips tremble. "Who sent you?"

Dirk shrugs. "No one. I'm with the FBI, but I'm not on the clock. The others, James, and Calvin, don't know I'm here. I came to warn you. And maybe get answers."

She steps back, the gun slowly drooping. She studies his face, the lines and the scars. Her own expression flattens to the blank slate of an interrogator. "You really think they'll kill me?"

"Yes."

Stephanie drops into a chair, the gun across her lap. She stares at the table, then at the prayer card, then back at Dirk. "My mother told me I was cursed. Even as a kid, I could never keep a friend. Never trust anyone. I guess I passed that down." She laughs, but it's only breath. "The man who came for me when I was sixteen said I was special. That I was pretty. That's when he raped me. It was a cruel joke."

Dirk watches, saying nothing. The way she talks, the weight of the story, feels heavier than any file in his case history. She's not acting. She's just exhausted.

Stephanie looks up, her eyes glassy but sharp. "If I tell you something, you swear you won't use it against me?"

"I swear," says Dirk.

"I killed a man once. He tried to rape me a second time, but I was ready. I didn't use the gun, just a rock from the fire pit. We were in the woods where he had taken me, and he smelled of sweat and alcohol. It was easy. I was sixteen." She pauses and lets the memory burn through her. "When Daddy and the others found me, they buried him behind a latrine. No one ever found him. After that, they treated me as if I were crazy. They were right, but not for that reason."

Dirk nods, lets the confession hang in the air. "Why did you come here? Why isolate?"

Stephanie shrugs. "Because everywhere else is worse. Because the mountain doesn't ask questions. Daddy said I'd be safe here. He makes sure I have everything that I need."

Dirk's mind races. The pieces fit. He had seen the pattern many times. Trauma, isolation, and then the slow, sick gravity of unfinished business.

A sound cuts through the tense peace, the crunch of tires on the gravel outside, slow and deliberate. They both freeze. Stephanie rises, shotgun in hand, and moves to the blackout curtain, peels it just a slit.

"Sheriff's Department," she whispers. "Lake County."

Dirk steps close, careful not to spook her. He sees the SUV in the driveway, engine running but headlights dead. "Did you call the sheriff?"

"No," Stephanie says. "They come by to check on me sometimes." She hesitated. "But never this early in the morning."

The vehicle sits there, windows blacked out, doing nothing. After a full minute, there's no movement no footsteps, and no flashlight beams. Just the car idling, exhaust curling like ghosts over the drift.

Stephanie's hands white-knuckle the shotgun. "This isn't normal."

Dirk's hand goes to his belt and pulls his service weapon. "Do they ever just park and not knock on the door?"

"No, never," says Stephanie. "I usually give them a cup of coffee and a piece of pie."

She walks to the door and turns on the porch light, but the SUV is too far down the driveway to get wrapped in the porch light.

Stephanie licks her lips, the skin cracking. "What do we do?"

Dirk's brain works through options. The simplest would be to walk down the driveway and see what the deputy wants. He edges up to the window, keeps his body off the glass, and squints at the SUV. The plate is real; the vehicle is standard issue. But there's still no movement.

Another sound, almost lost to the wind: a second engine, approaching from down the road. The headlights cut off before the curve. Whoever it is, they know how to move in the dark.

Dirk looks at Stephanie. "We stay here, keep the lights off until we know what's going on."

Dirk reaches for his back pocket and realizes he didn't bring his phone with him when he left the house. He keeps his pistol next to his leg.

She nods once, then turns off the lights so that only the glow from the fireplace casts light in the room. They wait, breathing shallow. Outside, a second vehicle door closes softly, then nothing.

Two minutes stretch like plastic wrap over the nerves.

Then, suddenly, a gunshot cracks the night, sharp and close. A yelp, part scream, part animal. Something heavy hits the ground outside. Stephanie flinches, drops to a crouch, and racks the shotgun.

Dirk puts his hand on her shoulder, his voice a whisper. "They're here."

They both stare at the door, hearts pounding, as the night closes in around the cabin.

Chapter Fifty-One

Jill drives the Bureau SUV up the pitch-black stretch of Forest Service Road, hands clamped on the wheel, and her jaw set hard enough to crack molars. She's had the emergency band playing in her head for the last twenty minutes, Leadville dispatch, Lake County ops, even the local Forest Ranger channel in case someone's dumb enough to get stuck out here on a night like this. She called the Sheriff's office for a welfare check on Stephanie Gormley, giving the address twice and spelling out the risk factors like a reading list for psychosomatic disorder. The dispatcher's voice was a reedy monotone, but he'd promised a car within twenty minutes.

Ahead, there's the Lake County Sheriff's SUV, parked nose-in to the driveway, just as promised. Jill feels a weird moment of relief: someone is here, someone with a badge and a gun and hopefully the will to use them. She slides her vehicle up behind the cruiser, kills the engine, and sits with the headlights off, letting the darkness reassert itself. The cold is so total it hammers at the windshield, making the interior of her car a kind of sensory deprivation cell.

She gets out, soft-footed, and stands in the hush between the vehicles. Every nerve is awake. No engine noise from the cabin. No dogs barking. No porch light. Only the sound of the wind making the pines scrape together in a language of dread. Jill double-checks her Glock, clears the holster in a single, silent move, and tucks her Bureau ID into her chest pocket where it can't flap loose.

The Lake County SUV is running, engine idling low, exhaust pulsing pale over the drift. She pads up to the passenger side, staying tight to the vehicle. There's a faint glow from the dashboard, but the windows are blacked out. She circles slowly, careful not to cast a silhouette against the snow.

That's when she sees them: a pair of boots sticking out past the front bumper, toes up, not moving. The brain processes it as a set of legs first, then as a dead body. She freezes. The air in her chest halts, suspended. Jill kneels, keeps her gun up, and angles for a better view. The legs belong to a Sheriff's deputy, sprawled face up in the rutted snow, hat missing, arms akimbo.

She circles to the left, keeping low, and that's when she sees the blood. A black slash from ear to Adam's apple, the collar of the shirt spread and gory, and the throat opened from side to side. The face is already bluing at the lips, eyes wide, mouth slack in a final what-the-fuck.

Jill's stomach knots. She ducks behind the bumper and tries to breathe through her nose. Training, she tells herself, training. The first rule is you're never alone. If this were an ambush, the killer is already behind her.

She pivots on a knee and brings the Glock up, but it's too late. The shape is there, a blur in the dark, silent until it isn't. The knife punches through the waistband of her jacket, low and hard, the point going in above the right kidney. The pain is white-hot, like nothing she's ever felt before.

She screams, not from the wound but from the rage of it. She jams the gun under her own ribs and fires straight back. The muzzle blast is a hammer to her eardrums. She feels the blade twist, feels a wet heat spill down the side of her leg.

The figure grunts and drops the knife. Jill sees the blade flash as it lands in the snow. She tries to rise, but her right leg buckles. The attacker, wounded, crashes away into the tree line, leaving a smear of blood and noise.

Jill clutches her side, fingers going numb in the cold. She looks down and sees her hand covered in blood. The wound is deep, not fatal yet, but if she doesn't get help soon, she's done. She crawls around the deputy's SUV, fighting for breath, using the front wheel well as an anchor. She pops open the door and hauls herself onto the seat.

The inside of the car is warm. It smells like burned coffee and a cologne she recognizes from her rookie days. She reaches for the radio, but the mike cord has been sliced through, the plastic dangling in ribbons. There's no time for curses or analysis. She fumbles for her phone in the left back pocket and nearly drops it twice before unlocking the screen.

She has one bar flickering. She wipes her fingers on her jeans, painting the denim a wet burgundy, and taps redial.

The dispatcher picks up. "Lake County, what's your emergency?"

"Officer down," she says, but it comes out a hiss, the syllables clipped by pain. "FBI agent down. Gormley cabin." She fights for the address. "Need backup, need ambulance. Suspect possibly wounded."

"Copy, ma'am. Help is on the way."

She tries to respond, but the phone slips from her hand, tumbling into the footwell. She slumps back, lets the blood run, and watches the world go gray at the edges.

In the last moment before she loses consciousness, Jill sees movement in the pines. Another shape, smaller than the first, moving in a straight line toward the cabin, head down, deliberate. She hopes it's Dirk, or failing that, someone with enough sense to finish this the right way.

Then everything is gone but the cold and the taste of blood and the memory of her first field office, the one with the old coffee and the plastic chairs. She thinks of Dirk, and the case, and the way the world always bends back on itself in the end. The cold is complete, and she lets herself fall into it.

Chapter Fifty-Two

For the last ninety-six minutes, I have not moved so much as a finger. My body is a node of patience wedged in a dry cradle of lodgepole pine, thirty yards up slope from the cabin. I've lined my watch cap with hand-warmer packets, counted my pulse to keep the blood from freezing in my toes, and exhaled only through my nose, letting the vapor curl, condense, and drop harmlessly onto my parka rather than plume into the night and betray me. No evidence. Not a trace. I live for these moments.

The cabin sits at the end of a long snow covered driveway, its porch sagging on the east side like it's bowing to the dirt. Two windows gape black on the interior, and a single blue-toned LED light is set into the soffit above the door. It's not on a sensor but a switch. The porch steps have been iced over, then salted; I see the patchwork through my spotting-scope. The path from the drive to the front door is unshoveled, a thin stride-width track flattened in the end-of-season snow.

I've seen Stephanie outside only once since she arrived just after midnight. She stands five-six, 137 pounds, though she walks like she's lighter. Her left hip juts, possibly arthritic, and she's left-hand dominant. The shotgun she cleaned was a Remington 870, 12 gauge, the barrel sawed at the legal limit, but the stock was still full length. She carried it underarm, a flashlight in her weak hand, the beam pointed at her feet, not outward, meaning she learned rural wariness so deeply it can't be unlearned. A light-blue Subaru wagon with current Colorado plates is parked on the far side of the house; its windshield is iced over.

At 04:07 a.m., a set of headlights appears at the end of the driveway. I shift the scope two millimeters and watch the approach. The vehicle creeps in at under four miles per hour; light discipline is observed; and the engine noise is minimized. The driver uses the foot brake to maintain a glide instead of shifting to park. It's a man, six feet tall, and 180 pounds. He exits near the front porch, hesitates, then moves forward. His footsteps are precise, the pace even, and he never looks up to the window where Stephanie is watching. I allow myself to smile as I track the curtain's threadbare movement.

At 04:10, Stephanie opens the door and brings the Remington to bear on the man's chest. He stops instantly, hands in view, and murmurs something I can't hear. They square off. After several minutes of conversation, she lets him ascend the steps. The gun doesn't drop, but she pulls it back two centimeters, barely visible to anyone who hasn't spent a lifetime tracking vectors. He enters, and she follows, closing the door behind them.

I reset my observation point, cycling my feet under my body to get the blood moving. I'm not worried about the man. He's a variable, but I've run the decision tree a dozen times, and I always win. My pulse settles. I close my eyes, a luxury only when surveillance is complete, and run through the plan. At 04:30, I will approach from the west, using the small shed as a blind.

My concentration breaks with the approach of headlights on the Forest Service Road and the sound of an approaching vehicle. At first, I suspect a snowplow, but within thirty seconds, I see the rolling approach of a law-enforcement vehicle. I switch my scope to the sheriff's SUV as it idles at the drive's entrance. The engine ticks, and the lights blink off. The driver's door opens, and a man steps out, backlit in blue. He is heavyset, in his late thirties, with gloves that are not uniform issue. He stretches slowly, as if signaling someone. He walks towards the front of the SUV. He appears to be looking at the SUV parked in front of the cabin.

I return the scope to the cabin. The Interior lights are on, sloppy, but whatever happens inside is now a formality. I see motion in the kitchen window: Stephanie is watching with her visitor at her side. Then, at the tree line, something flickers: a smear of black on black, lower than a human stride. I hold my breath before I realize it is a man moving in a low, direct vector. He paces the deputy with surgical precision.

"No," I whisper. "Not now."

The shadow intercepts the deputy at the woods' edge. No warning, no shout. The attacker slips an arm around the deputy's face, draws a blade, and with one swift motion, a brilliant jet of blood arcs across the snow. The deputy's head lolls; his legs go rigid, then slack. The attacker lowers him with almost tender efficiency, wipes the blade on the jacket, and moves to the SUV.

My scalp tightens. I don't like this. I trace the new

actor with my scope, cycling through my mental catalog of possibilities. His movement is angular, every motion studied, and no wasted energy. I've seen this in predator videos, in my reflection. For the first time in years, I'm shocked.

The figure opens the SUV door, leans in, and in less than five seconds is back in the trees. He's cut the microphone cable. Communications are dead. Efficiency is absolute.

I flip open my notebook and write in block capitals: UNKNOWN ACTOR. KILLS DEPUTY IN 5 SECONDS. KILLS POLICE RADIO. PROFILE: HIGH RISK, HIGH MOTIVE. REASSESS PLAN.

My heart hammers, not with fear but rage. "Who the fuck is this?" Out of nowhere, a second black SUV, identical to the first, pulls up with its lights off and parks behind the sheriff's SUV. "Who the hell is this now?" I whisper. "It's damn busy for a cabin way back in the woods."

I lower the scope and watch its occupant exit. Hunched, circling wide around the police cruiser, moving toward its front. The person leans over the deputy on the ground. A flashlight clicks on, goes out, and the person stands. A knife blade flashes, plunging into the person's lower back. The victim whirls, shouts and fires. The shot rips through the night. The attacker stumbles, hand to side, drops the knife and flees into the woods.

The victim, it seems a woman, drags herself around the cruiser, opens a door, slumps onto the seat, trailing blood on her hand as she grabs the mike to find the cable cut. She is wounded, possibly fatally.

Meanwhile, the attacker is not gone. He's trailing blood but moving north toward the cabin, faster now, like a fox fleeing a gunshot. I feel no fear. I am aroused by the violence, compelled to finish the job.

I flip my notebook closed, slip it into my coat, shoulder my kit, and melt down the slope, off the path, toward the cabin's east side, where the woods crowd closer. The plan is fucked, every expectation shattered, but I am more determined than ever. I will finish this. The only wild card is the man in the trees, and that, I decide, is a challenge worth meeting.

I draw the knife from its sheath, close it in my palm, and move through the dark with a precision no human has matched, except perhaps one, who is now less than a hundred yards away, leaking blood and purpose, drawing all eyes to the cabin at the end of the driveway.

Chapter Fifty-Three

I've lost feeling in my hands, which is a mercy, because the pain would be intolerable. It isn't the cold that worries me; it's how the wind finds the gaps in my jacket, needles in and cuts me until only bone and will remain. I've been lying flat behind a wind-felled pine for four hours, ribs pressed to the bark, heartbeat sinking reptilian slow. I've watched the windows of the Gormley cabin cycle through every glow, from candlelight to harsh LED, and I know the pattern well enough now that I can close my eyes and reconstruct it by the flicker on my eyelids. I've waited this long; a few more minutes of ice and tension won't kill me.

Good thing too, because my Arizona jacket wasn't made for this. It's meant for chilly mornings on a job site, maybe a December in Flagstaff, not the cold that pulls at you like it wants to break you into pieces and bury you in the white. I flex my toes to keep the blood moving. My boots are cheap, steel-toed, with thin socks, and I can't feel my feet anymore.

A crunch at the end of the driveway draws my attention. A dark SUV creeps up the drive. I stay in the shadows, one eye peeking over the log. I watch as the SUV stops several yards from the cabin. The driver steps out, his head on a swivel, shoulders up, and eyes scanning. Every motion is nervous and ready.

The cabin door opens next. An old woman emerges with a shotgun in her hands. Even from forty yards, I see her jaw set, boots planted, and her arms locked. I know a shooter's grip: tight enough to kill, thumb white, and finger hovering just off the trigger. She holds that gun like it's done its job before.

She and the man exchange hushed words that the wind can't carry. For a moment, it feels too familiar: a scared old woman, a man trying not to get shot, and the dark closing in around them. Almost funny, if you like that kind of joke.

They go inside. I shift to a crouch, every movement slow and animalistic. My pocket holds my knife. I don't have to look to remember the weight of the steel. I brought two, one folding for emergencies. I pull out the fixed blade.

I wait. If the man doesn't leave before I attack, there will be two victims. No problem. I've done it before. Several times.

Another crunch of snow, and a cop car glides up and stops near the end of the driveway. I don't know why a cruiser is here. Could it be a routine patrol or something else? I slide lower, wait for the driver to step out and trudge across the snow. He doesn't know what's coming.

He stops at the front of the SUV, staring at the SUV parked near the cabin. His hand moves to his pistol. I move: smooth and silently, using the trunk for cover. My boots whisper on the powder; the wind hides me. I'm on him before he smells danger. One of my arms snakes up to hook his neck; the other pushes the blade under the ear. I slash his artery and windpipe in one move, and there is a rush of blood that steams and spatters on the snow.

I hold him as he dies, feel his struggle go slack, then

ease him down like a sack of grain. His hat rolls away; I kick it into the shadow and wipe the blade on his shoulder. His eyes are already going glassy.

I let the clarity wash over me, not the kill, but the focus after, when the world looks sharper, more honest. I breathe it in. Then I go to the car, pop the door, grab the mic, and cut the cord with my knife, tossing it in the backseat. A box of stale donuts sits on the passenger seat. So fucking cop, I almost leave a note.

I duck back to my spot, check the cabin windows. Two silhouettes still inside, moving. The itch flares, the part of me that wants to strike now, but I wait. Something's coming I can't name.

Ten minutes later, a second SUV with blacked-out windows, creeping slower than the first, slides behind the cruiser. I stay hidden, my knife ready. The driver, a woman, slips around the front, circles the cruisers without making a rookie mistake.

She squats behind the dead cop, peering at him. That's my cue.

I launch forward in one straight lunge, blade low. She hears me too late; I catch her at the kidney instead of the spine, but it's deep. She snarls and spins. A gunshot cracks from under her jacket, splitting the night. The round finds me just under the ribs, and the pain explodes, electric and real.

I grunt and back off, knife still in hand but arm heavy. I drop the knife in the snow and run for the woods. I watch her crawl into the cruiser. I want to finish it, but the bullet has my number. I press a hand to the wound. It's not gushing, but it's hot and wet, and my knees shake.

I stagger toward the trees. I'm bleeding badly, but I'm not dead yet. I have work to do.

I spit blood onto the snow and head for the cabin, limp but steady. I stumble, fall against a rock, breathe through the pain. When the ringing in my ears eases, I push up again. The cabin sits dark, silent. There's nothing in the world but this house and the task at hand.

My primary knife vanished in the snow, so I draw my backup. Still sharp.

I move slowly at first, then faster as pain fades into focus. I cut across the snow, hugging the shadows, slipping between trees.

The final approach blurs. Pain is background noise now. I reach the porch, crouch, and wait. Every muscle tight, every sense attuned. The cabin is hushed.

I check my watch, not the time, but for the feel of the world slowing, right before it stops. I grin, all teeth and nothing behind them. I'm ready. The job's not done until the job's done.

Chapter Fifty-Four

For a full minute after the gunshot, neither Dirk nor Stephanie speaks. The echo, sharp, vibrates through the plywood floor, up through the table legs, and into the fragile stillness of the night. The stove throws heat that smells like old newspapers and burned sap, but it does nothing to push back the black of the glass. Dirk stands with his gun held tight to his chest, not for fear of her but for what might come next. Stephanie is still crouched by the table, one eye on him, one on the line of windows.

He listens. He filters everything except the creak and moan of the house, the cough of the wind, and that high, uncertain whine that means someone out there is not done. In the corner of his mind, Dirk counts the seconds between violence, like waiting for thunder after a lightning strike. His brain moves in loops, entry points, cover, and alternate exits, always scanning, always at the ready.

He checks his pistol, quick and silently, then looks at her. Stephanie's hands are gripping the shotgun so hard the knuckles are translucent, the veins on the backs of her hands the color of faded denim.

"What happens now?" she whispers.

Dirk answers in the flattest voice he can find. "Now we let it play out."

A clock on the wall ticks, its battery nearly dead so it hitches on every second, stuck in a slow-motion stutter. Dirk steps up to the table, keeping his line of sight to the door. "If we are to survive this, we must act first. As much as I would like to take these guys alive, we need to face the fact that it is us against them. We don't know who else is out there, so for now we are on our own."

Stephanie grins, but her teeth are clenched. "So, this is the point where you give orders?"

He shakes his head. "You know the cabin better. What's the best fallback if they breach?"

She nods towards the tiny bathroom. "It locks, and the window is nailed shut. It would take a grown man a while to get through. The floor under the toilet is solid."

"Good." He signals for quiet with a finger to his lips, then jerks his chin toward the hallway. She moves, not fast, but with the loping, self-contained shuffle of a person who's had enough fear to build an immunity. She vanishes down the hall, the gun angled at hip height.

The room is a pressure cooker: one cheap table, a folding chair and a threadbare couch. The walls are hung with a few cracked pictures; snowfields, a photo of a teenage girl in a choir robe, and a hand-painted verse: **For I Know the Plans I Have for You**. Dirk stares at it. For a heartbeat, he wishes he were the sort to believe in plans.

A new sound fills his ears. The crunch of snow, faint but clear, comes from behind the cabin. Dirk's skin tightens. He crouches in the shadow next to the bedroom door. He holds his pistol two-handed, elbow locked, knees flexed, and leans against the wall.

Another sound, closer. The front porch boards, warped and bowing under an unseen weight, creak in a language he understands perfectly. The silence that follows is absolute.

The doorknob turns with a click of cheap hardware. There is a scrape, like gloves on steel, then the knob moves again. Dirk angles for the perfect shot and waits.

The door explodes open and bounces off the inside wall. The icy blasts cut in like a thrown knife. The man flies through the door like he's been pushed from behind. He's hunched, clutching his ribs, blood covering the front of his coat, and blood soaks down the back of his coat from a fresh knife wound in his back.

The man's eyes are wide, not with rage but with animal panic. He lurches inside, staggers two steps, then collapses against the table. His hand goes out to steady himself, but misses, and he crashes to the floor, dragging a chair with him.

Dirk stays frozen for half a second, long enough to scan the entry, waiting for the second brother to appear, but nothing follows. The wind howls through the open doorway, and the sudden, keening wheeze of a dying man.

The man's jacket is open, shirt soaked red-black. There's a bullet wound in his abdomen, probably through the kidney. Blood pools and steams in the cold. The guy tries to look up at Dirk, but he's not all there. His lips work, but no sound comes.

Dirk kneels, grabs the man's shoulder, and rolls

him. There is a knife wound in his back and a knife lying on the floor next to him. Dirk kicks it away, then checks for other weapons. The man's breath stutters, then pauses. His hand comes up, a gesture so weak it barely creases the air.

For a second, Dirk wants to say something, but he doesn't know what. The man's eyes dart to the left, then up. He looks past Dirk, over his shoulder, at the cross on the wall. A wet cough, and then the man is gone.

Dirk stands and steps back from the body. There's still one more brother out there. He can feel it. In the kitchen, a river of blood is running towards the drain in the floor.

Time slows and nothing moves except the small shift of wind across the open doorway, drawing the smell of snow and copper-sweet blood into the entryway. Dirk is calculating the distance to the target, the odds of a first shot kill, and the angle of approach. He wants this over, but the hesitation that what's coming has his own face makes his arms lock for a fraction of a second.

He's expecting James to come through the front. He steps back to the bedroom door to be ready. Suddenly, his vision blurs, and in his mind, he sees himself standing in the doorway. Like he's looking through someone else's eyes. His vision clears, and he feels a shift in the air behind him, just a whisper, and then a shadow materializes from the other side of the room. It's silent but for the breathless, surgical grunt of impact. James slams into him, blade first. The knife arcs for Dirk's ribs, but he's already twisting; the blade catches only his sleeve and a shallow crease of bicep, the fabric going instantly wet.

James's free hand grabs Dirk's hair and smashes his head into the wall. Dirk's pistol is knocked loose, sliding into the dark under the table.

Dirk is not fast, but he is precise. He grabs the wrist, feels the tendons flex, and uses James's own momentum to roll him over his back and into the chair. James goes through it like it's nothing, but he keeps hold of the knife, even as splinters rake his hands. Dirk hits the ground on his knees, eyes gone starry with the blow, and then James is back, already upright, blood on his knuckles.

James is nothing like the photos. He is not calm or precise. His face is a ruin: mouth wet, eyes wild and his hair matted to his forehead in a streak of sweat and dirt. The resemblance is almost perfect except for the rage. James's rage is its own living animal, and it's out.

He closes in again, both arms forward, the knife set low. Dirk braces, pivots. James cuts for the gut, misses by a thumb-width, and Dirk smashes a palm into James's trachea. The move is clinical, but James absorbs it, coughs, and returns with a snap kick to Dirk's thigh. Dirk's leg gives, and he's down.

The knife comes up, bright and beautiful, ready to finish the job.

In the periphery, the world explodes in white. Stephanie flipped the wall switch, flooding the cabin with light. The sudden glare stuns all three. James sees Dirk, really sees him. The blood is forgotten; the knife held aloft but frozen. For three heartbeats, nothing moves.

He glances at the corpse on the floor, at the mouth gone slack in a mirror of his own, then back at Dirk, and he drops the knife to his side. His hands go up, not in surrender but in disbelief.

James backs away. "Is this some kind of joke?" The knife quivers in his hand. "Is this some kind of sick fucking joke? Who the fuck are you people?"

James moves towards Dirk who has nowhere to move. He braces for the assault.

James snarls as he attacks, but the shotgun blast fills the room with thunder. The pellets catch James in the hip and side; he's thrown back, knife spinning free, blood painting the inside of the cabin in a single, wild arc.

James slams against the wall, then scrabbles for the door. He makes it, trailing a comet tail of blood and pain, then disappears into the night.

For a full minute, no one breathes.

Stephanie stands shaking, the gun lowered, and looks at Dirk. His hands are soaked red, his shirt split open, but he's alive. He slumps against the couch, head down, listening to his own blood drip to the floor.

The wind comes through the door again, colder now, howling through the cabin like a last word.

Chapter Fifty-Five

Dirk's hand finds the grip of his pistol. The cabin is a horror show behind him. Stephanie, clutching the shotgun like it's the only anchor in the storm, the body of Calvin face down in blood, and his own blood making a second river down his arm. He staggers to the door and steps through it. The outside air hits him with a blast so pure it's almost narcotic.

He follows the trail of boot prints, blood and a single line in the snow where James's right foot drags. The woods are pale and dreamlike; everything is muffled under five inches of new powder, branches weighed down like mourners. Dirk blinks sweat out of his eyes, grits his teeth, and moves. Every step is a method: advance to the next tree, sweep, cover, listen. In the distance, the dawn is just beginning to light the sky, blue and indeterminate.

At fifty yards, the footprints angle hard to the left, up a grade. Dirk stops and crouches behind a granite boulder. He steadies his breath. His right arm is worse than he thought; the blood is pumping with every heartbeat, and his fingers are already numb. He tears the sleeve from the jacket, improvises a tourniquet with a belt, and keeps moving.

The next thirty yards are open, only small pines for cover. Dirk scans, then takes the risk and runs it. The snow makes him silent, but the cold drags at his lungs, sears the inside of his mouth. At the edge of a gully, the blood trail stops. No body and no prints, nothing but disturbed snow and the dark, waiting line of the treeline.

Dirk drops into a low crouch and sweeps the area slowly. He's finished his first arc when James hits him from the left, out of nowhere. The knife comes for his face, Dirk raises the Glock, but the impact drives both to the ground and the weapon is gone, lost in the snow.

They roll through the crust, limbs locking, breath exploding in clouds. Dirk catches James's hand, feels the bone under the skin, and twists hard. The knife drops, but James knees Dirk in the gut and drives the wind out of him. For a second, they're face to face, one eye each swelling shut, their mouths split and bleeding.

James gets a hand to Dirk's throat. Dirk bites the thumb, tastes blood and feels James jerk away in pain. The two break, scramble to their knees, each hunting for a weapon. James finds the backup blade first. He throws it, but Dirk's already rolling. The blade skims his shoulder, tears the flesh, but misses the kill.

Dirk grabs a broken branch and hurls it at James's head. It connects, thuds wetly. James slumps, but only for a heartbeat, then he's up and running, deeper into the trees, howling something wordless at the sky.

Dirk gives chase. He's slower now, dizzy, the world tilting, but he keeps the silhouette in sight. The trees crowd close, branches slashing at his face. He doesn't feel it. He's lost the pain, running now only on the old machine logic: follow, corner, and finish.

James leads him in a zigzag down a frozen wash, up a cut bank, into a thicket so dense it's all dark and motion and claws. Dirk gains on him, step by step. He sees James's breath steaming in the cold and launches himself in a flying tackle. They hit the ground together, slide through the drift, and crash into a half buried log.

James is first up, knife in hand again, but Dirk kicks out, sweeps the legs. Both go down hard, tangle, and roll. James's knife draws a red line down Dirk's thigh. Dirk feels it hot, then gone.

They slam to a stop at the lip of a ravine.

There's a pause, a single moment of shared, perfect hate. James's face is white with blood loss, lips curled in a snarl. Dirk sees himself, and he hates it. Hates the way the story ends.

James charges, and they crash through the undergrowth and into the ravine.

The fall is a blur, branches snapping, bodies spinning, snow, and rock and air and then a sudden, terminal stop. Dirk lands on his back, skids, and smashes into a deadfall. The world goes silent except for the rushing of blood in his ears.

He wakes up. It takes a moment to realize he's not dead.

He tries to move. Everything hurts, but his right leg is wrong. It's bent at an impossible angle, the pain radiating out in pulses. His arm is bleeding freely, and the cold makes the blood look black. He tries to sit up. His head is buzzing, and the world is out of focus.

Six feet away, James lies impaled on a branch, through the back and out his chest. His eyes are wide and staring, but not quite empty. Blood fans out beneath him, soaking the snow in an ugly halo. The knife is still in his hand, but it dangles, useless.

Dirk stares.

Above, the sky is brighter. The sun is creeping over the mountains, cutting the world into strips of shadow and light. Dirk laughs, a dry, broken sound.

He thinks he hears sirens, but maybe it's just his own heartbeat.

He lies back, lets the cold eat away at him, and waits.

The next time Dirk wakes, it's to the sound of voices.

Someone is shouting his name, distant but growing. There's the bright, urgent pop of a flare, the aroma of burning plastic and sulfur. He tries to move, fails, then feels strong hands lifting him and strapping him onto a rigid board. The hands work fast, methodically.

He sees the outline of the rescue team above him, orange vests, gloved hands, and a rush of faces he doesn't recognize.

Behind them stands Anthony Spinella. He's standing at the top of the ridge, an AR-15 slung across his chest, and his eyes hidden behind mirrored sunglasses. He looks at Dirk, then walks down the slope, picks up the Glock from the snow, and returns to where Dirk is being loaded onto the stretcher.

Spinella kneels, his face close. "You did good," he says. "You did what you had to do."

Dirk wants to answer, but all he can manage is a grunt.

Spinella pats him on the shoulder, and nods to the

EMTs. They haul Dirk up, out of the ravine, into the light.

Dirk looks up one last time, sees the sun. It's full and round, not warm but perfect in its own way.

He lets himself go, floating up through the snow and pain and the memory of blood, and up into the brightness of the world that waits on the other side.

Chapter Fifty-Six

Dirk wakes to the pulse of hospital monitors: a machine's idea of a heartbeat, constant and without compassion. The taste in his mouth is old coins and plastic. He tries to swallow, and the effort lights up his shoulder, then his bicep, and then his head. His first full breath brings a rush of pain that spikes behind the eyes and rolls down his body in icy cascades.

He lifts his head an inch and takes inventory. He's cocooned in a cotton straitjacket, bandages on his left shoulder and most of his right arm. His leg, the one that folded like wet cardboard during the fight, is set in a cast up to his hip, his foot hovering above the mattress like a flag on a broken pole. Every joint is wrapped, braced, or splinted. A morphine pump with a translucent tube runs to the crook of his arm, and there's a half-crushed ice pack seeping through the sheet at his ribs.

The room itself is shadowy and pale, lit only by the slow rhythm of dawn filtering through plastic blinds. There's an IV pole next to the bed plugged into him like a holiday display. The air is chilled, perfumed with disinfectant, and full of the quiet, authoritative whirr of climate control. A container of hospital Jell-O sits on the table next to a call button, the spoon standing straight up.

Dirk reaches for it and nearly screams at the way his shoulder disagrees, the noise that comes out more a whimper than a cry. He flexes his fingers and then tries again with the left hand. The spoon rattles against the plastic cup, the bite of lime Jello folding over itself and then bouncing off his lip as he misses. He tries again, gets a taste, and is working through the aftershock when he sees the shape in the chair.

Connie sits with her head propped on her fist, one arm hooked around her knees. Her shoes are on the floor, soles facing out, and her jacket is bunched in a defensive heap on her lap. Even asleep, she is vigilance personified: her neck bent, eyes half-lidded, and a line of tension at her jaw as if ready to intervene between Dirk and anything the world might send his way.

He makes a noise, tries to speak. The sound is enough, and Connie startles awake.

She stands, brushing the creases from her jeans, and walks to the bed. "Hey," she says, her voice thick from sleep. "You're awake." She sits on the mattress beside him, and her weight shifts the bed, rolling him a degree closer to her. She does not smile, not yet, but the lines around her mouth soften.

He tries to talk, but the first go is just a dry croak.

She pulls a cup of ice water from the table and raises it to his lips. He drinks cold and sweet, then licks his lips and tries again. "How long?"

Connie's hand smooths his brow, fingers warm and practiced. "A week and change," she says. "For the first three days, you didn't wake up. They said you had a severe concussion, plus all the." She gestures at the patchwork of injuries. "You know."

Dirk takes this in. The pain is real, but in a way that is almost a relief. He is alive. He is whole, more or less.

"You, okay?" he asks.

She leans back and gives him a look, something between exasperation and fondness. "I didn't fall off a cliff," she says, "so I think I'm doing better than you." She places her hand on his chest, gentle as a resting bird. "You scared the hell out of us."

He looks past her to the window. A thin band of sunrise works its way between the blinds, casting her face in vertical stripes. The two of them are alone in a world of hospitals and hush.

Dirk shuts his eyes, and memory fills the dark: the fight in the cabin, the twins, the knives and the impossible ache in his limbs. He can still feel James's hand at his throat, the bite of the blade, the way it all ended in a blur of snow and wood and blood.

Connie says, "They want you to try sitting up today." She nods at the wheelchair beside the bed, gleaming in the low light. "Do you want help, or do you want to show off and do it yourself?"

He looks at the chair, then at his body, then back at the chair. "I think if you could just…" He lets the rest trail off.

She stands, draws the rails down, and threads her arms under his back. Her touch is gentle but unyielding. On three, she helps him pivot upright. He bites his lip and fights the dark sparks that swarm his vision, but he makes it. He sits, dizzy but upright, and looks at her. She is only inches away, and her hair has escaped its knot, falling over her cheek.

She tucks a stray lock behind her ear and meets his

eyes. "Better?"

"Define better," he says.

She grins, this time for real, and wheels the chair closer. "I'm supposed to take you for a spin around the floor. Doctor's orders."

He hesitates. "Is there a parade? Balloons?"

"Nope," she says. "But there is a visitor who's been asking for you."

Dirk narrows his eyes. "Spinella?"

She smirks. "Not unless he's wearing lipstick and is five feet tall." She stands behind him and braces him as he slides onto the wheelchair. Every movement is pain, but the rhythm of her hands makes it bearable.

She grabs a robe from the chair and drapes it over him. "Ready?"

Dirk tucks his arms inside the robe and nods.

Connie wheels him to the door. She opens it, and the corridor greets them with the antiseptic tang of hospital cleanser, the click, and beep of distant monitors, and the flat white hum of a world designed to be invisible. The hall is lined with identical doors, some open, and some closed.

Dirk asks, "Where are we going?"

Connie leans in and whispers, "It's a surprise."

He lets her take him down the hallway, the world tilting at a manageable angle, the ride bumpy but slow. He tries to count the doors but loses track as the monotony lulls him. They pass a nurse who nods and calls him honey, and another who pushes a cart full of wound dressings. All along the corridor, there's the unspoken law of hospitals: keep quiet, keep moving, and keep hope on a short leash.

Connie stops outside a door. "You ready?" she asks.

He nods, and she pushes open the door.

The second hospital room is almost a carbon copy of the first, except the window is wide open and the sunlight is harsh, a line of blue cutting across the bed. In the center, Jill Quarters is propped at forty-five degrees by a phalanx of pillows, her right shoulder swaddled in fresh gauze and her left wrist taped to an IV. Her face is haggard, but her hair is clean, pulled back in a tight ponytail. Someone has brought her a vase of supermarket flowers, tulips already browning at the edges, and a stack of manila folders towers on the tray at her side. If not for the bloodless hospital pallor and the monitor leads trailing from her neck, she could be running a case review.

Jill looks up as the door opens. Her face cracks into a crooked smile, though her teeth are gritted in pain.

"Hey, hero," she says.

Dirk feels Connie's hand and the motion moves him an inch closer to the bed. For a second, he doesn't trust himself to speak. "What happened?" he asks. The morphine is wearing off, and his tongue feels like a fat, wounded animal, but he manages: "You look like hell."

Jill snorts and nearly laughs, the sound interrupted by a cough. "You should see the other guy," she says.

"Wait, you did."

Dirk glances at Connie, then back at Jill and repeats himself. "What happened? I don't remember…" The memory is spotty: snow, blood, James, a fall, and then darkness. He doesn't remember seeing Jill at the cabin.

Jill answers, but her voice is small. "Last thing I recall was hearing the Lake County dispatcher telling me that help was on the way, then everything went black. I woke up here after the surgery. They patched up the knife wound and told me I was at death's door when they brought me in. The rest is a blur."

Dirk stares at her. "Why were you at the cabin?"

"Connie called me. She was worried when you ran out of the house."

Chapter Fifty-Seven

Before Dirk can say anything, there's a knock at the door. Connie stands and steps aside as Anthony Spinella enters. He's in Bureau casual: blue FBI polo, jacket, loafers, his gun visible on his hip. The sight of him in sunlight is strange, like catching a bear in a Sunday suit. Spinella's face is grimmer than usual, but when he sees Dirk and Jill side-by-side, his mouth softens into a low-watt smile.

"Well, if this isn't a picture," Spinella says. He sets a box on the side table and approaches Jill's bed. "You look great," he tells her.

She rolls her eyes. "You're a liar."

He grins. "All my best people are in the hospital. That must mean the paperwork is done."

Jill sags into her pillow and nods at the folders. "They gave me a head start. The twins left quite a mess."

Spinella crosses his arms, leans against the foot of the bed, and surveys the two agents. "Dirk, do you know how lucky you are?"

Dirk shrugs, then regrets it as his shoulder barks in protest. "I have no idea, boss."

Spinella's smile doesn't fade, but the lines around his eyes tighten. "We got the whole story," he says, and it's all business. "We pulled the body from the cabin. That was Calvin, the Arizona twin. He bled out before the medics got there. James, the Denver twin, ran but left a blood trail a kindergartner could follow. We found both of you at the bottom of a gully. You had a busted leg and four liters of blood loss. He had a knife in his hand and a branch through his chest. If you'd been alone out there, you'd both be dead. As it is, only one of you made it."

Dirk looks down, hands gripping the armrest.

Spinella steps to the window, glances at the two wounded agents. "Stephanie Gormley is alive. Jill had called 9-1-1 before she passed out. As far out in the woods the cabin was, the cavalry arrived within fifteen minutes. Lake County called us when the 9-1-1 call came in, and I arrived with ERT forty minutes later by chopper. Jill was stabilized at the local hospital and then they choppered her here. She was in bad shape. Stephanie Gormley gave a statement, but most of it matches yours. She said you were the reason she survived."

Dirk looked at Spinella. "I don't think that's the case. She was handy with that shotgun if I recall correctly."

Dirk squints, the tension in his body draining out.

Jill speaks up, voice steadier. "What about the other evidence?"

Spinella paces, hands behind his back. "The search warrant for James's house turned up a secret space under the stairs, meticulously catalogued. Not trophies, but notebooks. Dozens of them. Twenty years of every kill, every compulsion and every moment he thought the world would catch up to him. He detailed eighty-four murders. It'll be a task force legacy for the next decade. Calvin's apartment was less organized, but same flavor, cutting and pasting news clippings, photos and a wall mapped out with victim names. He knew what he was, but I don't think he ever understood why."

He lets that hang. The room is all machine whirr and the perfume of tulips going to rot.

Jill says, "So it's over."

Spinella's voice is quiet, but it cuts through the haze. "It's never over, but the worst of it is. You did good."

Dirk can't think of anything to say. He just nods and stares at Jill's IV.

Spinella snaps the mood by clapping his hands once. "I want both of you cleared for return as soon as possible, but for the next couple of months your only job is to heal." He turns to Connie, gives her a warm but formal nod. "Mrs. Trainor." He pats Dirk on the good shoulder. "I'll leave you guys alone. But if you need anything, call."

Connie smiles, grateful but weary. "I think we're good. Thank you, Mr. Spinella."

He nods to them all, then leaves as quickly as he came.

Dirk sits in silence for a moment, then wheels himself closer to Jill's bed. She turns her head, fixes him with a look that is more alive than it has been in weeks. "This is not your fault," she says.

He wipes a tear from his eye. "I'll still feel like it was."

Jill reaches out and squeezes his hand, a flash of the old partnership in the gesture. They stay like that, silent, as outside the window the sun crawls up past the hospital roof, setting the line of snow beyond into a flare of orange and gold.

Connie stands behind them, watching both, her face unreadable but calm.

In that room, with the evidence of violence and survival all around, Dirk feels like the world has stopped spinning out of control.

After Spinella and Connie are gone, the room is as quiet as a church. The afternoon sunlight creeps down the bedrails and pools in a weak puddle on the linoleum. Dirk sits beside Jill's bed, hands in his lap, shoulders curled inward as if bracing for an aftershock.

He should say something, maybe apologize for getting her stabbed and nearly killed, but the words would only stain what's already a perfect silence. He glances over at her. Jill's eyes are open, but she's not looking at him; she's watching the window, the angled light, or the possibility of nothing at all.

For a long time, neither moves.

Dirk tries to remember how many times he's sat next to Jill in a state of shared exhaustion, post-interview, post-raid, and post-mess. But none of those times ever felt this absolute, this permanent.

Jill shifts in bed and adjusts her IV. The monitor beeps a little faster, then slows. She turns her head just enough to catch him in her periphery.

They watch the hallway through the glass in the

door. Someone pushes a cart past; there's the faint sound of conversation, the echo of a laugh, and then nothing again.

"Are you going to be okay?" Jill asks so quietly he almost misses it.

Dirk blinks. He gives a tight nod. "You?"

She closes her eyes for a moment, then opens them. "Yeah." There's a smile. "Don't let them put you on desk duty. You'd hate it."

He gives a dry laugh, the pain manageable now. "I'll keep that in mind, but I think it's going to be a while before I need to worry about that."

The silence resumes, not empty but full. They sit together, letting the guilt and the grief and the relief swirl and settle.

The sun moves another inch across the floor. In that light, they don't look like partners or survivors. They just look like people.

The spell breaks with a squeak of sneakers on tile. A nurse appears in the doorway, her face round and kind, and her badge gleaming on her lapel. "Mr. Trainor?" she says, voice as soft as a bandage. "Let's get you back to your room."

Dirk nods, braces himself as the nurse positions the wheelchair. He turns to Jill. "See you soon."

She lifts a hand, the IV tape pulling a little at her wrist. "Count on it."

The nurse guides him out, and the door hisses shut behind them. In the empty room, Jill listens to the echo for a long, long time.

The next morning, the world is less a disaster and more of a half-remembered dream. Dirk wakes to the slip of sunlight through the hospital blinds and the clean smell of newly changed sheets. For a moment, there's nothing, no pain, no noise, just the hush before the machines catch up and start their day.

He looks at the ceiling. It's the same as yesterday and the day before: rough texture, and a single dark mark in the paint. But the tension in his body is gone. His hands are steady.

The door opens with a whisper. Two women enter, neither hurrying, both holding hospital coffee in white foam cups. Maggie Trainor wears a blue cardigan and moves with the careful precision of a nurse on rounds. Stephanie Gormley's hair is freshly brushed, and she wears a white shirt with the sleeves rolled high on her forearms and a pair of jeans.

They approach the bed together and for a heartbeat, Dirk thinks the room is a trick of his broken mind, a hallucination of comfort. But they're real. And they're here for him.

Maggie sits on the right, the same side she's always chosen in every parent-teacher conference and doctor visit. Stephanie chooses the left, nearest the window. They both set their coffees on the tray and fold their hands atop the blanket, a mirror image, neither speaking first.

After a while, Maggie pats his arm, bare since the hospital gown rides up, and says, "You look better than you did yesterday, sweetheart."

Stephanie's mouth twists into something like a smile. "He looks like a freight train ran him over. But I guess that's an improvement." She reaches out and, with a hesitant thumb, brushes a stray eyelash from his cheek.

The gesture freezes him. It is not motherly, not exactly, but it is so strange and unexpected that he laughs.

The three of them sit, watching the sun climb up the wall. There is no need for words. For the first time, Dirk is not afraid of what comes next.

They talk about the hospital food (worse than Maggie's cooking), the color of the walls (Stephanie's old cabin was the same jaundiced yellow), and the future, an idea that feels out of reach.

Maggie tells a story about Dirk as a child, how he broke his arm in two places climbing a playground fence. She remembers every detail, from the ice cream she bought to the way he insisted he was fine until he fainted from the pain.

Stephanie tells a story about herself at sixteen, how she climbed out her bedroom window to see the night sky, and how she slipped on the shingles and nearly died. "I was always running from something," she says, and Dirk hears it for what it is: an apology.

They drink their coffee, and once, their hands touch over the edge of the cup. The moment passes, but the echo lingers.

Finally, Maggie stands. "You need your rest, honey." She kisses his forehead, as she always has.

Stephanie hovers, not quite knowing how to say goodbye. She settles for a squeeze of his hand. "You'll be all right," she says.

Dirk nods, and the two women leave together, their footsteps soft as feathers.

He sinks into the bed. The sunlight has reached the window, bathing the room in a thin, forgiving glow. Dirk nods off. His sleep is deep and empty. No dreams. No ghosts. No women being murdered as he watches through someone else's eyes. Just the slow, steady rhythm of the heart monitor, marking time for a life that, for today, at least, belongs to him.

Acknowledgments

A special thank-you to my daughter Christina J. Morgan, my unofficial collaborator.

. Any mistakes the reader may find are solely the responsibility of the author.

Special thanks to my daughter Stephanie Morgan, my beta reader. Stephanie has read every novel in its rough stages and rarely gets to see the completed product. Her insight and critique have been critical in making sure the stories make sense.

Also, I would like to thank my family for their encouragement. I have been telling them stories since they were little, and I always told them that someone should be writing this stuff down. I decided to write it down myself.

I want to thank my closest friend, Trish Moakler-Herud. She has been encouraging me for years to write my stories down. I hope this will make her proud.

A special thanks to my late wife, Jane. She pushed me for years to become a writer, and my biggest regret is that she didn't live long enough to see it happen. I love her with all my heart and miss her every day. I think she would be pleased.

Finally, thanks to the readers. Without you, none of this would be important.

About the Author

2019 Pacific Book Awards Best Mystery Finalist . . . *Crime Delayed*

2020 Pacific Book Awards Best Mystery Winner . . . *Crime Denied*

2020 Chanticleer International Book Awards: 1st Place Blue Ribbon, CLUE Book Awards for Suspense, Thriller Fiction . . . *Crime Denied*

2021 Chanticleer International Book Awards Finalist, CLUE Book Awards for Suspense, Thriller Fiction . . . *Crime Conspiracy*

2021 Chanticleer International Book Awards Finalist, Book Series, CLUE Book Awards for Suspense, Thriller Fiction . . . Crime Series, The Buck Taylor Novels

2022 Chanticleer International Book Awards Finalist, CLUE Book Awards for Suspense, Thriller Fiction . . . *Crime Exploded*

2022 Chanticleer International Book Awards Finalist, CLUE Book Awards for Suspense, Thriller Fiction . . . *Crime Spree*

2023 Chanticleer International Book Awards Finalist, CLUE Book Awards for Suspense, Thriller Fiction . . . *Crime Scene*

2023 Chanticleer International Book Awards Series Finalist, Mystery & Mayhem Book Awards . . . *Crime Series*

Chuck Morgan attended Seton Hall University and Regis College and spent thirty-five years as a construction project manager. He is an avid outdoorsman, an Eagle Scout and a licensed private pilot. He enjoys camping, hiking, mountain biking and fly-fishing.

He is the author of the Crime series, featuring Colorado Bureau of Investigation Agent Buck Taylor. The series includes *Crime Interrupted, Crime Delayed, Crime Unsolved, Crime Exposed, Crime Denied, Crime Conspiracy, Crime Unknown, Crime Exploded, Crime Spree, Crime Family, Crime Scene, Crime Victims, and Crime Unraveled.* He is also the author of *The Assassin's Heart, a romantic thriller and Preserve, Protect, and Defend,* a political thriller.

He is also the author of *Her Name Was Jane,* a memoir about his late wife's nine-year battle with breast cancer. He has three children and four grandchildren. He resides in Lone Tree, Colorado, with his Siberian husky.

Other Books by the Author

Dear Reader, thank you for reading this novel. Please enjoy the other books in this series and follow Colorado Bureau of Investigation Agent Buck Taylor and his team as they investigate new and sometimes unusual crimes in the Colorado mountains. Each novel is a separate story, and they can be read in any order, but you might find it more enjoyable to read them in order.

Happy Reading,

Chuck Morgan

"Crime Interrupted: A Buck Taylor Novel by Chuck Morgan is a gripping, edge-of-the-seat novel. Right from page one, the action kicks off and never stops, gaining pace as each chapter passes." Reviewed by Anne-Marie Reynolds for Readers' Favorite.

Finalist . . . 2019 Pacific Book Awards Best Mystery

"This crime novel reads like a great thriller. The writing is atmospheric, laced with vivid descriptions that capture the setting in great detail while allowing readers to follow the intensity of the action and the emotional and psychological depth of the story." Reviewed by Divine Zape for Readers' Favorite.

"Professionally written in the style of a best-selling crime novelist, such as Tom Clancy, Crime Unsolved: A Buck Taylor Novel by Chuck Morgan is a spellbinding suspense novel with an environmental flair. Intriguing subplots of fraud, survivalist paranoia and murder weave their way through the fabric of the plot, creating a dynamic story. This is an action-filled, stimulating tale which contains fascinating details that are relevant in our present climate." Reviewed by Susan Sewell for Readers' Favorite.

"Chuck Morgan has a unique gift for plot, one that makes Crime Exposed: A Buck Taylor Novel a hard-to-put-down book. From the start, readers know what happens to Barb, but they become curious as they follow the investigation, wondering if the characters will find out what happened to her. The descriptions are filled with clarity, and they offer readers great images. The prose is elegant, and it captures both the emotional and psychological elements of the novel clearly while offering vivid descriptions of scenes and characters. This is a fast-paced thriller with memorable characters and a criminal investigation that is so real readers will believe it could happen." Reviewed by Romuald Dzemo for Readers' Favorite.

Winner . . . 2020 Pacific Book Awards Best Mystery

2020 Chanticleer International Book Awards:
1st Place Blue Ribbon, CLUE Book Awards for
Suspense, Thriller Fiction

*"It's really progressive to see a female serial killer
portrayed with such intelligent writing and depth of
character*, and the cat and mouse chase dynamic is thrown off
nicely by the switching of genders. What results is a really
enjoyable thriller and crime mystery novel, and overall Crime
Denied is certain to please fans of both hard-boiled detective
tales and action/adventure crime novels." Reviewed by K.C. Finn
for Readers' Favorite.*

2021 Chanticleer International Book Awards
Finalist, CLUE Book Awards for Suspense,
Thriller Fiction . . . *Crime Conspiracy*

*"This makes for a truly dynamic story where anything is
possible, and a hero you can root for even when it looks like
all is lost." Reviewed by K.C. Finn for Readers' Favorite.*

*"This is a book you can't put down, which will entertain
you on many levels, and at times make your skin crawl; the
kind of book that remains in your thoughts long after you*

2022 Chanticleer International Book Awards
Finalist, CLUE Book Awards for Suspense,
Thriller Fiction . . . *Crime Exploded*

*"**Action-packed and fast-paced, I was sucked into the story
the moment I opened the novel.** The author built the story to
perfection. Chuck Morgan gave just the right amount of
suspense, mystery, and action to keep readers' attention on
Buck and his team. There was never a dull moment in the story.
The narrative ran smoothly until the end; it followed the
development of the story and the pace set by the characters. I
enjoyed the twists and turns. What I loved more than anything
else in the plot was how calculating Buck was. He was smart; he
didn't let the FBI discourage him and kept his head in the game.
The action gave me an adrenaline rush. Absolutely brilliant!"
Reviewed by Rabia Tanveer for Readers' Favorite.*

2022 Chanticleer International Book Awards Finalist, CLUE Book Awards for Suspense, Thriller Fiction . . . *Crime Spree*

"It is one of the best crime novels I have read in a long while, with real characters developed in a way to let you get to know them intimately, understand them, and appreciate their strengths and weaknesses. The plot is tight, exciting, and tense, with plenty of action, and it will grip you from the start. The bizarre storyline is enthralling, written in descriptive prose that lands you right in the middle of the action. Forget sleep; once you pick this book up, you won't want to put it down until it's finished. Fantastic story, and highly recommended for fans of high-octane crime thrillers." Reviewed by Anne-Marie Reynolds for Readers' Favorite.

"Crime Family is the tenth book in the Buck Taylor series. Chuck Morgan had me hooked from the first page until the end. There was never a dull moment with all the action; one chapter flowed into the next. The story was fast-paced and kept me on the edge of my seat. I kept turning the pages to find out what would happen next. I was intrigued, and with all the twists and turns, I could not predict what was looming. The characters were well-developed. Each had a background description, and it was fun getting to know some of them. The story was excellently written with a fitting ending." Reviewed by Alma Boucher for Readers' Favorite.

"Crime Scene is a must-read for lovers of mystery sleuth and

murder tales with a touch of conspiracy." *Reader's Favorite review.*

"**Crime Scene has a carefully designed intrigue that deepens with every unforeseeable turn of events and a dynamic narrative.**" *Reader's Favorite review.*

"**This is a great book. Holds your attention and you don't want to put it down. I would recommend this book to anyone who loves a good crime novel.**" *Amazon review.*

"**Spellbinding, gripping, powerful, and relevant are just a few words that come to mind after turning the last page of Crime Scene: A Buck Taylor Novel, Book 11, by Chuck Morgan.**" *Amazon Review.*

"**A riveting plot and good pacing keep the reader in suspense as Buck Taylor and his team establish evidence beyond a reasonable doubt.** *The author sustains interest by skillfully showing the art and intuition involved in crime investigation and the science behind it, as well as the elements that can delay or confound it. There are a lot of quirky characters in the novel and the author gives them mannerisms, voices, and descriptions that make them distinctive and realistic. The details and descriptions of the work and everyday life of the players are both pleasantly appealing and revolting, depending on the scenario. What's most captivating and intriguing about the character development is the backstory of the unhinged characters and how the author uses them as part of the perplexing trail of a horrendous crime. Themes of sadism, cruelty, grief, forensics, police procedures, and even a little bit of romance can be found in this installment of the Buck Taylor series. Highly recommended for crime story fans who especially enjoy the information as well as the twists, turns, and the untangling of intricate and cold case crime sprees." Reviewed by Carmen Tenorio for Readers' Favorite.

⭐⭐⭐⭐⭐ If you are looking for a mystery murder novel with a touch of crime, Chuck Morgan's Crime Unraveled is just what you should be looking for.

⭐⭐⭐⭐⭐ Chuck Morgan took me on a roller coaster ride with Crime Unraveled. The action started on the first page and continued until the last.

⭐⭐⭐⭐⭐ Filled with suspense and action, Crime Unraveled: A Buck Taylor Novel, Book 13, by Chuck Morgan delivers a compelling and realistic story with historical and legal elements.

⭐⭐⭐⭐⭐ The 13th book in the Buck Taylor series, Crime Unraveled by Chuck Morgan is a fantastic addition to the series. I've read a few books in this series and they never fail to leave me in awe. This is the type of high-octane, fast-paced thriller I've come to expect from this author.

Delia Cahill is one of the world's elite assassins, but her next assignment has gotten into her head. Will Delia carry out her assignment or risk everything, including her life, to protect her intended victim?

⭐ ⭐ ⭐ ⭐ ⭐ If you are looking for a thriller with brains, heart, and just the right amount of edge, this one is a must read. 5 stars, no doubt.
⭐ ⭐ ⭐ ⭐ ⭐ Chuck Morgan's The Assassin's Heart will keep the reader's heart thumping from the first page to the last.
⭐ ⭐ ⭐ ⭐ ⭐ Overall, I enjoyed the novel very much. If you're craving a fast-paced, action-packed thriller, you will not be disappointed!

"Preserve, Protect, and Defend by Chuck Morgan was intricate and enthralling, grabbing my attention from start to finish. This fast-paced, action-packed story had me turning the pages as quickly as possible, afraid to miss a single detail. With each twist and turn, the plot kept me on my toes, continually surprising me

with its unpredictability. The suspense had me sitting on the edge of my seat, making it hard to set the book aside. The engaging writing style made it easy to immerse myself fully in the story, and the characters felt incredibly genuine and relatable. Mike was a powerful force, and Stevenson had no idea what was headed his way. This book was masterfully written and maintained my interest throughout. It surpassed all my expectations, and I enjoyed every moment." Reviewed by Alma Boucher for Readers' Favorite.

www.ingramcontent.com/pod-product-compliance
Lightning Source LLC
Chambersburg PA
CBHW070313310726
48976CB00005B/1700